STARK'S COMMAND

STARK'S COMMAND

JACK CAMPBELL

WRITING AS JOHN G. HEMRY

TITAN BOOKS

STARK'S COMMAND

Print edition ISBN: 9780857688989
E-book edition ISBN: 9780857689573

Published by
Titan Books
A division of Titan Publishing Group Ltd
144 Southwark St
London
SE1 0UP

First edition: September 2011
10 9 8 7 6 5 4 3 2 1

Visit our website: **www.titanbooks.com**

What did you think of this book? We love to hear from our readers. Please email us at: readerfeedback@titanemail.com, or write to us at the above address.

To receive advance information, news, competitions, and exclusive offers online, please sign up for the Titan newsletter on our website: www.titanbooks.com

A CIP catalogue record for this title is available from the British Library.

Printed and bound in Great Britain by Clays Ltd., St Ives plc.

For Paul Crabaugh, a good friend whose own story ended far too soon.

For S., as always.

PART ONE

A STORM OF BATTLE

The organized violence humans call warfare takes many forms. An attack can be as sudden and brief as an earthquake, a surprise spasm of fury in which soldiers dash against defenses then fall away. Or an assault can be slower, gradually building in strength as soldiers cautiously push forward, seeking weak points in defenses, their efforts as continuous and unrelenting as a sea straining against barriers holding it from dry land.

So the attack began, slowly building in intensity. Like a flood of water, the pressure rose, in a place where the only real water rested eternally frozen beneath the lifeless rock of the surface. Gradually it increased. Testing here, pressing there, searching for any signs of weakness, any give in the defenses holding it back. Every probe met a firm barrier, each push repulsed with varying ease. But the pressure continued, shoving harder, the strength of barriers at some points herding it toward those areas where the defenses held with less strength. Not much less, but enough, as the flood pressure gathered at those points where resistance seemed softer, where trickles of advancing elements could push through. Slowly, so slowly as not to be apparent at first, but with increasing speed, the apparently firm wall of defenses began to crumble.

"Ethan, we got problems."

Sergeant Ethan Stark, acting commander of the rebellious soldiers still defending the American Colony on the Moon hastily donned his battle armor. "I'm still suiting up, Vic.

What's happening?"

"You don't need battle armor inside the headquarters complex," Sergeant Vic Reynolds, Stark's acting Chief of Staff, scolded. "I need you in the Command Center. Now."

"Okay. Okay. But I'm gonna be in armor." Stark sealed the last fastenings on his suit, grabbed his rifle, and darted out the door. The corridors around him still felt unreal, wood paneling where bare rock should be. *I'll never get used to the luxury here at headquarters. Maybe we can sell this stuff to pay the troops.*

Most of the personnel in the Command Center were unknown to Stark, experienced enlisted troops manning their consoles to maintain a constant stream of symbology, communications, and video feed between individual soldiers. All of it centered here, where until recently officers of every rank had tried to dictate their subordinates' every action. Now that those officers sat within the stockade under arrest, that role, if he wanted it, was Stark's.

"Wow." Stark paused to admire the massive main display screen on which a sector of the front glowed in enhanced 3-D. Green American symbols hung in a slightly ragged arc marking the perimeter, each group of friendly soldiers clustered around the heavy weapons fortifications symbology that indicated the presence of strong defensive positions. In front of those green markers, clusters of red symbols ebbed and flowed, shifting in a constant dance as sensors reported the presence of enemy soldiers trying to break through the American defenses. "They're pushing harder than before, aren't they?" In the three days since the horrible failure of General Meecham's grand offensive, forces of the enemy coalition had tested for weaknesses in the American line a dozen times as rumor of riot and rebellion came dimly across to them.

"Yes," Vic agreed, one clipped word which spoke volumes. "We should be able to hold it, though."

Should be able to. Stark studied the display again, scowling. "Why are those enemy units getting so close? Why aren't they being shoved back farther?"

"I don't know." Vic tried to keep her frustration hidden, but it swelled to the surface as the Sergeant tried to handle far more soldiers than her training and experience had ever prepared her for.

"I don't like 'I don't knows' in combat, Vic."

She fought down another sharp answer before speaking more calmly. "Neither do I, but I'm not sure what's happening on the line. Everything looks right, but our defenses don't seem to be as strong as they ought to be." Vic glared at him briefly. "We shouldn't have gone ahead with the unit rotations this early."

"Vic, we didn't have any choice. The units on the line had been extended there because of Meecham's offensive, and they were getting really ragged."

"They could have stayed on line a few more days. Another week. We started rotating units the day after we took over, for Christ's sake!"

"Everybody insisted on it," Stark reminded her. "What could we do?"

Vic set her jaw stubbornly. "Tell them no."

"I haven't got that authority, Vic."

"The hell you don't. They elected you commander, remember?"

Stark jabbed a finger at her. "Yeah, I remember. You helped that happen. And you know as well as I do that saying I've got full authority and actually being able to order people around at the drop of a hat are two damn different things. I can't buck every other Sergeant. Not yet. They're still gonna think about it before they do as I say."

She bent her head, then nodded wearily. "You're probably right. No, you *are* right, but I still don't like it. Everything is still too soft and rotating units made it softer. I've activated the on-call reserves for that sector," Vic added.

"Good move. How many soldiers is that?"

"Two companies."

"Where are you putting them?"

"I don't know!" The frustration surged into the open again as Vic waved at the display. "Where do we need them?"

"If you can't tell, I sure as hell can't." *Vic's the best tactical thinker I ever met, so if she can't read this mess, nobody can.* Stark watched the display, hundreds of symbols clashing together and moving apart, a constant stream of data scrolling along the sides of the display where it framed simulated terrain so real Stark felt he could fall into it.

She stared first at him, then back at the display. "I think that's because there's too much on here to think through, Ethan. They packed every bit of data they could onto these displays so it's just about impossible to see the forest for the trees. We've got to prune this junk back to essential data."

"Sounds like a real good idea. But we can't do that now."

Vic lowered her voice, barely whispering so only Stark could hear. "I wish the hell I knew what we *could* do."

The other enlisted were glancing back at them, expressions guarded. Stark smiled tightly, eyes on the display as if unaware of the attention. *Just like leading my Squad, only a lot bigger. People have to think you're confident. Even if you're scared as hell and don't have a clue what to do.* The distraction triggered an instinct as something nagged at Stark's mind. He stared at the display, green and red markers swimming amid the rapidly swelling and just as rapidly disappearing threat symbology that marked the flight of heavy shells. It felt like that odd itching between the shoulder blades when a sniper had you in their sights, as if the display were saying something his conscious mind couldn't grasp, but that caused a sub-consciousness honed in uncounted battles to shout alarms. "What else have we got for backup? What's the next reserve?"

"The next?" Vic frowned at the question. "Two battalions. But they're not on-call. We'd need to activate them, get them suited up."

The words felt wrong. Advice from Vic was always good, but right now it felt wrong. "Do it. Get them ready to hit the line."

"Ethan, there's no reason at this point to jerk around a lot of soldiers we'll probably need sharp later on."

Reasonable words. Reasonable advice. Vic playing her old role of guiding his decisions down the right paths. Stark kept his eyes on the display, almost unfocused, seeing the rhythm of movement rather than the details, and not liking the feel of it. "We don't have a handle on this, Vic. We need those troops ready."

"If we keep them suited up too long—"

"I know. I know. Let's get them activated."

"Ethan, I don't—"

The itching intensified, urging action. "I said do it!"

Vic halted in midsentence, face rigid. "Yessir."

The word hit Stark like a fist in the stomach. *We've always worked as equals, or I've deferred to Vic. Now I'm supposed to call all the shots, and I don't like it and neither does she.* He wavered, trying not to be seen noticing the angry lines etched on his friend's face as she transmitted the order to the on-call battalions. *Am I wrong? Am I just being a jerk? No. No. I've got to be in command and every instinct I've got says I'm gonna need those troops.* "Thank you," Stark stated softly, leaving anything else unsaid.

Vic glanced his way, startled by the reply, but still mad. "You're welcome. This isn't easy."

"It ain't for me, either. We'll talk later, figure out how to work this better. I still want you telling me what you think."

"You won't get it if you cut me off like I'm a stupid recruit," Vic noted, her tone still hard, but somewhat milder.

"You're right."

To Stark's surprise, the last words brought a smile to Vic's face. "Now, that's never happened. I never worked for a commander who told me I was right." She glanced at Stark, one eyebrow raised in question. "I've got two battalion commanders asking me why their people need to suit up and deploy."

"Because . . ." *I said so? Real bad answer.* "Because we've got some real strong probes hitting us. They're stressing the line. The guys holding the front might need backup." *Too soft.* "No. Leave out the 'might need.' Say we need backup for the front."

"Okay." Vic rapidly repeated Stark's words into her comm unit, then nodded. "They rogered-up. Ethan, that's a real vague reason for activating that many soldiers. What's got you so *I* worried?"

Even as she spoke the question, an answer appeared before them. "That." Stark pointed a rigid finger toward the display, where a small patch of their own soldiers had suddenly begun moving. "They're falling back. That squad. Retreating. Why the hell are they falling back?"

"Bunker status is okay," Vic muttered. "What's going on?" she called over the headquarters communications circuit. "Corporal Hamilton. Why did your squad abandon your bunker?"

Stark linked in to hear the reply. Hamilton's words came quickly, rushed with fear and the stress of rapid movement. "Too many of them. Too much pressure. Couldn't hold."

"Hamilton," Vic barked, "there's nothing out in front of you an entrenched squad can't handle. Return to your position."

"Negative. Too hot. Falling back."

Stark forestalled Vic's next transmission with one hand on her shoulder, using the other to point again. "Look how fast that symbology's moving. They ain't falling back. They're running."

"Running." Vic repeated the word as if she'd never heard it before and couldn't grasp the meaning. "Oh, God," she added in a whisper as the squads to either side of the abandoned bunker also left their positions.

"Over there, too," Stark observed through a tight jaw. "In another company's area. The line's crumbling." More symbology moved as soldiers broke from their defensive positions, heading toward the rear in ragged groups as the red markers of enemy soldiers began following, the enemy advance almost tentative, as if they feared ambush.

"What's going on?" Vic wondered, whispering the question, then glaring at Stark. "Why are they running?" She slammed her fist against the console before her. "Why the hell are they running?"

"I dunno. Let's ask again." Stark pulled up the ID on one of the Sergeants involved in the growing rout. "Srijata. What's going on? Why did you abandon your bunker?"

The wild disorder of combat only dimly echoed in Srijata's reply. "I don't know! Everybody just jumped up and started running!"

"Why'd *you* run?"

"I can't hold a bunker by myself! I could see the bunkers on either side going, too!"

Stark shifted comms. "Private Shanahan. Hold your position."

"Negative. Negative. Too hot. Can't hold."

"You're not under pressure right now. Take a stand."

"Why? I'm not gonna die for nothing!"

Vic stared directly into Stark's eyes for a moment, then called a soldier herself. "Corporal Delgado. Report in." Silence. "I know you've got comms, Delgado."

"Go to hell!" Delgado panted back.

"Hold your position, Delgado. There's soldiers depending on you."

"Nobody's risking their ass to save me, are they? They're all running, too."

Stark focused back on the Command Center, suddenly aware of

every eye on him. *Yeah. Like being a squad leader, but with one helluva big squad.* He keyed the general circuit, linking it to every soldier in the threatened sector. "Everybody listen up. This is Stark. Hold your positions. There's nothing coming at you we can't handle. I've got reserves moving up. Hold your positions," he repeated. Some of the symbology seemed to hesitate, but the breach in the front kept widening as more positions were abandoned and more units began running. The dam had broken, its individual pieces falling away under pressure, the enemy flood shoving at the ragged edges of the break to sheer away more defenses in an ever-widening rout.

Stark became aware of Sergeant Jill Tanaka, in charge of the headquarters staff, standing near. "How far will this spread?" she wondered, voice despairing. "Is the whole front going to go?"

"I'll tell you as soon as I know." Odd. To have so much power at his fingertips, yet to have so little ability to influence events.

"Dammit," Vic swore, punching another circuit to life.

"Where the hell's my brain. Artillery. Grace? We got problems. We need you to stop a penetration."

Far from the main headquarters complex, ensconced in a room where rested control of the big cannons, which infantry had feared for centuries, Sergeant Grace spoke carefully, spacing his words. "I see it. I can lay down barrages to slow the enemy a bit, but I can't stop them without ground troops forming a line."

"We'll form a line. We got reserves moving up. Start dropping shells on those enemy troops."

"Okay. I'll slow some of them down, like I said, but I can't hit the ones farthest forward without risking our own people. They're too intermingled."

Vic stared at the display, then at Stark. He nodded slowly. "Do your best, Grace. You're the expert."

"You don't wanna see my firing plan and sign off on it first?"

"Hell, no. What're you talking about?"

"Standard procedure," Grace explained, speaking rapidly now. "I develop a plan, then send it up the chain of command so every officer along the line can sign off on it and fiddle with exactly what target which cannon shoots at when. Then I get it back."

"After the damn battle's over?"

"Hey, I didn't make the system. You want to see my plan?"

"No," Stark declared forcefully. "Grace, you'll forget more about employment of heavy artillery than I'll never know. You do your job and if I see a problem from here, I'll talk to you about it."

"Command by negation?" Grace questioned. "Stark, you're my kind of wild-eyed radical. There'll be shells going out in a few minutes."

"Thanks." Stark glanced at Vic. "What the hell is 'command by negation'?"

Reynolds grinned, the expression rendered slightly unnerving by her tension. "That means you tell somebody to do a job, then just watch them do it. You don't interfere unless you see something you think needs done differently."

"Common sense," Stark muttered. "How the hell else can you—?" He stiffened, staring at the left flank of the collapse. "It's stopped on that side. There. Look, they're holding. Tanaka, get on with that bunker and hold their hands personal. Make sure they stay."

"Why there?" Vic wondered as Tanaka rushed to a terminal to link in. "Oh, hell, look at the terrain. They're on an elevation with a steep depression in front and rocks in front of that."

"Yeah." Stark smiled crookedly in recognition. "The Castle. We never got stationed there. Best bunker assignment on the perimeter. The enemy's being channeled away from them by the terrain so they're under no pressure at all." He shifted to gaze to the other side of the penetration, where a cluster of friendly symbols stood fixed on a piece of terrain shaped like a lopsided oval. "Vic, somebody's holding on this side, too. Thank God."

"Yes," she confirmed. "Mango Hill's holding."

"But that's just a low elevation. The enemy's gotta be pushing them."

"Ethan, look at the unit ID." Vic snapped the suggestion as if she knew he wouldn't like the information it provided.

He didn't. "Oh, Christ." Third Squad. First Platoon. Bravo Company. Second Battalion. First Brigade. His old Squad. The twelve soldiers he'd personally trained and led for years. His Squad until decades of poor leadership by their officers, culminating in the unthinking slaughter ordered during General Meecham's ill-considered offensive, had led the senior enlisted to finally mutiny; until those senior enlisted had elected Sergeant Ethan Stark to command them, so that he had to leave the Squad where his heart still lay. That same Squad, those same soldiers, had rotated back onto the line in the last few days and were now holding a position that had become the linchpin of the American line. Holding where the enemy was certain to hurl full force in an attempt to continue the unraveling of the American front. "Anita," he called.

"*Sí, Sargento.*" Corporal Gomez sounded absurdly cheerful.

Scanning her display, Stark could see the bunker combat systems shifting in a rapid blur to slam rounds at enemy targets as fast as they winked into existence on the local sensor net. A lot of targets probing, pushing, trying to work their way close enough to the bunker to pinpoint its sensors and weapon hard points. In one corner of the view from Gomez's command seat, Stark could see Private Mendoza hunched forward at his control station, an occasional quick gesture changing the bunker system priorities to concentrate on different targets or sectors. "You've gotta hold," Stark stated. "Right there. I can't trust anybody else to stand and fight right now."

"We gonna fight, *Sargento*. No *problema*."

"They're gonna hit you, hit you bad, but you gotta hold," Stark repeated.

"*Sí*. Nobody's leaving this hill. They're pushing us now, but we're pushing back plenty hard. You see? We ain't gonna run like those Earthworms." Stark called up a different direct vid feed, seeing through the eyes of another one of his old Squad members as Private Chen fired from a pit outside the bunker. Shadowy shapes moved among the scattered rocks, flickers of motion amid the solid black shadows and glaring white light overlying the dead gray of the lunar landscape. Chen fired coolly, steadily, as his Tac pinpointed target kill-points. His Heads-Up Display jittered as enemy jamming tried to confuse aiming and detection of targets, the symbology altering in a constant wild jig as combat systems tried to sort out real targets from false. Minor vibrations jarred the Tac display as a nearby chain-gun mount pumped out staccato streams of shells. So easy to be there, focusing on the moment, on one target at a time in the familiar routine of a leader responsible for one small group of soldiers. So hard to be back here, instead, worrying about thousands.

"Let me know if it gets too hot," Stark ordered, breaking the link to resurface in the Command Center.

Vic was watching him, eyes hard. "Ethan, they're going to catch hell."

"I know that. They're gonna catch hell because I can count on them to stand there and take it. That's the way it works, right? The ones who can take it and do the job, no matter how rough, always end up getting handed that job." He ran one hand through his hair, staring at the sector display once again where enemy forces were pushing deeper inside the American lines. "That's a big flippin' hole." New symbols appeared, heavy shells arcing in from the American rear to burst within the area where enemy forces were thrusting forward. "Grace is right. The artillery's not gonna stop them."

"That's not Grace's fault. He has to guess where the enemy will be and where our own troops will be. He's always going to be behind the curve unless you tell him to drop his stuff on our own people."

"Which we ain't gonna do. So how we gonna plug that damn hole, Vic?"

"I've got the two on-call companies." She waved at the display. "At least I don't have to wonder where to deploy them anymore. Delta's off to the left a long ways. I'm sending them in behind the Castle to hit the enemy flank," Vic advised, her fingers flying over the command console to transmit orders straight to Delta Company's Tactical systems. "The other company is almost dead behind the hole in the line. Maybe they can stop the enemy advance." She paused. "Okay?"

"What?" Stark questioned irritably. *Oh, right. I'm the boss.* "Yeah. Good moves. Do it."

"They won't be good enough, Ethan. Damn fine thing you ordered those extra battalions activated." Vic bit her lower lip so hard that a bright bead of ruby blood appeared. "Charlie Company. I need you in place fast." Even as she spoke, Vic rapidly updated positions to feed Charlie Company's Tacs. "Establish a defensive line."

"You want us to hold that alone?" Charlie Company's acting commander questioned incredulously. Another Sergeant with a lot more soldiers and a lot more responsibility than a few days before. "There's a lot of crap coming down that way." The enemy, caution evaporating, had begun chasing the retreating American forces, hurling more and more troops into the hole in the American line despite the artillery falling in their path.

"Negative," Vic soothed. "Delaying action. Don't try to hold firm until we get more people there. We've got two battalions on the way. Understand? You're not alone."

"Okay." The doubt behind the acknowledgmnt rang clear even through the distance of the comm circuit.

Stark fidgeted, unable to act for the moment, his available forces committed. The line of symbols representing Charlie Company seemed far too small compared with the mass of friendly and enemy soldiers rushing down at it.

The thin line of Charlie Company had barely taken up position when the first scattered symbols representing fleeing Americans began to stream past and through them. More symbols came, moving rapidly toward the rear in singles and small clusters, like debris in a river rushing against the small dam that was Charlie Company. "Ethan . . ." Vic began.

"I see it." Some of the Charlie Company soldiers had begun falling back as well, swept up in the retreat as another wave of panic-stricken troops hit their line. First the edges of the company line began peeling away, then segments of the center eroded, then the rest simply collapsed, joining in the rout. "We got big problems, Vic. Holding the flanks won't help if the center ain't there." *There's too much going on all at once. How do you decide anything with all this data in front of you and stuff happening faster than you can think?* Indecision ate at him, allied with a growing fear. *What do we do? Tell people what to shoot at like the officers did? That won't accomplish anything. Maybe there's nothing I can do. Nothing but watch and hope something happens to salvage this mess.*

A vision of bloodied grass suddenly mocked him, jeering at his inaction. Just like Stark's commanders had once waited indecisively at Patterson's Knoll as their troops died around them; until their options were all foreclosed. *Good Lord. Am I becoming my own worst enemy?*

Memories tumbled out, as if thinking of the hopeless battle on the Knoll had been a key to a locked door. One steadied, forming a vision of soldiers sitting around a glowing heat lamp somewhere near a nameless battlefield, the veterans swapping war stories while newer personnel watched and listened in something approaching awe. One of those inexperienced soldiers, then-Private Ethan Stark, venting his frustration. *It can't be done. There ain't no damned way to accomplish this mission.*

Corporal Kate Stein, his self-appointed "big sister," had grinned back. *Lemme tell you something kid. When you've tried everything you can think of, and nothing's worked, try something else.*

What? Stark complained. *You just said I'd already tried everything.*

No, I didn't. I said you'd tried everything you could think of. Think of something else.

Stark rapped his faceshield with an armored fist, drawing a surprised look from Vic. "What was that for?" she wondered.

"Me. Trying to shake a few brain cells loose."

"I hope it helps." Vic hung her head for a moment, both hands supporting her above the command console, then raised again to look at Stark. "Ethan, I don't know how to stop this. I don't even know why it's happening."

"I think I do." He knew it, now, somewhere down deep. *Some people fight for God, some for glory, some for country. Which of those are left for these guys right now, right here? But that's a long-range problem. Gotta save everybody's asses first.* Too much happening, too big a disaster in the making, and too many responsibilities on his shoulders, yet Stark felt oddly calm. *Think of something else.* He stood directly before the map display, pointing toward it. "We've been trying to deal with this penetration by throwing stuff straight at the enemy."

"That's how you stop them."

"Depends. Forget where the enemy troops are this second. Forget about trying to hold on to as much ground as possible. If you had your choice, where would you try to stop the enemy advance? Stop it cold."

"My choice? You mean the best terrain?"

"Yeah. Anywhere short of the Colony."

"Right here." She illuminated the spot, an isolated ridge of rock rearing up slightly off center from the enemy advance. A remnant of a very old crater, perhaps, the rest of its walls long since pulverized by subsequent minor impacts. "Great ground. But it's too far back. If that spot didn't hold we wouldn't have anyplace else to make a stand before the Colony."

Stark narrowed his eyes, studying the position. "That's its strength, Vic. It gives us time to establish a line before the enemy gets there."

"Ethan, if you don't hold the line there, we've lost."

"Yeah, but if we can't hold there, we won't be able to hold anywhere." He nodded, once. "Okay. Get those battalions on the way there."

"Both of them?" Reynolds questioned sharply.

"We gotta stop them and then roll them back."

"Not that way," she insisted. "Main force against main force? And what if all those running soldiers break a battalion the way they broke Charlie Company? Think, Ethan. You don't want every egg in one basket."

Every nerve demanded action, but Stark forced himself to stand before the display. "Okay, one battalion goes to hold the ridge. Where should the second go?"

Vic swung one arm along an arc, a planner in her element, the despair of a moment before lost in the rush of action. "Deploy them along this side of the penetration. Hit the enemy in the flank after you've stopped them. Or, if worse comes to worse, hit the flank and try to stop them that way."

"Good. Great." He turned to go. "I'm on my way."

"What!"

"I'm on my way," Stark repeated. He pointed again, this time to the retreating symbology. "Those running soldiers won't stop just because there's a battalion waiting at that ridge, anymore than they did when they hit Charlie Company. I've gotta be there to hold them."

"Ethan, you're all that's holding this entire army together! If you die, everything will come apart!"

"Vic, everything *is* coming apart." He turned away, leaving her groping for an answer. "Sergeant Tanaka, I need a ride out to the front. How soon can I get an APC here?"

She nodded and gestured simultaneously. "An Armored Personnel Carrier? You got one. Two, actually. The Commanding General's Mobile Operations Centers."

Stark scowled. "I said I wanted an APC."

"They are APCs. Just a little modified with extra command and control gear." Tanaka's fingers danced over several screens. "I've downloaded the directions to the APC loading dock into your Tac and alerted the drivers. Have a nice trip."

"Thanks Sarge." Stark ran, following the path Sergeant Tanaka had entered into his armor's Tactical Combat System, but deliberately slowing his pace from a mad dash to a quick jog. *No way I want people to see me running like crazy—* The APC loading access gapped ahead, much larger than Stark was used to and set into the side of the vehicle so he could board just by walking. *Why the hell did they compromise the armor and the camouflage by putting a door in the damn thing? Guess Generals don't like having to climb into their personal vehicles.*

Stark dove into the seat directly facing the command displays, fumbling with his restraining harness until he realized it had been much more heavily padded than usual. With a muttered curse he slammed the buckles home, then sat for a long moment. *Alright, already. Let's go!* He jacked in, cursing again at the delay. "Driver? What's the holdup?"

"Awaiting orders, sir."

"Orders?" *Ah, hell. All my career I've gotten on these things and they've gone where someone else told them to go. Guess I've got to break a few habits.* Stark pinpointed the ridge on his display and bounced it to the APC systems. "Here's a position. Get me there as fast as you can."

"Yessir." The APC rose with a smooth glide, unlike the wicked lurches Stark was used to experiencing when riding as a simple grunt. Accelerating rapidly, the vehicle shot down the wide lane leading through the lunar surface over the headquarters complex, only to slow significantly as it entered the broken terrain outside the developed areas.

"What's the problem?" Stark snapped. "How come you slowed down so much?"

"There's a lot of rocks out here, sir. I've got to be careful maneuvering around them."

"A lot of rocks?" Stark switched to an exterior view, watching the terrain scroll past. Tortured rock, interspersed with puddles of dust. Dead as only something that had never known life could be dead. The terrain didn't look too bad for a lifeless expanse of rock on the Moon. "How long you been driving up here?"

"Four years."

"Four—? Why don't you have more experience with driving around this junk?"

"I'm the General's driver, sir," the driver noted with a trace of annoyance. "I'm always on call if the General needs a vehicle."

And all those Generals probably only rode this thing around the Colony, if that. What a waste of a good soldier and a decent vehicle. One more thing to fix if and when I get the chance. "Well, mister, you're driving me, now. Get this thing moving. I don't care if the paint gets scratched or the fenders dented."

"Uh, standing orders—"

"Just got changed. Move it!"

"Yes, sir." The APC accelerated again, not to the pace an experienced driver could have maintained, but noticeably faster than it had been poking along at before.

Stark worked the controls before him, bringing up the sector display. He paused, one finger poised to call up direct vid from a frontline soldier, then lowered the hand. *Too easy to watch this battle through the eyes of the people fighting it instead of doing my own job of trying to watch the big picture. Blasted command and control gear is too good.* Without his willing it, Stark's memory flashed to the initial assault on the Moon. Years ago, the first time the command and control vid had been fed straight to the networks with minimal time-delay as another form of mass entertainment, the first time the brass in the Pentagon figured out that a public hungry for blood-and-guts entertainment would pay to watch the real thing going down. A clever way to boost the military budget and fund some more hyperexpensive weapons without inflicting pain on civilian taxpayers, never mind how the average soldier felt about it, and never mind another big wedge driven between civilian and military society. *Why'd we put up with it as long as we did? And how do I get my people to fight now?* He stared grimly at the sector display. *Still running. Lots of them. But the flanks are holding.*

Nobody's even bothering the Castle. He flinched at the sight of the forces massing against his old Squad's position on the other flank. "Anita," he called. "How's it goin'?"

"Been better, *Sargento.*" Only someone who knew her well could have detected the worry behind her grim words. "They lost a lot of people trying to push us out fast, and now they're trying to do it smart. Nothin' we can't handle so far, though. Kinda busy to talk."

"Understand." He broke the link, fighting off an overwhelming sense of dread. *What was that story my friend Rash had told me about? Spartans. Yeah. Hold 'til you die. Why did it have to be my old Squad?*

"Stark?" The voice could have come from beside him, but the command display highlighted a location on the other side of the perimeter. "What's going on?"

Stark took a deep, calming breath before replying in an even, confident voice. "We got problems in one sector. I'm heading there now."

"Problems?" another Sergeant queried. "Looks like the front collapsed there."

"Yeah. That's how it looks 'cause that's what happened. But the edges of the penetration are holding, and we got a coupla battalions headed to knock the enemy back on their butts."

"How come they're running, Stark?" a third voice wondered.

Count to five, slowly, before answering. "I'll ask them when I get there."

"We're getting some pressure, too," a fourth Sergeant added. "They're pushing us in front and the guys guarding our rears are running away. We can't hold our positions with that happening."

Stark stared bleakly at the display, feeling uncertainty rising on all sides, the small hesitations multiplying, every one inconsequential in and of itself, but together building into a force that could turn the defenders into a panicked mob. "I told you we're gonna seal this penetration."

"Maybe we oughta fall back a little."

"No!" Stark almost shouted it. *Start falling back now, and they'll never stop.* "Hold on! Everybody hold their positions."

"Why?"

Why. Simple question. One word. Very hard answer. Why get yourself killed for something and someone else? Just having that question asked meant trouble, because "why" was one of the things you were supposed to be able to take for granted that everybody knew. "Why" had been easier to answer before Meecham's offensive had slaughtered the Third Division in repeated attacks against strong defenses, before the long habit of obedience had been shattered as unit after unit in Stark's own First Division had revolted against their own officers in order to try to save the remnants of the Third. Now, every possible reply seemed to have too many words, explanations too lengthy to have meaning to someone staring at incoming fire. Stark spoke with forced calm even as his mind churned in futile search for the answer that would likely do the job. "If anybody falls back, they'll screw everybody on their flanks and everybody in the rear."

"We're getting screwed now, Stark."

"You're in fortified positions," Vic broke in. "If you run, you'll be out in the open and much easier targets."

"Sure, Reynolds. But you'd still be at headquarters, and we'd be just as dead either way. Why should we do that?"

Stark felt pain, looking down to see his fist clenched so hard the armored fist of his suit was forming a vise. What reason could he give these Sergeants, what cause, when so much they'd always believed in and depended upon had been swept away along with the authority of their imprisoned officers? But maybe "what" was the wrong question right now, right this moment. Maybe right now he could only give them a "who." Sometimes people who couldn't find strong enough reasons to fight for themselves could find the reasons to fight for somebody else.

Stark let his anger and frustration boil over, spitting out each word with accusing force. "Okay, Goddammit. You apes elected me to this rotten job. I didn't want it, but I said I'd do my best because you guys gave it to me."

"We trusted you—"

"And I trusted you! So now you're gonna leave me hanging while I try to do this damn job? Is that right?"

"Stark, we've got our butts on the line here."

"What the hell do you think I'm doin'? Looking at the damn scenery? I'm goin' out there. I'm goin' on the line. And I'm gonna hold that line. Because you gave me a job to do, and I'm gonna do it. So who the hell's gonna screw me? Who's gonna leave my backside hangin' out? You, Carmen? How about you, Jones? Or maybe Truen?"

A moment's silence as the APC swerved around obstacles, rocking Stark in his harness though his eyes stayed fixed on the command display. "We ain't gonna screw you, Stark," an answer finally came. "We just, you know . . ."

"No, I don't know. This is a battle. The enemy's in front of you.

Kill 'em if they come at you, and they'll stop coming. That idea too complicated for anybody?" Silence, maybe embarrassed, maybe defiant. "So, you gonna fight? You gonna hold? You gonna back me up?" Stark demanded.

"Yeah. We put you out there. We'll watch your flanks. Give 'em hell, Stark."

"Thanks." He'd meant it to come out at least half-sarcastic, but relief made it sincere. A moment later, the APC braked gently, coming to a carefully controlled stop. Stark waited, fuming at the delay until the vehicle finally halted, then popped his harness and the access hatch in one motion. With the ease of long practice in low gravity, he shoved off surfaces with hands and feet to drive himself out and down instead of depending on the Moon's gentle pull for impetus. "Get the APC back about ten meters," he ordered the driver. "Have the gunner cover the ridge, but don't fire without my say-so."

"Uh, sir, mobile command center-configured armored personnel carriers don't have any armament."

"You don't have a gun? Nothing?"

"No, sir. All the command and control gear takes up too much space."

"Oh, for . . . never mind. Get that damned thing back ten meters and try to look threatening." Stark stood on the surface, the unnamed ridge rising before him, blasted black rock merging into endless black sky lit with a trillion trillion tiny lights that offered neither heat nor comfort. On the other side of the ridge, panic-stricken soldiers were streaming his way. Behind him, a battalion of soldiers was rushing toward this spot. But here, now, everything around sat quiet, still, and empty. Shut out the frantic messages filling comm circuits, look past the HUD crawling with enemy and friendly unit symbols, ignore the APC resting a short distance back, and Stark might be alone on the surface, the only human on the otherwise dead lunar landscape. *Just like that first human here, the guy who made the speech about everybody cooperating to share the Moon. Too bad all the other countries thought we meant it and came up here to get their share. Too bad our greedy corporations couldn't be happy with owning everything on Earth and had to tell their bought-and-paid-for politicians to order us up here to take it all back, so we end up fighting an endless war that we can't win and refuse to lose no matter how much we bleed. Yeah, too bad that for every human who wants to cooperate in building something there's usually two willing to cooperate to destroy it.* Far above, the blue-white marble of Earth beckoned, gazing down serenely at the organized violence its children had brought from their home. *You ever feel a little guilty, Mother Earth? Inflicting your offspring on other planets? Hell, you ought to. Maybe if you'd treated the human race nicer when we were growing up we'd have turned out better.*

Stark's original intention had been to take a position on top of the ridge, giving him maximum visibility to help rally his panicked soldiers. But some instinct held him here, on the reverse slope, while he watched the symbols crawl his way from both directions. Off to his right, where the widest open gap lay, a field of jagged rocks littered the terrain. On his left, a smaller gap beckoned, but off the direct line-of-retreat of Stark's fleeing troops. *On Earth they'd run right or left, but here they'll go up the ridge. Easier in the low gravity. So we've got to hold the top of that ridge. Right? Wrong. That won't work. Not enough time to dig in and anyone on that ridge will be exposed to fire by every enemy soldier coming this way. Besides, I've got to stop all the apes running away, and my reserve battalion won't get here before some of them do. Just me and a lot of scared-witless soldiers. A whole lot of scared soldiers. Back here, I can handle them as they start coming over that ridge, one or two at a time. Yeah, much better odds. But how to stop them? A rousing speech?* Stark snorted in self-derision. *I wouldn't know how. So what do I know?*

I know how to tell people what to do.

A figure came panting over the crest of the ridge, movements jerky with fatigue and panic. Stark tagged the soldier's symbol, coming up with an instant ID. "Corporal Watkins!" The figure spasmed in surprise, staring toward where Stark stood. "Take up position on the right." Stark pointed, armored finger designating the spot.

"What? But—"

"Watkins, get your butt in position! Now!" The figure finally moved, instinctively obedient though still uncertain. Two more soldiers came scrambling into Stark's view. "Jurgen! Rodriguez! On the left! By that rock."

"There's an enemy army right behind us! We can't stop them!"

"You haven't tried! Get into position."

"Who the hell are—? Stark? You're Stark?"

"Yeah, I'm Stark. You gonna stand here with me or leave me to fight alone?"

The two privates began moving, descending the reverse slope to where Stark had pointed them. Another soldier came right behind them. "Steinberg! Get over there with Corporal Watkins!"

"I don't—"

"Shut up and get over there!" The words had barely cleared

Stark's throat when two more soldiers came into sight, but both of these paused on the top of the ridge, facing back toward the enemy. "Sergeant Ulithi, Sergeant Van Buskirk! Get down here!"

"We're going to stop them," Van Buskirk insisted, standing steady even though his voice shook with anger and frustration.

"Damn straight," Stark approved. "But do it down here. One soldier at a time." He felt something to his left, where Jurgen and Rodriguez waited by their rock, an unsteadiness, as if the soldiers were reeds wavering in a strong wind. "Sergeant Ulithi, get down on my left and hold those soldiers and any others I send you. Van Buskirk, same on the right with Corporal Watkins."

"Roger. They won't go nowhere, Stark." The Sergeants moved, and Stark's small line steadied a little more. More American soldiers now, coming in larger numbers. Too many to hail individually. Stark grabbed the ones he could, building up concentrations of troops who had stopped running. Gradually, they stiffened, out of sight of the enemy, surrounded by friends, with increasing numbers of Sergeants giving them alternate doses of encouragement and browbeating. Gradually, they became an armed force again instead of a beaten mob.

"Commander Stark?" Another voice, breathing heavily, from a symbol approaching from the rear. "Fourth Battalion. Sergeant Milheim commanding."

Stark broke his concentration on the situation to his front, switching scans and juggling responsibilities frantically. "Nice to see you. You got the positions in your Tacs?"

"Yeah, but I don't like them."

"What—?" Stark bit off the word, remembering Vic's anger at

being ordered around like a new recruit. *He's not some brainless, green private. He's a smart, senior enlisted. I'm not perfect, and I don't have time to think everything through the way a guy with less responsibilities can. I damn well better remember all that.* "What's the problem?" he continued, his tone clipped but respectful.

Milheim pointed along the ridge. "You want my battalion deployed in thirds. One third here in the center, and the others to the left and right. I want to put most of my people right here in the middle and only a company on each flank."

Stark considered the idea, frowning at the ridge before him. "Why?"

"Because the enemy ain't gonna come through that rough terrain on the left," Milheim argued. "It'd slow them too much, even in low-G. And the opening on the right is too far off their line of advance. No, they're gonna come charging right up the middle here, and I want enough force on hand to knock them back on their butts."

"Kinda risky if you're wrong," Stark observed. "But it makes sense." And it felt right on that level where his instincts operated. "Okay. Do it, Milheim. Update your battalion's Tacs and get them deployed like you want. Do it fast. We ain't got much time."

"You got it." Milheim's fierce smile somehow came through the comm circuit, then he switched circuits to start ordering his soldiers into position.

"Ethan?"

"Yeah, Vic."

"What the hell is Milheim doing?"

"Sorry. You weren't in on that conversation." Small wonder, with the entire rest of the battle to worry about. "We decided to deploy his battalion different than you'd told them."

"I see. You've gotten rid of the officers so now you have to disobey *my* orders."

"You think your original plan was better?"

"I don't know. But I do know I can't run a battle if you keep improvising and don't keep me informed!"

Stark winced. *She's right.* "I'll keep you cut in from now on."

"Thanks." Vic sounded only slightly mollified. He'd have a lot of fences to mend when this battle was over, assuming they both survived the experience. "Don't get me wrong, though. I'm not used to handling this many troops. I want input."

"Understood. Me, too."

"You sure you want that battalion deployed along the back of the ridge? The best place to hit the enemy is when they're trying to climb up at you."

"Yeah, and the best place for them to hit us is on top of that ridge. These guys are still shaky, Vic. I need them under cover."

"You're on-scene. It's your call."

The simple statement startled Stark, used to officers in the rear using the sophisticated command and control gear to literally try to call every shot he fired. *If we get through this, I bet I can make these apes ten times as dangerous as they were when they were micromanaged. Just give me a chance.*

A moment's respite, the line around him solidifying, Milheim's Battalion giving a spine to those soldiers who had fled the enemy. Stark switched circuits again. "Anita. How's it going?"

Her breathing came heavy, health indicators displaying stress markers across the board. "They're all over us, *Sargento*. This bunker ain't gonna last much longer. They've got its position, and there's a lot a heavy stuff being thrown at us."

Scan simply confirmed Corporal Gomez's report. The enemy had figured out that Mango Hill formed the hinge for the American line now. Break it, and the rest of line would probably fall apart. Stark bared his teeth as he viewed the forces assaulting the hill held by his old Squad. *Too much going on at once, but I'm not gonna forget them. Okay. Think it through. Try to find an option, maybe not a by-the-book option, but one that fits the problem.* "Anita. Put the bunker's chain guns and grenade launchers on continuous full auto, minimum target criteria."

"Sarge, that'll burn all their ammo in a coupla minutes, at the most."

"The bunker won't last much longer than that, anyway, and that heavy fire will roll back the troops closest to you. Hang in there a little longer. We've almost got this mess fixed up."

"*Sí, Sargento*. Got 'em on full auto. Uraaahhh!"

"Bail out of there, Gomez, before they take the bunker down. You and the weapon station sentries."

"*Comprendo*. See you on the surface, Sarge."

Back to where he stood, focusing on the situation around him, adrenaline making Stark shiver with reaction even as Vic Reynolds called in. "Got a problem with Fifth Batt, Ethan."

"What?" Stark scanned Fifth Battalion's symbology hastily, scowling as he did so. "Nobody's hitting them. Why aren't they moving?"

"Because Kalnick doesn't like his orders."

Kalnick. Sergeant Harry Kalnick. Not someone Stark had ever had much contact with. A vague impression of someone who didn't quite rub right, though. "Kalnick, this is Stark."

"Yeah." The response was surly, with a dash of annoyance thrown in for good measure.

Stark counted to three before speaking again, fighting off the pressure-driven urge to scream Kalnick into a primal state. *Give him a chance to explain.* "Why isn't your battalion moving into position on the flank of the penetration?"

"I'm not going to let my battalion get beat up because you and Reynolds lost the bubble. I think it's a lousy idea and lousy tactics."

"Okay, what's your idea? How do you think we should deploy Fifth Batt to stop and roll back this attack?" Silence. "Kalnick. Tell me what's wrong with the positions you've been ordered into."

"They're lousy orders! They won't help anybody!"

"What's your alternative?" Stark repeated with forced patience. "Kalnick? We haven't got all damn day. The tactical situation is critical, and every other soldier is counting on you."

"This situation isn't my fault, Stark."

"I'm not debating with you, Kalnick. Get your Battalion moving."

Another voice, one Stark recognized, broke in as other Fifth Battalion Sergeants joined the debate. "Hey, Kalnick. What's wrong with these orders?" Sergeant Stacey Yurivan questioned.

"Stark's trying to use us to bail himself out," Kalnick argued.

"The hell he is. Stark's planted right in front of the enemy advance along with Fourth Batt."

More Sergeants chimed in. "I got friends in Fourth Batt. I ain't leaving them hanging."

"Why are we just sitting here?"

"Kalnick, what's your plan?"

Another brief stretch of silence, finally broken by Stacey Yurivan's voice again. "Hey, Kalnick. Either lead, follow, or get out of the way."

On Stark's scan, units in Fifth Battalion began moving, breaking out of their neat alignment to head for the positions Reynolds had designated on the flank of the penetration. "Kalnick," he called, "I'm giving you one more chance. Get your Battalion in position. If you've got a problem, we'll settle it after this is over. Understand?"

Kalnick didn't reply directly, but as Stark watched, the rest of Fifth Battalion surged into motion. *Okay. Got that fire put out. Now look at the big picture. Got a battalion taking up position to hit the flank of the penetration.* Stark pulled up the command scan, chewing his lip as he watched the so-far victorious enemy swarm toward his improvised defensive line. *Got another battalion here behind the ridge.* Switch views again. *The Castle's still holding. Mango Hill's still holding. God, look at all the crap getting thrown at them.* "Corporal Gomez." Static answered, fuzzed with the staccato beat of enemy jamming. Stark swore in frustration.

"Use your command overpower setting to punch through the jamming," Vic suggested.

"I can do that? Sure I can. I got official access to it now. But what are you doing sitting on my shoulder?"

"Just lucky timing," Vic assured him. "Gotta go and make sure our reserve company is ready to punch out from the Castle. See ya."

"Likewise." Stark checked the options available on his

commander's scan, calling up the overpower and linking it to Corporal Gomez's call sign.

Chaos sprang to life around him. Stark twitched as another dose of adrenaline surged into his system, urging action against violence being played out far away. "Gomez. What the hell's happening there?"

"Damn all, *Sargento.*" The view from Gomez's remote swung dizzyingly as she pivoted to pump a round into an enemy soldier who reared up not a meter away. "Hand-to-hand," she added unnecessarily.

"Can you hold 'em?"

"I dunno. Real target-rich environment out here." Lunar terrain jumped wildly again as Stark watched a ripple of red warning lights spring to life on Gomez's remote. Grenade, maybe, exploding not far from her. The view jerked several times as she fired rapidly. "Damn. Too close, *Sargento,* and too many, I think. Bunker's been breached."

"Hang on," Stark repeated helplessly.

"*Sí, Sargento.* Hell. Murphy's down."

Murphy. How long's he been in my Squad? Forever. Stark stared at the situation projected before him on the command scan, trying to block out emotion.

"Ethan, Murphy's just one soldier," Vic advised quietly. She'd been listening in again, of course.

"Every grunt out there is just one soldier. How many one's add up to too many?"

"I don't know."

"Me, neither." Stark gazed up at the endless black sky overhead, the symbology on his HUD superimposed on the heavens as if a complicated and intricate new zodiac had sprung to life. "I can't let that position fall, Vic. That's not sentiment. It's got nothing to do with them being my Squad. The whole line will unravel on that flank if that hill goes."

"You can't weaken any other point. They've got to be watching for that."

"Maybe they are, but maybe they're already throwing everything they've got at Mango Hill and into the hole that's in our line right now. If they win at either place, they take us down. It must look like a sure thing." He toggled a circuit. "Sanch." Sergeant Sanchez, formerly one of the three squad leaders in their platoon along with Stark and Reynolds, now commanding that platoon.

"Yes, Stark." Very calm, as if he were discussing the nonexistent lunar weather.

"You see what's happening to Gomez's position?"

"Of course. They are taking a great deal of punishment. We are providing as much supporting fire as we can."

"Thanks, but you're gonna do more. I want you to strip every soldier you can possibly spare from your other two squad bunkers and get over there as fast as possible. That hill has to hold."

"You are aware the positions we leave will not be strongly enough held to withstand a determined assault." Sanchez made it a statement, not a question.

"I know. But everything else I've got available is committed. I can only get reinforcements to throw at that hill by robbing Peter to pay Paul."

"Understood. I am certain I can clear the hill of enemy soldiers," Sanchez stated, imperturbable, as if he were describing a minor difficulty, "but I cannot keep it clear. There will be too much pressure."

"I'll take care of that."

"Then we are on our way. I will contact you when I link up with Corporal Gomez." Left unsaid was the distinct possibility that Corporal Gomez might not be alive to link up with when Sanchez got there.

It added up to considerable risk, leaving only skeleton crews manning the other two bunkers in that sector. Even a small but resolute push from the enemy targeted at that weak point could widen the hole in the front considerably and sweep away the only troops Stark could really rely on in the bargain. *But it's either that or lose anyway.*

"Grace," he called Divisional Artillery.

"I know I'm not stopping the enemy advance, Stark. Didn't say I could."

"I know that, and you're doing the best anybody can. No, this is about saving one position. How long to set up a barrage onto this spot?" He keyed in the coordinates of Gomez's bunker.

"We got a unit there, Stark. Looks like more on the way, too."

"I know. They'll be in a bunker. How long?"

"How big a barrage?"

"Enough to sterilize the top of that hill and the immediate area. No penetrators, though."

"Just surface and near-surface? To protect the troops in the bunker? Stark, I can't guarantee that none of those won't have a fuse malfunction and go subsurface before it detonates. It happens."

It happens. Stark wavered mentally again, pondering bad

choices and worse choices. *You'd think commanders would have enough to worry about during a battle without wondering if their weapons will work as advertised. But it's probably always been that way. I'll bet weapons designers in the Stone Age managed to screw up some of the rocks they handed out to the other cave dwellers.* "We'll have to chance it, Grace. It's the only way to stop the assault there."

"Okay, Stark. You're the boss. It's on."

"Thanks. Stand by for my word."

Another scan of the oncoming enemy. Some were charging ahead of the rest, heedless of the risk as the fruits of victory danced before their eyes. A couple of those enemy soldiers crested the ridge as Stark watched, their shapes suddenly silhouetted against the stars, the symbology on Stark's HUD momentarily superimposed on the actual objects it represented. Perhaps the overeager enemy soldiers had a brief moment to realize the enormity of their mistake. Perhaps not. A hundred rifles fired almost simultaneously, the impacts of the bullets launching their targets backward into space to fall again in long, slow arcs down the reverse slope.

"Sanchez. How're you coming?"

"In among them. Wait one."

A small force of enemy soldiers, not more than a single squad, came around the ridge to the left, trying to avoid the broken terrain by clinging to the slope above it. The Fourth Batt company positioned there waited until the enemy cleared the slope, then opened up a withering barrage that cut down every soldier in seconds. A low snarl came across the comm circuit as the American soldiers reveled in the small victory. "Good job," Stark called. "There's more coming, and they're gonna get the same treatment."

"Stark." Sanchez, breathing heavily now, but otherwise nothing in his tone revealing he'd been in heavy combat. "We have cleared the hill of enemy soldiers. They are positioning for another assault."

"That's fine. They're gonna regret it."

"Then we hold."

"No. Not yet. Get everybody down into the bunker."

"The bunker has been breached."

"You won't be fighting from it. Get under cover! Fast!"

"Ah. I see."

On the scale Stark was using for his command scan, the enemy units hurtling to regain their foothold on the hill seemed to merge with the American symbology as he switched circuits. "Grace. Now. Lay it on."

"Okay, Stark. Those troops up there have got, uh, thirty-five seconds before they get turned into hamburger."

"Roger." Stark swapped circuits frantically. "Is everybody down in the bunker, Sanch? You've got thirty seconds!"

"Thirty seconds. Acknowledged. Our rear guard is entering now."

Stark watched the rounds arcing in from the rear, trying to imagine almost a platoon of soldiers crammed into a single bunker battered by enemy fire. They'd be lying on top of one another, almost immobile except for those closest to any openings, huddled in the dark, feeling that hopeless fear foot soldiers experienced when they know heavy artillery was coming down on them. At such a moment, only chance and the grace of God mattered as training and experience came to nothing. Counting down the last few seconds to impact. Very easy to do with their HUDs helpfully displaying the digits in bright red numbers. Ten seconds as sensors on the surface revealed enemy forces charging onto the crest of the hill, expecting desperate resistance from ground level, then pausing as their own sensors told them of the threat coming from above. Five seconds as the enemy began frantically scrambling into retreat, too late and too slow. Only a few of the incoming American shells blossomed into early death as a result of counterfire from too-distant enemy defenses.

Zero. Silence. Somewhere hell had come to rest on the Moon's surface, massive shells hurling their fury onto a single, small area. On Stark's HUD, streams of symbology converged on the elevation nicknamed Mango Hill, vanishing on impact. Clean, with no vegetation to block or divert the path of shells. Quiet, with no atmosphere to transmit the unbearable thunder of explosions. Precise, without variables like wind to mess up finely calculated trajectories. Someone who had never experienced a shelling would have no concept from the HUD display, from the serenity of the Moon even a small distance away, of the reality where those shells were falling. Blizzards of metal fragments cutting down everything in their path, explosions rearranging the rocks and dust in wild patterns, hurling high-velocity gasses against anything too close to strike with deadly force before those gasses dissipated into the emptiness around them.

No comm signal could punch through that interference. Stark could only wait while the fury ran its course, wait with the silence that marked so much of the violence of war on an airless world.

It'd only take one shell, one shell penetrating into that bunker. Collapse the whole thing, expose the troops inside to the rest of the barrage, kill 'em all. And I'm the one who ordered it. Please, God, let it be the right thing. From somewhere, a memory of Vic's voice came. *Sometimes even doing the right thing doesn't do a damn thing for your conscience.*

A larger force of the enemy, perhaps twenty, came over the ridge crest, firing as they came, and died in another concentrated fusillade.

"Stark?" He jerked at the transmission, realizing as he did so that it had not come from Sanchez. "This is Lamont. I've got three squadrons of tanks in position on the right flank of the penetration."

"You do?" He'd missed that, with everything else going on.

"Yeah. Reynolds sent us up. That's okay by you, right?"

"Sure as hell right." Stark opened his scan, viewing a larger area. Lamont's armor sat in a half-dozen clusters, ready to rip the guts out of the enemy flank. "You hold fire 'til I give the word."

"Sure thing," Lamont acknowledged. "Perfect targets out there. This is gonna be like shooting on a firing range."

"Ethan," Vic chimed in, "you've also got APCs moving up. I'm setting them behind the ridge to help cover it."

"Thanks." He'd completely forgotten about armored support in the rush of activity, a ground soldier instinctively depending upon his own weapons. "Good job. Damn good job."

"*Sargento?*"

Stark let out a breath he hadn't known he was holding. "Anita? Corporal Gomez?"

"*Sí*. Sergeant Sanchez, he got a little banged up during that barrage. Partial bunker collapse. Lost some suit systems, but he's okay otherwise. What do we do now, Sarge? Any more of that artillery coming?"

"Not ours," Stark vowed.

"*Gracias Dios.* I don't wanna ever sit through somethin' like that again."

"God willing, you won't. Now get out on the surface again. That last assault must have been wiped out, but the enemy's gonna try to put some fresh troops together and hit you one more time. Don't worry. I'm about to give them something else to worry about, so just hold on a little longer."

"*Sí, Sargento.* We'll hold 'til hell freezes over. This hill is ours. We paid for it, and I ain't letting no one else take it."

"Stark?" Milheim again, Fourth Battalion commander. "We just going to hold this line?" he asked doubtfully.

"No. Listen up, everybody." He could see them, in his mind's eye, armored figures still rushing into final position or poised on the line, waiting for his next words under the black sky and the endless stars. "They've come as far as they're gonna come. We're gonna hit them so hard they won't be back for a long time. We're gonna get even for some of what they did to Third Division."

"Does that mean no prisoners?" a voice inquired.

Stark had an image of Sergeant Grace, wishing to take personal revenge on General Meecham for the death of his brother. Now he could do the same, in spades, inflicting the same slaughter on the enemy that Third Division had suffered. He clenched his teeth in sudden anger. "Negative, negative, negative. We take prisoners. We are soldiers, ladies and gentlemen. American soldiers. Despite everything. Don't forget that. We do not kill people trying to surrender."

"Understood," Milheim rogered-up for the entire force.

Stark paused, wondering how to issue a single command to Fourth Battalion and also to the polyglot collection of soldiers who had been rallied here. "Listen up. Everybody behind this ridge. You are all part of Task Force Milheim. Understand? Vic, can you link them all?"

"Roger. Wait one. Okay. Got 'em linked. They're all part of one command circuit, now."

"Good." Stark called up another circuit, speaking to every unit bordering the penetration. "Everybody hold fire until I give the word." Stark switched scans rapidly, seeing the battle from the perspective of other soldiers on other parts of the field. From one of the tanks hidden to the right, threat symbology highlighted shadowy figures gathering below the opposite crest of the ridge from where Stark stood with his line of troops. Better than company strength this time, he estimated, and getting stronger by the moment, preparing for another shove, which the enemy doubtlessly believed certain to shatter the remaining resistance to their advance. "Hold it." Over on the left, an anti-armor team tracked enemy APCs rushing forward to catch up with their infantry, the anti-armor team's HUDs painting a bright aim point along the flank of one APC. "Hold it." Up on the hill, Gomez held the remnants of her Squad and Sanchez's reinforcements among the newly rearranged landscape, firing steadily at enemy soldiers trying to regroup below for another push at Mango Hill, but ignoring enemy forces scrambling through the gap. "Hold it." The right side of the penetration again, where Delta Company had gathered in the lee of the Castle, chafing like racehorses awaiting the starting gun. "Hold it." Back to the tank, watching as the enemy soldiers swarmed up the slope toward him. Easy, far too easy, to imagine himself among those troops, charging to the attack, doped on adrenaline, elated and scared at the same time. *They're not monsters. They're grunts like me, and soon they're gonna get cut to ribbons in a crossfire. Hell. But I didn't start this war, and I didn't launch this battle, and I'm damned if I'm gonna lose either one. Or one more soldier than I have to.*

Stark waited, waited until the charge had almost reached the crest. "Now. Open fire. General engagement."

The enemy attackers hit the top of the ridge and ran head-on into a concentrated barrage from Fourth Battalion and the rallied soldiers from other units. The charge halted as abruptly as if it had hit a brick wall, the leading elements hurled backward by the impact of the American fire, their fall back down the slope dreamlike in the low gravity, bodies slowly spinning from the impact of bullets and the venting of atmosphere, limp arms and legs occasionally striking the slope to generate small falls of dust and gravel to drift gently down in tandem. The scene had all the weird beauty and horror of a mad painter's vision of hell, set against a landscape of dead black shadows and blinding white sunlight.

The enemy rallied just beneath the crest, but before the assault could resume, fire swept in from the flanks, raking the exposed troops once more. The enemy ranks seemed to dissolve, vanishing from the ridge, a few survivors frantically racing downward. Stark switched vid feeds rapidly, viewing other areas, seeing enemy armored vehicles erupting into flowers of metal fragments and gasses, soldiers hesitating in their charge, falling under fire, then beginning to drop back. "Alright, you apes. We've taken enough punishment. Let's hand out some. Task Force Milheim, let's go! Everybody forward. Keep going until we reoccupy every position we lost. Vic, get Fifth Battalion and Delta Company moving to seal the penetration."

Stark was charging up the slope, aware of the soldiers following even without checking the symbology on his HUD. To the top and over with one smooth motion, one free hand shoving him down the reverse slope. A figure rose nearby, IFF painting it red for enemy. Stark's rifle swung and fired without his conscious thought, hurling the soldier back against the dead rocks. Maybe the soldier had been trying to surrender. Maybe trying to fight on and buy time for friends running for their lives. Stark would never know.

"Ethan! You don't have to lead the damn charge!" Vic shouted at him, her faraway presence sounding next to his ear.

"Yes, I do. They're following me, Vic. How's Delta Company coming?"

"If you weren't in the middle of combat you could check for yourself! Geary's pushing her company out, but she's scared of mines and enemy forces that might have occupied our bunkers."

"She's got a right to be scared."

"Ethan, I can't give her company detailed orders for their Tacs when we know so little about the threat there."

"Then don't. Let Geary handle it bunker by bunker."

A pause. "Right. I'll tell her to run her company from where she is."

"Fine, but make sure she knows we're depending on her to retake those positions so these people we're chasing don't get away."

"Roger. I'll keep a fire going under her."

Down the slope, his feet pushed off outcrops with the skill born of experience, driving him downward in rapid surges that altered direction at each push to confuse anyone trying to target him.

Other soldiers raced alongside, literally running over a few of the enemy caught in the motions of throwing aside their weapons. Ahead, the bulk of the enemy forces had reversed direction, falling back as fast as they'd advanced, trying to escape the trap they could now see closing in from all sides.

A section of broken terrain ahead suddenly began spitting bullets at the advancing Americans, and Stark's HUD screamed threat warnings as it highlighted the threat symbology heading his way. The soldier closest to Stark came to an abrupt halt, his forward motion stopped by the impact of bullets, then was punched backward by several more hits. Stark fell behind a small mound of lunar dust, piled up by who-knew-what forces over uncounted years, and wished those forces had managed to build a higher pile in all that time. Shouts rang out over the circuit, orders and warnings intermingling. An attempted rush of Americans to the right was met by a flurry of fire, driving the attackers to ground. The charge faltered, hesitating as the retreating enemy pulled away behind the cover of their rear guard.

Stark scanned the surrounding terrain, cursing. *Perfect defensive position. I either lose a lot of people charging straight in or lose a lot of time working around the flanks. I wish—*

A boulder detached itself from the moonscape, sliding forward as the tank's main gun swiveled to bear on the enemy strongpoint. The cannon twitched, lobbing a shell into the center of the enemy firing. Dust and rock flew in a swelling geyser as the tank's round created a new crater, then a second shell dug another hole not far from the first. A few figures rose, scrambling for cover or trying to target the tank, only to be cut down by bullets from Stark's soldiers.

The tank slid to a halt, its secondary cannon spraying the enemy position with fire as the main gun continued to leisurely hurl heavy rounds onto any point that might hide a concentration of enemy soldiers. A moment later the terrain seemed to erupt armored figures as the enemy broke, leaping up to flee. Rifle fire claimed several before they could travel a meter, then most of the others halted, raising their arms in the universal gesture of surrender.

"Milheim," Stark called out, "detail somebody to guard those prisoners."

Before Milheim could reply, Vic Reynolds came on line, speaking in cool, clear tones. "All prisoners are to be instructed to drop safeguards on their suit systems so we can take them over.

"What if they don't do it?" someone demanded.

"Tell them that anyone who doesn't has not surrendered. Give them five seconds to comply and then open fire again." She altered subjects smoothly. "All APCs forward. Even sections proceed just behind the infantry line to provide fire support. Odd sections break off to assist guarding prisoners."

A flurry of questions sparked by the order flew over the comm circuits. "How many prisoners should each APC guard?"

"What if an odd section is closer to the front line right now?"

"Should we break the sections down if we have to?"

"Dammit!" Stark bellowed. "Think for yourselves!" Silence followed his order. "Vic, did that go out?"

Her chuckle answered him, incongruous against the battle flaring on all sides. "Yeah, Ethan, it went out."

"Why didn't anybody acknowledge it?"

"They're probably in shock. God only knows the last time that particular order was given by anyone in the U.S. military."

Forward again, Stark no longer literally leading the charge as younger, less cautious soldiers moved faster, running down groups of the enemy before they could establish new defensive positions. Other groups, in familiar armor, appeared as well—Americans captured in the rout now shocked to find themselves free and pressed into guarding their own former captors.

"Vic! Has Geary reoccupied the entire front?"

"Negative. Too much resistance. I'm angling a couple companies from Fifth Batt up toward the front to reinforce her and close the gap from the other side."

"Can we push some tanks in from the right, too?"

"I'll ask Lamont."

Down and through a small crater, a group of soldiers appeared with shocking suddenness off to the left. Stark's rifle was already steadying as his IFF chirped a reassuring "friendly," then the new arrivals opened fire on the nearest retreating enemy forces. *Fifth Battalion*, he realized, scanning his HUD. *We've linked up.* "Keep moving, everybody. Don't stop. Keep pushing them hard so they don't have time to dig in."

Pull out the scan, viewing the entire area, symbology swimming in dizzy patterns as friendly positions shifted around the entire penetration and enemy positions popped up, vanished, then reappeared in fleeting sensor detections. A gaudy sensor display to Stark's left, throwing out wild bursts of infrared, resolved into an enemy APC as he reached visual range, its fuel and ammunition burning in an erratic bonfire. Figures lay scattered among the rocks, some in suits still broadcasting feeble signals, some silent and unmoving. He tried not to look, beyond ensuring none were enemy soldiers playing possum, and tried not to personally tally the losses suffered so far this day.

Victory or defeat. Each had a momentum, becoming self-sustaining as confidence or despair skyrocketed. Stark wasn't leading the charge anymore; he was caught up in it, swept along as the counterattack surged forward.

Not far now. The front beckoned, crowds of enemy soldiers milling about in confusion, raising their arms toward the dark heavens or making desperate attempts to break out through the reoccupied bunkers. American armor, rushing forward in a highly risky dash, had reached the bunker line and formed a moving cordon, tracking back and forth to overawe or fire into small pockets of resistance. Stark's troops swept forward, filling the circuits with cries of triumph as they turned defeat into unlooked-for victory.

Some of the troops kept moving, reaching the bunker line and going beyond to chase the retreating foe. Stark felt it, then, a force born of exhilaration and heedlessness, pulling at him and the others, urging them forward. *The enemy line must be thin. They must have weakened it to push troops into the attack. Their own panicked troops are running into and through it. We can take them. We can break their line.*

And then what? Stark checked himself with a muffled curse. *What the hell would we do if we did break that line? We can't exploit it, and we couldn't hold an isolated section way out in front of our own line. And what if it isn't weakened? What can I win here that would be worth what's it's likely to cost?* "Everyone, do not pursue past our own front. I repeat, do not pursue."

"But we got 'em! They're running!"

"So were we not so long ago, and what'd we just do to them? Nobody's touched the enemy line yet, and you apes are running right at their bunkers! Anybody forgotten what happened to Third Division?" The question, invoking the deaths of thousands of soldiers who'd tried to break that same enemy line, seemed to have more force than Stark's earlier command. His units suddenly braked, but those forward of the American bunkers held their ground instead of falling back.

"Stark," someone beseeched, "we can do this. End this damn war."

Tempting, but only if your thoughts remained focused on the here-and-now. Stark mentally braced himself, then triggered a change in the unit scans. New symbology sprang to life on everyone's HUDs, phantom units arrayed for battle, the better part of a brigade of soldiers frozen in midcharge against that same portion of the enemy front. "Everybody see that?" Stark demanded. "Those are dead soldiers from Third Division, still out here because we haven't been able to recover them yet. Look at them. They thought they could take those defenses, too. Remember?" *How could they ever forget? Alarms screaming threat warnings, that brigade dying out in front of us and nothing we could do but watch. Dear God, never again.* "Now get back inside our lines!"

His troops moved at last, pulling back slowly and cautiously, keeping to cover as best they could. The so-far silent enemy line began spitting angry shells in their wake, hastening the withdrawal to the safety of the American defensive umbrella.

Enemy artillery reacted, throwing shells into the area, the barrages losing much of their force to American defenses, but some rounds making it through. *God, I hate artillery. Enemy artillery, anyway.*

I'm sure I've lost too many people today already, and I've got too many soldiers out in the open rounding up enemy prisoners . . . . "Vic, is there any way to talk to the enemy from headquarters?"

"I don't—yes. Tanaka says there's a red line direct from here to their headquarters. Why?"

"I want someone to get on that red line and tell them we've taken a lot of prisoners and right now their own artillery is dropping shells on those prisoners. They better lay off hitting that area unless they want to kill a bunch of their own people."

"Roger."

It took a few minutes, but the enemy fire lifted, avoiding attempts to hit deep targets and contenting itself with pounding the American front. Stark stepped carefully downward, working down the slope, making his way to a position screened from direct enemy observation. *I'm forgetting something. Something important. Ah, hell.* "Anita."

"Yes, Sarge." Her voice shook slightly, reflecting overwhelming fatigue of mind and body.

"The enemy's gonna start hitting your hill with artillery, just as soon's they think of it. The bunkers to your left have been reoccupied, and we've got this situation stabilized enough so you can come down. Get everyone off Mango Hill and into those other two bunkers to your right. We'll be able to cover the gap."

"No."

"No? What the hell do you mean, 'no'?"

"I ain't leaving here." Her voice shook more, beginning to quiver as Stark knew her body must be at that moment. "We paid for this hill."

"Corporal Gomez, we are not giving up the hill. We will retain possession. But leaving infantry up there exposed to enemy bombardment would mean throwing their lives away."

"I can send most of the other troops to the bunkers—"

"Corporal Gomez, you and every other soldier on that hill will reenter the bunkers to your right, and you will do it now, or I will personally come up there and kick your stubborn damn butt into the nearest bunker! Is that understood?"

A long moment later, she answered, voice ragged with apology. "*Sí.* Sorry, *Sargento.* Will comply. Been a long day. I—"

"Got nothing to apologize for. You did great. Now, get your people under cover." Stark watched the symbology on Mango Hill begin to move, sliding back and sideways in sections as the defenders finally relinquished their hold. *Have I forgotten anything else really important? God, I don't know. So close. They almost had us. Just figured they'd keep charging deep, and we'd keep throwing in small groups of reinforcements to try to stop them as soon as possible. But we thought of something else. Thanks, Kate. That's another one I owe you.*

The debt never seemed to lessen, Stark reflected grimly. So many years ago, his fellow soldiers dying all around, trapped by superior forces on the hellhole forever to be known as Patterson's Knoll. Corporal Kate Stein, also surviving until night fell, but critically wounded, ordered Stark to leave and try to escape in the dark. He'd promised her then, promised to save other soldiers someday even though he couldn't save her that night. And he'd kept that promise, despite the risks, despite the anger of officers who cared more about sticking to a plan than fighting smart and keeping their people alive. Kept it until it had led him here, with no idea of where it might lead next.

That man-created line on the lunar surface, which had been the front, then fallen, and now become the front again, seemed curiously peaceful. Stark stood below the top of a low rise, protected from the enemy artillery that sought belated vengeance by targeting anything moving among the American positions. A tank, its multiton bulk gliding with incongruous delicacy among the rocky terrain, took up position about half a kilometer away. With its massive curved carapace, it resembled a giant, mutant beetle hiding in the lee of the ridge, although fortunately for humanity no beetle had ever been armed with such an impressive array of heavy weaponry.

"Yeee-hah," Sergeant Lamont remarked in a conversational tone. "That there was the best fun I've had in all my years up here. We gonna do it again?"

"Dear Jesus, I hope not," Stark responded fervently.

"Ethan?"

"Yeah, Vic." He had to keep reminding himself that she wasn't somewhere nearby, guarding his flank. No, Reynolds sat far away at headquarters, guarding both flanks and his rear as she helped oversee the battle.

"Could you do me a small favor?"

"Sure, Vic, what?"

"Get the hell away from the front line!"

"Okay, okay." He tagged the tank's comm circuit again. "Hey, Lamont, I gotta go. My mom's calling. Can you use your armor to stiffen the front until we get all the bunkers back on-line?"

"Sure. No prob. You ain't gonna get that bunker on Mango Hill working anytime soon, though."

He shied away from the implications. "I know. We'll have to figure out how to fill the gap."

"Heck, I can use my tanks as mobile bunkers. Rotate a half-squadron at a time up right behind the front, keep 'em moving behind screening terrain so the enemy can't pinpoint 'em. Good practice for us, and it'll make anybody think twice about trying to annoy us around here again. That is," Lamont added, "if that's what you tell me to do with the armor."

"Lamont, *you* tell *me* how to use armor. How come I haven't seen you armor apes do that kind of thing before?"

"Because anytime you take one of these tanks out of the storage hangar there's a chance it'll get hurt, and they're so blasted expensive no general ever wanted to let them out of the hangar. Let me tell you, I'm pretty tired of only driving these things in simulators."

Stark nodded, unseen by Lamont. "Those tin cans'll see plenty of action, now. Work out your plan and just shoot a copy to Reynolds and me."

"You're the boss. See you in the Out-City."

"Yeah." Stark shook his head, eyes suddenly blurring so the symbology on his HUD fuzzed into unreadable blobs. "Vic?"

"Here."

"What's happening out there? Is everything else okay?"

"Check your command scan."

"I . . . can't. Look, just tell me. We got things fixed here, right? Any problems anywhere else on the perimeter?"

"No, Ethan. No problems. When the other enemy sectors saw how hard we hit back, they pulled their own forces out of contact. Relax."

"Thanks." Stark started trembling, first his arms, then his legs, shaking so badly he couldn't stand and had to kneel, then lie on the rough lunar rock, eyes looking past the symbology on his HUD to the empty black sky beyond. After awhile, the cold began to seep through his suit's insulation, but he lay still except for the tremors running through his body. The stars swung slowly overhead, scattered points of light blessedly free of meaning, indifferent to the woes humans inflicted on one another.

"Commander?" The voice had some vague familiarity. Stark shifted his head slightly, seeing for the first time the bulk of an APC looming nearby, its curved armored shell black-on-black against the rocks rising behind it. "Sergeant Reynolds sent me to bring you back to headquarters. Commander?"

That command-configured APC. Forgot about it. "Yeah." He struggled to rise, submitting finally to aid from the driver as his stiff joints refused to cooperate. Inside the APC, he strapped in, looking past the status displays as the vehicle rose and swung around on to a course back to headquarters. This time, its speed didn't really matter.

Stark walked slowly through the headquarters complex, unaware of those around him, until he reached the room he'd chosen for his own living quarters. It had belonged to a Colonel once, which made it large enough to cause Stark some embarrassment, but it had quickly become apparent that he needed that room to handle the work his new responsibilities had brought. Now, though, he ignored the work reminders blinking on the desk, palmed off the lights, and sat silently in the dim illumination of the room's nightlight.

Sometime later, Vic pulled the door open, letting a shaft of light from the hall lance into the room. "Hey, Ethan."

"Hey."

She leaned against the door frame, arms crossed. "What're you doing?"

"Trying not to think."

"Jeez. One battle in command, and you're already trying to act like a General." When Stark didn't rise to the joke, she shook her head, then extended a hand. "Come on. We're going for a walk."

"Why? What good will a walk do?"

"A helluva lot more good than sitting in a dark room. Let's go, soldier."

Stark stood reluctantly, yielding to the pressure as Vic steered him out of the headquarters complex, along corridors whose rock walls grew less finished and whose width shrank as they approached the Out-City. The bars and corridors were filled with soldiers celebrating with the curious joy of those who have stared death in the face, yet somehow come away living once again. Amid the larger groups, small clusters of more sober men and women marked those discussing the loss of friends and relatives. How, when, and where. Knowing those things didn't help the dead in the least, but they meant a great deal to those left behind.

"Who are these apes?" Stark wondered.

"Fifth Battalion," Vic replied, "and the units that broke on the front. I pulled them off the line and left Fourth Battalion to cover the area for a little while."

"Good idea." These soldiers might look happy, but he could feel their brittleness, the fragile equilibrium under their surface gaiety.

"Milheim did a good job."

"Sure did. Got a real solid outfit, there, and a real solid commander."

"Glad they're holding the line right now." A deep breath. "Any casualty count, yet?"

Reynolds twisted her mouth. "Things are pretty confused, but we ran a system inventory and came up with about a hundred dead. Wounded? God only knows. It'll take us days to sort that out."

"A hundred dead."

"About. Hundred and fifty, max. Ethan, most of those died running. We could tell by where their bodies are lying."

"That's the way it usually works." They'd kept moving as they talked, and as he walked past some of the soldiers recognized Stark, grinning as they brought right hands up in sharp salutes. "We kicked butt!" one called, to a chorus of agreement from nearby listeners.

Good morale, Stark realized with surprise. *They survived, we won, and the butcher's bill wasn't too bad. Pretty damn small, truth be told. One will always be too many, but at least I kept the casualties down.* "Maybe I didn't do too bad, after all," he muttered under his breath.

"You did real good, Ethan," Vic stated.

"How the hell did you hear that?"

"I didn't. I read your mind."

"I always figured you could do that." Stark shook his head, slowly smiling. "Okay. I did okay. Could have been better. There's a whole lot of stuff we gotta work out before another battle like this happens. Coordination. Getting a lot of the detail off those damned headquarters displays. Setting up people to support you and me when too much is happening at once." His smile faded into a frown as he caught sight of one soldier slumped against a corridor wall, face reflecting some internal wound. Stark veered to come face-to-face with the man. "What's up, soldier?"

"Huh?" The question had obviously shocked the soldier out of an internal reverie, and now his expression screwed up in total misery. "Stark. Sir. Damn it all. I let you down."

"*You* let me down? Just how did that happen?"

"I ran." The two words seem to choke in the soldier's throat. "I ran away. My unit broke, maybe because I ran."

Vic moved forward, face concerned, but Stark waved her back. "How far? How far did you run?"

"I . . . I dunno. As far as that ridge."

"The ridge. The one where I was? The one we held, and then hit back on?"

A flash of pride broke through the pain. "Yessir. That one."

"Let me tell you something, soldier." The man braced himself in obvious expectation of a severe tongue lashing at best and arrest at worst. "If I'd seen you running on the field I might have shot you to stop you, because I have to worry about a lot of people and sometimes that's the only way to get their attention. Yeah, it's bad you ran. Real bad. But you stopped. That counts, too. You stopped, you fought. That means you've still got the makings of a good soldier."

"It's okay?" The man obviously didn't believe it.

"No, it's not okay," Stark snapped. "You let me down, you let down all the other soldiers in this unit, and most importantly you let down the soldiers on either side of you who depended on you to guard their flanks. Don't do it again. Ever. Or I'll make you regret the day you put on a uniform."

"I won't. I swear."

"Good, because the enemy gives me enough to worry about. You apes are too damn good to let me down. You're too damn good to let your friends down."

"Yessir. You don't have to worry about me." Still unhappy, but determined as well, now.

"Good. I won't forget you. Carry on." The soldier saluted stiffly, standing rigid as Stark and Reynolds walked on.

"You're mellowing," Vic remarked.

"Am not." Stark glared at her. "Didn't I sound mad enough? 'cause I sure as hell was mad."

"Right now, that soldier's a lot more afraid of you than he'll ever be of the enemy," Vic assured him. "But he confessed to running, Ethan. That's a court-martial offense."

"I know that." He scowled down the corridor. "A lot of people ran. I can't court-martial them all. Don't want to. That'd do more damage than their running did. Rip outfits apart. No. The shame, knowing they let everybody down, that'll make 'em fight better next time. They'll want to prove themselves."

She nodded judiciously. "The Uniform Code of Military Justice doesn't leave a lot of room for discretion, but you were never big on the letter of the law, were you?"

"Vic, the letter of the law is for people who don't have enough sense to know what's right unless it's spelled out for them. I am not going to lead these people at the point of a bayonet. They'll follow me because they want to, or I'm doing something wrong."

"Not a bad philosophy." She chewed her lower lip, gazing upward at the rough steel-and-rock ceiling over the corridor. "So, you told me during the battle you had some idea why they started running in the first place."

"I think so, yeah."

"Care to enlighten poor ignorant me?"

"Let's get a beer, first." Stark veered again, heading into one of the literally hole-in-the-wall establishments to grab two beers. Waving off a small group of soldiers who tried to surrender their seats at the only table in the tiny bar, he led Vic outside again, leaning against the rough rock wall, oblivious to the cold, which somehow managed to seep into the stone no matter how well insulated or how warm humans made their living areas.

Stark took a long, slow drink, pausing to order his thoughts. "You want to know why they ran? Because they didn't have a good reason to fight. They haven't figured out their cause, yet, Vic. They don't know what they're fighting for."

"Hmmm." Vic pondered the statement, taking a drink of her own beer. "You'd think they'd fight to save themselves."

"Sure. But saving your skin is a lousy combat motivator. That's why mercs make rotten soldiers, right? They're fighting to stay alive and draw their pay checks."

"Yeah." It was Vic's turn to scowl, though she aimed the gesture at her beer. "This stuff really sucks. Ethan, you and I and any veteran knows the best way to get yourself killed in combat is to start running."

"But that's just it! It doesn't make any sense. It's crazy. The way to stay alive is to stay in combat? No, every instinct we've got says to stay alive you run away from danger. You've gotta have a reason to override those instincts."

"Good point." She looked down at her beer again. "I'm empty. You should've gotten more than two."

"I thought you said it sucked."

"It does. But it's still beer."

"Anyway," Stark continued, "we've spent our lives fighting for . . . what? The U.S. of A.? Protecting our families? The Constitution? Or just plain trying to do the right thing in a world full of wrong things. So which of those still apply? Right here, right now?"

Vic rubbed the tip of her nose with one forefinger as she thought. "Doing right," she finally concluded.

"I sure hope so. But you had to think, didn't you?"

"Sure did." Vic stared outward, eyes fixed somewhere and somewhen else. "The only way to handle combat is to not think about things, like how maybe you're going to die at any moment, but if you don't have much of a clue why you're fighting in the first place I guess people can't stop from thinking."

"Maybe." Stark snorted in sudden derision. "That'd fit. The only people who can't handle the mil are the ones who can't stop thinking."

"So, what are you thinking right now?"

He looked around, taking in the troops filling the corridor and the cramped bars that lined it. "I'm thinking we got off lucky. That battle was too damn close to lost. How can we know the same won't happen again next time somebody pushes us hard?"

She laughed. "Ethan, you gave them a reason to fight that'll be good enough until we come up with some others. Okay, two reasons."

"And those are?"

"You. And one another."

"Me?" Stark stared in disbelief. "What the hell are you talking about?"

"People need heroes and leaders, Ethan. You're both. Think about it. Think how you held things together when the other sections of the line started getting real nervous. You told them they were letting you down."

"That's not what I said. Was it?"

"Maybe not exactly, but it was the general idea. And they didn't want to let you down because you've never let them down. Whenever things start to fall apart, Stark is there, holding the line, looking out for everybody. You can't ask for much more in a commander."

"Yeah. Right." Stark looked away, but every direction held soldiers offering smiles and salutes. "How about a commander who knows what the hell he's doing?"

Vic grinned. "Hell's belles, Ethan, we've *never* had one of those."

"I've let a lot of people down, Vic. They're dead, and I was responsible for them."

"You can't take the blame for those guys running—"

"I didn't mean them. I meant the people in my Squad. God, how many have died? I can still see them all."

Her smile vanished as she stared down at her empty beer. "We've all got those kinds of ghosts, Ethan. Some more than others. If you never wanted anyone who worked for you to die, you're in the wrong line of work."

"I guess. Damn strange way to make a living." He crumpled his beer, tossing the empty container into a nearby recycling bin.

"Which reminds me. There's something I gotta do."

"Okay," she agreed as he began to go. "Ethan?"

"Yeah."

"You did a good job. Don't torture yourself because it wasn't perfect." One corner of Vic's mouth twisted upward. "Who am I kidding? I'm telling Ethan Stark not to sweat the fact he's not perfect? Why don't I just tell the Moon to grow an atmosphere?"

"Why don't you? You seem attracted to hopeless causes." He left her laughing again, heading back to headquarters, not stopping until he reached his room again. Stark sat carefully before the terminal, bracing himself, knowing he'd put off one last task for too long already, then activated his comm unit. "Corporal Gomez."

The reply came after a few moments, thin but steady. *"Sí, Sargento."* She looked like hell, face pale and drawn, but tried to draw herself as erect as possible.

"Relax, Anita. How you doin'?"

Her body drooped very slightly. "Okay. Pretty tough battle, huh, Sarge?"

"I've been in a lot easier ones. You did one helluva job. Damn good."

Color flooded back into her face as Corporal Gomez flushed. *"Gracias, Sargento."*

Stark hesitated before speaking again. "How many did we lose, Anita?"

It took a moment for her reply. "Kidd. She fought real good, but there was just too many targeting her. Hit six, seven times. Hoxely. Got a big hole blown in his chest. And Maseru. Too green, that kid, he made one mistake too many. Not his fault, I guess. Didn't have time to learn the ropes."

Three dead. Surprisingly few. "That's it?"

"Dead, yeah. Then there's wounded. Just about everybody got beat up some. The worst ones, well, Billings took a hit in the shoulder that broke everything all to hell. The docs are building her a new shoulder joint and stuff. Chen got another round in his hip. He must have a target painted on there."

"What about Murphy? He was down . . ."

"Oh, yeah." Her eyes widened. "Man, I'm really wasted, I guess, to forget him. Murphy, he lost an arm."

"An arm?" Not dead after all. But—"He lost a whole arm?"

Gomez nodded. "Yeah. Don't know for sure what hit him, maybe he got in the way of a bunker-buster. Blew away everything up to the shoulder, and some of that, too, I guess, and filled his side with shrapnel."

"How the hell did he survive that?"

Gomez's tight grin spoke more of remembered tension than of humor. "Real lucky guy. Somebody was close enough to him to slap one of them economy-size battle bandages on the wound. You know, the ones that clot the blood automatic. That sorta sealed the big hole in the suit, too, long enough to get Murphy into a survival bag. Still don't know how he lived long enough to be stabilized, but he's tough, eh, *Sargento?*"

"Yeah, he's tough," Stark agreed, knowing that he was probably talking to the "somebody" who'd saved Murphy.

"They can grow him a new one, right? A new arm? We got that up here?"

"Yeah. Either the mil docs or the civs can handle it. I'll make sure they do."

"Good. Murphy was worried about that." She grinned again. "While he was being medevac'd I told him, 'Murphy, you're damn lucky that Sarge ain't here, 'cause if he was, he'd tell you too bad you lost that arm instead of your head, since sometimes you use that arm.' "

Stark laughed, too, unable to hold it back. "Anita, you are one hard-ass bitch."

Her grin widened. *"Gracias, Sargento."*

"Take it easy, all of you. Get all the rest you need."

"Don't got no choice. The docs, they wanted to stick us all in medical, but they're still full up with more serious wounded so they had to confine us to our bunks. Pretty good, huh? Getting ordered to stay in bed all day."

"Enjoy it. I doubt it'll ever happen again." The connection ended, Stark palmed the lights off again, but this time he lay on the bunk, closing his eyes to sleep, trying not to see the faces of Kidd, Hoxely, and Maseru.

He was still nursing a cup of coffee the next morning in the nearest rec room when Vic came in and plopped down at the same table. "Good morning, sunshine."

"Likewise."

"What you been up to this morning?"

"Working out." Stark rolled stiff shoulders, wincing. "Haven't done a resistance workout in way too long."

Vic drew herself a cup of coffee, smiling archly. "We've been busy."

"I know. I also know what'll happen to my muscles if I drop off the daily workout routine for any length of time. Speaking of which, when was your last workout?"

"You got me. Right before we enjoyed front-row seats for the death of Third Division." She nodded several times at Stark's expression. "I'll get back in the routine. Cross my heart. You don't have to look so disgusted."

"I'm not disgusted by you. It's this coffee. With all the luxuries here at headquarters, I always figured the officers also had good coffee. Boy, was I wrong. How come I've never found a decent cup of coffee in the mil?"

"I think there's a regulation against it." Vic sipped her own cup. "Ugh. This is worse than the stuff we get. Okay, Ethan, we got some issues to talk about."

"We've got about a million issues to talk about. Which ones in particular do you mean?"

"Officers."

Stark winced again. "Vic, we haven't had time to work out how to get them back to Earth. As soon as—"

"That's not what I meant. We need new ones. Some of the acting commanders are okay, some aren't. We need to appoint officers, and the only place we're going to find them is from the enlisted ranks." She glanced around until her eyes focused on the terminal imbedded in the wall nearby. "I knew there had to be one of these in here. Look. This is the table of organization for our division. How are we ever going to locate enough enlisted good enough to fill all these officer positions?"

"We won't, and we don't need to. You told me, remember?

There's too many officers. So we only need to fill the positions we, uh, need to fill."

"Elegantly expressed, Ethan," Reynolds noted with a smile. "Good point. Still, that leaves a lot of job openings."

"What's wrong with the people holding those jobs now?"

"You're kidding, right? There's nothing wrong with some of them. But some of the others are way out of their depth. Others can handle the job but don't want it."

"Tough." Stark leaned back, pitching his empty cup expertly into the recycling chute. "My heart bleeds for them. Nobody better complain to me about having to do a job they don't want. I know all about it."

"Then," Vic continued, "there's the ones who just don't belong in their positions."

"Like who?"

"Like Kalnick."

"Oh, yeah." Stark scowled. *Unfinished business. Gotta deal with that, and soon.* "Okay, you've made your point. But how do we turn Sergeants, Corporals, and Privates into Colonels, Majors, and Captains?"

"There's on-the-job experience," Vic pointed out, "like we had yesterday."

"I'm not sure I could take many more experiences like that. And since I don't intend launching any offensive actions, there ain't gonna be a lot of opportunity for people to learn that side of the job in the field."

"Agreed. So we need to set up a training program."

"A training program? What kind of training?"

She shrugged. "Large unit command and control, I guess. We'll have to depend on the simulators up here to teach maneuvering large units. Once we get the sims fixed, that is."

"Fixed? What's wrong with 'em?"

"Nothing if you prefer fairy tales to reality."

Stark frowned. "I thought they were supposed to have the latest and greatest combat sims up here."

"Nah. These are pretty damn good, but the latest and greatest never goes to the front lines. It always ends up in the Pentagon or somewhere else in the rear. You want to know what's wrong with the sims?" Vic leaned to trigger the display again. "You can access them from here." The display sprang to multicolored life, cluttered symbology marking American and enemy positions. "This look familiar?"

"Yeah." Stark fought down a shudder. "That's what things looked like just before Meecham sent Third Division forward."

"Very good. This is the sim they ran to, if you'll pardon the term, 'test' Meecham's plan. Watch." She activated the sim, letting Stark watch as the initial brigade assault began.

Stark shut his eyes, trying to block out memories of futile slaughter. "Vic, I don't think I can watch this."

"This is the sim, Ethan. Look."

It took a lot of effort, but Stark forced his eyes open again, then almost immediately furrowed his brow. "This shows the enemy, too?"

"Uh-huh."

"How come those units in their rear are jittering back and forth instead of heading to counter our attack?"

"Because," Vic explained patiently, "Meecham's theories said they'd be confused by our little diversionary actions. Remember those? So the enemy, in the sim, can't decide where to commit its troops."

Stark snorted in derision. "Hey, there's a lot of enemy positions missing. Meecham's plan needed that to work, too, right?" As Vic nodded, Stark pointed at the symbols marking the advancing American brigade. "Look at that! They're maintaining perfect formation! That's ridiculous. Those soldiers were incapable of that up here."

"They had to be able to maintain perfect formation for Meecham's plan," Vic reminded him. "Ethan, I talked to the ape geeks who run the sims. Their orders are always to make the plan work, so they program the sim so the plan works. Get it?"

On the display, only scattered enemy fire met the American charge, then enemy units began falling away, retreating in ironic mimicry of the recent disaster Stark had narrowly avoided. "No. I don't get it. These sims are supposed to be so good they show exactly what would happen in the real world."

"Uh-uh," Vic chided, wagging one finger at him. "Not the 'real world,' Ethan. Whatever world needs to exist to make the plan work. See? To make Meecham's plan work, the enemy needs to react just the way his theory says they have to. Our forces have to perform just the way he needs them to, regardless of things like terrain and training. And when push comes to shove, the enemy has to be overwhelmed by the force of our . . . what'd they call it, our clustered paradigms?"

"Somethin' like that." Stark shook his head, jaw slack. "I don't believe it. Those damn Generals really did think they were gods. If the world don't match the plans, you change the world to fit."

"Right. Then you declare the plans good because, hell, you ran them on a state-of-the-art simulator, right?"

Stark rubbed his palms into his eyes. "Then the sims have always been run like that? That's why so many real-world ops went to hell even after they'd supposedly been sim'd to death?"

"I expect. Most people figured the sims were being run to get real answers. Instead, they've been designed to produce whatever answers the guys in charge wanted to get."

"Why didn't we hear anything about this?" Stark ground out. "Those ape geeks are enlisted. How come they never passed word around?"

"Security, Ethan. Everything about the sim designs has been slapped with high-level, compartmented security protection. The ape geeks were subject to the highest levels of security screening so they couldn't breathe a word to anyone for fear of flunking the screens. That was supposedly so the enemy wouldn't learn anything about us from the sims. I guess it was also to keep *us* from learning about the sims."

"Nothing like security rules to cover up mistakes, arrogance, and just plain stupidity," Stark agreed sourly. "Okay, but the sim guys can fix this junk? Program sims so that they reflect the real world?"

Vic hesitated. "They say so."

"But you don't think so. Why not?"

"Because I've been thinking about it, and I'm not sure we can ever make a sim do what's advertised." Vic leaned back, apparently watching the sim unroll as the virtually unscathed simulated

American troops continued to simulate triumph in every direction. "Take terrain. You ever walk someplace where the map exactly matched the ground?"

"Hell, no. There's always differences. Even up here where nothing's supposed to change and the whole surface is supposed to be digitized to hell and gone. There's always a rock where one ain't supposed to be, or no rock where the map says there is one."

"Right. The Rock Gremlins." Stark laughed at her reference to the mythical creatures that altered terrain every time an allegedly definitive map had been produced. Since senior officers always insisted the maps had to be right, the enlisted joked that there had to be something moving rocks, hills, trees, buildings, and bodies of water around after the maps had been created. "So even terrain in a sim can't be exactly right," Vic continued. "What about fuzzier stuff, stuff you can't just scan from orbit and digitize? You know, how well a weapon works, how fast a soldier will move, how much ammo they'll need, how often they'll hit what they aim at. And that's fuzzy enough for our side. Now think about trying to input that data for the enemy. What the hell's so precise about any of it?"

Stark thought about it. "Not much. You're saying a sim's just a bunch of guesstimates being run against other guesstimates, right?"

"Exactly. Guesstimates precise to the tenth decimal point, but they're still guesstimates. Even when you're trying your damnedest to make it reflect some impartial reality, which apparently docsn't happen all that much."

"Huh. I guess that's why the fantasy games some of the troops play seem just as real as the sims."

"Yeah. As far as the computers are concerned, they're the same thing."

"Great. So the sims aren't a magic bullet, even if we do our best to make them realistic. How else can we teach our people to be officers?"

Vic canted her head to indicate her terminal. "I've been browsing around a little. There's a whole mess of Staff Education Courses in the files. I guess officers were supposed to do them in their free time."

"Staff Education Courses? SECs?" Stark pronounced the acronym as one word in standard military fashion. "Who thought up that name for the courses?"

"I wouldn't care to guess, but I'd bet somebody suggested it as a joke, and when some Generals liked it, everybody was afraid to tell them."

"So what kind of SECs did our officers enjoy?"

"Ethan, behave. Look. Here's one on *Effective Battle Management.*"

"You're kidding." Stark leaned to look closer, twisting his face skeptically as he did so. "How the hell do you 'manage' a battle? I always thought they were too big a mess for managing."

"No idea, Ethan. But they apparently not only figured out how to 'manage' a battle, they figured out how to do it 'effectively,' too."

"Uh-huh. If our officers were so good at managing battles, how come our battle plans were usually screwed up, and we had to fight like hell to win?"

"You can't have everything, Ethan. Do you want your battles well-managed or do you want them well-planned?"

"You're right. What was I thinking? What other kind of courses have they got in there?"

"Let's see." Vic paged rapidly through menus. "Here's a whole bunch of courses on leadership."

"Leadership? Officers were supposed to learn leadership from education courses?"

"Guess so. We got *Leadership Fundamentals, Leadership for Commanders*—"

"Who else leads? They got a 'Leadership for Followers' course?"

"Haven't seen one yet, but it might be there. Then there's *Advanced Leadership, Basic Leadership*, which must differ somehow from fundamental leadership, *Leadership for Field Grade Officers, Crisis Leadership, Effective Leadership*—"

"All the other kinds of leadership aren't effective?"

"Based on our experience with officers, I'd say no. Hmmm. Here's *Total Quality Leadership.*"

"Which is also different from effective leadership, I guess. Do they have to call it 'total quality' so nobody will think it's half-ass quality?"

"*Midcareer Leadership!*" Vic continued, ignoring Stark's latest jibe, "for those officers who haven't learned any leadership during the first half of their career, I suppose. *Leadership Case Studies*—"

"Oh, for cryin' out loud," Stark complained. "These guys were supposed to be leading us. Who the hell thought they'd learn more from 'case studies' on their computers than they would from actually spending time with their troops?"

Vic made another face. "I guess it was one of those 'sounded good when it started' things that got out of hand, like they usually do. Oh, I don't believe it."

"Now what? More how-to-be-a-leader-on-your-computer junk?"

"No." Vic leaned back so Stark could see the screen. "New course series, I guess. *Combat Management*"

Stark found himself laughing. "Sure. When it comes to actual combat, all that leadership garbage just doesn't apply. For combat, you gotta be a manager. Or if you want to run an effective battle. Why in God's name would anyone waste time on this stuff?"

"I don't know. Maybe one of these codes along the top . . . ah, here you go. 'Course completion mandatory for promotion eligibility to O4.' "

O4 was the rank code for an Army Major or Navy Lieutenant Commander. "So an officer couldn't make Major unless they took all these courses?"

"A lot of them, anyway. Now we know some of what our officers were doing when they were supposed to be leading us."

Stark pressed his fingers against his temples, trying to push away an incipient headache. "Okay, then. These courses are mostly crap. The sims are self-justifying junk. And we already know that officers were taught that command and control somehow meant the same thing as micromanagement. So, basically, we gotta throw out just about everything that's already there and build our own training system."

"Ummm, yeah," Vic agreed reluctantly.

"I guess we do all that in our copious free time?"

"Ethan, it's not like we have a choice."

"Yeah, we do. I could just shoot myself. Or surrender and let our former officers shoot me. But I ain't gonna do either one."

"You're not alone in this," Vic pointed out.

"Which is probably the only thing keeping me sane." Stark

reached out to grab her wrist, giving it that brief squeeze that signified friendship. "Okay. We'll get it done. Somehow. Right now, you need a workout, and I need a shower."

"I wasn't going to call attention to either fact." She stood, smiling wryly. "Guess we're both going to be doing a lot of things that are unpleasant, but good for us."

"Guess so. See ya later." Stark slumped in his chair after Vic left, wondering why lunar gravity sometimes seemed so heavy. He closed his eyes, trying to shut out memories of battle, but seeing them replayed in the dancing lights behind his eyelids, explosions and swarming symbology mingling in a never-ending dance. Opening his eyes revealed the unfamiliar surroundings of the headquarters rec room, an unmistakable reminder of endless current problems. The buzz of his comm unit came as a welcome distraction and relief. "Stark?"

"Yeah. What's up, Bev?"

Sergeant Manley sounded apologetic. "I know you're real busy, Ethan, but the civs are calling again."

"The civs." Civilians. Inhabitants of the Colony. The people Stark and his soldiers fought to protect, but met only rarely.

"Yeah. They want to talk to somebody in charge. That's you."

"That's me," Stark agreed wearily. *Guess I can't put the civs off any longer. One more thing I gotta deal with.* "Any administrative issues need addressing right now?"

"Sorry. My office is humming with its customary awesome efficiency, so I can't give you any excuses for not calling the civs."

"Okay, okay. Give me their number, and I'll call them." The vid screens here in headquarters were bigger and fancier than Stark was accustomed to, so that he needed a few frustrating seconds to figure out the extra controls. Eventually, the screen cleared, showing two civs seated at a metal conference table. One of the civs, a man, had a harried but determined look that somehow matched his graying hair. The other civ Stark recognized immediately. He'd met her once, an eternity of a few days before. "Ms. Sarafina. Long time no see."

Sarafina stared back in obvious surprise, then whispered quickly into the man's ear. He nodded, then looked straight at Stark. "My name is Campbell. James Campbell. I'm the Colony Manager."

"Pleased to meet you. Ms. Sarafina told me a little about you."

"Are you an authorized speaker for the lunar military forces?"

Stark mustered a half-smile. "I suppose you could say that. Sorry I've been too busy to talk before this. We've had a few problems."

"So we've guessed." Campbell visibly hesitated. "There's been a very large amount of military activity in the last few days. Our sensors have picked up a tremendous level of surface explosive activity."

"We've been fighting like hell, if that's what you're trying to say."

"Is the Colony . . . that is, how secure—"

"We're holding, Mr. Campbell. The Colony's safe."

"Thank you. Now . . . your proper title is Sergeant?"

"It is if you want to get on my good side."

Campbell looked briefly puzzled. "Sergeant Stark, exactly what has happened to your leaders?"

"You mean our officers?" Stark found himself reluctant to speak or even look directly at the civilians. *First time I'm talking to somebody who wasn't in on it all and shares the guilt. God, what have we done?* "They're safe."

"I don't understand. We haven't seen or been able to communicate with any officers for days. Our only contacts have been with enlisted personnel such as yourself, and they've refused any information. Normal communications with Earth have been cut off without explanation. Shuttles have been blocked from departing and no new shuttles are arriving. What is going on, Sergeant Stark?"

Stark lowered his gaze, concentrating on the lower frame of the comm terminal. "Mr. Campbell, I regret to inform you that our officers have been disarmed and imprisoned. We are no longer following their orders."

The statement seemed to confuse both Campbell and Sarafina, who looked at each other for possible enlightenment before focusing back on Stark. "Whose orders are you following?" Sarafina finally asked.

"Our own."

"Your own." Comprehension suddenly entered Campbell's eyes as he held up a hand to forestall any further questions from his aide. "Sergeant Stark, are you telling us you are no longer acting under lawful authority? That your forces are in a state of mutiny?"

Stark closed his eyes momentarily, then nodded. "Yeah. Yes, sir. It's a long story," he added as Campbell's and Sarafina's faces paled with shock. "Let's just say things got too bad. Way too bad. It came down to taking over in order to survive."

"I don't . . . but all those new soldiers we've seen arrive recently ——"

"Are mostly dead," Stark stated bluntly.

Campbell looked down at his hands for a moment, plainly gathering both his thoughts and his composure. "But if you are no longer obeying your officers, who is in charge?"

"Me." This time Sarafina looked ready to pass out. "It wasn't my idea," Stark added rapidly. "Well, maybe a lot of it's my fault. I don't know. But afterward, everybody wanted me in charge. So I'm the commander."

Another pause, then Campbell fixed Stark with a demanding but anxious stare. "Then I must ask you what your intentions are regarding this Colony."

"Our job is to keep the Colony safe. We're going to keep doing that."

"But if you're no longer American soldiers—"

"We're still American soldiers!" Both civilians jerked away involuntarily, hitting the backs of their chairs as they tried to distance themselves from Stark's outburst. "Sorry," he apologized gruffly. "There's a lot of things we haven't worked out. But that hasn't changed. We'll defend the Colony. We already have. We just won't die senselessly anymore just because some idiots with stars on their shoulders want to make names for themselves and won't listen to common sense."

"I apologize. I didn't mean to imply . . ." Campbell took a deep breath. "This is totally unexpected news. We weren't prepared for it."

"Neither was anyone else."

"You will not surrender the Colony to any foreign powers?"

"No."

"You will continue to defend us as vigorously as ever?"

"Yes."

"You still consider yourselves Americans?"

"Absolutely."

"But you are not accepting orders from the authorities on Earth or their representatives on the Moon?"

"No."

"And your long-term objectives are . . . ?"

"Undetermined."

"Sergeant Stark, I understand if you are unwilling to share that information with me, but it is of critical importance." Campbell shook his head, lips a thin line. "Let me explain. We're under martial law, Sergeant. It's been that way as long as the Colony has been here. We've been allowed a very small degree of local independence as long as it didn't affect whatever got labeled a 'security issue,' but we don't rule ourselves. We also have no means of effectively resisting your forces no matter what actions you decide to take. To put it bluntly, it appears you are our new master, and I need to know what you intend to do."

"I've told you all I can tell you right now."

Campbell glanced despairingly at Sarafina, then back at Stark. "I have responsibility for every civilian on this Colony. I cannot protect them if you will not provide me with basic information."

Stark kept his face impassive. *Responsibility talk. From a civ. And a politician. Does he mean it? Everything I've learned in life says no, don't trust him.*

As he sat silent, Sarafina leaned forward, her own expression pleading. "Sergeant Stark, please. Our people are depending on us."

Two civs, both of whom seem a whole lot more concerned about "their people" than they do about themselves. And Sarafina, near as I can tell, kept her promise to me not to tell any of our officers what I'd said to her. If I can't respect that, what can I respect? Stark rubbed his chin, pondering his response. "You want to know our long-term objectives? I don't know," he finally admitted. "That's the truth. Nobody's had time to think about that yet, or about what we'll do regarding you civs.

Civilians. We don't want you stabbing us in the back. But I don't think any of us want to tell you what to do, otherwise."

"Sergeant Stark, there are any number of things I cannot do without approval of the designated military authorities."

"I can patch you through to the stockade if you want to talk to any of them, but it doesn't much matter right now whether they approve what you want or not."

Campbell maintained a poker face now, sitting silently, then glanced over as Cheryl Sarafina began speaking again. "Sergeant Stark, are we to understand you have no interest in exercising control over the civilian portion of the Colony?"

"I told you, I can't have you people doing stuff that would cause problems for my people. But I've got a full plate just trying to run the mil side of things. And the military isn't supposed to give orders to civilians. Things are supposed to be the other way around, right? So, I've got no interest in telling you what to do, and to be perfectly frank, I don't think any of the other mil want anything to do with you."

Sarafina railed at the words, her expression angry. "We've done nothing to the military personnel up here. We've provided a tremendous amount of support to you. We appreciate your sacrifices. Just because we haven't been allowed—"

"Sorry. Didn't mean it to sound like your fault." Stark forced another smile. "Not you specifically. My people, the military, don't know civilians. They grew up separate, they work separate, and they die separate. Mostly, they get treated real bad when they meet civilians. Back on Earth. So they don't like you. I think, maybe, you guys are different. But it'll take time to convince my people of that."

Campbell nodded. "I believe I understand. You're a separate

subculture. Perhaps we'd appreciate this better if we'd been allowed to view the military vid shows—"

"No. We hate the mil vid. It's a vid show put together from our command and control systems during combat. We're dying, the civs are watching and having a good time, and the government rakes in revenue from the ads it sells. Understand?"

Sarafina looked horrified now. "Gladiators. You've been treated like gladiators."

"Hey, it made money for the government and kept the civs entertained. Who cared how we felt about it?"

"I begin to understand," Campbell stated slowly. "You've been used."

"That's one way of putting it."

"But what are your goals, Sergeant Stark? What exactly are you trying to accomplish?"

Stark found himself laughing, bitter and angry all at once, "Damned if I know." He sobered, looking downward for a moment. "All those new soldiers you asked me about, Ms. Sarafina?" The brief meeting seemed ages ago. "Most of them are dead, like I said. That idiot General Meecham threw them against strong defensive positions, and when that didn't work, went ahead and did it again a few more times. We stopped that. That's why we took over. But stopping the slaughter meant we had to handle a lot more, and we're still working all that out."

Campbell's eyes narrowed. "Then you really *haven't* thought this out. It happened, spur-of-the-moment, and now you're trying to deal with the results."

"I guess that's a good way to sum things up."

"Sergeant Stark, you've done a very foolish thing." Campbell paused as Stark felt his face flush with anger. "I'm not referring to your decision to seize control of the military forces up here. Only you can judge the wisdom of that action. No, I'm talking about your discussing this with me. By combining your words with what I can see between the lines, I know far more about your situation than you should want to disclose to someone whose loyalty to you is an unknown."

He's right. Me and my big mouth. I shouldn't have made this call without Vic here to tell me when to shut up. I don't know this guy and don't really know Sarafina. They're civs. And they're political types. Or corporation types. I'm not sure which, but I've never found reason to think either type cares a damn about the best interests of me or any other mil ape. "So why are you telling me this? Why not milk me for more information before telling me I oughta shut up?"

"Because I believe the military and civilian communities up here need each other. I'll be as honest with you for a moment as you've been with me."

"You're a politician," Stark pointed out coldly.

Instead of triggering animosity, Stark's words brought a laugh from Campbell. "Yes, I am. But that doesn't mean what you think it does in this case. Why do you dislike and distrust politicians? No, don't bother, I'll answer for you. They manipulate the laws they write to benefit themselves and their friends. They take large contributions from corporations and then do pretty much what those corporations want. They steer government money to pet projects. Is that a good summary?"

"It's a start."

Another laugh, tinged with bitterness. "Yes, I suppose it is. Sergeant Stark, I have no voting power, anywhere. Every penny of the Colony budget is set in stone by Congress. The corporations direct every aspect of the Colony that the military hasn't wanted to control. I can't make laws, and I can't spend money. All I can do is go hat-in-hand to the people who do control those things and ask for a decent shake for the people of the Colony, whose only vote is to choose the person occupying my position."

"Then why do you do it? Why get elected?"

"Because it's important. Because if I don't, some hack who cares nothing for the Colony except as a stepping-stone for ambition might be elected instead. Not that actually gaining any political points are likely, given the powerlessness of the position, but it's possible if you were willing to sell the Colony's inhabitants even further down the river."

"Huh." Stark thought about that, then nodded. "Thankless job. I'm familiar with the concept. Okay, so let's assume you're being honest with me. What is it you want to say?"

"That this event is totally unexpected. I have no idea how the rest of the Colony will react to the news. However, I believe your actions offer my people an opportunity to finally alter their own status vis-a-vis the authorities back on Earth." Campbell glanced at Sarafina, who nodded. "My aide here told me she explained to you our situation."

"She said something about you being, uh, wage slaves?"

"That's essentially correct. Nearly every civilian up here signed agreements to repay the costs of our transportation to the Moon and subsequent upkeep. Everyone thought this offered a great opportunity, that the money to be made working in the Colony would allow eventual repayment of those debts followed by a life filled with more promise than the employment opportunities back home."

"I guess things haven't gotten any better for civs since I joined the mil," Stark observed.

"They've gotten worse. Vertically and horizontally integrated corporations have locked up so many jobs they can exercise almost total control of working conditions and wages. Back home, the government long ago 'got off the backs' of the corporations, which has meant the corporations have been on our backs ever since. Up here, where we thought things would be better, it turned out to be a lot worse. There's nowhere else to go for work, and no place to shop except company stores charging prices exorbitant even by lunar standards. And, of course, the transportation and upkeep contracts turned out to contain hidden interest on outstanding debt."

Stark remembered, long ago, overhearing his mother and father during anguished conversations. "So every day you wake up poorer, right?"

"Exactly."

"Sounds like the corporations have been killing you slow while our leaders killed us fast."

"That is an excellent summation, Sergeant Stark."

"So what does what we've done have to do with your problem?"

Campbell stared. "You really don't know, do you? Sergeant Stark, we've had no choice but to endure these conditions. No lawyer we could hire could prevail against corporate legal teams, we are denied our own political representation in Washington, no politician from back home would act on our behalf because they are in pay of the corporations, and if we had ever tried to act unilaterally the military forces up here would have simply enforced the will of the authorities back on Earth. But, now, you are no longer following the orders of those authorities."

"Not at the moment, though I don't know how much they've realized that so far."

"Sergeant Stark, I know very little about the military, but I assume you require the same things most people do in the way of food and shelter, and somewhat the same things a corporation would, supplies to meet your specialized needs. You'll need this Colony to help provide all that for you."

"I expect that's true."

Sarafina leaned forward again. "We need each other. Whatever you decide your long-term goals are, Sergeant Stark, you'll need the Colony's cooperation. And we can provide that cooperation in exchange for your protection and support when we demand political and economic redress."

Stark twisted his mouth, trying to think the offer through. *I don't know enough. Bottom line, I just don't know enough to know if this is a good offer or a good idea. Besides, I'm already scared of what I started. Do I want to have a colony in revolt on my conscience, too?* He sat silent, thoughts going nowhere.

"Sergeant Stark?" Colony Manager Campbell finally asked. "I understand you may need awhile to consider what we've said, and you'll no doubt want to consult with your own advisers. Can we arrange another conversation tomorrow, or perhaps a face-to-face meeting?"

My advisers? I haven't—Yeah, I do. People like Vic, and Manley, and other grunts with experience in things I don't know. "That sounds like a good idea. Let's talk again. Maybe not tomorrow, but soon. There's a lot going on." He moved to break the connection.

"Wait." Campbell raised a hand to forestall Stark. "There's something else. You told us you've had many soldiers killed."

Stark froze for a moment, then nodded slowly. "Yeah. A lot. What of it?"

"I assume that means many others are injured?"

"That's right."

"We know the military medical facilities are limited. There is a state-of-the-art hospital for treating civilians up here." Campbell mustered a derisive smile. "The corporate VIPs and politicians who visited the Colony wanted to be sure we could handle any problems they might have. If you need more space, or specialized care, for your soldiers, we can take them."

"You can? That's great, but I don't know how we'd pay for it."

"Pay?" Campbell shook his head firmly. "It's us who are repaying you for your defense of the Colony all these years.

If you need medical assistance for your soldiers, we'll provide anything we can free of charge."

But still put us in your debt. I sure wish I knew if I could trust these civs. I know we could use their help, though. My wounded soldiers can use their help. And Campbell did volunteer it without me even hinting at it. Stark smiled with what he hoped looked like genuine gratitude. "Thanks. That's very nice of you. Tell me how to contact your medical people, and I'll have our docs call them right away."

The screen dark again, Stark hesitated, then punched in Sergeant Reynolds's address, frowning as the image stayed blank.

"You there, Vic?"

"Yeah."

"What's wrong with your vid?"

"Nothing. I just got out of the shower, and I'm not offering a free vid show to anybody who calls."

"How 'bout if I input a credit access code?" Stark teased.

"Soldier, you'll never have enough money to buy a look at this show. What's up?"

"We need another staff meeting."

"Can't we just go on a suicide mission instead?"

"Sorry. Let's combine it with lunch so at least we'll get one useful thing accomplished."

A late lunch, as it turned out. Stark shoveled down a last soggy french fry, then looked around the table. "I got a big issue, but let's save that for last. Anybody else got anything really hot?"

"Everything's hot." Sergeant Gordasa tapped his terminal with one rigid finger. "We've got a lot to worry about in Supply. Let's talk basics. Food. Water. Environmental systems."

"We know we're not self-sufficient," Vic stated. "Why does this need to be handled now?"

Gordasa shook his head. "We're probably closer to self-sufficiency than you think, and we got a lot of rations stockpiled on the surface. Stuff Third Division apes were supposed to consume and won't be needing." He ignored the anger his words triggered, knowing it was aimed elsewhere. "But it's still limited, and we've no idea how long this situation is going to last. And we've got lots of officers we've got to feed until we can off-load them. So what happens yesterday? You heroes snag a whole bunch of prisoners. Prisoners we've got to feed. What the hell are we going to do with them?"

"You got a suggestion?" Stark asked.

"You're damn right I've got a suggestion. Give 'em back. They're not worth the supplies they'll consume."

"Prisoners are extremely valuable," Vic objected.

"Not to us," Gordasa disagreed. "Sure, our officers wanted them for intelligence so they could plan the next offensive, but we're not planning any offensives, right? So aside from asking for any of our own prisoners back, what else can these guys do for us?"

Sergeant Manley looked up suddenly, frowning thoughtfully. "Hey. That's it. Swap."

"Swap prisoners? That's already a given, but we've got a helluva lot more of theirs than they do of ours."

"No, no. Trade 'em. The enemy wants their people back. We want food and environmental supplies and stuff. Fine. We do a swap."

Something about the suggestion disturbed Stark. "Trade people for food? A human isn't a sack of potatoes."

"Some might as well be, but that's not the point. We need the potatoes. We don't need the people."

Vic smiled. "Ethan, I like this idea. We get rid of the prisoners, we get more of what we need, and we probably get humanitarian points for letting the prisoners go pretty quick."

Stark tried to think of problems with the proposal, glaring down at the table surface, then nodded. "Okay. We'll do it. Tanaka, use that red line to enemy headquarters to set up the swap. Make sure we've got a smooth operator running our end of things so we get a good bargain."

"Sure. Gordasa? You a good scam artist?"

"Me?" Sergeant Gordasa questioned indignantly. "I work by the rules. Which you apes usually complain about."

"If we want a scam artist," Manley suggested, "we ought to get Yurivan involved."

"Stacey Yurivan?" Vic cocked one eye toward Stark. "You want to give her access to headquarters?"

"What's the worst that could happen? Never mind. Forget I asked that." Stark glanced around at his improvised staff. "Can we trust her with something this big?"

"Pair her with a straight arrow," Gordasa suggested. "Somebody to watch whatever deal she's working up."

"Make that two arrows," Vic amended. "Gordasa, you keep an eye on the technical side of the deal. Tanaka, you keep an eye on Yurivan. Every contact with the enemy includes all three of you."

"Stacey wouldn't betray us," Jill Tanaka protested.

Stark nodded again. "You're right, but she would try to work a deal that'd turn her a fat, juicy profit. We can't afford that. At the very least, it'd make us all look bad if she got caught."

"I'm not going to lie to her about why I'm involved," Tanaka insisted.

"Not asking you to. Besides, Yurivan will know why as soon as she sees the setup."

"And," Vic added dryly, "she'll be proud we posted two sentries to watch her. Alright, Ethan. Enough stalling. Let's handle this big issue of yours."

He fidgeted a moment, aware of the eyes on him. "It's the Colony. The civs. They wanna know what we're doing."

"Screw 'em," someone murmured.

"No," Stark objected. "We're all in the same boat up here. We can't hold out if the civs go against us. Anybody ready to shoot American civs who don't do what we say?"

Silence.

"I didn't think so. And like I told Vic awhile back, these civs seem a little different. They've been right behind the front lines long enough to realize we're not playing some fancy vid game for their entertainment."

"Even if you're right," Gordasa noted, "and my own experience sort of confirms it, so what?"

"The head civ, a guy named Campbell, wants to know if we'll back the civs against the government."

Everyone stared, half-startled, half-scornful. "I think," Vic finally suggested carefully, "that starting one rebellion is enough for us for now. Why get involved with a bunch of civs?" Most of the others around the table nodded in agreement.

Stark clenched his hands on the table, looking down at them for a moment. "Not too long ago I asked Vic what we were fighting for. She said if nothing else, at least we were doing the right thing. Well, near as I can tell, so are the civs. They're being used. They want to be treated right."

"What they probably want," Tanaka stated icily, "is to use us, and treat us the way they always do." More nods. "You can't trust civs."

"I grew up civ." Stark's words shocked some of those around the table, while others simply stared back, unresponsive. "I know. You all grew up in Forts with mil parents and mil friends. But I didn't."

"You're mil now," Vic objected.

"I grew up civ," Stark repeated. "They're not necessarily bad.

I've been through the same treatment you guys have in uniform. Stay out of the civ neighborhoods 'cause they don't want any violent lowlifes around. Get cheated by civ merchants. Get sent to lousy places to get shot at because the corporations think they can wrangle a few more bucks that way. And I was in on the action the first time we got an op sent to vid for entertainment. So I know. But I know the other side, too. They're people. They're our people."

"What do you want from us?" Vic asked. "Don't expect us to trust these people, these civs, at the drop of a hat. It's not going to happen. We've been screwed too many times."

"Like I said, I know. All I want is to talk to them. Find out if they're for real. See if we have stuff in common. We should, by God. What's wrong with talking to them?"

"That's probably what Eve said to Adam about the snake," Vic observed.

Stark took in the expressions around the table, unconvinced, and not willing to be convinced. "Fine. Then let's put it in terms of self-interest. Anybody around this table think we can survive up here without the cooperation of the civs? Anybody care to think what'll happen if the civs are actively working against us? Anybody want to take over running the civ Colony?

"How about you, Bev? That'd be a great administrative challenge."

"Uh-uh," Manley demurred. "It'd also be a nightmare for me. I don't know their systems." She looked around sourly. "Stark's right. We might wish they'd go away, but they won't. We've gotta deal with 'em."

"I'll set up a meeting," Stark continued. "Like this one, but with the civ reps here, too. And we'll talk. No promises. No deals beforehand. That okay with everybody? Vic?"

"I'll talk," she glowered back, "but don't expect hugs and kisses."

Gordasa raised one hand slightly and waved it. "This looks decided, and I've got too much to do and too little time to do it in. Is there anything else for now?"

"No," Stark informed the group. "I'll let you know when we'll meet the civs."

"Oh, goody," Vic whispered not-quite-under-her-breath, evoking laughter as the others filed out. "Sorry, Ethan," she added when the last of them had left. "It just kind of slipped out."

"Yeah. Right. Just give me a chance on this."

"Sure. You, I trust. Civs, on the other hand . . ." Vic let the sentence trail off meaningfully. "Speaking of trust, are you sure you're happy with having Stacey as our lead on the prisoner negotiations?"

Stark snorted a brief laugh. "I haven't been happy with anything for a long time, now. But if anybody can get us the best deal, it's her." He checked the time, exhaling heavily. Over half a day gone. Unreal. *I spent most of yesterday fighting for my life and most of today in meetings wishing I was handling something as simple as yesterday.* He paused, face suddenly tight. "And, speaking of Stacey, now I've got to do something real hard."

Vic raised a questioning eyebrow. "What's that?"

"Kalnick. She's in his battalion."

"Uh-huh. What're you going to do?"

"Only one thing I can do. He didn't follow orders, and he won't in the future. I've got to get another commander for that battalion."

Vic nodded decisively, taking a step toward the door. "Okay, let's go."

"No." Stark stopped her with an outstretched hand. "I've got to do this alone. Do me a favor, though. Set up a meeting over at Fifth Battalion for me. All their senior enlisted."

"Not just you and Kalnick?"

"No. He wants this to be personal, and a one-on-one would make it personal. If he's gotta defend his actions in front of a lot of other people, he won't be able to claim they railroaded him."

She nodded. "Truth. Good luck."

"Thanks." The wood-paneled walls of headquarters were getting entirely too familiar; so that increasingly Stark was surprised when they gave way to the lunar rock of the corridors in the rest of the city. *Gotta get rid of that junk. Embarrassing. Worth ten times its weight in titanium back on Earth, I bet. Just have to get it down there.* Still, he found a sense of liberation in leaving headquarters, as if walking awhile alone among his peers somehow kept him a part of them.

A standard briefing room, once used primarily for officers to explain the latest version of universal and everlasting truth from headquarters, the versions changing roughly every time a new General replaced the old one. Now, the Sergeants from Fifth Battalion sat stonefaced before him, except for a crooked smile on the face of Stacey Yurivan several rows back.

"First of all," Stark began, "I want to thank all of you and all your people for how good they did in that last engagement. We really hurt those bastards. They won't try anything again for a long time." Some of the hard expressions eased slightly. "But I gotta talk about something else." The faces hardened again perceptibly.

"We had a real delay getting your battalion into position. It almost didn't get there in time. Not because you couldn't, but because your commander wouldn't move you. That coulda cost us a lot of lives. It coulda cost us the whole battle."

Kalnick sat silent, scowling, as another Sergeant spoke. "So? What's your point here? What do you want, Stark?"

Keep it respectful Treat these apes like you'd have wanted to be treated. Stark chose his words carefully, avoiding loaded terms like "order" and "command."

"I want a commander for this battalion that I can count on. I want a commander that every other soldier here can count on. They, and you, deserve a commander who'll look out for them when the chips are down."

Kalnick flushed, then stood. "What you really want is the same thing the damn officers wanted, enlisted troops who only do what they're told. Isn't that right, Stark? Or should I say General Stark?" Stark stared back, keeping his face impassive with great effort, remaining silent to keep his anger from showing. Kalnick's defiance seemed to waver under Stark's steady gaze. "Well?" he finally demanded. "Should I?"

"No."

"You just want me gone because I thought for myself!"

"No."

Another Sergeant stood, mouth and eyes tight. "Denials are fine, but how about more detail, Stark? How do we know Kalnick isn't right, that this isn't about making us follow every order exactly again?"

"Ask Milheim." A ripple of reaction ran through the crowd.

"Acting Fourth Batt commander, right? He didn't like the way his troops were supposed to deploy, told me and Reynolds that, and suggested another way. We let him do it. Or Geary. We let her pick her own routes for her company when we sealed the penetration. She was on the scene, we let her make the call." Stark raised his right arm, leveling an accusing forefinger at Kalnick. "Your commander didn't make any suggestions. He didn't offer alternatives. You heard me ask, right? Anybody hear Kalnick say what he wanted to do instead? That's 'cause he didn't. No, he just wanted to sit on his fat ass while Fourth Battalion and the rest of the soldiers up here got blown away. *That's* what this is about. We're a team, but Kalnick doesn't want to play with a team. If he doesn't like the moves, he just wants to go home and let the rest of us get beat."

"That's a lie!" Kalnick went white with rage, raising his own trembling arm. "Who died and made you God?"

"Third Division died," Stark shot back coldly. "Most of them anyway, and the Sergeants made me Commander. I didn't want the job, but by God I'm going to do it to the best of my ability. That means I can't have a battalion commander who ignores orders." The word slipped out at last. Stark tensed, waiting for the inevitable reaction, but it didn't come. The debate had passed that point.

"Stark's right." Yurivan was standing now, her smile gone. "Kalnick, I never played by the rules, but I never screwed my buddies in other units, either."

"I didn't do anything!"

"Yeah, well, that's the problem, ain't it? I just realized, someday I might be out on the line, getting hit, and depending on you to come to help. And that scared the hell out of me." She scanned the crowd. "We need another commander, people. Not just because Stark can't trust him. We need one *we* can trust."

"I second that."

"Me, too."

"Anybody still want Kalnick in command?" A small scattering of hands responded to Yurivan's question. "Who else can do the job? You got any suggestions, Stark?"

Stark shook his head, trying to keep his relief from showing. *Give 'em a chance, they'll do the right thing. Just lead 'em instead of shoving 'em.* "That's not my place. I guess someday it'll have to be if we're to stay an army, but for now, you guys choose a commander you trust."

"I nominate Demetrios, then."

"What?" Demetrios protested. "What the hell did I ever do to you?"

"What about Falco?"

"Hey!" Kalnick faced his own peers now, staring at them in unconcealed outrage. "You all elected *me* to this job! I'm the battalion commander, and you can't just toss me out because Stark and his stooges say so."

"I ain't nobody's stooge."

"Me, neither."

"You mad 'cause we ain't following *your* orders, Kalnick?"

"Kalnick, why don't you get your butt out of here before we kick it out?"

"You can all go to hell. Which is exactly where Stark is going to lead you." Kalnick pivoted on one heel, exiting the room in a low-gravity stalk.

Stark nodded to the now-silent ranks of Sergeants. "Thanks for backing me up. During the battle, and now. This is a good outfit. I don't have to hang around for the rest of this. You guys let me know who you want to lead this unit."

A thin Sergeant stood, his face familiar from the meeting that had elected Stark to command. "Are you going to accept the name we give you or approve it?"

A very loaded question. Stark felt the room tense again, then swept his eyes across his audience. "Approve it." A murmur of comment arose. "Look. You made me commander. If I don't command, I'm not doing my job. And 'command' means I gotta call the shots on big issues. Important issues. You don't like it, you can all toss me out and find someone else dumb enough to take the job. So you tell me what you want. You tell me why. I better listen, because you apes know what the hell you're talking about. But I may not do what you want for a lot of reasons. I won't apologize for that."

A long silence stretched, then the thin Sergeant nodded, a tight smile on his lips. "Spoken like a Sergeant. Okay. But if you reject our choice, we'll want to know why."

"Deal. Now, if you guys will excuse me, I got about twelve more alligators to wrestle today." Stark left, his stomach slowly releasing the knot he hadn't realized had been there. Almost dizzy with reaction, half-happy, half-nauseous, he passed through the doorway, turned right, and saw Sergeant Kalnick standing in the hall, his arms crossed defiantly.

Kalnick glared at Stark, eyes radiating hate. "Congratulations, 'General.' I guess I'll go back to my squad now."

"Wrong." Stark moved closer, eye-to-eye with the other man. "I don't need a snake like you within striking distance. You've just been assigned to administrative duties under Sergeant Manley." If Kalnick felt tempted to cause more trouble, he wouldn't have much scope within the Admin offices. "Once we get the procedures worked out, you'll get on one of the shuttles and head home with the officers."

"You can't do that. I'll be shot!"

"No, you won't. Just tell the truth, that you never accepted my authority and didn't follow my orders. You'll pass any security screen they care to run. I would like to know one thing, though. What the hell did I ever do to you?"

"Besides thinking you're better than the rest of us? Besides being a glory hound? Besides starting something you have no idea how to finish?"

Stark shook his head slowly. "I guess I gotta admit the truth of that third thing. None of us knows how this is gonna come out, and, yeah, I started it. But the rest? I'm not better than anyone, not as a person. Maybe I'm better at being a Sergeant than some people, and a lot of Sergeants seem to think I'm the right guy to lead them, but the day I start thinking I'm better is the day I prove myself worse."

"Nice words. I don't believe any of them. I'll be back, Stark, to try to save the others from this unholy mess you got them into."

Stark smiled the way a wolf does when challenged. "You do that, Kalnick. But you try to hurt a single soldier up here, and I'll have your head on a platter. Got me?" Without waiting for a reply, Stark walked away.

PART TWO

COURAGE OF THE SECOND KIND

An open plain, desolate and empty as only a lunar field could be. Long, shallow pools of fine dust lay interspersed with low islands of bare rock. To one side, the mounds of the Colony pimpled the Moon's surface. To the other, emptiness ran off to the too-close horizon, where it vanished against the black of endless night. On Earth, such a field would be farmland, or a park, or quickly overrun with housing. Here, it was just a useless piece of real estate, without concentrations of minerals or subsurface ice to lure human enterprise. Someday, the Colony might expand in this direction, taking advantage of the openness for another landing field. But for now, this dead plain was useful for only one purpose.

An object flew slowly across the sky. Its armored limbs, long since frozen stiff, extended at awkward angles as they cartwheeled in a languid, tumbling flight until the dead soldier fell onto a pile of similar remains. Even before it had ceased motion, another body followed with only three extremities to stand out against the bright cascade of stars. It landed, finally, coming to rest with an arm locked upward, armored fingers splayed as if the fallen soldier were making a last, futile appeal to the blue-white orb of home, where it hung in silent sentry overhead.

"What the hell is going on here?" Stark demanded.

The members of the work crew halted, turning toward him, their posture even in battle armor that of someone caught at something. No one spoke.

"I asked you what you're doing," Stark repeated coldly. He strode over to the heavy mover being used as a transport for the dead, finding bodies piled haphazardly within its open bed, indicating they'd been tossed inside in the same fashion as they were being unloaded. "What's the matter with you?" He felt his voice begin to tremble with rage and tried to tamp it down.

"Uh, we've got an awful lot of these to recover," one of the work crew finally and hesitantly began explaining.

"'These'? You mean the remains of your fellow soldiers? Is that what you mean, Corporal?"

"We . . . we didn't mean—"

"I don't want to hear it. You listen to me, all of you." Stark raised an arm, one finger extended to point toward the several piles of dead. "These are the remains of your friends, your brothers and your sisters. You will treat them with respect. You will carry each one individually. You will set them in neat rows. If I see any more remains treated like sandbags, I will make every last one of you wish you'd never been born. IS—THAT—CLEAR?" The last three words came out in a roar, each one slamming home across the comm circuit.

A long silence answered him, then the members of the work crew carefully picked up the nearest bodies and began arranging them in a precise row, as if in a cemetery with no graves or headstones. Stark stood a moment, watching them, trying to calm himself, and then turned and stalked away, not slowing until he had entered the headquarters complex. He went past the door to his quarters, past the command center, until Stark reached the rec room that had become an informal staff office and meeting area. "Vic?"

She looked up from her palm unit, bleary-eyed. "Just a sec. Yeah. What's up?"

"Who the hell is supervising the work teams recovering all the dead?"

Reynolds didn't answer for a minute, first draining a cold cup of coffee dregs next to her with an involuntary shudder at the taste. "What happened?" she finally asked.

"Nothing, just them treating the dead like they're sacks of laundry. That's all."

"Damn. Sorry, Ethan. I got a lot of things to watch over right now."

For some reason the frank admission calmed him. "I know. We all do. I never thought to check on this until just now, either."

She rubbed her eyes, somehow looking weary and apologetic. "Ethan, you know what burial details are like after a lot of deaths. Remember that place in Asia? Where they threw the human wave assaults against us? So many enemy dead we couldn't bury them all proper."

"These aren't enemy. Not that that'd make it right. They're ours."

"After enough of them it doesn't matter, Ethan. People get numb, start treating the bodies like, well, like laundry. Maybe it's a defense mechanism, dehumanizing the dead. You know that. The first time you shoot someone you get physically ill. The next time, it's easier. After awhile, you've learned not to think about it."

"That's no excuse." Stark slumped in a chair, his face flushing with anger again. "You look after your dead."

"I know that. I'm not making excuses, just explaining how it happens." She squinted to look into his eyes. "This is about Patterson's Knoll, too, isn't it?"

"Everything in my head isn't about that worthless damn knoll," Stark denied, even as his flush paled.

"Of course," Vic agreed in tones which implied the opposite of her words. "Our dead on the Knoll didn't get buried, if I remember right."

"Not until we got to them." Stark stared sightlessly ahead. "After the position was overrun, they'd stripped them of everything they wanted, mutilated some, then left them there for the animals and what all."

"Sorry."

"When we retook the position," Stark continued in a thin voice, "they sent work details in to recover the bodies. I got assigned to one."

"What?" Vic couldn't hide her incredulity. "What kind of idiot would assign a survivor to that kind of duty?"

"I don't know. If I ever find him or her, I'll beat the hell out of them." He shuddered briefly as memories cascaded. "I want the dead treated right."

"I understand. I'll make sure of it from now on. Personally." She leaned forward enough to lock a tight grip on his biceps. "Wish I could make the hurt go away, Ethan."

"No, you don't. I wouldn't be the same guy, would I?"

"Wounded animals are dangerous, Ethan. No, I don't mean I'm scared of you. I'm scared for you. Not that there's much more you could possibly do at this point."

Stark quirked a brief, sardonic smile. "I still got a chance to start a full-scale revolution in the Colony up here, remember?"

"I remember."

"But," Stark continued, "'wounded.' That reminds me. Something else I shoulda already done." He stood again, eyes wandering nervously around the room. "Gotta visit a friend."

"Rash Paratnam?"

"Yeah. He got beat up some during Meecham's offensive, but he's recovering okay. I oughta stop by and say hi."

"That all you going to do?"

He paused, then glanced at her with a slow smile. "I need all the friends I can get right now, Vic."

"Amen," she agreed. "Good luck. Say hi to the big ape for me."

"Sure." Out again, along corridors that suddenly changed from gray rock to white-painted walls, the universal red cross sign marking the entry into the military medical complex. Stark paused to ensure his helmet was off. Nowadays, anyone who made it to medical was almost certain to live, but you still made that small gesture in respect for the dead. Biting his lip, Stark oriented himself, walking through crowded wards toward his objective.

"Sergeant Stark?" The woman's voice was vaguely familiar. He turned to see tired eyes in a weary face. The medic who'd checked him out of here an eternity of a few weeks ago.

Stark nodded. "Nice to see you."

The medic smiled crookedly. "You promised you wouldn't be back again soon."

"Hey, this time I can walk in instead of being carried. How's it goin'?"

A shrug. "Lots of work. Your boy Meecham broke a lot of soldiers, and the fun a few days later sent us some more."

"Meecham ain't mine. Hopefully, you won't see many more casualties from now on."

"I'll believe it when I see it." The medic inclined her head in the direction of the Colony. "You set up the deal to send some of our wounded to the civ hospital?"

"Yeah. The head civ suggested it first, though."

"No kidding? They got good facilities. We've already sent a bunch of people over there. One of yours in the batch. Guy named Murphy."

Murphy. Still alive, which meant he'd stay that way. Stark felt one of the knots of tension in him slowly unravel. *Too many questions I just don't want to ask. Afraid of the answers. Thank God some of the answers are good.* "How'd you know he was mine?" Stark wondered.

"He told us." Another grin, sparking a small response in her tired eyes. "Kept asking if 'Sarge' knew about him going to the civ hospital. Wouldn't settle down 'til we told him you'd ordered it."

"I didn't. Not specifically, anyway."

"I know."

Stark smiled at the shared joke. "Mind if I ask you something?"

"Go ahead. But I'm busy Saturday night."

"That wasn't the question," Stark laughed. "Do you ever get any sleep?"

The medic pretended to ponder the question. "Sleep? Used to. I think. Been a long time." She sobered abruptly. "Too damn much to do. You know."

"I know." The bays around them, full of wounded, emphasized the simple statement. "I'm gonna do my best to keep soldiers out of here from now on. There'll always be some, as long as we're fighting, but I'll keep the numbers as low as I can."

"Trying to put us out of business?" the medic challenged. "I'll believe it when I see it. Good luck, though. Who you looking for here, anyway? Somebody specific?"

"Paratnam. Sergeant Rashamon Paratnam, in, uh, Bay 16C."

"Take a right, then the third left. You'll be there."

"Thanks." Stark paused. "For everything. You guys are . . ." He fumbled for the right word.

"Angels?" The medic finished for him, putting a sarcastic lilt on the word. "Yeah, we keep the wings in storage so they'll look nice during inspections. Keeping those white feathers clean is a real bear."

"I bet. See ya."

"Hope not, unless you're walking in."

"Deal." Stark left her, wending through the aisles of the medical complex until he reached Bay 16C. Paratnam lay on a bed there, eyes fixed on a vid screen he obviously wasn't really watching. His husky body was thinner and paler than Stark remembered from their last encounter. He took a deep breath, then stepped closer, drawing his friend's attention.

"Hiya, Rash." Stark sat near the bed, chewing his lip nervously.

"Hi, Ethan." The reply lacked noticeable enthusiasm.

"How you doin'?"

"Fine. All things considered."

"They takin' good care of you?"

"Yeah."

"How's the leg?"

"It's fine."

"Uh, Rash, look, I—"

"Tell me about my sister," Paratnam interrupted.

Stark stared at the floor, clean white stone merging into spotless white walls. "Nobody's told you?"

"You tell me."

"She's dead, Rash."

"I know that. How'd it happen?"

"Rash—"

"Tell me, dammit!"

Stark raised his head, his eyes on Paratnam's for a brief moment. "Best we can tell, she took a burst from a chain gun dead-on during the first enemy barrage. Cut her in two. Never stood a chance. Sorry."

Paratnam looked away, face grim. "You didn't do it."

"That's what you're saying, but that's not what I'm hearing."

"Can't help what you hear."

Stark gazed at him for a moment, eyes questioning. "Okay. Look, I got something to ask you, Rash. You know what happened, right? After you got hit?"

"You mean you guys taking over? Yeah, I know."

"Geez, Rash, you don't have to sound so damn grateful. We did it to save what was left of Third Division."

"We didn't ask you."

"No, because you idiots were too busy proving that even the thickest skulls in the Army can't stop bullets." Stark glared at his friend. "Rash, we need good leaders now. I wanted to ask if you'd stay on and help us."

Rash finally met Stark's gaze again, staring back with some unreadable emotion. "That'd make my folks real happy, wouldn't it? Their daughter's dead and their son's a traitor. You wanta tell 'em?"

Stark closed his eyes, fists slowly clenching tight in his lap. "No. I wouldn't have wanted to've told them you were both dead, either. So I did something about it." He stood, nodding, eyes averted from Paratnam. "Okay. I guess I got my answer. Don't worry. Rash. You'll go home with the other Third Division guys who want that. I'm sorry you won't be up here with me. I really could've used you." He turned away.

"Hey, Ethan . . ."

Stark paused, not turning back. "Yeah?"

"Nothin'. See you around."

Stark walked out of the hospital, threading through crowds of soldiers, wounded and healthy as well as the many personnel dedicated to healing and caring for the injured. *How can I feel so alone with all these people around me? Need a drink. No. Beer never held any answers. Need to talk to Vic.*

Vic watched Ethan as he walked back into the rec room and collapsed into a chair in the slow-motion, low-gravity maneuver long since grown familiar. "Should I ask how it went with Rash?"

"No."

"Sorry, Ethan."

"Vic, I have never felt so damned lonely. Not even on that ridge when I held off the enemy to let the platoon escape. Sometimes it seems like there's nobody else there."

"You've always got me, big guy."

"What exactly does that mean?"

Vic exhaled in a quick burst, raising her eyes heavenward in pleading fashion. "Down, boy. It means comrade in arms. Comprendo?"

"That's what I figured. And, hell, that's what I really need. Just like always."

She grinned as if at an inner joke. "Good boy. They told me you were untrainable, but I knew I could manage it."

"Gee, thanks. What's my reward?"

"My smiling face in your dreams."

Stark started laughing, realizing as he did so that some of the weight seemed to have lifted from his shoulders. "Vic, if nothing else, there's nobody who can pull me out of a funk the way you can. Thanks."

"Heck, Ethan, I've got to give you some reason to keep me around."

"Here's another. When we meet with the civs I want you helping. I'm not the sharpest guy in the world when it comes to negotiating stuff."

Vic made a face. "We still got to meet with the civs, huh?"

"What's so bad about that?"

"Gee, let me think. Abuse. Mistrust. Being looked down on. Are any of those bad things, Ethan?"

Stark bit off an angry retort. "Look—"

"Oh, yeah. I forgot the entertainment factor. Will any of us have to shoot each other to amuse the civs?"

"That's enough! I've told you more than once these civs aren't that bad."

"This from the guy who admits he's not the sharpest in the world?" Vic flinched exaggeratedly at Stark's expression. "Okay. Sorry. Don't detonate on me. Do you want my honest opinion or do you want me to treat you like a General and just say 'yessir, yessir, that's right, sir'?"

"What I'd like," Stark explained carefully, "is for you to keep an open mind and evaluate the situation, not approach it with your mind already made up. You're a good tactical thinker, and you don't fight battles that way, do you? You see what things are like before you commit your forces."

"You do if you're smart," Vic conceded. "I'll do my best, but I've seen a few too many 'no dogs or military' signs to be completely dispassionate. When is this wonderful meeting?"

"Tomorrow morning. Like I said, I'm gonna need you there helping me."

"I'll be there," she partially promised.

Stark stared toward the gray emptiness of a blank display screen. *Looks like it'll be me against the world. Just like always. I used to have friends standing beside me, though, before those friends decided to make me their boss.* He searched his heart, trying to ignore Vic where she worked nearby, trying to ignore him, but came up with no better answers. *I've got to go with my instincts. Do what seems right. What the hell else can I do?* The blank screen offered no reply.

× × ×

A long night hadn't generated any special wisdom, either. Stark grumbled internally as he took his seat. The meeting room sat near the edge of the headquarters complex, close enough to the rest of the Colony that Stark thought it qualified as neutral territory. *And I sure as hell ain't gonna let the civs see that wonderland the General used for conferences.* Besides, in Stark's experience uncomfortable conference rooms made for quicker meetings and decisions than comfortable ones did. He sat along one side of a standard-issue metal table, forged from lunar ore, his makeshift staff seated to his left and right. On the other side of the table, Colony Manager Campbell sat opposite Stark, his aides also ranked to either side.

Campbell looked nervous, though he hid it pretty well. Sarafina, seated next to him, smiled briefly at Stark. The other civilians either stared at the table top or glowered upward. Stark turned to whisper a comment to Vic, the words dying unuttered as he realized his own people all mirrored the attitudes of the Colonists. *Oh, man. This is gonna be as bad as I feared, ain't it?* "I guess we ought to start," Stark finally suggested. "But I'm not sure how this should work."

"None of us do." Campbell smiled tightly. "It's been a long time since Americans staged a revolution."

A wide-featured man down the table from Campbell sat straight at the words. "I was not aware any decision had been reached regarding this situation. The potential for extremely serious—"

"Yes, yes," Campbell interrupted wearily. "This is Jason Trasies, Chief of Security for the Colony."

"And I take that responsibility very seriously," Trasies insisted sharply.

Stark's staff exchanged cold glances with Trasies, who stared back as if he was imagining them all in prison garb. "I assure you," Stark stated evenly, "that the Colony is secure."

"Thanks to us," Vic added. "We also take our responsibilities very seriously."

"Our own Navy almost attacked us!" A woman to Campbell's left leaned forward, eyes flaring like a deer watching a party of hunters. "We don't have normal communications, we aren't getting regular supply shipments, I'm told we're under heavy attack—"

"Ma'am," Stark broke in, "the heavy attacks are over. We beat them back and hurt the enemy bad enough that they won't be returning soon."

"You killed them! You killed a lot of them! And now you want to run this Colony?"

"Ms. Pevoni." Campbell glared down the table. "As I explained earlier, the military has made it clear to me that they do not desire to run the Colony. Indeed, they have indicated they want to grant us far more freedom than we have ever experienced to date."

"And you trust them?" Trasies needled. "Did they take an oath to respect your decisions?"

Stark felt his face grow hot, but Bev Manley spoke before he could. "None of us need ethics lessons from corporate storm troopers," she noted, smiling mock-pleasantly as her words slid into Trasies like a stiletto.

"I work for the Colony," Trasies stated stiffly.

"You work for me," Campbell corrected, his own face flushed. "I will not tolerate any further insults directed at the military representatives."

Pevoni leaned forward again. "It's not insulting to bring up their own recent behavior. That's their track record—"

"Who the hell are you?" Vic demanded icily.

"Yvonne Pevoni, Corporate and Government Liaison," the civilian responded with more than a trace of hauteur. "As such, I am responsible for evaluating the character of those we deal with, and I cannot imagine rendering a favorable assessment of armed criminal elements—"

"That's enough," Stark cut her off sharply. "Campbell, your people are out of line."

Trasies purpled with anger. *"We're* out of line? Just who the hell do you—"

"Sergeant Stark's right." Campbell, his jaw muscles tight, glanced around the table. "This isn't getting us anywhere. We need a time-out."

Stark nodded back. "Good idea."

"And privacy while I talk to my staff, if that's acceptable."

"Sure." Stark stood, ignoring the daggerlike glances from Trasies. "We'll wait in the hall, if it's not too long. How much time you want?"

"Half an hour. If we can't settle a few things by then, we'll probably need a lot longer."

"Okay." Stark stood, leading his people out of the room, then turned to face them in the narrow corridor.

Vic leaned against one wall, pulling out her palmtop. "Might as well get something constructive accomplished," she remarked in an idle tone as her fingers began tapping the palmtop's surface.

"I'd like that, too," Stark suggested bitingly. "Alright, people.

What happened in there?"

"You know as well as we do," Bev Manley replied with a bitter smile. "Civs are trying to roll us. It happens in bars all the time."

"I know that security chief is bad news, and I could do without that pure-as-driven-snow liaison broad, but—"

"They're all bad news, Ethan. They think we're dangerous. They want to use us for whatever they need and have nothing to do with us otherwise."

"The rest of you agree with that?" Stark looked at each soldier in turn as they nodded, Vic glancing briefly up from her work to add her assent. "Even Campbell and Sarafina? They didn't seem hostile to me."

"Campbell also didn't seem in control," Reynolds suggested dryly.

"He hasn't had a lot of real power up to now. He's got to get used to that."

"If any of *my* subordinates acted like that little slimeball Trasies," Manley noted, "I'd take him apart and feed the pieces to rats."

"Commander," Gordasa chimed in, "those civs need us, just like always. We don't need them."

"Huh." Stark looked around, eyeing each soldier in turn. "I got a funny feeling in there, you guys. I felt like I knew how Campbell felt. I felt like I could talk to the civs. But you guys are telling me you didn't feel any of that."

"Nope," Manley answered for them all.

"So why should I feel different about them?"

Vic grinned wickedly, though her eyes remained fixed on her palmtop. "You were born a civ, Ethan. You're just reverting to type."

Gordasa frowned. "Stark ain't no civ now."

"Not like them," Stark agreed. "Joined the mil a long time ago, just like you apes. But I grew up like them. So maybe I understand the civs just a little because of that? I dunno. I do know we're gonna need those civs even if we don't need them right this minute. Who's gonna talk to the authorities on the World about us sending the officers back and getting our people sent up in return?"

Silence for a moment, then Manley nodded reluctantly. "The authorities won't talk to us, that's for sure. As far as the Pentagon's concerned, we're poison."

"Verdad," Gordasa agreed. "And, you know, if we really want spares, and we're going to need them eventually if this drags on, we'll have to find a backdoor into the corporations that make them."

"Backdoor?" Vic questioned. "There's a way to get suit spares through unofficial channels? Those parts are all classified, official-sales-only equipment."

Gordasa shrugged and smiled simultaneously. "There's ways to get anything unofficial. You guys know that. I never played those games, but I know about them."

"So," Stark continued, "all you apes agree now that we need to talk to these civs?" *I should've laid better groundwork for this meeting. But it all just seemed to make sense. Next time I'll know better.* "That we need to work with them?"

"To some extent." Bev Manley glanced around as the others nodded with varying degrees of reluctance. "Nobody likes it, though, Stark."

"Nobody likes Administration, either, Bev, but we need it." Stark eyed his watch, then the door. "When we go back in there, I'll handle Trasies if he shoots off his mouth again. Maybe show

Campbell how it's done. Vic, give that Pevoni woman a death-stare if she looks like she's gonna talk again."

"Can't I just follow her out of the meeting until I can catch her alone in an alley?"

Stark stifled a laugh, trying to look stern as the others guffawed. "Okay, it's not like I don't know how you feel. But let's see what we can get done with the others in there."

Time finally up, Stark led his people back inside the meeting room, where Campbell wore the expression of a man trying not to reveal serious exasperation. He stared down his side of the table, eyes lingering on Trasies. "It appears there are some issues which require considerable coordination prior to successful agreement."

"We don't have considerable time," Stark reminded him. "What's the sticking points? Where's the hang-ups?"

"I'm afraid the specific issues are inflammatory enough that further discussion here would add nothing to our chances for working together." Campbell exhaled heavily, looking weary. "It's not your fault. This is something we have to work out ourselves."

"I understand. If you need any information or assistance from us while you're working things out—"

Trasies broke in. "We're quite capable of making decisions on our own."

Stark narrowed his eyes as if sighting in on the Security Chief. "And I'm sure Mr. Campbell is quite capable of speaking for himself. Or do you think you're in charge?"

Campbell held up his hands to forestall further conversation. "I believe it's best if the meeting end at this point."

Stark raised his own palm in objection. "No. There's one thing that needs to be addressed right away, and we need your help on it. We've got our officers locked up, and we want them gone. Sent back to Earth."

Sarafina looked eagerly toward Campbell even as she addressed Stark. "So the officers are still safe? None have been injured?"

"They're safe, but not happy, not with being in confinement. I want them home where they're no threat to us." *And where none of my soldiers can go berserk or get drunk and hurt one of them. Even I fantasize sometimes about finding Captain Noble and bouncing him off a wall a few times.* "But nobody back home is going to talk to us. You can negotiate with them, though, work out the deal so we can shuttle the officers home."

Campbell frowned even as he nodded. "That shouldn't be hard to arrange if you allow us to use the communications circuits again."

"There's more. In exchange for the officers, we'd like our family members sent up."

"Families. Of course. We'll need a list of officers and another of the people you want in exchange—"

Yvonne Pevoni waved her hands frantically. "I do not advise getting involved in this. We'd be in the middle of a critical situation—"

"And acting on behalf of these individuals," Trasies finished coldly.

Campbell flushed again, looking to either side, where his advisors watched expectantly. "This," he stated slowly but firmly, "is a humanitarian issue. We are not acting on behalf of anyone if we facilitate a transfer of confined officers for family members of people remaining up here."

"I do not—" Pevoni started.

"No further debate is necessary," Campbell snapped. "Ms. Sarafina, work with Sergeant Stark's people as necessary to facilitate the negotiations."

"Thank you," Stark stated, the emotion behind the simple words apparent despite his best efforts. He glanced over at Vic, who made a brief okay-Campbell-showed-he's-in-charge expression. "Sergeant Reynolds will be our POC." The civilians stared blankly back. "Sorry. Point Of Contact. The person you should work with, Ms. Sarafina."

Campbell stood, looking downward, face grim. "There is much to resolve. I'm sorry this meeting couldn't have been more productive."

"Me, too." Stark reached out to offer his hand, gripping firmly as Campbell shook it, then watched the civilians file out before holding out the same hand to his staff. "See. I touched him and nothing horrible happened."

"Have you still got your watch?" Vic wondered. "If you do, it's because he didn't want it."

Stark glared back. "I can't do anything about the civs' attitudes, but by God I expect my own people to back me up."

"We didn't say anything—"

"No, but your negatives were obvious to the most casual observer! I'll say this one more time. We gotta work with the civs. Anybody who isn't ready to do that just let me know and I can find you a job where you'll never have to see one!"

A storm rumbled down the halls of the headquarters complex. Stark wore a thundercloud on his face, ready to spit lightning at the slightest provocation, but everyone who saw him hastily veered aside before they came within range. *I cannot believe everybody is being so damn stupid and stubborn. Working with these civs is* important. *Why am I the only guy who sees that? When the hell did* I *become the most reasonable person around?* He turned a corner near the empty suite of rooms once occupied by the Commanding General, coming to a halt as his anger locked on to three soldiers standing by a small door. "Who the hell are you guys?"

"The gardeners," the Corporal answered rapidly. The two Privates accompanying him nodded vigorously even as they stared at the Corporal in an obvious attempt to keep Stark's attention focused on him instead of them.

"The . . . ?" Rubbing his forehead, expression now pained, Stark paused before speaking again. "Gardeners. There's a garden here?"

"Yessir. Two gardens."

"Two gardens." Stark waved the Corporal on. "Show me." As the Corporal fumbled with the door, Stark looked around. "Isn't this near the Commanding General's rooms?"

The Corporal nodded. "That's right. This is sort of a back door so we wouldn't tromp through his rooms on the way to the garden." He opened the door, leading the way inside.

"A back door into the General's quarters," Stark muttered, thinking darkly of security violations, then stopped as he saw the garden. The layout resembled courtyards found scattered around the Colony, a square room with windows set in the ceiling or one wall to view the outside. Instead of a view of the bleak lunar landscape, however, these overhead "windows" projected images of cloud-speckled blue sky. Stark blinked in amazement as his gaze wandered away from the windows. The walls had been worked with smooth stone and carefully painted to resemble an outdoors scene with rolling hills and ruins vaguely similar to those Stark had seen in the Middle East. Against the walls with their painted-on trees and other vegetation, real planters filled with bright flowers or carefully trimmed bushes stood neatly ranked. Full-spectrum lights overhead mimicked sunlight. On the ground, a carpet of bright green grass beckoned, its individual blades grown thin in the low gravity, but dense and finely manicured.

He gradually became aware that the Corporal and his assistants were standing watching him, their own expressions guarded. "This was just for the Commanding General?" Stark finally wondered.

"This one," the Corporal nodded. "The other one's for the Chief of Staff."

"The other one. Is it just like this?"

"Pretty much, except it's exactly two square meters smaller and has one less planter. The painting's not quite as good, either."

"'cause the Commanding General had to have the biggest and best garden, huh?" The Corporal nodded again. "And this is what you guys do up here?"

"That's right."

The absurdity of it all drained away Stark's anger like a lightning rod. *What a waste of good soldiers. Ain't their fault, though.* "Looks like you've been doing a fine job here, but what the hell do we do with it now?"

"Uh, excuse me?" The Corporal looked baffled as his accompanying Privates exchanged worried glances. "It's . . . for the Commanding General."

"Right now, that's me," Stark stated patiently. "And I don't want and don't need a garden." The other soldiers' faces tightened with an odd mix of sorrow and outrage. "I'm not saying you haven't done one helluva good job. But we gotta justify this, right? What would I do with a garden?"

"Generals would usually entertain VIPs here," one of the gardeners suggested. "You know, little parties and stuff."

"Little parties."

"Yeah. You know. Drinks and finger food. Swedish meatballs and those little weenies you stick with toothpicks and lumpia."

"Lumpia?" The little Philippine egg rolls were nearly mythical treats, especially for soldiers whose snack food usually consisted of chips made from Moon-grown potatoes, cut very thin, baked, then salted so lightly that they tasted like stale paper. "They had lumpia up here?"

"For the Generals. Yeah."

Stark sagged against the doorway, rubbing his eyes this time. *Why does this stuff keep surprising me?* He palmed his comm unit. "Vic."

"Here," she responded warily.

"Need you where I am."

"Gosh, Ethan, I'd love to, but I've got all this work just piling up—"

"Vic, I'm not still mad!"

"Uh-huh. You sound really calm."

"Vic, you're gonna have to see this to believe it."

"See what? The last time a guy said that to me I wasn't nearly as impressed as he thought I'd be."

"I'd rather not hear about it. Look, Vic, come here and see this."

"Okay, okay. Be there in a minute." She actually showed in about forty-five seconds, walking with the brisk glide lunar veterans used to cover ground fast. Stark stepped aside from the door, waving her forward to look into the garden. Reynolds stared for a long moment, then, instead of frowning, began laughing so hard she had trouble standing. "Hey, Ethan. You got grass."

Stark favored her with a level glare. "I hate grass."

"That's what makes it so funny. Oh, God. The only grass on the Moon, and it ends up in the hands of the one guy who'd want to trample it all." She went into another laughing fit, trying to catch her breath.

"Glad you like it," Stark muttered, then triggered his comm unit again. "Tanaka. I need to see you at the General's garden."

Sergeant Tanaka arrived in even less time than Vic had. "You found it, huh?"

"You knew about this?"

"Sort of. Not that any of the enlisted at headquarters, except the gardeners, ever saw it. But we'd all heard about the garden." She craned her neck to look inside. "Nice. What're you gonna do with it?"

"Tearing it up and dumping the remains on the surface come to mind."

"You can't do that!" Vic and Jill Tanaka protested simultaneously while the Corporal and his two assistants paled with shock.

"Why not?" Stark waved his hand toward the flowers. "I can't have something like this that nobody else gets to use.

Even if I liked the stuff, it'd be too, uh, imperial or something."

"We could let everyone visit the garden, now," Tanaka suggested.

"I don't think so, Jill," Vic demurred. "Thousands of boots on that small patch of grass, even in low-G? It'd be a mud patch in no time." The Corporal nodded in vigorous agreement.

"So, hold a lottery, maybe?" Stark wondered. *Ought to get some use out of it. I can't imagine how much getting this garden set up and maintaining it have cost, while we couldn't always get the spares we needed because the damn budget supposedly couldn't support it. Did anyone buy a bullet because of this?* "Hey, that's it."

"What's it?" Vic demanded.

"We've already got soldiers who've lost a lottery. The combat lottery. They're wounded. This would be good for them while they're recovering, right? And nobody can say they haven't earned the right to a few hours in the garden."

Vic smiled approvingly. "Fair and appropriate. Nobody can complain about the wounded getting a special deal. I like it. I'll talk to medical about setting up a regular visit schedule." She pointed to the Corporal. "You need to tell us how many people we can run through this place every day without wrecking it."

"I don't know," the Corporal protested. "It's never been used that way."

"Then take a guess," Stark suggested. "We'll modify it if we have to after we see how everything is holding up." He scowled. "Guess we'll have to post guards, too, to keep everyone from picking souvenirs and leaving trash."

Tanaka nodded. "That's prudent. We're not posting ceremonial guards outside senior officer quarters anymore, so we've got people free to assign to that job."

"Ceremonial guards? No. I don't want to know." Stark took another look at the flower planters, his eyes calculating. "Hey, Jill, one more thing. I've noticed you palling around with Sergeant Yurivan a few times."

She nodded again. "Sure. We've hung together. Stacey's a lot of fun."

"That's one way to describe her, all right. I want these plants kept safe here. You tell Stacey Yurivan that if I hear one word about fresh flowers being sold on the black market, I'll post her on sentry duty at the lunar pole for so long she'll think she's a space penguin. Understand?"

"Stacey wouldn't do anything like that," Tanaka protested.

"Not unless there's a way to turn a buck in it. You just make sure she understands what I told you."

Vic followed as Stark headed away. "Hey. You're human again."

"No thanks to you."

"Look, Ethan, you saw how Trasies and Pevoni acted. I don't trust them. Is that unreasonable?"

"Them? Hell, no. That'd be like trusting Yurivan with that flower garden."

She grinned. "Unlike Trasies, Stacey wouldn't hurt a soldier. Too bad we can't harness her for the forces of good."

"Maybe we oughta."

Reynolds's eyebrows shot up. "You serious? What kind of job would suit her special talents?"

"Keeping an eye on rats like Trasies."

"Tell me you're not suggesting her for our Security Officer."

"That's exactly what I'm doing." Stark half-smiled. "I'm basically a squad leader at heart, Vic. And what's a squad leader do? They match the job to the individual. Pick the best guy for the assignment. Okay, so we gotta counter a bunch of sneaky, devious people who're gonna try to take us down. And who's the sneakiest, most devious mind we got to outguess them?"

"Stacey Yurivan. But do you think she'd agree to work on your staff? She's not exactly a close friend."

"I dunno. She did back me against Kalnick, but that might've been more about self-preservation than supporting me." Vic pulled out her comm unit. "Who you calling?"

"Stacey. She'll take the job request better if I make the offer. Besides, it occurred to me that having someone who's definitely not one of your inner circle here in headquarters might benefit you. There's already been talk that you're surrounding yourself with too many friends who're loyal to you."

"What?" Stark, exasperated, took a moment to slam his palm against the nearest wall, the sharp sound echoing down the corridor to shock anyone within hearing distance. "If you guys are totally loyal to me I'd hate to see how my enemies would act."

"Thanks."

"You know what I mean. Who's starting this talk? Why is it happening? Like Kalnick. We never had enlisted working against one another in the past."

"In the past, Ethan, we had the officers as a common enemy. Working against another enlisted would've meant allying yourself with the officers. Know anybody who would've done that?"

"No one who'd survive long on a battlefield."

"Right. But now the officers aren't in charge. Now we can play nasty little games against one another. And some people are just out of their depth in their new jobs and looking for someone else to blame for their problems. Like Gabriel in Second Battalion, First Brigade."

"Sergeant Gabriel? I haven't heard about any problems in her battalion."

"That's because Sergeant Gabriel isn't telling you about any problems. She's letting her subordinates run amuck, either because she can't or won't control them."

Stark absorbed the news, shaking his head. "If she's not telling, how'd you find out?"

"I got sources, remember? We're going to have to replace her, Ethan."

"No." Stark paused to enjoy the look of surprise and annoyance on Vic's face. "You and I ain't gonna do it. First Brigade's being run by Nageru. I'll tell him to either whip Gabriel into line or replace her with someone who can do the job."

Reynolds smiled ruefully. "Right. I'm so used to watching officers micromanage things that it comes too naturally. Thanks for keeping me honest." She tapped her comm unit irritably.

"Where the hell is she? Stacey? This is Vic Reynolds. I want to meet with you right away."

"Why?" Yurivan questioned.

"It's a surprise."

"I'm not involved, Reynolds."

"Involved in what?"

"Whatever it is you're calling me about."

"I'm disappointed, Stacey. Generic denials from you?"

"They save time. So, should I pack a toothbrush for this meeting?"

"I don't see why. Just come on over. I got something to ask you."

"Roger. I've been wanting to scope out all that luxury where you friends of Ethan have been living. See you in a few."

Vic glanced at Stark. "Want to wait in the rec office? We could grab some coffee."

"I'd prefer a beer," Stark noted, "but I guess I oughta keep all my wits about me when we meet Stacey."

"We'll still be outclassed, but that's a good idea." They waited, passing the time by using their spoons to nudge the congealed blocks of nondairy creamer floating in their cups. Thanks to the Moon's low gravity, the lumpy off-white rectangles danced over the surface of the coffee, not penetrating the dark liquid unless forced under by a well-aimed utensil. Like most of the other supplies, the creamer came from stocks whose "use by" dates had long expired. It was just one of the things you got used to in the military and perversely took a certain pride in. Competitions had been known to occur over which unit had the worst coffee and the oldest fixings.

"Hey, Vic," Yurivan stood in the doorway, eyes wary as they shifted from Reynolds to Stark. "What's up?"

"Relax, Stace, this isn't about the illegal gambling joint being run out of a storeroom in the Buford Barracks."

"There was gambling going on in the Buford Barracks?" Yurivan asked, her face reflecting wonderment. "I'm . . . shocked."

"Sure, Stace. Save it. How would you like to be Security Officer?"

"Huh?" Yurivan's expression shifted to disbelief. "What's the joke?"

"No joke. We need someone who can outthink our enemies. That's you."

"Then no thanks. I'm not interested in running loyalty screens."

"Wouldn't ask you to. Loyalty screens are dead. No, we need to worry about external security issues. Spies. Sabotage. Finding out what the enemy's planning, including any mischief any of the Colony civs might try. Interested?"

Yurivan made another sidelong look at Stark even as she answered Reynolds. "Why would I be interested?"

"Because you'd be trying to outthink and out scheme the best minds our enemies can throw at us. C'mon, Stace. No more playing games with the military police and the local security officer. You'll get to see if you can beat the boys and girls from the national agencies."

Yurivan kept a poker face. "That's a pretty big league to play in, Vic."

Stark favored her with a taunting smile. "Hey, Stace. No guts, no glory."

"Uh-huh, and no brain, no gain."

Vic shrugged, fingers wandering idly over her palm unit. "Well, Stace, if you figure the job's too hard . . ."

"Reynolds," Yurivan laughed, "you'll have to do better than that. I've been psyched by experts."

"Any of 'em figure you out?"

"Hell, no."

Reynolds smiled politely. "Big surprise. So, do you want the job or not?"

"Maybe. Gotta think about it."

"Fine. You let me know." Stacey Yurivan flipped an elaborate salute, smiling at some hidden joke as she did so, pivoted precisely on one heel, and marched out. As her footsteps faded down the hallway outside, Vic began laughing softly.

"What's so funny? She's not going to take it," Stark declared gloomily.

"Sure she is," Vic assured him. "Stacey just wants time to shut down her other illegal scams before she becomes Security Officer. She's got her own code of ethics. You watch. In a couple of days she'll call and accept."

Stark squinted at the empty doorway as if it held some answers. "How do you figure that? I couldn't read her."

"That, Ethan, is because you're a man and because you're blessed with a wonderfully straightforward and uncomplicated mind."

"I'll assume that's a compliment."

"Sort of. It lets people take advantage of you, but earns you a lot of trust. Stacey's different."

"That I knew. 'Trust' isn't a word that comes to mind with her."

"But she's never hurt another soldier," Vic reminded him. "Except in the wallet. And she will take this job. The chance to stick it to the system in the biggest way possible will be irresistible for her—irresistible enough for her to become part of our system."

Stark found himself smiling. "You know, this has been a really rotten coupla days, but right now I'm thinking about Stacey Yurivan being sic'd on people like Trasies and Pevoni, and that's making me real happy."

"Good. While you're happy, start thinking about how we're going to find all the officer candidates we need from the enlisted ranks."

"Thanks for the reality kick." Stark finished his coffee, glaring defiantly toward the dispenser. "I'm gonna have a beer. You should, too."

"Way to be in charge," Vic applauded. "Keep making decisions that good and people'll be talking about Stark's Big Victory someday."

"Sure. Right now this feels more like Custer's Last Stand."

"You're not Custer, Ethan. If you ever start acting like him, I'll whap you upside the head." She stared upward, pensive. "Speaking of that battle, and officers, funny how you never hear much about Captain Benteen."

"Who the hell was he?"

"One of Custer's subordinates. I know about him because I grew up in Fort Riley, Kansas, where the old Cavalry Museum is located. In the histories, it's always Custer this, Custer that. Right before the battle, Custer split his regiment into three parts, taking one himself, giving one to Reno to charge straight in to attack, and telling Benteen with the rest to just wait around. But if Benteen hadn't chosen to disregard the last orders he'd received from Custer, if he hadn't guessed that things were going to hell, then picked out a strong defensive position and been already digging in when Reno's troops came running back with the Indigs at their heels, well, the whole Seventh Cavalry would have been wiped out instead of just the troops with Custer. Benteen saved them, but you never hear about him."

"Vic, if you made a big deal about some officer who disobeyed orders and instead did what he thought was right and smart, you'd have other officers thinking that might be a good idea, too. Then where'd you be?"

She smiled lopsidedly. "You're right. What was I thinking?"

Stark's own smile shifted, his face growing thoughtful. "But you know what? You got something, there. Why does the mil have to work that way? Why can't we let people run their units smart instead of following orders blindly? And if they can't run their units smart, why have them in charge in the first place?"

"If they don't follow orders, how can you run a battle?"

"Maybe better. Look, I really gotta think about this, how to balance the need to keep people focused on the same objective and also let 'em use their brains. Maybe it can't be done."

"I'm not sure it's ever been tried. Maybe the technology wouldn't permit it before now. I mean, signal flags or horns or walkie-talkies can't provide the information you need to run things any way but top-down." Vic sighed, smiled at the beer Stark placed before her, then downed it in one long drink. "While you're thinking up a new way to fight, I'll arrange a meeting with that Sarafina civ to talk about the exchange. Maybe she'll bring her little friend along."

"What little friend?"

"Your date, remember? What was her name?"

"Robin?" Stark chuckled, reaching to take away Vic's empty. "It wasn't a date. It was an interrogation. A nice one, but all I did was answer questions. I haven't heard from her since."

"Poor Ethan. No luck with the ladies."

"Probably because you're scarin' 'em off, Sergeant Reynolds. Besides, I don't have time to date nowadays."

She smiled and sighed simultaneously. "Yeah. Running an army is no fun. At least you still get to sleep."

"Yeah. Sometimes."

Another day. Another meeting. Stark's staff sat back in their chairs, rigidly proper, like sentries guarding their own welfare, while Campbell's assistants hesitated or flung insults. Minor points were raised, debated endlessly, each one dying out in a fog of tiny deviations of definitions. Stark checked the time, trying for the hundredth time to keep himself from exploding. *I thought forcing this meeting to last until something got decided was a good idea. Wrong. Real wrong.* While the arguments raged inside, outside the conference room the normal workday came to an end, dinner was eaten, evening leisure enjoyed, and late-night shifts came on duty.

Stark fixed his eyes on Campbell, who stared back with exasperation dulled by exhaustion. "I'm not hearing anything that makes me think we're gonna decide anything."

Campbell nodded, the weary gesture barely moving his head. "Everyone go home," he ordered his staff shortly. They stood with varying degrees of apparent fatigue, edging out with barely a glance at the military representatives. Only Sarafina remained, gazing bleakly at Campbell.

"You apes go, too," Stark told his people, not watching as all but Reynolds left the room.

Reynolds exhaled, a long and slow gesture. "If it means anything, I'm not happy."

"Thanks much," Stark grumbled. "Campbell, you don't have to hang around. It's been a real long day."

"I agree," Campbell replied, with a wave toward his remaining assistant. "But I needed to give you some good news."

"I could use some."

"Ms. Sarafina has made a great deal of progress on the negotiations for the exchange of officers for your family members,"

Campbell reported. "I'd meant to tell you about it in the morning," he continued dryly.

"It's morning," Stark noted. Outside and overhead, the blue-white Earth hung as always, uncaring that her rotation from day to night still governed the lives of humans no longer directly affected by it. "How come you didn't bring this up before?"

Campbell visibly hesitated. "I am no longer sure how my advisers will react to even apparently good news. I felt it best to keep this issue separate from any contentious ones."

Stark managed to muster a smile. "Can't argue with that. Everything seems to be contentious. No big hang-ups, then?"

"No. The authorities in Washington apparently want those officers back pretty badly. Are you sure you want to let them go? They must be very good if the Pentagon needs them . . ." Campbell halted as Stark and Reynolds started laughing. "Something is amusing?"

"Just the idea that our officers are very good," Vic gasped. "The Pentagon wants them back for two reasons. First, to find out what's happened up here. They've probably got only the barest information, which must be driving them crazy. Ninety percent of the Pentagon is devoted to regurgitating information for senior officers who don't really need it, and those officers must be getting pretty tired of seeing variations on 'nothing new to report' for the umpteenth time."

"I see. Gathering information makes a great deal of sense. What's the other reason?"

"Scapegoats," Stark answered matter-of-factly. "They want to hang Meecham and maybe some others. Otherwise, they'll take the blame. Can't have that, even if they did send him here and approve his plans."

Campbell hung his head, shaking it as he did so. "And to think I once lectured you on politics. It appears you've had plenty of exposure to the bad side of it."

"There's a good side?"

"Yes. Perhaps I'll be able to show you someday."

"I won't hold my breath. Hey, Vic, where's that data coin with the latest list of family members?"

Reynolds smiled thinly. "Last I saw, on your desk, where you put it after I gave it to you."

"Oh. Yeah. Thanks." Stark stood, beckoning to Campbell and Sarafina. "Come on. My room's down the hall a little ways. I'll give you that coin so you can set things up." The hallways, normally the scene of numerous personnel hustling on errands, were quiet and empty in that curiously deserted way buildings got after midnight, even though the midnight up here was totally artificial. Palming open his door, Stark rummaged over his desk until he held up a coin triumphantly. "Here it is."

"You found it?" Vic questioned. "Miracles do happen."

Campbell took the coin, staring at it for a moment, before handing it to Sarafina. "Odd to hold the fate of so many in my hand for even a moment. Do you ever feel that burden, Sergeant Stark?"

"Not too often. Only once every day. All day."

The words brought an understanding smile to Campbell's face. "If there's nothing else, I'd like to get back to the Colony proper before too many observers wonder why I'm lingering here to hatch nefarious plots with you."

"Good idea." Instead of stepping out the door, though, Campbell paused, staring at Stark's battle armor where it stood against one wall. "Something wrong?" Stark finally asked.

"No." Campbell shook his head. "I've just never seen your combat equipment up this close." He reached out a hand, then hesitated. "Is it all right to touch it?"

"Feel free. You can't damage the outside."

"That's odd." Campbell frowned as he pushed fingers against the armor's chest area. "I thought it would be rigid, like steel. But it gives very, very slightly."

"That's right." Vic stepped forward to punch an arm of the armor with a light tap. "It's designed to be a little flexible."

"But I thought armor would be made as strong as possible."

"Yes and no." Vic slid easily into the instructor role every veteran had to fill for new personnel. "Things which are technically very strong are also very brittle. When they break, they shatter all to hell. That'd be bad in the case of our armor. So the composite material it's made of flexes a little when it's pushed, enough to help absorb and distribute the force of an impact, but hopefully not enough for the shock to injure us as bad as a penetration would."

"We get bruised a lot, though," Stark added with a laugh. "Beats a hole in your body, but after a battle we sometimes look like we've been run through a line of guys with clubs."

"Think of it as a trade-off," Vic continued. "Ideally, the armor would be very light, very strong, and very flexible. In the real world, we have to accept a compromise of those traits."

"The best compromise you can get?" Campbell inquired, smiling. "Odd. Here we'd been discussing the good side of politics, and your armor is a very concrete example of just that."

Vic raised one eyebrow. "What do you mean?"

"That's how politics works at its best," Campbell elaborated. "Everyone wants something. Some people insist they have to have that something, and exactly that, no matter what. But other people insist on having other things, which don't match what the first group wants. To really get anything done you have to compromise and find a middle ground that isn't everything you want but satisfies most of your needs."

"Great," Stark observed. "Our armor's like politics? I'll never trust the damn armor again."

Campbell laughed once more, then sobered abruptly. "Sergeant Stark, are the compromises in your armor a bad thing? Or do they make it work?"

"They make it work," Stark admitted after a moment.

"Ideally, that's how politics should be as well. Not a perfect thing, but not a bad thing. Something which makes things work in an imperfect world."

Vic bared her teeth in a humorless grin. "From what I know, our armor does a helluva lot better job of that than politics has recently."

Campbell nodded back, still somber. "I must agree. Technology is much more straightforward than human relations."

"Your armor is dark gray," Sarafina pointed out. "I did not think it looked that color in the vids I saw before I came up to the Moon."

Stark shook his head. "No, it wouldn't've. Gray's the default shade. In action, the camo's activated."

"Camo?"

"Sorry. Camouflage. That means anything that helps hide us. We use the word *camo* to talk about any active or passive countermeasures."

"On a battlefield," Vic interjected, "survival is often a matter of not being seen. If you can be spotted and engaged with aimed fire, your chances of survival drop dramatically."

"Yeah," Stark agreed. "So when the camo's on, the suits scan their surroundings and alter color and shade to match. Like a . . . what's that lizard?"

"A chameleon?"

"Right. Only better. If we're on a field of snow, it'll be white. If the snow's melting in patches, it'll have dirty brown or green mixed in with the white."

Campbell eyed the armor judiciously. "It must make you very hard to see."

"Sure, but the enemy's got targeting systems designed to spot us anyway. Sometimes we win, sometimes they do."

Campbell and Sarafina stared back at him. "I do not see how you can discuss that so casually," Sarafina finally stated.

Stark shrugged. "It's the way things are. We do our best to survive and beat the other guy."

"You mean 'kill the other guy,'" she corrected, eyes wide.

"Yeah. I guess I do. If we have to. Sometimes you don't, but basically the job's about killing other people." Stark reached to pat his weapon, resting ready in its rack. "That's why a rifle has always been a soldier's best friend. At least, since they invented rifles."

Campbell bent to look, examining the rifle without attempting to touch it as he had the armor. "It looks just like the weapons I've seen portrayals of back on Earth."

"It does because that's pretty much what it is. The muzzle velocity has been lowered considerably so there's a lot less chance of firing slugs into orbit. Of course, we've got inhibits built into our suits' targeting systems that keep us from firing straight up, but you could be aiming at someone above you and miss a little. Anyway, back home, high velocity is necessary to give you long range and accuracy, but up here there's no air the bullet has to punch through and the gravity doesn't drag it down near as fast. You don't want to be able to shoot a bullet around the Moon."

"But if the bullets don't go as fast, can't your armor defeat them?"

"Good question. The answer's no, because the bullets aren't just solid metal. Armies haven't used solid slugs for a couple decades, I guess. There's an explosive charge inside every round, so when the bullet hits something it fires a super dense sub-caliber penetrator at high velocity into the target. Punches through most personal armor and hurts like hell. On the other hand, if the bullet doesn't hit anything for a long time, like if despite the aiming inhibits it does go high enough and long enough to threaten God-knows-what, then that same charge goes off a little different and just blows the bullet into little pieces."

"Very neat," Campbell approved.

"When it comes to killing people, humans are extremely clever," Vic agreed dryly. "Look at the whole war we've been fighting up here. Everything's pretty much nice and peaceful on Earth where a major war might inconvenience folks and break stuff, but up here, where everything's dead anyway, we just add a lot of new craters."

"Not everything is dead," Sarafina declared, her voice thin. "The Colony is alive."

"True. So are we. For a while, anyway. I guess some lives count more than others."

"Hell, Vic," Stark noted, his voice harsh, "we've known that for ages."

Sarafina shook her head, eyes downcast. "It appears we must also learn that same lesson."

Vic's expression softened momentarily. "You've got to work with the world as it is, and that's the reality we have to live with."

"Wrong." Stark flashed a grim smile. "Reality's gonna change, and we're gonna change it."

"That," Campbell observed, "is a rather high goal to aim for."

"We've been putting our lives on the line for longer than we care to think about. And you know what I think? If you're gonna risk your life for something, it might as well be something big. Something really worth dying for."

"This is big," Vic agreed.

"Worth mutually pledging your lives and your honor?" Campbell asked.

"Is that some sort of quote?"

"Sort of, Sergeant Stark. Sort of."

Open, yet closed in. Like a passenger concourse in an airfield, the main spaceport terminal for the Lunar Colony was dominated by a large room, which extended in all directions, interrupted by stone pillars supporting a metal-reinforced Moon-rock ceiling above. A very thick ceiling, just in case one of the shuttles using the spaceport had the worst kind of accident. On Earth, the pillars would have been described as having been hewn from the living rock, but somehow the phrase didn't fit for lifeless lunar matter. Among the pillars, clots of people stood or moved in patterns that appeared chaotic at first, but slowly resolved into a sort of ballet of three parts, one of those moving to the exit, one of those arriving, and one of those holding their places to guard or guide the first two. Groups of civilians stopped to stare at the soldiers crowding the terminal, unfamiliar faces in unfamiliar garb intruding on the isolated small-town environment that no longer existed back home. An environment inadvertently recreated on the Moon, which those fabled small towns of yesterday had once gazed upward from on clear, quiet nights.

Stark smiled at a nearby gaggle of civs, a few teenagers wide-eyed with faked nonchalance at the military presence. *I could've been one of them. That punk in the short jacket. Funny where life leads you. And,* the disquieting thought arose, *if I screw up this situation I may ruin their lives along with mine.*

Fitful movement started up to one side of the concourse, a long line of uniforms shuffling forward. Officers. The former leaders of Stark and his troops, now under guard and on their way home. Some of the officers stood tall, gazing around defiantly as if still in charge of all they surveyed. Others huddled small, ashamed or frightened of their changed roles, eager to get on the shuttles that would return them to a world where they still commanded. Stark's eyes narrowed as one of the enlisted guards gave a passing officer a shove with a rifle butt, creating a stumbling ripple down the line heading for the exit. He took a dozen quick steps, closing on the incident. "You."

The guard looked around, worried eyes clashing with his hastily forced look of innocence. "Me?"

"Yeah. You." Stark reached to grab the shoulder of the officer who'd been shoved, a female Colonel who seemed torn between terror and outrage. "Your orders are no mistreatment. Right?"

"Uh, yessir."

"So you will apologize to this officer for striking her without cause." The other guards were watching Stark now. "If she gets out of line, you are authorized to discipline her. If she tries to grab your rifle, you are authorized to shoot her. But you will treat her with courtesy otherwise."

The guard flushed, his mouth tight. "They never treated us with no courtesy."

"That's the point. We're supposed to be better than that. And we will be." Stark paused for a moment. "I'm waiting."

"Okay. I mean, yessir." Gulping, the guard nodded toward the Colonel. "I apologize for striking you without cause, Colonel."

Stark shifted his gaze to the officer. "Now, you accept the apology."

The Colonel turned a brighter shade of red than the guard had. "I don't—!"

"Yes, you do. Get out of here." Stark turned her with casual force, placing the Colonel back into the flow of officers headed outward, then faced the guard again. "We're better than that," he repeated. "I'm not asking you apes to respect people like this, but give them courtesy. Make it automatic. It's called discipline, and nobody better forget it. We've got our own officers coming along, and I don't want anybody out of the habit of listening to them."

"Where we gonna get our own officers?" another guard wondered.

"From apes like you. The best ones." Expressions of incredulity met

Stark's words. "I mean it. You guys all know somebody who's good enough to lead, and good enough that you'll follow. Tell them word's gonna be coming down for volunteers, and we'll want the best."

Silent nods and scattered "yessirs" acknowledged Stark's words as he stepped away, heading toward another column whose members' awkward shuffles marked them as new arrivals to the Moon. He watched them, half-curious, half-envious of the soldiers whose parents had shared their lifework and could now share their lives again.

One man, slim and elderly, locked his eyes on Stark, evaluating him in a fashion that caused Stark to automatically stiffen his posture. The man detached himself from the file, ignoring a hasty call from one of the escorts, walking with the wobbly awkwardness of a new arrival to the Moon until he reached Stark and stood at rigid attention to render a precise salute.

Stark returned the gesture as professionally as he could. "Do I know you?"

"No, you do not, Sergeant Stark. My son, however, had the good fortune to serve in your Squad for some years. He often spoke of your leadership qualities."

"Your son?" The man's face, his mannerisms, his carefully controlled speech, suddenly clicked into focus. "Private Mendoza. You're his dad."

"That is correct."

Stark smiled broadly. "Lieutenant Mendoza, I guess I should say. Damn nice to see you, sir."

"I was not aware my son had spoken of me to you." Hard to say how the elder Mendoza felt about it. Like Mendo, it seemed he kept a quiet, disengaged front before the world.

"Just once. He's a good soldier. Your son's okay, Lieutenant. Minor wound during a recent action, but nothing that kept him off duty."

"Thank you. I am grateful for the news. But I am retired now, as you must know, Sergeant Stark. Mr. Mendoza is sufficient."

"Sorry. From what I've heard, you're a fine officer, so you're still a Lieutenant to me." Stark spotted Reynolds walking down the incoming line, scrutinizing the arrivals. "Hey, Vic. Mendo's dad's here. This is Lieutenant Mendoza."

Reynolds saluted automatically. "Pleased to meet you, sir."

Lieutenant Mendoza quirked a quizzical smile. "I was informed discipline had failed on the Moon. How odd to be met by proper military courtesy."

"Just what were you expecting?" Vic challenged.

"The authorities at home warned that an officer, even a retired one, might well face a lynch mob here."

"Can't lynch people on the Moon," Stark noted sardonically. "Gravity's too light. They just hang there, yelling at you while their neck muscles automatically tense to keep them breathing. Takes a few hours before their necks get too tired to keep the windpipe open. We haven't tried it," he hastened to add as Lieutenant Mendoza raised an eyebrow. "Every once in a while some guy tries to suicide that way. Never works. When they get found, people make fun of them for a while before they cut them down."

"I see I have much to learn of the environment up here, but it appears that soldiers are much as they have always been."

"I'll take that as a compliment," Stark smiled. "Once you're settled in and have had a chance to meet your son, I'd like to talk to you, sir. I think you could help me with some ideas, if you're anything like Mendo. Excuse me, like your son."

"Certainly." Lieutenant Mendoza saluted again, then turned to cautiously make his way back to the incoming file.

Stark glanced at Reynolds. "That was a nice surprise. What brings you here, checking out the incoming? Expecting anybody?"

Vic shrugged, projecting indifference. "You never know when a familiar face might turn up." Turning slightly, she gestured toward the outgoing column. "All officers today."

"Yeah. General Meecham and all his little sub-generals were loaded onto the first shuttle. I doubt he'll ever be back to the Moon."

"What a shame," she noted with a total lack of sincerity. "Did you say good-bye?"

"Hell, no. I said everything I wanted to say to that guy a while back."

She grinned humorlessly. "I understand the next batch of shuttles is supposed to start taking off the Third Division enlisted apes who preferred going home to staying with us."

"I know." *Rash. Have a good flight, pal. I'm gonna miss you, but I sure hope you don't come back. How long has it been since we two Privates hid behind rocks while the enemy tried to see how well our armor worked? Or since we got into that bar fight and ended up being chased by half the Indigs in the city? Man, been a long time. And if he comes back here, he'll be with an army trying to defeat us. Shooting at us and getting shot at. Rash, don't come back.* "How many decided to bolt, anyway?"

"You mean how many Third Division soldiers chose going home

to staying with us? About two-thirds of the survivors." She paused, face carefully composed. "Which is so small a number I can hardly stand it."

Two-thirds. Two-thirds of how many? They were still trying to tally the dead from Meecham's ill-advised offensive. Far, far easier to count those from Third Division who still lived. It wasn't supposed to be that way. Third Division wasn't supposed to have been gutted by being thrown against unshaken enemy fortifications. But things never did happen the way Generals planned. "How can they go back?" Stark asked softly. "After what was done to them?"

"Don't blame them, Ethan. They're not lunar veterans at heart. Home is still home to them. Plus, they're still shell-shocked from getting cut to ribbons during Meecham's offensive, and before that they were confused and disoriented from being rushed up here."

Stark managed a small, self-mocking smile. "They ain't the only ones who're confused. I don't blame 'em, Vic. Everybody makes choices. I'm not exactly in a position to claim my choice is the best one."

"Not yet, anyway." She nodded toward the incoming line. "Hey, here comes another visitor aiming for you. You're popular today."

"Just my luck." Stark stared at the man approaching, uncertain legs marking him as another new arrival, trying to shake off a feeling of familiarity. *I never met that guy. Why does he seem like somebody I used to know?*

The man, some years younger than Stark, saluted cheerfully. "Private Grant Stein, reporting for duty."

"Stein." The half-familiar face fell into context, matching half-buried memories. Stark held his expression with difficulty, noting as he did so the tight glances Vic shot toward him and the new arrival. "You related to Kate Stein? Corporal Kate Stein?"

"That's right. I'm her little brother."

Stark swallowed, fighting off shock. "I never knew she had . . . that is, you're a lot younger than she was when . . ."

"I was just a kid when she, uh, fell at Patterson's Knoll. Maybe you could tell me about it sometime, Sergeant?" The grin shifted to eager shyness.

"Uh, sure, I don't usually . . ." Stark shook his head, emotionally off-balance, angry at the disorientation fogging his thinking. "How'd you get them to let you up here? The exchange is only supposed to be for family members."

Stein grinned again, the simple gesture sparking memories of his sister in Stark. "Civs are running the exchange. For the right bribe, you can do anything. Somebody altered my record to show I had a relative up here. Easy."

"Easy?" Vic questioned sharply. "You're a Private? An active duty soldier and you got up here? Family member or not, why would the authorities allow that?"

"I'm not the only one," Stein protested. "I don't know why they allowed it, but there's maybe a half-dozen of us."

"That's very odd." Vic looked at Stark as she said it, even though her words were apparently aimed at Grant Stein. "Why send us reinforcements?"

Something about her tone aggravated Stark. "How the hell should I know? For that matter, most of the family members we're getting are retired mil. They're sort of reinforcements, too. Maybe not good enough for the front line, but they could free up a soldier to fight."

Reynolds chewed her lip, then nodded reluctantly. "That's true. Welcome to the Moon, Private Stein. I'm sure you and Sergeant Stark have a lot to talk about." She saluted Stark, uncharacteristically formal. "With your permission, I'll get back to work."

"Sure." Stark returned the salute, looking questioningly at her, but Vic simply nodded before heading off across the concourse.

"Is she a friend of yours?" Private Stein asked casually.

"Yeah. Real good friend." Stark focused back on the man who carried a ghost from the past in his features. "Look, you've gotta settle in. Attend the orientation briefings. But you call me after that. I'll tell you what I can about your sister."

"That'd be great. Thanks." Private Stein beamed happily, snapped a sharp salute, then returned to the file of incoming personnel.

Never expected to see a brother of Kate's. Stark fought down a shiver. Every night, the long-ago-lost battle raged in his mind. Every night, Kate Stein and his other fellow soldiers died. Now here was Grant Stein, somehow forcing that nightmare into waking hours. *Why now? What's it mean?* He suddenly imagined Vic talking to him, expression exasperated. *Maybe all it means is that you've met Kate Stein's brother.* Maybe.

Stark eyed the nearby window warily despite the thickness of its synthetic "glass" and the gleaming knife edge of the emergency seal barely protruding on one side, ready to slam shut in an instant through any obstacle if the window somehow cracked. Thinking of the airless waste outside, he couldn't appreciate the bleak beauty of the dead landscape painted in shades of gray. Off to one side, the spaceport landing field was visible, a large flat plain leveled and painstakingly swept clear of dust. On the field, the squat shapes of shuttles pointed upward from the centers of blackened patches, access tubes latched on like remoras temporarily linking them to the Colony.

He stole another glance, intrigued despite himself by the view. Many times he'd been out on the surface and seen the few Colony towers built of excavated lunar rock, but he'd never been inside one. "Why are we here?"

Stacey Yurivan gestured toward the closed door. "I found a shuttle commander willing to talk, but only in a nice place near the spaceport."

"A shuttle pilot'll talk to us? Is he corporate or government?"

"Neither. Our former bosses wanted our former officers back so bad they hired some foreign shipping to help on the pickups this time."

"What's he got to say?" Reynolds wondered. She stood near a corner, even farther from the window than Stark. "The officers from the first exchange should be home by now, and they were probably debriefed all the way back."

"You can bet on it," Stark agreed. "Most of the senior officers went on that first exchange. I wish I coulda been a fly on the wall when they were being talked to. This second is mostly junior officers, right?"

"Mostly. And like Stacey says, there's more shuttles in this one. We'll still need a third shuttle exchange to get everybody back, though, counting the Third Division survivors who want off this rock. What does this guy know, Stace?"

Yurivan shrugged elaborately. "Stuff about the situation on the World. I figured you'd find it interesting."

"Can't wait," Stark agreed dryly. "Did you invite any of the civs?"

"Do I have to?"

"Yes, you have to. Just a couple, though. Campbell and his chief aide."

Vic nodded in agreement. "They deserve to be here. Those two made this exchange happen." As Yurivan made the calls, Vic turned to Stark. "What do you think they've been saying about us? Back home?"

"We'll know in a few minutes. I'm sure it ain't good."

Reynolds screwed her face up thoughtfully. "They'll probably try to make us out as renegade scum. I imagine they'll paint you as a beer swilling, insubordinate warlord-wanna-be." She squinted at Stark. "Which won't take too much work."

"Very funny. What'll they paint you as, Whore-Empress of the Moon?"

"You think? I always wanted to be a Whore-Empress. Maybe they'll enhance my figure when they fake the vid."

"Your figure don't need any enhancing."

"Says you," she laughed. "You been admiring me in my battle armor all this time, Ethan Stark?"

"Yeah. That's it. The battle armor. I got a thing for women shaped like over muscled gorillas with really big heads. The civs on their way, Stace?"

"Yup." Yurivan strode over to a nearby duffel bag, fishing inside for a moment before she emerged with a bottle filled with dark liquid.

"What," Stark demanded, "is that?"

His Security Officer smiled back. "A bribe. Also a way to keep our shuttle commander's lips flapping."

"Rum," Reynolds observed. "Good stuff. Where'd you get this, Stace?"

"The Officer's Club stocks."

"I didn't know you had access to the Officer's Club stocks. Sergeant Gordasa never mentioned it."

Yurivan shrugged. "Ah, well, I haven't bothered Gordy about it. He's pretty busy, you know."

"Uh-huh," Vic agreed with a sardonic smile. "He's going to be a little busier now, running an inventory on those stocks."

"Whatever." Stacey carefully set up the bottle and a shot glass on a small table next to a seat at one end of the room. "Your civs should be here by now. I'll get them and the shuttle guy."

A few minutes later, Licensed Shuttle Commander James Plant leaned back in his chair and took an appreciative sip of the rum, smiling as he did so. "This is excellent, though I suppose its virtue is enhanced by its rarity, eh? Not many people have drunk rum that has journeyed this far from the Caribbean. From the Commanding General's private stock, I imagine?"

Stark shook his head. "Officers' Club stock. I guess they kept this stuff for the Generals, though."

"I can see why." Plant took another taste. "What is it you want to know?"

"What makes you think we want to know something?"

"I am not a fool. I also am not privy to any secrets, but I have no loyalty to your superiors. I am only a temporary hire. And my time here is limited. So, if you have questions, you should speak them without further games."

Stacey Yurivan nodded nonchalantly. "What are they telling you? About things up here?"

Plant sipped again, face thoughtful. "Not much, really. Certainly not enough to satisfy those curious about the situation, which is almost everyone. Initially, there were claims of security clampdowns associated with enemy action. Then statements that technical problems associated with sunspot activity had halted communications with this Colony. No one believed it, naturally. Finally, official American sources declared a breakdown of law and order here, attributed to unnamed criminal elements in the pay of foreign powers." Plant smiled again. "Though not, of course, *my* particular foreign power."

"Of course not. What're they saying about Stark and the rest of the leaders?"

"Very little." Commander Plant spread his hands. "The official story is that anarchy reigns. For a brief time, it was stated that Colony Manager Campbell had died at the hands of a mob. All other lawful authority is in hiding, it is claimed, fearing a similar fate."

"You look pretty good for a dead guy," Stark observed to Campbell.

Campbell smiled back as Plant continued. "However, Mr. Campbell's continued existence apparently became obvious during the negotiations for this exchange of prisoners, so your government has shifted their tack and now decided he is not dead after all."

"That's good to hear," Campbell noted sarcastically.

"Thank you. Unfortunately, I must inform you they are now

claiming the stress of the lunar environment has rendered you mentally unstable."

"I see. Then it's sort of a good news/bad news thing."

Plant nodded, took another sip of rum, then reached into the thigh pocket of his coverall. "I have a recording here which might be of interest to you." Extending the screen of his hand unit, the Shuttle Commander turned it so his audience could see. "This is a copy of a vid released by your government. It has become somewhat valuable for reasons I will disclose in a moment." He tapped the terminal, bringing the vid replay to life. On-screen, a small group of men and women in dirty, torn military uniforms were shown brandishing weapons and firing randomly, pausing only to drink from variously shaped and colored bottles. The perspective jerked repeatedly as if the operator of the vid cam were shaking in fear.

"Looks like none of those soldiers have shaved or bathed in weeks," Yurivan observed facetiously. "They get these guys from the Ranger Battalion?"

Stopping before a doorway, one of the men kicked viciously, causing the portal to slam open. Ducking inside, he quickly reemerged with a screaming, crying woman. "What is this supposed to be?" Stark wondered.

"You," Plant stated. "Or rather, the soldiers up here. According to the back-story for this vid, an unidentified but deranged renegade has set himself up as the nominal leader of otherwise out-of-control, mutinous soldiers. This," he added with a wave toward the screen, "is allegedly a covertly filmed incident in which his minions are seizing civilian women for a slave harem."

"You're kidding," Vic chuckled. "Well, Ethan, it looks like you've finally figured out how to get women."

"Very funny," Stark observed. "At least Campbell and I can be 'mentally unbalanced' and 'deranged' together."

On the vid, the scruffy soldiers were shoving the woman around with their rifle butts. Suddenly, a small figure darted from the open doorway, obviously a child rushing to cling to her mother. With a wicked smile, one of the soldiers kicked the child away, then raised her rifle. "Hey," Vic began, her laughter dying. Before she could say anything else, the rapid bark of automatic fire came from the vid screen and the child was tossed back to lie motionless in the street.

"This ain't funny, anymore," Stacey Yurivan growled. "That's just sick. Am I the only one who's noticed these apes are moving like they're in Earth gravity?"

"No." Stark stared at the now-blank screen, his eyes hard. "Even if those plug-ugly so-called soldiers weren't a giveaway, the normal G would be. I'd like to get my hands on whoever faked this vid. I'd show them a damn atrocity."

"Not to worry," Commander Plant advised, replacing the unit in his pocket. "A good number of people on Earth noticed the gravity problem, too. Quite a stupid mistake, apparently the result of rushing to create the vid within a short time. Your government quickly shifted from saying it was real footage to claiming it was a reenactment of actual events, but any credibility it might have had was long gone by that point. It has since attempted to reclaim every copy of the vid in existence, a task remarkable for its scope and futility."

"You'd think our government would have at least learned how to lie right by now," Reynolds observed angrily. "Commander Plant, there hasn't been any effort to publicly identify the leaders up here? None at all?" Plant shook his head. "It's odd they haven't named us so they'd have someone to demonize."

"Not really," Plant lectured. "If you consider, any leader can be a focal point for either hatred or admiration. I believe there is a great fear that the public would come to admire the leaders up here if they were identified and given faces and personality."

"They think we're that great?" Stark laughed shortly.

"No, I believe they realize how weak they measure as leaders against you. Bold action, risking life and fortune for fellow humans, no deception or half-measures masquerading as sacrifice for the welfare of others. You see? The moral opposite of your country's current leadership on Earth. One need not be a giant to stand tall beside dwarfs."

Stark looked down, plainly uncomfortable at Plant's words, then glanced over in relief as Campbell began speaking. "What else is happening? Have events up here had any other impact?"

"Ah. Impact." Commander Plant seemed to find the word amusing. "Let us see. The loss of revenue from lunar investments caused the profit projections for a number of large corporations to fall significantly. There is also fear they might have to completely write off those investments. Their stocks have fallen as a result. Those stocks have dragged down the general market. The average citizen, I am told, is worried, and since so much of the American economy is based on services, which are not necessities, people are not spending money on such services."

Sarafina closed her eyes briefly. "We're triggering a recession?"

"Apparently. Your government has instituted a number of measures to increase confidence, but a government lacking in credibility cannot easily generate confidence, eh?"

Campbell nodded, eyeing the pilot narrowly. "What about other countries, such as yours? What do they think?"

"What do they think?" Plant pondered the question for a moment. "They wait. America is too powerful. What will become of you here? Can you withstand the pressure from your home, as well as that from the coalition that has fought you all these years?"

Stark smiled in a manner that had nothing to do with humor, the barest curling of the corners of his mouth. "That coalition got a nasty bloody nose and several black eyes when they tried us. They've been a lot quieter since."

"I see. There have been rumors, of course, but actual information has been censored. Yours is not the only government which seeks to control what its citizens know." Plant glanced at his wrist as the chronometer there chirped rapidly. "I fear my time here is up. I must return to my ship to prepare for liftoff." He glanced at the bottle of rum regretfully. "Alas, since our ships are in hire to your government they are being monitored by your customs inspectors. We have been told any contraband will be seized."

"Booze isn't contraband," Yurivan observed.

Plant shrugged. "As far as your government is concerned, any item from the Colony is contraband until the situation is resolved."

"Is that right?" Stacey grinned at her companions. "Then it's all worth a lot more than usual, huh?"

"That is so. I see you have a merchant's eye for markets."

"We'll be getting shuttles in again, you know. The blockade's not perfect. Potential profits will be . . . pretty large."

"I imagine so. I will keep this in mind and ensure my own superiors are aware of the opportunity this offers." Commander Plant rose, nodding to everyone else present as they stood in turn. "I thank you for the hospitality."

They watched him leave, escorted out by Stacey Yurivan, then sat silent for a few moments, digesting the information. Vic finally turned to Stark, shaking her head. "Ethan Stark, you have kicked over one helluva lot of dominoes."

"All I did," he protested, "was try to stop something stupid, try to do the right thing, and save people's lives."

"Like I said." Vic walked toward the door, waving toward Campbell, Sarafina, and Stark. "If you all will excuse me, I need to get a little rest before I get as deranged as our leaders."

"I believe," Campbell stated with exaggerated dignity, "that I personally have been characterized as 'mentally unbalanced,' not 'deranged.' "

"True. My apologies. Ethan, I think you've got another meeting scheduled in less than an hour."

"A meeting?" Stark groused. "Which one?"

"Personal business. Remember?"

He grimaced. "Oh, yeah. I remember. Guess I better get going."

Grant Stein stood at the main sentry station leading into the headquarters area, smiling as usual as Stark walked up. "Here early, huh? Come on." Letting the younger man follow slightly behind, Stark headed for his quarters, then changed his mind. *I need neutral ground. And someplace quiet, where we won't be interrupted. I know just the place.* He continued on, past his room, until he reached the wood paneled, double-wide door which led into the former Commanding General's suite.

Stein looked around eagerly as they entered. "Fancy digs. I bet you enjoy it here."

"I don't get much free time," Stark answered cautiously. "Sit down. You want anything? Coffee or something?"

"No, Sergeant. Or I guess I should say Commander."

"Whatever. Titles aren't as important as the people carrying them." Stark rubbed his neck, then smiled ruefully. "Funny. I remember so much about Kate, but I don't know what you want to hear. I imagine you've heard all about the battle."

"Patterson's Knoll?" Grant Stein shook his head. "Not many details. I mean, not many people can talk about details, can they?"

"No. I guess not. Only a few of us survived." Stark sat carefully, chewing his lip. "Basically, our outfit was sent in to beat up some Indigs who didn't want to sell their ore supplies cheap to a corporation that'd given a lot of money to our politicians. The sort of thing that happens a lot, right? These particular Indigs had a decent mil of their own, but our commander, just a Colonel 'cause the General was off with the rest of the brigade, he figured we could just roll over them. Maybe we could've, but we found out too late that the Indigs had gotten foreign backing. A lot of weapons, a lot of ammo, even some half-decent troops."

Grant Stein nodded, intent, as Stark continued. "Well, even our Colonel couldn't avoid getting the hint when we ran head-on into a major Indig force. All kinds of ammo getting thrown at us from all directions. He only had two companies of troops with him, and he'd run us way forward of the other columns. Wanted to get himself a lot of press coverage, I heard. The Colonel only let us fall back a little, even though we were too far from any supporting forces. We stopped in this open area, I guess 'cause he thought we could evac from there if worse came to worse. But our air couldn't get through. Too many antiaircraft defenses, and we were too far from the big air bases. I dunno what that idiot Colonel Patterson was thinking, but we just sat there, all night. There was just a thin layer of dirt over solid rock so we couldn't dig in, just had to sit there while the officers held meetings. Then we started taking fire again, from all sides. Then word came around that our comms back to headquarters were being jammed. After that the jamming got bad enough to disrupt all our comms."

Stark paused, fighting down a wave of memory-induced panic. "All morning. All afternoon. They just kept hitting us. Small arms. Heavy stuff. We could've broke out in the morning, I think. Fought our way through. But the officers just locked up. I don't even know how long Patterson lived, or if he got nailed before noon. By afternoon, we'd lost too many people. Just had to sit there." Stark suddenly became aware of pain, looking down to see his hands clenched so tightly they were mottled red and white. He relaxed them with an effort.

"I didn't see Kate most of that day. We were all just hugging the ground and praying. Nobody moved, not unless they were trying to take care of wounded, and after awhile we ran out of medical stuff, and all the medics were dead anyway. But somehow, I didn't get hit except a few minor wounds. Come night, they finally let up. I went looking for anybody else. I found Kate." He stopped, unable to speak for a moment.

"She'd been . . . hit bad." *Why can't I tell him she'd had her legs blown off? God, I can't say it, not even now.* "Couldn't move. Couldn't be moved, and wouldn't let me stay. She didn't survive the night. I know that. She couldn't've."

Stark stood, turning away and facing the wall, his head lowered as he gathered his thoughts. "I had to run away. I had to get together any other survivors who could move and run. Not my fault, nothing I could have done, but I relive it damn near every night. Wish I could have done something. Anything. But it always ends the same, because that's the only way it could've ended. Kate knew that. She gave me the last, best advice she could. Saved my life when I couldn't save hers. Ever since, I've been trying to make a difference, but none of it changes the past."

He pivoted suddenly, facing Grant Stein again and catching his expression in midchange, just settling into lines of earnest sympathy. *Didn't want me to see how awful he felt about losing his sister, I expect. Can't say I blame him.* "There isn't much more I can tell you. Sorry there weren't last words or anything. I guess we were just too much in shock to even think straight."

Stein waited for a long moment after Stark finished, then nodded, his expression open, sorrowful. "It was hard to leave her, then?"

"Hard? Hardest thing I ever did. Let me tell you, dying's easy. Too easy, sometimes. Kate wouldn't let me take the easy way. She was like that."

"I never got to know her that well."

"Oh." Stark bent his head again. "Sorry. Wish I coulda . . ."

"I'm sure you did all you could," Stein assured him. "But, now, look at all this. You're really in charge? There's not, like, some council you answer to?"

"Council?" Stark squinted as if trying to gauge Grant Stein's seriousness. "No. I'm in charge. Got voted into it, but the voting stopped there. I guess if I screwed up bad enough, they'd get rid of me, but that hasn't happened yet. Until it does, it's just me."

"But Sergeant Reynolds, she seems pretty close."

"She's a damn good soldier and a damn good friend."

Stein smiled. "I understand."

Stark fought down a wave of irritation. *What do I care what this guy thinks? He's not Kate. But, God, he's so much like her. On the outside, anyway.* "Well, I can't think of anything else. You settling in okay up here?"

"It's really different. I can see why new arrivals need a lunar veteran to help them adjust."

Stark hesitated, aware of the half-request in the younger man's statement. "I'll make sure you've got a decent soldier paired with you. Me, I'm so buried in work I can't spare the time. Sorry."

"Oh. That's okay. I'd heard that Kate took you under her wing, and I thought maybe . . ."

Damn. That's a debt I owe. "Being close to me right now might not be the smartest thing a soldier can do. I'll keep an eye on you, though. If you're anything like her, you'll do fine."

"Thanks," Grant beamed. "It's all right if I come to see you every once in a while, isn't it? You're sort of a living link to Kate."

"Uh, sure." Stark checked his palm unit ostentatiously.

"Looks like you got some more familiarization briefings coming up. Better get going. You need an escort out?"

"No, thanks, Commander." Stein stood, saluted smartly,

then headed out. Stark stared at the door after he'd left, sitting silently in the expansive room once used as a front office by the Commanding General.

Sometime later, Vic Reynolds stuck her head in, frowning around. "Ethan? Somebody told me they saw you go in here. What're you doing?"

"Thinking."

"Will wonders never cease?" Vic came inside, flopping into another chair and looking around. "Nice place. So, how'd your meeting with Grant go?"

"Okay, I guess."

She raised both eyebrows. "Doesn't sound okay. What's the problem?"

"I dunno." Stark shrugged uncomfortably. "Brings up a lot of memories, you know?"

"I can imagine. If I'm lucky, I'll never really know. That's not all, though, is it?"

Stark shrugged again. "Everything seemed fine, but also a little off. I can't really explain."

"You sure he's for real?"

"Huh? You mean, is he really Kate's brother? Yeah. No doubt."

"But he's not his sister, is he? Look, Ethan, you don't know this guy."

"If he's anything like Kate—"

"If. That's a big if, right?"

"Sure it is. But I still owe him. For Kate's sake."

"I can't tell you different, not from the little I know about her. But let me ask you this. If Grant Stein has admired you for so many years, how come you never heard from him until now? Why no letters or calls or visits in all the years since his sister died on Patterson's Knoll?"

Grass. Flecked with blood. Swaying and trembling in the wake of explosions on all sides. Stark shook his head to dispel the vision. "I don't know. Maybe it hurt him too much to talk about."

"Something you'd know all about, huh? He doesn't seem the type, but you could be right." She sighed, pulling out her palmtop. "Ready for some administrative issues?"

"Ah, geez, Vic. Hasn't my day been hard enough so far? What kind of administrative issues?"

"Our new officer candidates. Got the first batch of names in for screening." Vic leaned back, keying her palmtop to display a welter of data. She peered at the screen, clicking through a few items, then smiled. "And we need a final disposition for disciplinary action against one of those new officer volunteers."

"Already? What'd he or she do?"

"A couple of days ago he turned his living cubicle and the adjacent cube into a duplex."

Stark chuckled in disbelief. "You're kidding. How'd he do that?"

"Seems he had a shoulder-fired weapon with a defective firing mechanism. He decided to fix it himself by welding the firing circuit back onto the propellant charge."

"In his cube?" Stark stifled another laugh. "He's lucky he wasn't killed."

"Which he admitted," Vic noted. "Said he'd screwed up, couldn't believe he'd done that, etc., etc., etc., and so on. It's up to you," she leveled a slim finger at Stark, "to decide his punishment and whether he should become an officer candidate."

"Huh." Stark rubbed his chin, staring toward the ceiling. "He admitted he'd made a mistake. Hell, he *knew* he'd made a mistake. That ranks him better than most of the officers we got rid of."

"You've got a point there."

"Give him another chance."

"No punishment?"

"He's gonna be an officer, a real officer, one held accountable for what he does and how he does it. That's a tough sentence. Let's see if he's learned his lesson."

"Another good point." Reynolds tapped a few more times. "How's it feel playing God?"

"Usually pretty bad. Most decisions are harder than that one."

"Right, like this next one."

"Ah, hell," Stark groaned. "Now what?"

"We've got about twenty officers who've been stalling being exchanged. Not one big group, just a lot of individuals and a couple twosomes or threesomes. Now they say they want to stay up here."

"Huh? Why?"

"So they can be officers. In our division. They're all junior officers, of course, mostly Lieutenants with a few Captains."

Stark stared at Reynolds, shaking his head at the same time. "Never expected that. Sure, I've met a few decent officers, but . . ."

"So what do we do? Send them back anyway?"

"I don't . . . no. We can use good officers. People with training. But how can we be sure they mean it?"

"We could take their words for it," Vic suggested. "But then we haven't had a lot of luck with doing that in the past, have we?"

"No." Stark raised a palm, brow furrowed in thought, to forestall Reynolds before she continued. "That's probably it."

"What's probably it?"

"The past. We know how these volunteer officers treated their people in the past, right? We just ask their units. If they were decent officers when every rule of the game said they didn't have to be, that's a good sign they might be sincere."

"An excellent suggestion, Sergeant Stark. Hmmm."

"Hmmm? Hmmm what?"

"One of the officers who wants to stay. Her name's Conroy."

"Conroy? Our Conroy?"

"Looks like it. Yeah. Her record shows she commanded us at one point."

"I haven't seen her since she led our platoon on that blasted raid."

"Uh-huh. The one you got to play rearguard hero on."

Reynolds ostentatiously ignored Stark's scowl. "And the one Lieutenant Conroy got fired for."

"She got fired for leading you guys back to get me, right?"

"Yup. I thought they'd sent her home, but I guess she got parked in a warm-body job up here."

Stark closed his eyes, remembering lying alone under a barrage of fire while he covered the platoon's retreat, wondering if any friendly reinforcements would arrive in time to help him; seeing figures flit forward in a red haze of memory, shooting at him as they came. "I guess the Generals figured it'd be a worse punishment to make her stay on this lifeless hunk of rock."

"So," Vic asked quietly, "does she stay a little longer?"

"I'd sure as hell think so. Check her out, though, with the

people she's been working with lately."

"Don't even trust Conroy, huh? Not that I disagree."

"Vic," Stark declared heavily, "I haven't trusted any officers for so long I don't know how it feels. I'd like to change that, but it's gonna take awhile." He fell silent.

Reynolds glanced at Stark, sitting slumped in his chair, staring morosely at the far wall. "What's the problem, Ethan?"

"I got a million problems, Vic."

"I know. We just talked about two of them. What's the one that's got you so down right now?"

He thought a moment, face puzzled. "I'm surrounded by soldiers, Vic. How come I feel like I'm isolated?"

"Ah." She nodded wearily, placing her palmtop to one side. "Because you *are* isolated. Everything we do is about running this situation. There hasn't been time for just shooting the bull, except between you and me and a few other guys we see fairly often."

"Yeah. That's it, ain't it?" Stark sat up suddenly, face determined. "I still want to get with Lieutenant Mendoza. And when's the last time I talked to Mendo, or Corporal Gomez or anybody from my old Squad? Let's set some time aside, Vic."

"We haven't got time to set aside."

"We'll make some. How about having a dinner here at headquarters and then just relaxing awhile afterwards with those apes?"

Reynolds grimaced, then smiled softly. "That might be a real good thing. I'll get an invite list put together. You want Stein on it?"

"Stein? No."

She raised both eyebrows. "I thought he wanted to spend time with you. The whole hero-worship nine yards."

"Yeah."

"What's the problem? Can't handle an admiring puppy?"

"That's not it." Stark frowned, his gaze fixed on the floor as if the surface held some sort of intriguing but confusing picture. "Kate Stein died a long time ago, Vic. No matter how much that damn battle on Patterson's Knoll torments me, I know she's gone. But here's her brother all the sudden, and every time I look at his face or watch him do somethin', he reminds me of her. It don't feel right. The dead oughta stay buried."

"Yes," she agreed gently, "they should. I can send Grant Stein to some assignment where he'll be out of sight and unable to visit here."

"No. Why punish him 'cause I can't handle this? But I don't need a ghost sittin' there at the table when I'm tryin' to unwind. *Verdad?*"

"*Verdad. Comprendo.*" Vic stood up, reaching for Stark's hand. "Come on, soldier. Let's get out of this gilded cage and hang out with some people."

"Sounds good. Don't forget about that dinner."

"I won't. But it'll take a few days to set up."

"A few days? When's that third shuttle exchange scheduled for?"

Vic winced, then checked her palmtop. "Cheryl says one week from today."

"Cheryl? You mean Sarafina?"

"Who else would I mean?"

Stark grinned wickedly. "On a first-name basis, huh? You friends with a civ, Vic?"

She feigned indignation. "Ms. Sarafina has rendered us a great deal of assistance."

"Can't argue with that," Stark agreed, still grinning. "I'll be glad to get rid of the last of the officers and the Third Division types who didn't want to join with us. One more week? Can't think of anything that might screw up the exchange between now and then."

"Stark! Commander Stark!"

He halted in midstride, unable to miss the urgency in the call. *Guess that late lunch I was heading for is gonna be a little later.* "Here. That you, Jill?"

"Yes," Sergeant Tanaka agreed hurriedly. "Yes, sir. Got a real mess. We need you in the Command Center fast."

"What is it?" Stark had begun moving again even as he asked the question, threading through startled groups of soldiers. "Another attack?"

"No. I don't think so. It's the Navy."

"The Navy?" Warships had guarded the Colony since its founding, tangling with enemy warships, trying to blockade other colonies and the enemy armed forces. Since Stark's troops had rebelled, the Navy ships had blockaded the Colony instead, though at a distance rendered respectful by the Colony's surface defenses. "They're not attacking?"

"I don't think so. I don't know."

"Is Reynolds there?"

"No. I'll call her right now."

Stark accelerated a little more, trying to look urgent, but not worried, as other soldiers watched him pass. *Okay, so your boss has to get somewhere fast, but that's nothing to worry about. Right?* He took the time to look up and smile briefly at several soldiers, earning grins and salutes in return. *When I was a squad commander I only had to worry about keeping twelve guys calm. Now I gotta worry about thousands. It's like living in a fish bowl almost full-time.* For the first time, he realized just how seductively attractive the restricted access of the headquarters complex could be. *It would be easier if these guys couldn't see me, except when I felt like it. But usually something that looks easier is also wrong. I want these apes to see me, and I wanta see them, and so what if it makes my job a little tougher? It's still my job.*

Inside headquarters, he walked down corridors growing grander with every step until he confronted the wood-paneled access to the Command Center. Inside, the watch standers twisted in their chairs to eye him with confusion and worry. On the main display, which normally portrayed a section of the front on the lunar surface, a weird image twisted in 3-D. Its glowing symbology moved in patterns with no reference to the ground, intertwining and spinning like fireflies in a vast empty arena instead of following the flow of terrain. As the display shifted slightly to follow the action, a huge arc appeared to one side, glowing with hazard markers and threat symbols.

Stark eyed the display suspiciously. "What the hell is this?"

Tanaka ran a pointer around the display, highlighting different symbols. "These are Navy warships. Our Navy. The size of the symbology is tied to the size of the ship."

"So big symbol means big ship."

"Right."

"What's the real big thing?"

"That? Us. The Moon."

Suddenly things made a sort of sense. Stark tried to recall the approach to the Moon during the period before the first assault, long ago now, but still vivid in the way unique memories remain. *Yeah. We were out there in the troopship, and the Moon looked like that when we started getting close.* "What's going on?"

"There's a group of ships calling us. These two, over here."

Stark squinted. "They're being shot at."

"Right again. Shot at by this bigger group of warships."

"Why is one group of Navy ships being shot at by another group of Navy warships? Vic," he called as she entered, blinking away the effects of an afternoon catnap, "you understand this Navy stuff?"

"Hell, no. Do I look like a damn sailor?" She studied the unfamiliar symbology distrustfully. "Why are those ships shooting at each other?"

"I dunno. Neither does Tanaka. They're trying to call us, though."

"Then answer up! Aren't you the guy who wants to understand what's going on?"

"Yeah, but. . ." Stark waved toward the display. "I don't get this Navy stuff. There's no front and no rear."

"And no up or down. I know. It's weird."

Tanaka raised an urgent hand. "They're calling again, and they insist on talking to you, Commander Stark."

"They know me by name?"

Sergeant Tanaka flushed slightly. "I informed them you were in command when they asked."

"That's okay. It ain't a secret. I just wanted to know where they heard it. Okay. Link me in." The vid flickered once, then steadied into a view of a woman inside a room that shuddered and moved. She focused on Stark.

"You Stark?"

"Yeah." Enlisted, obviously, though Stark couldn't see any rank markings from this angle. "Who're you?"

"Chief Petty Officer Wiseman. Alex Wiseman. No jokes about the name, okay? We need your help." The room around her jerked suddenly, triggering a cascade of alarms.

"We?" Stark tried to concentrate over the unfamiliar scene and events. "Who's we?"

"Enlisted on these two ships. We got the *Subic Bay* and the *Guantanamo Bay*."

"Whatdayya mean you got 'em?"

Wiseman glared angrily, her expression changing to worry as another series of shudders yanked around the sailors to the cries of more alarms. "This is the *Subic Bay*. We took it over. The enlisted on the *Guantanamo Bay* did the same. Right now, the other ships out here are attacking us, and we're trying to defend ourselves without shooting back."

"Don't look like that's working very well."

"No, it's not. We need protection. Can you give it to us?"

"Vic?" Stark wondered. "Can we?"

"I doubt it," she came back.

Wiseman glared again. "You got real strong surface defenses. If we can get inside the range of those, the other ships won't be able to come after us."

"Commander Stark!" Tanaka seemed to be whispering in his ear, but from Wiseman's lack of reaction she couldn't hear this transmission. "If we let those ships inside our defenses they could do a huge amount of damage before we took them out."

Wiseman fidgeted, snapping a command unheard by the soldiers before turning back to address them. "We're taking hits. Nothing critical so far, but I haven't got a lot of time, here. You mud-crawlers gonna help us or not?"

"How do we know you're for real?" Stark demanded. "How do we know this isn't a trick so your ships can get in close and then open up on us?"

"Can't you tell we're in real combat?" Wiseman shouted.

"No. I see your room shaking. I hear alarms. I don't understand any of it. I'm a ground soldier."

Wiseman stared, then nodded rapidly, holding up her hands. "Okay, okay, I understand. I'm on the Bridge. The, uh, Command Center for the ship. We're maneuvering to avoid weapons being fired at us. Torpedoes. That's some of the shaking. Some of the torpedoes are getting too close for comfort when they explode. That's other shaking and the alarms."

"You could fake that."

"Yeah." Wiseman looked down for a moment, then over to the side as someone shouted a suggestion. "Hey, that's right. I'm opening my ship's systems to you. Take a look. You'll see we're taking real damage."

Tanaka's voice whispered in Stark's ear again. "If they open their systems to us we can take them over."

"So they either trust us or they're desperate," Stark noted back over the same private channel. "Do it. Whatdayya see?"

"Just a min . . . yeah. Got some systems down. Looks real to me."

"Okay." Stark focused back on Chief Wiseman, sitting tensely as her figure rocked to the ship's movement and the hammer blows of torpedoes. "What happened? Just tell me quick why you're being shot at."

"Because of you, I guess! We don't know much about the situation down there. Something about you enlisted taking charge. All the senior enlisted on the ships have been locked down for weeks. No explanation, but we figured the officers on our ships were worried about mutiny."

"Sounds like they knew what they were doing."

"I guess they had to be right once. But nothing probably would have happened if they hadn't tried to do our jobs themselves. Anyway, they couldn't run things right. Our Captain finally killed a half-dozen sailors in one of the machinery rooms by giving bonehead orders and causing an explosion. That's when the junior enlisted let us out of lockdown. The officers panicked at that point and tried to break out the small arms, so we locked them down in self-defense. It'll still look like mutiny to any court-martial, though."

"Makes sense," Vic said over her circuit. "Can we let them under our defensive umbrella?"

"How would I know? Does anybody know anything about Navy stuff?" Stark called over the circuit. "Anything?"

"I know enough to say they can't bring those big ships in close," Sergeant Gordasa in Supply offered.

"Huh? How come?"

"'cause I know logistics. Navy ships burn a lot of fuel when they're trying to hold a position near the lunar surface. We've had to do emergency refuels a few times out of our stocks. If those big ships try to fix themselves over the Colony, they'll run out of fuel in no time."

"Wiseman." Stark waited until the Chief looked directly at him, her expression grim. "My people say you can't bring those big ships inside our defenses and keep them there. It's a fuel issue."

"Fuel? Damn!" Chief Wiseman slammed her fist against her leg, glaring angrily offscreen. "Damn right you shoulda brought that up before now!" she barked at someone. "Snipes," she muttered. "That's Engineers to you guys. Okay, there's nowhere else to run, so that means we only got two choices. We either fight, or we abandon ship. You guys ready to shoot at other Americans?"

Stark paused, thinking for a moment, even though his instincts had instantly provided the answer. "No. Not if we got any choice at all."

"Didn't think so. Then we leave."

"You got enough, uh, life rafts and stuff?"

Wiseman responded with a tense grin to Stark's stumbling terminology. "We got lifeboats. And armed shuttles. Two on each ship. We'll bring 'em all."

Vic broke in again, this time speaking directly to the Chief. "What about your ships?"

"Guess our former shipmates will blow them into little pieces to make sure we don't put 'em on auto and keep 'em fighting. Good riddance. I won't have to worry about patching together worn-out equipment any longer."

"And your officers?"

"Like I said, locked down."

"So they'll get blown away, too?"

Wiseman smiled humorlessly. "Oh, well."

Stark shook his head. "We don't do business that way. We keep our hands clean."

"I let those officers free, and they'll open fire on the lifeboats!"

"Can't you disable everything? Wreck the ship?"

"Scuttle?" Chief Wiseman glanced sideways, then nodded. "Yeah. We'll set it in motion, then release the officers on our way out and leave them a coupla lifeboats so they can get away. That satisfy your tender little heart, mud-crawler?"

"Yeah, squid." Another alarm began sounding behind Wiseman, squawking with belligerent urgency. "Sounds like you better get going."

"For once, I agree with a soldier. I'll call you from a shuttle."

"Roger." Stark broke the connection, focusing back on the symbols looping over the huge arc of lunar surface. It made a little more sense now, the smallest threat symbols obviously representing the torpedoes battering the two ships. "How'd they survive so long? They're outnumbered six-to-one."

"At a guess?" Vic offered. "The other ships are being fought with their senior enlisted still locked down, and the officers can't do the job very well without them."

"That's right," Tanaka nodded. "But you've got another problem now, Commander."

"Great. Now what?"

"Those armed shuttles. They've got some serious weapons, since they're designed for things like commerce raiding and supporting their mother ship in combat. Are we going to let them land on our spaceport?"

"Have we got a choice?"

"What happens if they start shooting? It could still be a trick."

Stark watched the display wordlessly, then pointed as one of the large symbols glowed with sudden critical damage markers, before being replaced by a grim image indicating destruction. "They just blew up a ship. That's a damn expensive trick."

"There goes the other," Vic added. "Did the lifeboats and shuttles get away?"

"Yeah," one of the watch-standers piped up. "See those things?" A cluster of bright symbols swam out from the markers designating the deaths of two ships. "Lifeboats are made to show up real easy on scans."

"They're trying to get away in somethin' that's easy to see?" Stark asked, appalled.

"You're not supposed to shoot at life rafts," the watch-stander added worriedly.

"You're not supposed to shoot at your own ships, either," Vic pointed out. "Can they get to us safe?"

"I think so." Several symbols were suddenly highlighted. "Maybe not. These ships are heading after them."

"Are they trying to catch 'em or kill 'em?" Stark wondered aloud.

"Can't tell. Not until they get within weapons range."

"Torpedoes, you mean? Anybody know what the difference is between a missile and a torpedo?"

"They're pretty much the same thing," another watch-stander advised, "but aircraft or ground installations fire missiles while space warships fire torpedoes."

"What? Why?"

"I dunno, Commander. It's a Navy thing."

Stark glared over at Vic. "With all my other problems, now I gotta try to understand how the Navy thinks."

"Don't ask me. I've never figured them out."

"But we have to let those lifeboats come down. They're counting on us."

"No argument here." Vic favored Stark with a sidelong look. "But, what about the shuttles? Are you going to let them come down, too?"

"Damn, Vic, what the hell else can I do?" He waved wordlessly at the display, where a half-dozen large symbols lunged after the lifeboats and their escorting shuttles. More symbology flashed to life, tracing the paths of defensive weaponry fired by the shuttles to slow their pursuers, seeding a temporary minefield to drift far above as the Moon turned below it. "Mines?" Stark asked, recognizing the threat symbols by their similarity to those used for land mines. "How long do those space mines last?" Blank looks met his question.

"It can't be long," Vic noted. "They'd drift right into commercial space in no time."

"Variable lifespan," Tanaka shouted from a terminal as her fingers danced over the tactical database screen. "Maximum thirty minutes."

"Not long," Stark muttered. "But those other ships are almost into them. Wait. What're they doing?"

Symbology flared, marking short-range fire from the Navy ships as they targeted the minefield. Mines burst into premature death as the Navy ships braked short of the minefield to give them time to blast a channel through the threat area. "I guess those ships could track our own mines, but that still bought the lifeboats some time," Vic approved.

"Not enough time," Tanaka announced grimly. "Here's the

projected intercept plot." Long arcs curved across the display suddenly. "You see? Those big ships have a lot more mass than the shuttles, but they've got much bigger drives to push it all, and the lifeboats don't look like they're designed for speed. It'll be close. Real close."

"The lifeboats will get clear," Vic stated firmly. "I can read a tactical plot, and that one says they've got enough time to get under our defenses."

"Yeah," Stark agreed, "but those shuttles are behind the lifeboats, protecting them, and they're gonna have big ships right on their tails when they get near us. I've got to worry about them."

"You've got the entire Colony to worry about."

"I know that! What if I tell the shuttles not to land and they try anyway? I can't shoot my own people!"

"Sometimes you have to. To save the rest."

Stark froze at the cold words, his eyes involuntarily shifting to stare at the Silver Star ribbon on Vic's left breast. *She knows. She shot a Lieutenant to save the rest of her platoon. No other way. Is this the same thing?* "Vic, we owe these guys."

"I know they've kept the route to the Colony open—"

"That's not what I mean. Remember when the enemy counter invaded? Way back at the beginning of this mess?" New stars blossoming in the endless black above the still-unfamiliar lunar terrain. Fearful soldiers staring upward, knowing the Navy was buying them all the time it could. "They held off the invasion force long enough for us to set up defenses. If those sailors hadn't stood and fought and died, we'd have been creamed down here. We *owe* them, Vic."

Momentary silence, then a single nod. "We do. How do we pay a past debt without endangering present responsibilities?"

Stark glowered at the display, thoughts running through his mind. *Let 'em come down and the hell with risks? Or leave 'em out there to die? No! That's not gonna happen. Not as long as I'm in charge. Why don't I have another option?*

"Commander?" Sergeant Tanaka asked urgently.

"Yeah, Jill."

"I've got the head civ on the line. Campbell. He says it's real urgent and sounds real unhappy."

"Welcome to the party. Put 'im on."

Campbell stared out of the vid display, face almost frantic. "Sergeant Stark, my people at the spaceport say there's a space battle going on near the Colony."

"I know that." Stark spoke evenly, trying to calm the civilian as he would a panicky Private. "There's some kind of trouble on a couple of Navy ships. Their crews are heading for the spaceport."

"Trouble?" Campbell didn't seem the least bit reassured by Stark's demeanor. "You mean mutiny? Dear God. And they're coming here?"

"That's right." Stark glanced at the display to one side of Campbell's image. "Mostly in lifeboats."

"Sergeant, this is a very serious escalation of events. If the authorities think we are actively trying to export some sort of revolution they'll — "

"I can't help what anybody thinks. I'm just dealing with this situation."

"Letting those lifeboats land here could have serious implications for the agreements on exchange of your families for the officers. And a Naval battle involving our own ships right over the Colony will greatly increase the threat to everyone here. You can't permit it."

Stark kept his face rigid, though he felt his jaw tightening in anger. "Don't tell me I can't help people who need help."

"The Colony—"

Can go to hell. "Don't push me, Campbell! I'm dealing with a big problem here, but I'm not leaving anyone outside the perimeter just to make my life easier."

Campbell stopped speaking, his face that of a man who'd run into a brick wall that had come out of nowhere, then tried again, voice pleading. "Sergeant Stark, please—"

On the display, weapons flew, symbols tracking out from the pursuing Navy ships toward the shuttles and their herd of lifeboats. Counterfire flared in return as the shuttles spat out their own barrage of defensive munitions aimed at the other weapons. "I don't have time for this," Stark interrupted bluntly. "I'll notify you when the crisis is over." He broke the connection, glaring toward Reynolds. "Just what I needed right now."

"Don't expect me to comment on the civs. But we've only got about five minutes left before those shuttles get close enough to threaten us."

"Damn." *This wouldn't be a problem if those blasted shuttles weren't armed. Wish I could frag their . . .* "Hey, Tanaka."

"Yessir."

"Those Navy ships opened their systems to you. Could you disable their weapons when they do that?"

"Uh, yes, Commander," she affirmed after a hasty glance toward another watch-stander, who was nodding repeatedly. "We're set up to remotely control any weapon system in any unit from here."

"Get ahold of those shuttles. Tell 'em we're taking control of their weapon systems and shutting them down before they enter our defensive umbrella."

"What if they don't agree?"

"Then they don't get in. No negotiating."

It was quiet for a while then, as they watched the symbols arc gracefully through space. The bright swarm of lifeboats was herded by four bulkier symbols representing the shuttles, their offensive and defensive weapons clashing in an insect ballet of multicolored symbology. Tanaka's voice in the background spoke urgently. "Commander?"

"Yeah."

"Wiseman doesn't want to do it. She says those hostile ships are too close, and they might nail her if her weapons aren't working."

"Hand me the circuit. Chief Wiseman?"

"Give us a break, Stark! We're fighting a damn battle up here, and you want to take away our weapons!"

"I'm giving you a break. I'm letting you inside our defenses. But I'm not letting you inside unless your weapons are disabled from here."

"What if we get blown away because of that? Huh? I'm telling you, we may well get killed if you insist on this."

Stark's eyes shifted away from the symbology, staring into a dark corner of the Command Center, remembering black shadows on the lunar surface and the brilliant white light around them. *Black and white. Like life and death. Separate. Somehow intertwined. There's a gun pit you've got to take out. Who do you send to die so the other members of the squad don't? Simple math. One is less than three or four. But the math never made the decisions easy, and they never got any easier.* "Chief Wiseman. I've got thousands of people depending on me. That's my first priority. Right now, you're second. I can't change that."

A moment's silence, then Wiseman came back, voice deflated. "Yeah. You got your wish, ground ape. Take over our weapons when you think you need to. Just leave them to us as long as possible, okay?"

"We'll do our best."

"If I make it down, you owe me a beer."

"I'll be happy to pay off that bet." Stark felt Vic's hand on his shoulder, a firm squeeze that transmitted reassurance and approval before dropping away. He fought down a shudder, maintaining an impassive stance as the fleeing vessels drew closer to the Colony's surface defenses, and the pursuing ships closed on the mutineers. "Have the anti-orbital defenses been told what's going on?"

"Yes, sir," Tanaka confirmed. "They don't want to shoot, though."

"I don't blame 'em. But I bet some warning shots will do the job. Tell them to let loose before the Navy ships really get within range. If we're lucky, that'll scare 'em off before things get any worse."

"Got it. Systems are estimating we're getting within range of the shuttle weapons about now."

"Take 'em over. Shut 'em down."

"Yes, sir. Shutting down now."

He'd never had to do that before. Take weapons away from someone being shot at. There'd always been a way to work the system, avoid leaving someone with their butts hanging out. *I gotta plan better. I need to look ahead so I know how to handle this stuff without getting my options blocked.* "You still got vid from Wiseman's shuttle?"

"Uh, negative. The Navy ships are close enough to jam comms now."

"Use the command overpower, then."

Tanaka shook her head. "Those ships are big enough to carry real powerful electronic warfare gear. When they're jamming at that close a range, we can't punch through it."

"Do we still have control of the shuttle weapons?" Vic snapped.

"It doesn't matter," Tanaka insisted. "We finished shutting them down before we lost contact. They can't reactivate without overriding the command system watchdogs."

"Which we know how to do on our systems," Vic reminded her. "Ethan, those shuttle weapons might be hot again."

"Yeah." Watching the lifeboats falling toward the spaceport. Watching threat symbology climbing past them as the Colony surface defenses slammed warning shots at the big Navy ships. Watching the shuttles desperately evading fire from the big ships.

"Ethan?"

"Let 'em land." Closer now, everything closer. The big ships snapping at the heels of the shuttles. Another volley from the Colony batteries. A shuttle symbol flickered amid the swarm of threat symbology, hazing out. "Did we lose one?"

"We can't tell," Tanaka reported. "Too much jamming, too much junk from all the weaponry. We might have just lost track of it."

The three remaining shuttles seemed to halt their downward path, as if preparing to go to the defense of their fellow shuttle. *We're gonna lose them all. Damn. I blew it. Sorry, Chief Wiseman.*

"The fourth shuttle's still there!" a watch-stander sang out. The symbol reappeared, flashing damage status. The other shuttles rallied around it, then dropped toward the lunar surface. Above, the big ships fell back, maneuvering drives pushing them onto new courses, curving out, back into empty space where the Colony defenses couldn't reach. It took a moment for it all to sink in, the sudden lack of threat warnings, the strangely peaceful trajectories of the shuttles falling toward the lunar surface.

"It's over?" Vic questioned, incredulous. "The battle's over?"

"Looks like it." Stark exhaled, suddenly aware he hadn't been breathing. He scanned the display again, searching for the scattered exchanges of fire that would have been part of the slow wind down of a land battle. "I guess Navy battles are neater than ground fighting."

"They look neater, anyway."

"Stark?" Wiseman's voice was ragged with audible relief. "You owe me more than a damn beer."

Stark glanced at Tanaka. "We got comms again. Their weapon systems still cold?"

She consulted her display, then looked up in surprise. "Yessir. It doesn't look like they even tried to reactivate them."

Stark took a moment to flash a told-you-so look at Vic, who nodded back in exaggerated agreement. "Welcome to the Moon, Chief Wiseman. Park your shuttles where the spaceport authorities direct." A sudden focus on damage markers near the shuttle symbology. "Do you have any wounded?"

"A few. We're mostly just banged up from being tossed around, but some took heavier hits."

"We'll have medics on the way." Stark looked toward Tanaka,

who nodded and turned to her console to pass on the orders. "Are you in charge, Chief Wiseman? Of all the sailors comin' down?"

"Uh, I guess so."

"I need that for sure. I also need to be sure you can maintain discipline."

"If any sailors get out of line, one of the Chiefs will bounce them off a bulkhead."

"Good. I'll be at the spaceport soon to meet you. Keep your people there until then. We'll work out barracks assignments as quick as we can."

"Okay. See you in a while. Wiseman, out."

Stark hung his head a moment, leaning on his console with both arms rigid, letting the tension drain from him. "Vic, make sure we have enough troops on hand at the spaceport to handle anything."

"You mean combat troops?"

"Yeah. There might still be trouble. Maybe these sailors won't want to accept my authority. Maybe they'll be ready to riot. Whatever it is, I want people there to keep a lid on things."

"You got it." Reynolds laughed suddenly. "Well, Ethan Stark, congratulations. You had an Army, and now you have a Navy."

"A Navy. Great. Want to be an admiral?"

"No, thanks. I don't look good in blue." She saluted briskly. "I'll take charge at the spaceport. The ready reserve company in that sector ought to be enough to handle anything the sailors might try."

"I said *I'd* be there."

Vic pointed an unyielding finger at Stark's chest. "You are too damn important to be on-scene when some crazy sailor might decide to blow his shuttle to hell and take half the spaceport with it."

He stared back stubbornly. "I oughta be there."

"So you don't trust me?"

"Of course I do." *And trusting subordinates to do their jobs is part of leading them right, isn't it? I can't be everywhere. I shouldn't have to be.* "You're right. I'll try to make Campbell feel better while you deal with the sailors."

She grinned. "I think I've got the easier job."

"You do." Stark grimaced. "I handled that wrong."

"What do you mean? He was a civ sticking his nose into mil business. You told him to butt out. What's the problem?"

He brooded over the question a moment, oblivious to the multicolored displays and the chatter of relieved watch-standers around him. "It's not right. Don't ask me why right now. I gotta think. But it wasn't right. You get going while I apologize."

"Apologize?" Vic looked disbelieving, then shrugged. "Ethan Stark apologizing? Hell must have just frozen over again. Have fun."

"Yeah." Stark punched in a code as Reynolds hurried out, waiting just a moment until the reply came. "Mr. Campbell? I'm sorry. It was a very tense situation with a lot going on, but I shouldn't have blown you off."

"Sergeant?" The shift in Stark's tone had obviously confused the Colony Manager.

"I'm sorry I didn't acknowledge your concerns," Stark stated in formal tones. "The space battle is over. We've got a bunch of lifeboats and four shuttles, all full of sailors, coming in to land at the spaceport. I'll have troops on hand to keep things under control."

"What happened to their ships?"

"Blown up. By the sailors and by the other ships out there."

Campbell rubbed his forehead with both hands, looking weary. "The government is going to be very unhappy. Warships are extremely expensive, and the implication that your revolt may be spreading to the fleet—"

"I didn't have anything to do with it. They didn't even know who I was until they talked to me."

"You'll never convince the authorities of that, Sergeant Stark." Campbell shook his head slowly. "You're sure it's over?"

"There's no shooting going on, and the big Navy ships have pulled back to their long-range blockade positions again. As far as I can tell, it's over."

"I'll have Ms. Sarafina contact the government negotiators. She's the one you ought to apologize to, Sergeant Stark. She's going to catch hell, and it's going to take everything she's got to get the next personnel exchange to take place as scheduled. Don't be surprised if the government says no way."

"I'll be surprised," Stark stated calmly. "Mr. Campbell, there's a whole lot I don't know about things back home right now, but one thing I do know; the government needs those Third Division soldiers back and they need them back bad. They're trigger-pullers. Frontline combat troops. And right now there's an awful shortage of those in the U.S. military. I guarantee it."

Campbell's eyes narrowed, then he nodded. "I see. I'll make sure Ms. Sarafina is aware of that. Thank you, Sergeant. We'll have to work out better procedures for future crises."

"No argument here." Stark glanced over at the display again. "The shuttles and lifeboats are coming in. I've got to monitor that."

"I understand. We'll talk later."

Stark broke the connection to Campbell, watching impatiently as the refugee spacecraft dropped toward the Colony spaceport, the lifeboats falling long and fast before their braking drives jerked them into rapid deceleration and abrupt landings. The shuttles followed at a more sedate pace, using their greater fuel reserves to brake in a relatively gentle fashion as they fell toward the Moon. Stark triggered remote vid feed from Vic's battle armor, scanning past her HUD symbology to the visual picture of the spaceport. The blunt shapes of lifeboats lay scattered around, their simple shells unadorned by weapons or sophisticated sensors. *Just big trash cans, I guess, good for getting sailors back on a planet in one piece and not much else.* As Stark watched, the shuttles came down, spaced to avoid the lifeboats, their landing drives kicking up thin clouds of the fine dust, which could never be kept completely off the landing field.

Stark checked the symbology on his headquarters display, matching it to the visual picture from Vic's battle armor. She had dispersed the available company of infantry into three platoon-size blocks around the edge of the area where the lifeboats and shuttles had come to rest. "Vic, you coulda covered more area if you'd broken those guys into squads."

"I know that, but I want to stop trouble before it starts, and a platoon is a lot more visually intimidating than a squad. Right?"

He studied one platoon, three rows of menacing figures, impassive in their battle armor as so many figures on a chessboard, rifles held at port arms. "Right."

"I know how to do this, Ethan." The words were stated in unemotional tones, but Stark still felt the implied rebuke.

"Okay. Sorry. I'll try to keep my mouth shut."

"That'll be the day." Switching circuits, Reynolds called the Navy personnel as Stark listened in. "Chief Wiseman? Go ahead and exit your vehicles."

"Vehicles?" Wiseman asked sarcastically. "Okay, ground ape. I'll tell the guys in the lifeboats to debark first." A few moments later large hatches dropped open on the sides of the lifeboats, the weak lunar gravity offering only a feeble assist to the process. Sailors spilled out, most in their own shipboard battle equipment, but a few sailors were carried out, sealed into clear survival bags. Staring at the formations of ready ground troops, the clusters of sailors hesitated outside their boats. "Get those sailors into formation," Wiseman ordered over the common command circuit. Figures moved, other Chiefs standing separate to bark commands and gesture sailors into ragged ranks.

"Oh, God," some soldier commented. "I hope those sailors ain't gonna try to march. That ought to be good for some laughs."

"Knock it off," Stark ordered. "Those sailors just fought a battle against tough odds and came through. They deserve their pride and our respect. Keep your jokes to yourselves."

"Get the medics forward," Reynolds commanded.

Two APCs rose at her command, gliding forward toward the startled sailors, who watched with obvious nervousness as the armored shells of the ambulances came to rest near them. Medics spilled out, heading for the bagged wounded, throwing the sailors' formations into greater disarray. Chiefs could be seen gesturing angrily toward them, bringing an involuntary smile to Stark's lips. *I know exactly what they're saying to their people, and I'm sorta glad I can't hear it.*

"Chief Wiseman," Vic called again. "You can exit the shuttles at any time."

Stark caught an undertone of tension in her voice, something no one else would have detected. *She's still worried about those shuttle weapons. Or maybe she's just afraid some sailor will push the wrong button and level half the spaceport.* "We still have control of the weapons from here, Vic."

"Thanks, Ethan."

Chief Wiseman came on once more, her voice carrying some of the fatigue she had to be feeling after recent events. "I'll be out in a minute. We gotta secure the shuttles."

"We handle security at the spaceport," Vic insisted. "Or is there some sort of internal threat you're worried about?"

"Internal threat?" Wiseman didn't bother to disguise her annoyance. "What the hell are you talking about?"

"You said you're securing the shuttles. That means you think there's a threat."

"No, it doesn't."

"Then why," Vic questioned, grinding out the words, "are you worried about security?"

"We're not! We're just securing the shuttles!"

"Wait a minute," Stark broke in. "Chief Wiseman, what do you mean when you say you're securing the shuttles? What exactly are you doing?"

"Turning off the lights. Powering down systems. Closing hatches. What the hell else would it mean?"

Vic made a strangling sound, then spoke in carefully controlled tones. "Securing something means establishing a perimeter and posting guards."

"Maybe it does to you," Wiseman shot back, "but that's not what it means to me. I guess it just figures the ground forces have a totally different meaning for what *securing* involves."

Vic shifted to a private circuit with Stark. "How are we supposed to work with these people? They don't speak the same language we do. The words sound the same, but they don't mean the same things."

"Everybody's got their own special lingo," Stark argued. "Even in the mil. Go talk to Gordasa about supply stuff. Or talk to a lawyer."

"No thanks. I have enough problems at the moment dealing with Wiseman. She rubs me the wrong way."

"Gee, Vic, I hadn't noticed." Stark looked over as Tanaka waved urgently. "What's up?"

"They're trying to shut down the shuttle combat systems, Commander. Should we let them?"

"Absolutely. Vic, the sailors are shutting down their weapons. How's everything feel there?"

"You can see it as well as I can."

"I didn't asked how it looked. I asked how it felt to you."

"Sorry, Commander." Stark could feel Vic's grin. "It feels safe. The sailors are acting a little shell-shocked. We'll break them into smaller groups and get them billeted and fed fast. Sergeant Manley's getting sections of a couple of barracks ready."

"Great. Make sure Manley sends word to those barracks that anybody picking fights with the sailors will get to explain it to me personally." Stark took a calming breath. "Any more crises scheduled for today?"

"Just your dinner party."

"Oh, man . . ."

"Right. I wouldn't hold my breath on that dinner going down."

"Sergeant Stark?"

Stark frowned, looked toward the query, then stood quickly. "Lieutenant Mendoza. What brings you here?" He checked the time, stifling a yawn. "At this hour?"

"I will state my reason simply, Sergeant. I fear your social occasion was cancelled to avoid any appearance of impropriety in dining with an officer."

"What?" Stark's fatigue shifted to aggravation. "Who the hell told you that? Sir?"

"No one stated a reason explicitly . . ."

"That's 'cause they didn't know any reason." Stark shoved his palmtop aside, collapsing back into his chair. "Please have a seat, Lieutenant. Hasn't word of our little Navy problem made its way around yet?"

Lieutenant Mendoza took his own seat gingerly, still moving carefully in the low gravity. "Of course."

"Then people should know that's why I couldn't spend tonight socializing. Wish I could've, but the Navy screwed things up for me. We'll reschedule."

"Then you have no concerns about meeting with an officer?"

"Lieutenant, I never cared much what people thought about what I did before, so I sure ain't gonna start caring now. My apologies for having to cancel, and we *will* reschedule."

"Thank you, Sergeant."

"But," Stark continued, forestalling Lieutenant Mendoza as he began to rise from his seat, "as long as you're here, there's something I'd like to ask you." He paused, gathering his thoughts. "Your son's a real sharp soldier. He could be a lot more aggressive, but he thinks good and he's dependable."

Lieutenant Mendoza smiled with restrained but obvious pride. "Thank you again, Sergeant."

"No. Thank you. It's been a pleasure to have your son in my unit. And I figure you've got to be sharp, too, but you've also been trained as an officer, with a lot of experience."

"I have spent many years in the field, yes."

Stark hunched forward, speaking with quiet intensity. "Here's the deal. We got rid of our old officers, so now we need a lot of new officers. Good officers. We want to do things right. Promote for the right reasons, train the right way, all that stuff. We know what we don't want; a lot of politicians in uniform just looking to please their bosses by saying and doing whatever they think their bosses will like the most. And to hell with the job and the people they command if they think their bosses want that. Getting what we want means doing things different. I hope you can help us figure out how to do that."

Lieutenant Mendoza nodded once, slowly, his eyes fixed on Stark. "I will be happy to offer suggestions, Sergeant. Like you, I have had much experience with the negative side of the current system." He smiled, brief and bitter. "I still recall the particular document that triggered my decision to retire. The Pentagon issued a directive whose purpose, in these exact words, was to 'enable process improvement in warfare and warfare support.' "

"Process improvement." Stark repeated the words, his voice flat. "In war? They actually said that?"

"I have never been able to forget the phrase, Sergeant."

"Well, Lieutenant, I've gotta tell you, I've been doing a lot of fighting, and I personally haven't noticed a lot of improvements in the process of war in the last few years."

"I am sure your perception is correct. You see, though, that an organization which can speak in such terms has lost sight of its true function and is instead following bureaucratic imperatives focused on 'process' instead of common sense."

Stark shook his head, reaching for the half-forgotten coffee on his desk, then flinched as he drank the cold liquid. "I'd offer you some of this, Lieutenant, but I don't think you'd ever forgive me. So, you're telling me you've seen plenty of the bad stuff, too. Can you show us how to avoid that kind of junk?"

"I can do my best, Sergeant. However, nothing I can do or say will really matter."

"Individuals can make a difference, Lieutenant. It may hurt a lot, but—"

"That was not my point. I am not in command. You are.

"Only you can create the results you seek. Many people can alter them for the worse, but only you can push them through."

Stark blew out a long breath, then laughed softly. "I should've expected to hear that. Is there anything I'm not responsible for?"

"A commander must bear responsibility for many things, but few are harder than these matters you discussed. You have heard of von Clausewitz?"

Stark thought a moment. "He's that German that Mendo, excuse me, that your son mentions every now and then."

Lieutenant Mendoza smiled. "I have spent many hours discussing von Clausewitz's work with my son. I am pleased he is sharing that learning with his comrades-in-arms."

"He shares, Lieutenant, but he's pretty careful about it. He doesn't like to talk much. A lot of times I have to drag stuff out of him."

The smile shaded into a mild frown. "That is regrettable, but understandable. I was forced to become more outgoing by my responsibilities as an officer. It appears my son's similar introversion has instead been encouraged by his low rank."

Stark nodded. "I did my best, Lieutenant, but it wasn't my job to remake the personalities of my soldiers. Right? But I want Mendo to speak up more. He's got a good head and knows a lot of theory I never picked up."

"Thank you. I would suggest placing my son in positions where his opinions are required. He will rise to the occasion. As for theories, their value can be overblown, but von Clausewitz has a deserved reputation, in my own opinion."

"So what's he say that applies to me right now?"

"Sergeant, one of the things von Clausewitz proposed is that there are two kinds of courage a good commander must have. The first kind of courage is the type everyone thinks of—the courage of fighting well on the battlefield. The second kind of courage, though, applies off the battlefield. It is the courage to make the right decisions in leadership away from combat, in all the matters of training, equipping, and planning. To make the right decisions and to stick with them despite all the political and bureaucratic forces seeking to corrupt them. This second kind of courage is in many ways more difficult than the first, for decisions must be made and held to without the force of enemy action driving and enforcing them."

"Huh." Stark took another drink, grimaced, and shoved the cold coffee away. "I've got to do that? Since I'm in command, I've got to make everything stick?"

"I am afraid so, Sergeant. There are many ways to fail in command positions. I cannot claim to have been a perfect officer in any sense of the word, and I made my share of mistakes, but I like to believe I did so out of inexperience or lack of knowledge, rather than failure to adhere to higher principles when it mattered."

Stark rubbed his eyes with one hand. "The more I learn about this job, the less I like it."

Lieutenant Mendoza leaned forward slightly, eyes intent. "If you succeeded in everything you desired, it is not impossible that you could reach a higher command position, perhaps even command of a national military."

"Jeez." Stark didn't bother to hide his shiver. "Don't scare me like that. You're supposed to be motivating me, Lieutenant."

"The prospect is truly unwelcome?"

"Damn right. I'd go back to my Squad in a heartbeat."

"Then why don't you?"

Stark looked around helplessly. "I can't. I've got a job to do. There's people depending on me. I can't let them down."

Lieutenant Mendoza rose, nodding with evident satisfaction. "Sergeant Stark, I will do my utmost to aid you. Because I know what you do is right. And because I believe you when you say you neither want this 'job' nor would seek another. If you can hold to that despite the temptations of rank, you will succeed in your effort."

"Thanks." Stark stood in turn, shaking Lieutenant Mendoza's hand as it was extended. "There's so much I've got to straighten out. It's good to know I'll have help like yours."

Lieutenant Mendoza smiled again. "Do not discount the help of your friends, Sergeant. They appear to have aided you well in the past."

"Well, yeah. Hey, I just figured something out. You came here to evaluate me, didn't you? Find out how I was really handling this job?"

"You are correct. I never doubted my son's assessment of you as a squad leader, but many lower-echelon commanders have been overwhelmed by the demands of greater responsibility."

"That I can understand," Stark chuckled. "And it might still happen. Good night, Lieutenant. We both need sleep. And don't worry, I'm gonna have that dinner."

"I no longer doubt that, Sergeant. Good night."

The ground trembled, quivering erratically beneath Stark as enemy shells landed all around the Knoll. Someone nearby had been screaming for a while, suffering from pain too intense for their med-kit's drugs, or maybe their med-kit had simply exhausted its supply. The screaming had that thin, wavering quality that meant the soldier making it didn't have much longer to live. Everything Stark could see seemed to be viewed through a gauzy haze formed of smoke, dust, fear, and exhaustion. They'd been under constant fire and bombardment for hours now. His system buzzed with fluctuating static from heavy jamming, providing no link to however many other soldiers still survived. Over Stark's left shoulder, the sun still hung above the tree line, crawling slowly down the sky, oblivious to the soldiers praying for the partial concealment darkness would offer.

A hollow-eyed figure a few meters from Stark turned her head, shocking him since her extended immobility had convinced Stark she was long since dead. She'd lost her head armor somehow, and blood from a jagged wound along her temple had run down the side of her face to dry in a mottled red mask. Her lips, chapped and torn, moved, forming words that couldn't be heard over the thunder of explosions and the stutter of small arms fire. Stark stared, trying to read the words. Where. Where's. Oh. No. Our. Coming? Commander. Where's our commander? The other soldier shuddered suddenly, then buried her face in the faded green grass, oblivious to the blood spotting it.

Stark's eyes shot open, his breath coming in heavy gusts, sweat spotting his skin. *Damn. That was a bad one. Vic might have been wrong when she said I never left Patterson's Knoll, but I sure as hell visit that godforsaken spot every night.* Silence reigned in the room, a strange counterpoint to the long-ago explosions he could still hear in his mind. Instead of harsh sunlight, darkness surrounded him, relieved only by the pale glow of the night-light. The air felt cool, tasteless the way only reprocessed lunar air could be.

He frowned, grasping at a fleeting fragment of his dream. The other soldier. She hadn't been there. Not really. Had she? Asking for their commander. No, she would have said Lieutenant, or Captain. Now, he was the commander. Had she been asking him for help? *Great. My flippin' subconscious is merging the Knoll with my problems right now. Just what I need.* The only thing missing from the dream had been a gaggle of civs looking on and applauding the quality of the entertainment.

But civs hadn't put him on that Knoll. Not directly. And they weren't the ones shooting at him. *Real basic stuff. Who's the enemy? Why's that so hard to figure out sometimes?*

Stark lay on his bunk, staring upward, imagining the layer of rock above, the thin patina of dust above it, then the airless, empty expanse running away forever, dark and silent. *People. We're alone out here, as far as we know, the only minds able to realize we're surrounded by endless nothing. Which should make us important. It should make us want to huddle together like Earth was our campfire, the only real light and warmth in a real big night. But we don't.*

He was missing something. By every measure Stark could think of, his soldiers and the civilians of the Colony should be natural allies, working together. Instead, they were usually at each other's throats. *So, how come I don't think the civs are out to use us? How come I can talk to them? I've had the same experiences everyone else has in uniform, so it can't be just that. Was growing up civ so much different than growing up mil?*

A very long time ago, it seemed, blurred by intervening years and intense experiences since enlisting in the military. Stark tried conjuring up memories. *I used to think about going places. Anywhere I wanted. Yeah. Walk out the door, go across town or across the country. No big deal. Did Vic grow up that way? No. Mil kids grew up on Forts and Bases. Walls around them. Gates. You go a lot of places, but they're all on the Fort, and even there are a lot of other places that are off-limits.*

He had something there. *I think that way now, too, right? The world has fences around it. I live inside the fences. Outside, if I get sent overseas, there's people who're trying to kill me. If I'm at home, people still want me inside the fence.* Even the kids, he now realized. *Never met one, but we told jokes about them. Saw a few, didn't I? Can't remember, now. But I never talked to one. They were different. Huh. So you grow up thinking everybody outside the fence doesn't want you, and when you're all grown up and go outside on your own they want you even less.*

That's it. At least part. Mil grows up inside. Civs don't want them. But what about civs? Hell, my life wasn't perfect. Freedom. Do whatever I want—as long as I have the money to pay for it. Money makes the civ world go around. Got a lot and people listen to you. Don't got a lot, and . . . nothing you do really matters.

He sat up, face unfocused as memories came to life. High school. A teacher, given the thankless task of instructing teenagers on American history and civic responsibilities. Stark remembered, suddenly clear, as if he were sitting in that uncomfortable chair again, bored, almost automatically downloading bits of data into his brain so he could spill it out during the mandatory learning standards exams and then delete it all to make room for the next batch of trivia. Funny how your mind could learn to do that. No wasted effort, and no bother trying to understand the mass of detail they were expected to "learn."

The teacher, his name lost somewhere in the past but his face still clear in Stark's mind, had been sitting at his desk. Like most teachers, his eyes spent most of their time on the display built into the desk, reading out the learning standards for the day. This day he'd suddenly stopped, looking up at his students, who'd taken a few moments to realize that fact, and look up from their own displays where the same data scrolled by.

"What does all this mean?" he'd asked.

A pause while students frantically searched their displays for the answer and came up negative. "Sir?" one of the girls finally ventured. "Where's the answer?"

"Inside you. Or, it should be."

Blank stares, until one of the boys raised his hand. "Do we have to know this if it isn't going to be on the tests?"

The question made the teacher shake his head slowly and sadly. "No. That's rather odd, isn't it? I mean, here I am supposed to be teaching you about civic responsibilities, and yet nothing I teach you really matters unless it matches one of the test questions, does it? I guess that means your civic responsibilities are limited to passing that test, doesn't it?"

Silence, students eyeing one another now. Stark recalled going through the emergency drill in his mind, wondering if the teacher was about to go violent on them.

But the teacher simply stood, looking around pensively. "Now, there's tests and there's tests. Some tests you take on a terminal, punching in whatever answers we've previously spoon-fed you. That way you get a diploma, the school looks good, and we get teaching bonuses. Everybody wins. But there's other tests. Tests of citizenship. Someday, you'll be eligible to vote. How many of you are planning to do that?"

A few hands raised tentatively, bringing a weary smile to the teacher's face. "You see, we teach you all sorts of trivia about something called civic responsibility. But the fact of civic responsibility, the duty of voting, somehow doesn't get taught, does it? Do you know how many of your ancestors died so that you could vote?" He leveled a finger toward one student. "How many of your ancestors died fighting for freedom?"

"Fighting? You, mean, like, in the *military*?" The student seemed scandalized at the concept. "We're not . . . my family wouldn't do that."

"I'm sure they did, once. Listen to me. All of this information you're supposedly learning means nothing if you don't make use of it. You, what's the difference between someone who doesn't vote and someone who can't vote?"

"Uh, I . . . that's not on the test."

"So why should you know the answer?" the teacher asked rhetorically. "Let me ask this. You will be able to vote when you reach your eighteenth birthdays. It's not very hard. You can do it on-line, from the comfort of your home or office. They've made it very easy to vote, but very few people bother. Why?"

"Why bother?" one of the students had shot back, sparking laughter. "I mean, it don't mean nothing."

"Nothing? The ability to choose the most powerful and influential humans on Earth means nothing?"

Another student piped up. "It's all rigged. Big money chooses the candidates. It doesn't matter what we vote. Everybody knows that."

"Why do you have to vote for those candidates? Why not vote for whoever you think is best instead of letting someone else choose?" The teacher's voice had risen, becoming more agitated. "You, Mr. Stark, do you agree with your classmates?"

"Yeah. I guess so. Why bother voting? I'm not rich, so I'm not important. Politicians don't care what I think, so nothing I'd do would matter."

The teacher's head sagged for a moment, and he spoke softer, so the students had to strain to hear. "If you truly believe that, it has a way of coming true. If you do not try, you can never succeed. No one can take your right to vote away, but you can give it away." When he looked up again, his eyes had been glistening with something Stark and his classmates had been shocked to realize were unshed tears. "You are citizens of the United States of America. What you think and what you do are important! Every one of you can make a difference if you just work at it!"

Neither Stark nor any of his classmates had believed a word of it, of course, sitting silent as the teacher left the room. He'd been back the next day, reading from his display once again, his face and voice a little duller than before.

Wonder why I haven't thought of that since it happened, but remembered it now? But that's what it's all about. And the mil kids never saw that, 'cause growing up they could pretend being isolated was actually being in some special club. He slapped the light on, then keyed his comm unit, waiting impatiently while it buzzed several times before being acknowledged. "Campbell?"

"Yes." Unlike Stark, the civilian Colony leader obviously hadn't been having trouble sleeping. "Who is . . . Sergeant Stark?"

"Yeah. I need to see you and talk about some things."

"We can schedule something in the morning—"

"No. Now. How soon can you be over here?"

"It'll take a lot of time to assemble my assistants at this hour."

"No assistants. Just you and me." Stark paused, reconsidering. "On second thought, there oughta be a larger audience. Bring Sarafina. I'll bring Reynolds."

"What is this about?" Campbell demanded. "Getting along. I'll have an escort meet you at the main entrance to the military area and bring you to my room. Just a nice, low-key, informal get-together." *Where I'm gonna rant and rave at everyone present.*

"Very well, Sergeant. I'll be there as soon as I can." Less than an hour later, two rumpled civilians sat irritably confronting two rumpled military personnel. Vic appeared torn between annoyance at Stark and disdain for the civilians, though she did greet Sarafina with a thin smile. Stark paced restlessly for a moment longer after the door sealed, then glared at his companions. "Let me say this right off. Neither the civs, the civilians, or the military are angels. Both are screwed up in their own ways." He pointed a finger at Vic as she started to speak. "Wait'll I've had my say. Now, you, Campbell, and you, Sarafina. Deep down, you don't trust us because you don't trust anybody with any power over you. You're looking for our angle. You figure we've got to be planning to screw you, because that's all that's ever happened to you. You know people with power in the civilian world, politicians and corporate types, can be bribed if all else fails, but you don't have the money to do that with us anymore than you did with them. And anyway, military like us don't play by those rules, which is something you don't understand either. And you're scared. You're scared because you don't think you can really manage to do this right because all your lives everybody and everything has told you that you don't matter, that the game's always rigged so you lose. That's been life for little guys in the U.S. of A. for a long time. You got something to say, Campbell?"

The Colony Manager glowered back for a moment. "This is a very difficult, very dangerous situation. It's prudent to be cautious. I might add that in the last several years we've devoted a tremendous amount of effort to gaining better treatment for the Colony."

"Uh-huh. And how much better treatment have you managed to get for the Colony in all that time? Don't get madder, for Christ's sake. You're smart. You're sharp. You just didn't have leverage. Now, you got leverage. Us. The best damn military force on or off Earth. And we can't be bought, unlike just about everything else these days, because if money really mattered to us we wouldn't be doing this job in the first place. But if you keep us at arm's length because you don't think you can really win, then you *will* lose."

Sarafina's face was a carefully composed mask, but her words carried some acid. "You are saying we suffer from some sort of inferiority complex?"

"Whatever you want to call it. If you don't think you matter, then you don't. I've been there. I remember being a civ, seeing all these great things I could supposedly do, and knowing I was really in a big glass box so I could see all that stuff but never reach it. I knew that, but maybe what I knew was way wrong. Think about it."

Stark turned to Reynolds. "The mil's a little different, but basically we're also sure we're gonna get screwed. We live inside walls and everyone outside the walls is against us. Especially the civs, right? But you know what? We've got something they don't understand. Everybody in the mil figures they make a difference. We figure we're doing something important. It doesn't make any sense because most of the time we're just being used and we know it, but even when we're being used we're still proud of who we are and what we do. We take an oath! Civs don't take oaths, except the politicians and everybody knows how much they believe in their oaths."

Vic eyed him, face as guarded as Sarafina's. "What's your point?"

"The point is that they," Stark pointed at Campbell and his aide, "don't understand that. Don't understand people who believe they make a difference. It scares them to see people devoted to a cause they don't understand, so they're always a little scared of us. Sure, they're scared of our guns, too, but guns are just tools. It's the people who use them that don't make sense to civs. And civs are all stepped on every day by people with big money, or people working for people with big money, so there's nobody else for them to look down on but us. So we get used, for a lot of reasons. But these civs won't use us, Vic, because they need us too bad. We're the only thing that'll ever let them break out of that glass box I talked about. We can blow it into little tiny fragments for them."

"So they need us. Why do we need them?"

"To give us a reason! What's the cause, Vic? Who're we protecting? What's the oath? The mil needs a reason for being, something more than just killing people who want to kill us and trying to stay alive in the process. Otherwise, we're like priests without a religion. We can go through the motions all we want, but none of it means anything and none of it makes sense. The only way we do make sense, the only way we're complete, is if we're part of a whole. Part of them. Maybe it's different in some other countries, but we're American soldiers." He pointed to the civilians. "Unless we're working for them, we got no reason for being."

Reynolds sat silent for a long moment, then quirked a small smile. "I've been trying to figure out our endgame. Our objective. Can't just hold the perimeter for the rest of our lives. We can't set an objective on our own, can we, Ethan? We're not trained for it, we're not supposed to do it, so even when we could do it something holds us back. And I sure miss fighting for 'we the people.' " She looked over Campbell and Sarafina. "It's our job to do what we're told. So, what do you need us to do?"

The civilians stared back, momentarily thrown off-balance.

"You're asking us for instructions?" Campbell finally wondered.

"Not instructions. Orders."

"But . . . *you're* the ones with all the power. Sergeant Stark is absolutely right about that. You should be giving *us* orders, just like he did yesterday when that naval battle was going on over the Colony."

"We're mil," Vic explained patiently. "American military. Push us hard enough, and even we'll break eventually, but we won't be happy or proud about it. Ethan Stark is right, something that happens more often than I can account for. We don't give orders to civilians. We don't run the country. We take orders, even orders that don't make much sense. It's not that I trust you, because I don't. I fully expect you to use us for your own purposes. But that's your right. What is it you want us to do?"

Campbell looked baffled. "We don't know what we want, yet."

"We're used to that." Vic looked up and over at Stark. "You got everything mapped out for the civs?"

"No." Stark finally sat, enjoying the sensation. "That's their call. I'm here to give advice."

Sarafina stared at him. "And what is your advice to us?"

"You got a lot of power, now. Use it. Use it smart. There's nothing wrong with the American system. There's a helluva lot right. We just let the wrong people take over running it." Stark canted his head toward Reynolds. "Like voting. Nobody in the mil votes. We figure we're hopelessly outnumbered."

Vic uttered an exaggerated sigh. "Ethan, we are. There aren't very many mil. There's a whole lot of civs. We can't outvote them."

"You don't have to." Stark switched his gaze to Campbell. "How many people vote in elections? Back home?"

"You mean what percentage of eligible voters actually vote?" Campbell questioned. "The average runs between twenty and thirty percent these days."

"Like when I was a kid," Stark confirmed. "Vic, we're not competing with every civ, just those who vote. And it only takes one vote to win."

"That does improve the odds," she admitted. "But, right now, voting is no help. We're felons. If the civs join us, they're felons."

Campbell glared back defiantly. "We have rights, rights which have been trampled for too long. Sergeant Stark, you're a much shrewder man than I had estimated. I promise you, I'll get my advisers in line soon and arrange a vote within the Colony which will hopefully give me a mandate to officially join with you."

"I'll take your word for it," Stark stated, "but I'll be blunt. I don't trust Trasies."

"I know he's been very difficult during our meetings—"

"That's not what this is about. I don't like him, but I can work with people I don't like. Trasies feels wrong to me."

Campbell glanced at Sarafina, who shook her head tiredly. "Sergeant Stark, we have checked repeatedly for any evidence that Chief of Security Trasies has acted against us or against you. We've found nothing."

Vic chuckled. "Did you really expect to find evidence in your files? If Trasies was working against you, the files wouldn't have been kept in the civ systems where anybody could trip over them. They'd have been protected in—" She stopped speaking abruptly, then swore. "They'd be in the military systems someplace."

"Wouldn't we have found them already?" Stark demanded.

"No, no, no. We've got a gazillion files in long-term memory, Ethan. And security documents would be protected by passwords, fake file names, firewalls, and special security compartments. Just finding the damn things would take a special effort, and if you didn't know they were there you'd never think to try looking for them."

"*If* there's anything there, I'd certainly like to see it," Campbell advised softly. "You realize, of course, any derogatory information would be questioned. Files can be faked."

"We don't have anybody who can—" Vic bridled, then broke off. "Maybe we do," she conceded. "Hell, probably we do. But we won't fake anything."

"You understand people will suggest that anyway."

"Yes, but if we just wanted to fake files to implicate Trasies why wouldn't we have done that right off the bat? Why wait until now?"

"That's true," Sarafina agreed. "And your Sergeant Stark couldn't pull off such a deception, I believe," she added with a smile. "He is not a good liar."

Vic grinned. "Well, we agree on one thing, at least. That and getting our officers sent home."

Private Murphy lay strapped onto a wide bed, well-cushioned despite the low gravity, his right shoulder and side rigidly locked into a gray box with gently blinking lights and bundles of tubes snaking into outlets in the wall. His face, drawn and pale, lit with surprise and happiness as he caught sight of Stark. "Hey, Sarge! I mean, uh, Commander." His words came rapidly, as if from a recording played back too fast, reflecting a metabolism sped up to accelerate healing.

"Knock it off." Stark sat next to Murphy's left side, forcing a smile. "To you I'm still Sarge."

"Thanks, Sarge. How come you're here? You oughta be real busy."

"I'm never too busy for you apes. How you doin', Murph?"

Murphy grinned, swinging his left arm up to indicate the gray box. "Lost my arm, Sarge. Part of the shoulder, too. Guess I earned another Purple Heart, huh?"

"I guess. There's easier ways to do that, Murph." Stark squinted at the readouts, vainly trying to interpret their data. "Everything goin' okay? They growin' it all back? No problems?"

"None they told me about." Murphy's smile grew a little strained. "But, man, I hate the itching."

"Itching?"

"Yeah, Sarge. The stuff they're growing back itches like crazy. Especially the stuff that ain't grown back yet! I told them my thumb was giving me hell and the docs said that thumb still hasn't, uh, regenerated. That's weird, huh?"

"Yeah." Stark took another look at the box. "But you can't scratch. Jeez."

"Nah. They have to dope me up so I can sleep at night. But I'll be okay, Sarge," Murphy vowed. "I'll be back in the Squad before you know it, good as new."

"That's the idea, Murph. But try not to catch heavy rounds bare-handed next time. I'd hate to lose you."

"Really? Hell, Sarge, I ain't goin' nowhere, not with you and Corporal Gomez looking out for me."

Stark forced another smile. "Neither one of us can work miracles. You just think about getting back in one piece right now. Anything I can do for you?"

"No, I . . . uh, Sarge, okay if I ask you somethin'?"

"Sure, Murph. What's up?"

Murphy fidgeted as much as his restraints would allow, his eyes wandering to the far corners of the room. "Well, Sarge, it's, uh, we've had some women come and visit."

"That's nice."

"Civ women, I mean." Private Murphy, veteran of a hundred battles, blushed. "Sarge, is it okay to, you know, get to know civ women?"

Stark hastily moved to rub his mouth with one hand, hiding his smile. "You want to date a civ, Murph?"

"Yeah. She's really nice, Sarge."

"Nice, huh? What kinda nice? Ginger or Mary Ann?"

"Mary Ann, Sarge."

"Really? A nice, wholesome farm girl type? You always seemed interested in the glamorous movie star Gingers before, Murph."

Murphy grinned. "I guess I was, but this one's really special, you know?"

I know. "Yeah."

"And she really seems interested in me."

"Stranger things have happened."

"Right." Murphy nodded briskly, missing the irony. "But is it okay?"

"Sure it's okay."

Murphy grinned again, this time with relief. "That's great." The smile vanished as quickly as it had come. "Man, how do you treat a civ woman?"

"Come on, Murphy, I know you've had a lot of dates."

"But with mil women, Sarge! You know, other soldiers, or daughters of soldiers. Civ women are different, aren't they?"

"Murphy, I've never understood any of 'em, but civ women and mil women are exactly alike in most ways."

"Even Corporal Gomez? I never—"

"Okay, Corporal Gomez is a little different from your average civ woman. Not that that's a bad thing. You just remember, dating a woman's just like anything else. You get back what you give. If you give 'em a grope session on the first date they're gonna think you're not interested in anything else. Take your time to learn 'em, listen, and talk to 'em, and maybe they'll do the same back."

"Uh-huh." Murphy frowned thoughtfully. "Kinda like learning to shoot, huh, Sarge? You gotta really get the feel for your weapon, how it's gonna react and everything, or you won't get any hits."

Now, that's a helluva analogy. Murphy, dating a civ may be real *good for you.* "That's right. And remember, you get careless with a weapon or mistreat it, and you're liable to shoot yourself in the foot."

"Right, Sarge. You respect your weapon. I'll do the same with this civ. I promise."

"Never doubted it, Murph." Stark slapped Murphy's visible shoulder lightly. "Take care of yourself, you ape. You're a good soldier."

Murphy blushed again, avoiding Stark's eyes. "Thanks, Sarge. I know I ain't the best."

"You're damn good when you wanna be. I'll be back to check on you." Stark smiled encouragingly as he left. *Good kid. Is this what my dad felt like when he talked to me, tried to give advice? Not that I listened. I guess soldiers are old enough to learn listening never hurts and might even help a little.*

Stark walked slowly through the corridor of the civilian hospital, its white walls comfortingly similar to those of the military medical complex, until his reverie was interrupted by the buzz of his comm unit. "Stark here."

"Where are you?" Vic Reynolds demanded.

"Civ hospital complex. Visiting Murphy."

"Oh. How's he doing?"

"His missing arm itches."

"Ouch. Listen, you have to be at the civ government complex in half an hour. Don't forget."

Stark frowned, checking his scheduler. "I thought the meeting wasn't for another hour."

"It isn't. I just want to make sure you look decent. I don't want any sailors saying the ground force Commander is a slob."

"I look decent," Stark complained indignantly.

"Sure. You'd say that if you'd spent a week straight in battle armor."

"Is everybody else ready?" Stark questioned. "My whole staff's going to be there, right? If we're going to be dealing with sailors, I want anyone who might know anything about them on hand."

"I can't guarantee knowledge, but the warm bodies will be there.

You want anybody besides your staff present?"

"No. Wait." *Lieutenant Mendoza? Can't do that, have an officer in the room, even though I think he'd offer some good advice. But the Lieutenant said his son would speak up if he had the responsibility. Okay, then.* "Yes. Mendo."

"Private Mendoza? From your old Squad?"

"Yeah. He knows lots of stuff."

"So I hear, but he never volunteers any of it."

"He'll tell me if something important comes up. Make sure he's there."

"You're the boss," Vic acknowledged. "Remember, half an hour."

"Alright, alright. Half an hour."

Chief Petty Officer Wiseman and her newly selected second in command, Chief Gunners Mate Melendez, stared around with prickly defiance at the group Stark had assembled. Stark's staff eyed them back, while the two civilian representatives. City Manager Campbell and his chief aide Cheryl Sarafina, watched both sailors and soldiers with careful neutrality.

Stark reached to shake Wiseman's hand after briefly introducing everyone present. "I guess I ought to formally welcome you to the Moon."

"Thanks. Love what you've done with the place."

"Any questions?"

"Yeah. Where's my beer?" Chief Wiseman grinned at her own joke. "I don't know what your plans are, but we've got four armed shuttles at our disposal. They've all took some damage, one took a lot, but it's nothing we can't fix. What do you need from us?"

Everyone was looking at Stark. He glanced down at the table for a moment before focusing on Chief Wiseman again. "Right now, it's a purely defensive mission. Defending the Colony."

"You gotta run supplies in, don't you?"

"Sure. We're working on that."

"Then you'll need escorts, or at least some way of keeping the big ships off your supply shuttles. We can't fight a pitched battle against ships of the line, but we can complicate a blockade somethin' fierce."

Vic hunched forward, speaking to both Navy representatives. "What about defending the Colony against longer-range Naval threats? Do you have any capability there?"

Wiseman shrugged, looking toward Gunner Melendez. "What kinda threats you talkin' about?"

"Bombardment."

Melendez shook his head scornfully. "Torpedoes can't make it through your defenses. This place is a flippin' fortress."

"I wasn't talking about torpedoes," Vic continued patiently. "I meant big stuff."

"Big stuff?" Wiseman questioned. "They ain't gonna do that. We've got firm orders not to employ Mike Delta Delta's under any circumstances."

The military nodded in understanding while the civilians looked bewildered. "Mike Delta Delta's?" Sarafina questioned.

"MDDs. Mass Destruction Devices," several of the military explained simultaneously.

"How do you know about these orders?" Vic demanded. "That doesn't sound like something that'd be shared with enlisted."

Chief Wiseman grinned. "We weren't supposed to know about it, but the Chiefs' Mess had copies of the messages before the

Officers' Wardroom did. You know how it works."

"Yes, I guess we do."

"Wait a minute!" Campbell objected. "What difference would those orders make? None of the Navy ships carry those, uh, MDDs. The Space-Based Armament Treaty prohibits it."

Gunner Melendez uttered a brief laugh. "No, it don't."

"I know that treaty," Campbell insisted, looking to Sarafina for support. "Space-BAT specifically outlaws weapons of mass destruction on orbital or transorbital space vessels. I cannot believe we would blatantly violate that treaty."

"Nah, we ain't violating it," Melendez assured him. "Listen to the gunner. Yeah, that treaty says no orbital or transorbital Earth bombardment weapons allowed, but somewhere in the fine print it defines 'weapons' as stuff with warheads. Nuclear, conventional, whatever. Don't say a damn thing about a hunk of solid metal with a guidance device stuck on the end. Of course, that hunk of metal dropped from orbit can put a good-size hole in the middle of a city, but as far as the treaty's concerned, it ain't a weapon."

"Convenient," Vic noted dryly. "I assume the authorities back home are scared we'll do just that, even though we don't have the warships to drop stuff on Earth even if we wanted to."

"We don't need warships," the gunner noted with a dismissive wave. "Hang a rock on the outside of a shuttle. It'd maneuver like a pig, but you could do it. Or just modify some of your maglev lines here on the surface to lob objects into space, aimed at the Big Blue. Your terminal guidance wouldn't be great, but cities are big targets."

"We're not dropping rocks on cities," Stark objected heatedly. "Not American cities. Not anybody else's."

"I'm not sayin' we should. I'm just pointin' out why the brass don't want to start a pissin' contest with big bombs. Heck, the Moon's already full of craters. Back home, they wouldn't want the same landscapin' job."

Sarafina looked puzzled. "How odd that we would negotiate a treaty with such a large loophole."

"Hey, we wanted to claim the moral high ground and still be able to bomb people, so we came up with a treaty which let us do both. What's odd about that?"

"I still don't understand." Campbell shook his head, eyeing the military representatives. "The authorities on Earth surely want to defeat the military forces up here. Why wouldn't they use any weapon available to them to do that? A massive attack would certainly overwhelm our defenses and prevent us from retaliating."

Private Mendoza, sitting quietly to one side, now looked up, suddenly animated. "A weapon employed must match the objective." His expression shifted to alarm as he realized he had the attention of everyone else in the room. "That is," he continued hesitantly, "there is no sense in the government using weapons which would not be consistent with their goals."

"Which means exactly what?" Stark wondered.

"The principle was set forth by von Clausewitz," Mendo explained.

"That German guy your dad likes?" *I gotta read that guy's book.*

"Yes. My father often discussed his theories with me. Clausewitz stated that war is a continuation of political policy by other means. So, armed conflict only makes sense if it furthers a political goal."

"Like us trying to take over the whole Moon for the last few years?" Manley suggested.

"Exactly," Mendo agreed, becoming more confident as he spoke. "The goal need not be achievable, but it must be understood. Now, the objective of the authorities in Washington, D.C. is to retake this Colony. If it is simply destroyed, America loses its foothold on the Moon and all efforts to establish a dominant presence here will have been negated. If the defenders, ourselves, are destroyed from long range, the enemy forces besieging us will immediately seize the Colony, thereby achieving the same result."

"And," Campbell added as he nodded, "in either case, the corporations which have invested up here would lose a huge amount of infrastructure and other assets."

"Yes, sir. Which means the only strategy the authorities can follow is to try to retake the Colony with ground forces, or force our surrender under terms which ensure they can immediately reoccupy the Colony."

Vic shook her head, face skeptical. "What if our brilliant former leaders don't do the smart thing? They're not exactly famous for making great decisions."

"It is a question of self-interest," Mendo insisted. "They cannot win by destroying us. The politicians seek to remain in power. Losing the Colony, to us, to the enemy, or to bombardment, would be such a setback that they would certainly lose the next election. They must retake the Colony to get what they want. Nor will the corporations acquiesce to any decision to destroy what they have invested up here."

Campbell nodded again, face thoughtful. "That makes a great deal of sense. Your man is right, Sergeant Stark. I don't know military issues, but I do know politics. The upcoming elections will drive this. The two main political parties need to win those elections, and they need corporate contributions to do so. The only way to achieve both goals is to retake this Colony intact. That does explain why they would rule out the use of certain weapons."

"Politicians lose elections," Manley objected. "What's the big deal if a few go bye-bye this time? They'll just be replaced by a couple more of the same."

"No. If the two main parties are totally discredited by losing this Colony, and they will be I assure you, the winners will be the current secondary parties, which have long claimed the mantle of political reform. The last thing the politicians currently in power want is for someone with a crusading agenda to replace them and overturn all the rocks that their various illegal and immoral arrangements have been hidden under for decades."

Stark suddenly grinned. "Then they're gonna talk to us, right? Not just you civilians, but the mil as well. You and Mendo are telling us the politicians and the corporations back home want this Colony back intact, and they want it bad. So it don't matter if the Pentagon hates our guts, which they must have even before this Navy stuff."

Campbell nodded grimly, looking around the table. "That's true. They'll talk to us. But what exactly are we going to say to them?" He centered his gaze on Stark. "Sergeant Stark, issues of civilian primacy aside, you hold the power up here. Nothing can or will happen unless you agree. What should our goal be? Compromise? Revolution? I don't think anyone here wants to break our ties to the United States, do they? So what is it we're after?"

Stark stared back mutely. *What the hell do I say? What do I really want besides a little respect and bosses who think of me as human instead of a piece of hardware? What kind of answer protects the people I'm trying to protect and doesn't betray everything I want to believe in? They're all looking at me. They're all depending on me. What the hell is the right answer?*

PART THREE

NO GLORY LEFT

They sat off the Colony spaceport like harpies out of some ancient myth, their very presence accusing Stark of oath breaking and dishonor. Official shuttles under official orders. Stark paused in front of a monitor, staring at its screen. *Not so long ago, a visit from VIPs like that would've had me and all my troops scrambling to paint, polish, and clean anything the bigwigs might come within several kilometers of. Now, they're coming to meet me. I'd rather be painting walls.*

He took another long look at the monitor, wishing it could somehow see inside the shells of the spacecraft. *Who exactly is in the delegation? What're they gonna say? Will they offer us a deal or just threaten us? Will our own civs from the Colony back us up, or jump ship if they get a good offer from the delegation? Ah, hell, I'll find out all that soon enough.* Stark walked away, heading for the corporate conference room Campbell had recommended using. *Neutral ground,* the Colony Manager had said, *or the closest we're going to find up here, and the best meeting facility in the Colony.* Stark had refrained from describing the Generals' conference room in headquarters, suspecting in any event that a top-of-the-line corporate hall would be very plush indeed.

Stacey Yurivan stood alone in the hallway outside the meeting room, a half-mocking grin on her face. "How's life, Commander, sir?"

"Just peachy. Anybody else here yet?"

"As far as I can tell, the other groups are all inside already. Just waiting for us mil to show up."

Stark felt his face getting warm with anger. "It's not scheduled to start for another half-hour. We're not late."

She grinned wider. "Guess everybody else is eager for this meeting. And we're not."

"I'd rather be leading a suicide raid," Stark admitted. "I take it everything's goin' great in your job?"

The grin slid away, replaced by an expression of mild annoyance. "Oh, yeah. Everything's perfect."

"Which bothers you for some reason."

Yurivan shrugged. "Look, suppose you were my boss—"

"I am your boss."

"Yeah. Right. I forget. Anyway, suppose maybe two months had gone by and you hadn't caught me doing anything against regulations. How would you feel?"

"Grateful?"

Stacey grinned again. "Wrong. You'd be worried, 'cause I'm always doing something, right? And the fact you haven't caught me means you haven't figured out what the latest 'something' is."

Stark frowned in response, his eyes straying to the conference room door. "Who you worried about?"

"The big guys. You know, the national agencies."

"I thought we hadn't detected any activity by them against us."

Yurivan sighed heavily. "Okay, do I have to explain this again?"

"No, no. I get it." Stark rubbed his chin, thinking of the sort of operations he'd known the national agencies to pull off in the past. "You figure they're up to somethin'."

"I know they're up to something! Those people do not sit on their butts when a big problem is going down, and we're a pretty big problem. But I haven't detected any serious attempts to mess up our systems or to send in saboteurs or spies. So what have I missed?"

"Maybe they've got orders to lay off. Maybe the politicians and the Pentagon are worried about making us mad, especially with these talks going down now."

"Oh, sure. All that theory requires is that the politicians and Pentagon are actually thinking about all this instead of going off half-cocked or treating it like another game of king of the mountain! Heck, that happens all the time!"

Vic Reynolds leaned into the conversation, glancing from side to side. "Hi, Ethan. Hey, Stace. How's the snark hunt going?"

"As usual." Yurivan dipped a hand into one of her pockets, surfacing with a data coin. "But my people did find this stuff this morning."

"Oh?" Reynolds took the proffered coin, turning it in her hand. "What stuff might this be?"

"The stuff you asked me to look for."

"That certainly narrows it down." Vic popped the coin into her palmtop, read briefly, then grinned. "Ah. I believe Mr. Trasies will no longer be a problem."

Stark smiled in turn. "You found the dirt?"

Stacey looked smug. "Those programs that keep data storage all neat and well-organized made it a lot easier. The dirt was hidden, but thanks to the clean-up programs that meant we had an apparently big empty space sitting in the middle of lots of nice, compacted, defragmented data. Stood out like a sore thumb once we went looking, then it was just a matter of cracking the access codes. Your little slimeball Trasies used to report regularly on people and events up here until we locked up his mil officer contacts. Looks like he was on the payroll of a couple national agencies and a few corporations as well."

"Think Campbell'll be sufficiently ticked off over that?"

"He will be when he reads Trasies's assessments of him. Not that Trasies spoke highly of anyone but his own bosses from what I could scan this morning. But he's been downright nasty about the Colony Manager."

"Good work, Stacey."

"Don't bend yourself out of shape thanking me," Yurivan noted sarcastically. "It might go to my head." She stepped closer, eyes intent. "Look, Stark, I might be able to do my job a little better in there," her head tilted to indicate the conference room, "if I knew the endgame."

"Endgame?"

"What's your plan? What exactly are you aiming for up here?"

Stark smiled crookedly. "Soon's I figure it out, I'll let you know."

"Sure." Yurivan made a face, shaking her head. "You trying to make me believe you started a major military revolt without any idea what you'd do next? Stark, nobody's that stupid."

Stark glanced over at Reynolds, who was staring at the ceiling overhead while her cheeks twitched in a mostly successful effort not to break into laughter. "I can't tell you anything else, Stace."

"Something really big, huh? You can trust me with it."

"I swear, right now there's nothing else—"

"Okay, okay. Don't tell me. But I'll find out, Stark. Just you try to keep it a secret." With a wide grin, Yurivan turned to greet the other members of Stark's staff as they strode up.

Reynolds sidled close enough to Stark to whisper. "Hey, if Stacey finds out what your plan is, do you think she'll tell you and me?"

"I sure hope so." Stark took a step toward the other soldiers, speaking loud enough for all to hear. "Okay, boys and girls. This is likely to be real tough, and it's sure to be unpleasant as hell. Keep your heads. Let Vic and I do the talking. We want to look sharp, disciplined, and tough. Any questions?" His staff exchanged glances but remained silent. "Okay. I got one, though. Where's the Navy?"

"Here." Chief Wiseman hurried up, hastily smoothing the front of her uniform into inspection quality. "I was giving my armed shuttle crews instructions on what to do if those rust buckets the official delegation came in turn out to be Trojan Horses."

"Good idea, as long as they don't start shooting if someone looks cross-eyed at 'em."

"They won't shoot unless someone shoots them first. I made sure no nervous types are at the combat systems."

"Thanks. Alright, let's go, people." Stark turned on one heel to face the door, took a deep breath, then pushed through to confront the official delegation and whatever demands they planned on making.

It was a large room, not quite a duplicate of the luxurious conference room in the headquarters complex, but in the same spirit. Half of the pictures lining the wall seemed to be of real facilities on the lunar surface or in Earth orbit, while the others appeared to be very realistic conceptualizations of planned future projects. One, Stark noted, displayed a city somewhat like the Colony, but set in reddish terrain against a deep blue sky. Vic followed his gaze. "Mars," she murmured.

"They plan big, don't they?" Stark replied softly.

"Guess so. Don't forget it."

Standing stiffly about the room were several distinct groups. One, consisting of Campbell, Sarafina, and a number of aides, nodded toward Stark's group. Several meters from Campbell, another group of civs in finer clothing, their faces generally young yet hard, pretended to be studying the outside views on the nearest monitors. A few feet from them stood the military representatives from Earth, uniforms bright and sharp, multicolored rafts of ribbons on their chests glistening under the overhead lighting. Farther on waited the next group, some older men and women, all their faces fixed in expressions of automatic yet meaningless bonhomie. Finally, hovering attentively near the older group, a gaggle of younger civs watching their elders like hawks.

Stark stopped, eyeing the groups sourly.

"Who are all these people?" Vic whispered.

"You can't tell?" He glanced from her to the clusters of people. *She should know, easy, because . . . hell. I know because I grew up civ, seeing these people all the time. To Vic, Yurivan, and the other mil, they probably look like identical civ unknowns.* "You know the civs from the

Colony. Try to remember they're on our side. That next group, the ones that look like they eat their young for breakfast? That's the corporate reps and their lawyers. Then comes the uniformed mil from the Pentagon."

"Yeah. Them I knew, too. All officers. Funny, they don't have a bunch of enlisted personnel in tow to do all the lifting and toting."

"Guess they're worried about exposing any more enlisted to us. Now I know what a virus feels like." Stark inclined his head slightly toward the farthest groups. "They're the politicians and their assistants. Staff members, sort of, who try to keep their politicians from saying and doing dumb things."

"Sounds like a thankless job."

"Also a hopeless one. Campbell will probably handle the civs, and leave the mil to us."

Chief Wiseman smiled slowly. "I know that Admiral with them. Had the misfortune to serve under her for a few months when she was doing her command tour on my ship."

"You think she remembers you?"

"Nah. I wasn't important enough. Bet she pays attention to me now, huh?"

"Good bet," Vic agreed, "but the Admiral's only a three-star. Anybody recognize the four-star General leading that group?"

Sergeant Manley nodded. "Wilkinson. Came through Lunar Command on his war-hero tour four or five years ago."

There'd been so many Commanding Generals, coming and going like clockwork at six-month intervals, that it had been easy to forget most of them. "You remember what he's like?"

She made a dismissive gesture. "Lots of bluster. Minor-league screamer." The rest of the soldiers nodded in understanding. Screamers were officers who "led" by erupting into tirades. All of the enlisted had encountered many of them. "Scared of screwing up," Manley added judiciously. "Spent most of his six months up here trying not to actually do anything so he wouldn't risk making a mistake."

"I remember that," Yurivan chimed in. "We had a lot of pressure from the enemy in the sector my unit occupied then, and we kept getting beat on hard because Weak Willie wouldn't let us react. How'd he get this job?"

"I'll bet it wasn't based on merit," Stark noted dryly, "but then, promotions in the mil haven't been based on merit for a long time, have they? I'm sure Willie sucked up the right way to the right bosses at the right time."

"But that's not so good for us," Vic objected. "If Willie's afraid of doing anything, we might not get any results out of this conference."

"Maybe. With the corporates and the political types here, I don't think the mil's gonna be running things. But I guess we'll find out real soon. Let's go give Campbell that little present Stacey dug up. He might want to change the membership of his team after he sees it." Stark led the way across the room, pretending to ignore the subtle and overt looks from the other groups as they followed the progress of the soldiers. *Take a real good look, people. We can move here. We know this place. It's been home awhile. Don't even think about sending Earthworms to fight us.*

"Sergeant Stark." Campbell smiled briefly, only a tightness around his eyes revealing the tension he must feel. "This should be interesting."

"Uh-huh." Stark held out the data coin. "So is this. You oughta read it."

Campbell frowned down at the object. "The first chance I get after this meeting—"

"No. I strongly suggest you need to see it right away. Before the meeting."

Security Chief Trasies stepped closer, face belligerent. "We won't be bullied by you, Stark. Don't try to give orders to us."

Stark returned Trasies's gaze calmly. "Wouldn't dream of it. Care to read that, Mr. Campbell?"

"I fail to see what could be so important we need to address it *now*."

"Then you oughta find out."

Campbell stared back, then took the coin, his other hand forestalling Trasies's attempt to grab it. He popped it into his palmtop impatiently, quickly calling up text. As Campbell read, his face flushed, then grew darker and harder, until he finally looked up and around at his assistants. "I see."

Trasies held out a hand, eyes narrowing with suspicion. "If I could review—"

"That's perfectly all right." Campbell smiled tightly at his security chief. "You are, I assure you, totally aware of the contents of the files I have just reviewed, since you drafted all of them."

Trasies stiffened. "Lies. Forgeries. Faking files is simple for—"

"Ah, then you do know the contents of these files." Campbell's words froze Trasies in midsentence. "As for validity, the files I've already reviewed contained information on past meetings with my assistants which I know these soldiers could have had no knowledge of." His gaze switched to Yvonne Pevoni. "I'd also doubted your loyalty, Ms. Pevoni, but according to Security Chief Trasies, you are too indecisive and intellectually challenged to have been a partner to him."

Pevoni's jaw dropped, then snapped shut. "You said that about me?" she hissed at Trasies. "I trusted you!"

"So did I," Campbell stated icily. "Sergeant Stark, I do not believe it would be wise to place Mr. Trasies in the custody of Colony police. I would appreciate it if you could place him under military detention."

"We can do that. Vic, get some MPs up here."

She smiled mock-pleasantly at Trasies. "They should already be outside. I anticipated the need for MPs."

"Thanks. You want to go quiet, Trasies?" The former Colony Security Chief glanced toward the other groups in the room as if gauging his chances of reaching them. "Just in case you're wondering," Stark continued, "I know all those sort of people, and none of them would help you unless they figured it'd help them. Right? And getting into a fight with us over you right now wouldn't help them at all." Trasies bit off whatever reply he had been considering, yielding to Stacey Yurivan's grip on his elbow to steer him to the door. Once again, Stark was aware of eyes following the small procession, until the door opened on a brace of military police.

Yurivan handed the former Colony Security Chief over to them with brief, whispered instructions, turned, smiled merrily at the other groups, then rejoined the rest of Stark's group.

"I'll bet that's given them something to talk about," she suggested gleefully.

Campbell gestured to his assistants, then walked to the grand table, which dominated the center of the room, its highly polished lunar rock surface shining like a solid sheet of black gemstone. "If everyone else is ready, we should probably begin. I am Colony Manager Campbell. As you can no doubt tell," he added with a small flash of anger, "I am having no trouble with my mental balance. These," he added as he indicated Stark's group, "are the representatives of the Colony's military defenders." Cold expressions shifted from Campbell to Stark, weighing and evaluating. "Please, everyone be seated."

General Wilkinson glared as Stark and Vic moved to take seats at the table. "I will not sit with traitors. Nor will any of my officers. Either those criminals leave or we do."

Stark kept his face emotionless as he and his staff watched Campbell for his reaction. The Colony Manager paused halfway into his own chair, reversing motion to rise slowly until he was standing straight. "Then we have nothing to discuss," Campbell stated firmly. "These soldiers have earned a place at this table by their defense of this Colony. If they are not permitted to stay, I and my assistants will leave as well. I'm sorry you wasted your time on this journey," he added to the other civilians with apparent regret.

"You are not in a position to dictate to us," one of the corporate representatives announced bitingly.

"That's to be seen. If you wish to talk, everyone here must remain."

Cold silence hung for several seconds, then some of the civilians in the official party turned to glower at General Wilkinson. "Sit down," one ordered.

Wilkinson flushed slightly, his mouth working with silent rage. "I do not wish—"

"Sit down!"

The General choked off whatever further words he had been planning on speaking, shooting a brief death-ray look at Stark and Reynolds as he waved his officers to their seats, then seated himself with overstated dignity.

Stark kept from smiling with an effort, noticing the ripple of unease among the more junior officers in Wilkinson's group. *He's gonna give his staff holy hell after this is over, not because they screwed up but because he lost face, and they know it.*

Campbell spread his hands, looking around the table. "Thank you. I know there's a lot of issues to discuss. Who wants to begin?"

A thirty-something woman who radiated an air of ruthless competence tapped her palm unit irritably, then looked straight at Campbell. "We're prepared to grant partial forgiveness of accumulated debts for corporate personnel on the Moon, assuming full control in accordance with ownership rights of every facility is returned immediately."

Campbell waited in obvious expectancy, then frowned when nothing more was forthcoming. "That's your entire offer? Nothing pertaining to the Colony's status? Nothing regarding our rights? Nothing in the way of redress for past suffering caused by corporate and government policies?" He gazed down the table to the political representatives. "Have you nothing to add?"

A middle-aged politician with smoothly handsome features shook his head, smiling reassuringly. "Your grievances with your parent corporations are internal matters. It would not be appropriate for the government to intervene in such matters, would it? We are merely here to assist in bringing this unpleasant state of affairs to an early and appropriate conclusion. I urge you to accept the generous offer which has been made by the corporations with financial interests up here."

Campbell sat silent for a long moment, drawing an impatient scowl to the corporate speaker's face, then spoke briefly. "The offer is not acceptable."

The corporate speaker flushed slightly. "This is not a negotiation. Our parent corporations are willing for the sake of good relations and expedient results to grant limited relief to personal indebtedness. Period."

Campbell shook his head, looking vaguely regretful, but keeping his words even. "That's not acceptable," he repeated.

"Failure to accept this offer *will* result in serious consequences. Our parent corporations *will* pursue all available options to compel compliance with our rights of ownership. As you are no doubt aware, your employment contracts bind you to arbitration of our choosing. In your absence, that arbitration has already occurred, and you have been found in violation of all aspects of your contracts. I don't need to tell you just how serious the legal and financial penalties for those violations can be, if we choose to demand them."

Instead of responding directly, Campbell looked at Stark. "Commander, do these people have the ability to carry out their threats?"

Stark had been trying not to look directly at Wilkinson and the other officers, fighting the unease his role generated inside. Now he made a very brief movement of his mouth that might have qualified as a fleeting smile. "No."

"Can they regain control of this Colony without our full assent?"

"No."

"Are the military forces protecting the Colony prepared to defend its citizens against any coercive actions by these corporations?"

"Yes."

Another one of the politicians leaned forward, raising an imperative hand. "Sir, you are playing with fire here. I trust you have fully examined the consequences of your actions! To place your faith and the security of this Colony in the hands of renegades is frankly beyond my understanding. You have received a fair and, if I may say so, generous offer from these corporations which have done so much for you and our great country. You would be well advised to accept that offer before these . . . these dishonorable mutineers decide to turn on you!"

Campbell's smile resembled Stark's earlier gesture. "I assume you are claiming we'd be better off placing our faith in you, Senator? Just how much have you received in 'campaign contributions' from the corporations you are now telling us to trust?"

"That is entirely beside the point! Every penny I receive is in full accordance with the laws governing campaign finance!"

"Which you write." Campbell shook his head. "So far, I haven't heard any constructive offers, or any reason to respond to blatant and unenforceable threats."

Corporate and political representatives turned as one to glare at their military counterparts. "Perhaps," the corporate speaker suggested icily, "you should inform these people of the consequences of failure to comply with our offer."

General Wilkinson nodded briskly, projecting confidence and bravado once again. "We will break the will of the so-called defenders and retake this Colony. We will reestablish the rule of law by whatever measures are necessary. Civilians who defied lawful authority will be delivered into the hands of law officers for punishment under the legal system. All, I repeat, all rebellious soldiers will be dealt with to the full extent of the Uniform Code of Military Justice." He glared fiercely at Stark. "The appropriate penalty being death."

Stark stared back, his eyes locked on Wilkinson's, his face rigid as granite. "Who's going to carry out that mission, General? Who's going to retake this Colony? Where are your troops? Third Division got cut to ribbons, and some of the survivors joined us. You got one helluva lot of officers, but they ain't worth a damn without enlisted troops to pull triggers, are they? Or maybe you're planning on sending Second Division up here? But then the U.S. back on the World wouldn't have any defenders, would it?"

Wilkinson and his fellow officers glowered back. "We will not discuss classified military matters in this environment," the General stated stiffly.

Stark shook his head, his gaze scanning down the table. "You mean you haven't told your civilian bosses how many casualties Third Division took, General? I know you, and I know your type, and you hate telling your bosses something they really don't want to hear. But this time you'll have to."

The corporate and political delegations were now staring at the military officers as well, faces hardening perceptibly. "General

Wilkinson?" the corporate speaker inquired acidly.

As Wilkinson paled and groped for words, Vic pulled a data coin from her palm unit, sliding it across the table toward him with the ease of long practice under lunar gravity, the coin coming to a slow halt just short of the General's hand. "Here, General. That's the best we've been able to come up with in the way of a casualty count from General Meecham's big offensive. You might want to share it with the others, but I have to warn you there's a lot of bodies left to tally, so it's far from complete, I'm afraid."

Wilkinson stared at the coin as if it were a snake as Reynolds continued speaking. "Perhaps you'd like to take your political and corporate bosses on a tour of the front lines. We could show you the places where Third Division's brigades got cut to ribbons in an offensive I assume you helped approve. No, wait." She leaned back, reaching to key the nearest monitor. "Right here. See?"

The screen displayed a long, open area, sloping downward gently before rising to meet a crater rim. Bright white light glared off elevations in vivid contrast to the knife-edged black shadows where sunlight couldn't reach. Motionless objects, resembling clumps of oddly similar-size rocks, littered the plain in front of the crater rim. Reynolds tapped a key, bringing the objects into high relief. "Just a low spot near the enemy lines. Second Brigade of Third Division went forward here. We call it Death Valley, now. All those objects I've highlighted are bodies of American soldiers we haven't been able to recover yet."

Stark watched narrowly as the others in the room reacted to the sight. The corporate honchos just seemed to get colder and madder. Expressions of concern, outrage, dismay, and a dozen other emotions chased across the politicians' faces as they tried to gauge which reaction would draw the best response. The politicians' handlers simply stared, faces intent, as if they were calculating a difficult problem. Campbell and the other lunar civilians bent their heads, faces grim.

Wilkinson rallied, even as he and the other military officers avoided looking at the scene on the monitor. "We can, and we will, carry out our ordered mission."

"Really, General?" Campbell questioned. "Are you guaranteeing your superiors that you can retake this Colony?"

"Our exact mission statement has not been promulgated and is of course subject to a careful staffing process to ensure that mission is defined precisely."

Sergeant Reynolds spoke into the brief quiet following Wilkinson's statement, her voice calm and professional. "General. I know you're used to wordsmithing the mission definition so you can claim victory regardless of the outcome, but that won't work in this case. That system depends on enlisted soldiers somehow executing the mission in such a way that declaring victory has a veneer of legitimacy."

"I will not tolerate being spoken to in this manner."

Stark raised one forefinger toward Wilkinson, instinctively rising to Reynolds's defense. "You haven't any choice this time."

"Sergeant, I *order* you—"

Anger flooded Stark, toppling the barriers he had tried to erect to maintain an even temper. "In case it hasn't sunk in yet, General, we're not going to follow your orders. We also don't intend dying or watching our friends die trying to carry out poorly conceived missions just to protect your reputation. You want miracles done, do them yourself." He felt Vic's hand reach under the table to grip his leg in silent admonition to calm down, and he tried to tamp down his emotions.

Wilkinson flushed scarlet. "I don't know who the hell you think you are, soldier—"

Another flash of anger dissolved Stark's good intentions. "I'm Sergeant Ethan Stark. Who the hell do you think you are?"

Before the General could formulate a reply, the hard-eyed corporate representative slapped one hand on the table. "This is getting us nowhere. Mr. Stark—"

"Sergeant."

The representative paused, obviously fighting for composure. "Sergeant Stark. Your confidence is misplaced. Your weapons need ammunition and spare parts. Neither will be coming. This Colony is not self-sufficient for food and water. Those won't be coming, either."

"We have plenty of spares," Stark stated, swinging one arm to indicate the monitor Vic had activated. "There's a lot of damaged battle armor to cannibalize, as you can see. We've also got lots of ammunition, and we know how to get more."

Campbell cleared his throat as if apologetically. "As for food and water, we have substantial stockpiles, thanks in part to our defenders. Aside from their own resources, they arranged to trade a large number of enemy prisoners for necessities like foodstuffs. In terms of water, we're in very good shape thanks to the recent discoveries of new subsurface ice deposits."

"That ice belongs to our corporations! Further, the existence and location of those ice deposits is proprietary information belonging to your parent corporations."

"Yes," Campbell noted, in tones that suggested no real agreement, "well, our parents have been somewhat abusive, so we no longer feel bound by their rules."

Another man leaned forward. "Sir, your words are condemning you to certain fines and imprisonment. As you are aware, subclauses of your employment agreement limit your ability to make public statements regarding your employers."

Cheryl Sarafina spoke for the first time, arching her eyebrows in surprise. "We were not aware this was a public forum."

The man smiled triumphantly. "The definition of *public* as set forth in paragraph four, section a, subsection five of your employment contract—"

"Oh, shut up," Campbell snapped, his own temper obviously fraying. "We're not here to split legal hairs. I believe it should be clear by now that you do not have the means to coerce our cooperation and should therefore be trying to negotiate a truly fair outcome."

The first politician who had spoken shook his head. "Our armed forces aren't as dependent on individual soldiers as you believe. I have been assured by the Pentagon that our new weapon systems provide many times the combat capabilities of older systems, yet require far fewer personnel. Perhaps you should enlighten Mr. Campbell, General Wilkinson, and also these, uh, enlisted persons as well."

Wilkinson licked his lips, eyes uncertain, then smiled confidently. "Of course. Take the new-generation Armored Fighting Vehicle, the Kilpatrick Tank. It can engage multiple targets in a high-threat environment, has unprecedented ability to operate against enemy countermeasures, utilizes a uniquely capable active-passive armor system providing unparalleled protection, and requires only one operator." He paused, looking around the table triumphantly.

Sergeant Reynolds held up her right hand questioningly. "How many personnel does it take to maintain this new tank, General? How often do its subsystems break?"

Wilkinson glowered at her. "Exact logistical and other support requirements are still being determined by operational testing and evaluation sequences."

Stacey Yurivan waved her own hand. "General. I assume one operator means that tank is very highly automated. If the enemy inserts a worm into the tank's operating systems, can the single operator override and countermand all functions in time to prevent fratricide?"

"How big is this thing?" Chief Wiseman wondered. "Can it fit on our existing orbital boosters and landing craft?"

Stark gestured to his staff for silence. "Sorry about that, sir," he apologized with barely veiled insincerity. "Those are the sort of questions veteran soldiers are likely to ask. As for me, I'm just wondering how well that tank's armor will do against the new sequential warhead anti-armor systems being deployed against us. They've been able to pretty much punch through anything we've got, which is why our tanks need good infantry screening to survive. We captured a number of those systems not long ago," Stark added, "during an enemy offensive."

Wilkinson's jaw muscles stood out for a moment. "The Kilpatrick Tank is far superior to existing weapons and has none of the weaknesses you have alleged." One of the other officers, a Colonel, leaned toward the General, whispering frantically in his ear. "Of course," the General continued, "the, uh, operational environment may not be favorable for the employment of specific weapons systems depending on, uh, required operational parameters—"

"General," Stark interrupted again. "It's a new weapon. You don't really know what it can or can't do. But none of us have ever met any weapon which lived up to its press releases, so we won't be impressed by claims of what any new weapon can maybe do in the future."

Another politician spoke, her tone pleading. "Are you all really prepared to risk death? This is a very serious course of action you're following. I never expected to be telling fellow Americans they would be attacked by our own military unless they agree to follow the basic rules of our society."

Colony Manager Campbell looked back at her, then around the table. "We do not want to fight. We do not want to defy authority. What we do want is some basic, elementary, fair treatment in accordance with our status as citizens. Why is that so hard? Why can't we be allowed to vote?"

"You're in a war zone! How can we conduct elections in a war zone? Campaigning, voting, it would all be impossible."

"No, it would not! If you bothered to actually walk around the Colony, you'd find it is a completely safe environment. I ask again, why can't we vote?"

"The timing and nature of that decision is not, and cannot be, left up to you. Look at your current actions. You are inviting attack by our own military because of irresponsible and ill-considered decisions."

Vic spoke, drawing attention away from Campbell. "I keep hearing threats to attack the Colony. The use of U.S. military forces against U.S. citizens or territory is prohibited by law unless those citizens or territories are declared to be in a state of rebellion. Are we to understand such a declaration is pending?"

The politicians exchanged glances, then all looked toward their so-far silent staffers. One of those staffers cleared his throat, speaking as if reciting from a memorized text. "A declaration that the Lunar Colony is in a state of rebellion against lawful authorities of the United States is in abeyance pending the results of this meeting. Failure to conform to the commands of duly authorized representatives of the government will be taken as evidence of rebellious intent and actions."

Campbell stared, eyes wide with disbelief. "You're telling us that we must submit to all the demands made today? That asking for the most basic rights of a citizen is being declared an act of rebellion?"

"That is a very prejudicial formulating of the government's position. Of course, what I just stated applies only to the Colony. The military personnel who have failed in their duties have already been declared rebellious."

Ms. Pevoni stood, her face reflecting shock. "You can't be serious! There is no need to escalate this dispute to the level of . . . of . . . war!"

The senior politician spoke, his voice harsh. "On the contrary, this is a very serious situation. We have been very patient with you. The former defenders of this Colony have already been informed that they must surrender immediately. No negotiations are being offered them. As for the Colony itself, you must either agree to the offer set forth by the corporate representatives present at this meeting, or we will be forced to call for appropriate measures."

"That is the only choice you offer?" Campbell swiveled to look back at his assistants, reading some unspoken consensus. "Then we must take the only choice we can."

"I'm very glad sanity has prevailed—"

"We thank you for coming," Campbell continued, his tone dripping acid. "Please gather your personal possessions. You will be escorted back to your shuttles. The citizens of this Colony will overlook your attempt to unjustifiably characterize our demands for fair treatment and will await an offer which reflects our rights and provides adequate compensations for our sacrifices. Good day." He stood abruptly, his back to the corporate, political, and military delegations as they first stared, then began arguing in low tones among themselves.

Stark, trying to ignore the ball of lead that seemed to have taken up residence in his stomach, nodded approvingly to Campbell as the Colony Manager glanced his way, earning a slightly shaky look of appreciation. "Good job, everybody," Stark murmured to his staff.

"They really gonna do it?" Bev Manley questioned. "It's like they don't realize what's actually going on."

"They don't. Maybe it's time they had a reality check."

The tight groups of official representatives broke into looser conglomerations as they intermingled and debated. Sergeant Reynolds stepped to one side, shutting off the monitor with its accusing picture of the lunar terrain now and forever to be known as Death Valley. A female Major took advantage of the distraction to leave the confines of the official military group, stepping quickly over to Vic to stand before her with a rigid face. "May I help you,

Major?" Vic asked with poorly concealed curiosity.

"I . . . yes, Sergeant. My brother. Captain Kutusov. Peter Kutusov."

"Kutusov," Vic repeated, hauling out her palm pad. "Second Brigade, Third Division?"

"Yes." The Major tensed visibly, casting a nervous look toward the brass still engaged in their own conversation. "That area you showed us." Her voice seemed momentarily lost, as if words couldn't form. "That's where his unit attacked?"

"I'm afraid so."

"I haven't received any word on him. He hasn't been among the officers repatriated."

"No." Vic's voice softened, her face impassive but eyes still betraying sympathy. "He won't be. We recovered his body just a couple of weeks ago."

Major Kutusov couldn't quite hide her flinch. "I see."

Vic consulted her readout. "He was pretty far forward with his unit. I'm afraid I can't tell you a lot about it. That unit was effectively wiped out, a lot of suit systems were destroyed, and we just haven't had enough time or resources to analyze existing system records for all the casualties Third Division suffered."

"I see."

"I can try to locate any survivors of his unit who might have stayed up here if you want to talk to them."

"No. There won't be time."

"Do you want to take the body back with you?" Vic asked gently.

"That won't be permitted." Major Kutusov bit off each word.

"We're sorry we haven't been able to publish full casualty lists, but there were just so many dead, and it's taking a very long time to recover them all."

"I assume that wouldn't be all that hard under truce conditions."

"Yes, Major, it wouldn't be, but not all the enemy forces have agreed to truces. We've had to pull a lot of our dead out from under enemy guns."

"Major Kutusov!" General Wilkinson bellowed the command from the other side of the room, not looking up from the palm pad he was punching repeatedly. "Where the hell are you? Where are my briefing files?"

Major Kutusov, pale with worry and reaction, spun on one heel to return to the General's side. "We'll take care of your brother's remains," Vic murmured, stepping close behind the Major. Kutusov hesitated for half a step, then nodded once, almost imperceptibly, before continuing on to stand stolidly before General Wilkinson while he loudly berated her for failing to anticipate his wishes.

Stark came up to Reynolds, frowning at her, as the official delegations trooped out of the room en route to their shuttles, each of the various representatives ostentatiously ignoring the Colony civilian officials and Stark's people. "What was that about, Vic?"

"I think I feel sorry for a Major."

"You're kidding."

"No. Her brother bought it during Meecham's offensive. Way up forward with his unit."

"Up forward? He a Lieutenant?"

"No. Captain." Reynolds shook her head, face saddened. "Ethan, we needed an officer like that to live."

"Officers like that are usually the first to die. That's why tin-plated jerks like Meecham and Wilkinson get to be Generals."

"Are you looking for an argument from me? I never met a General officer who didn't think the sun rose and set on his or her whims." She screwed up her face in distaste. "We probably shouldn't have baited Wilkinson that strongly, though. He can cause us a lot of trouble."

"He'd cause us trouble regardless."

"True enough, but if it wasn't personal it might not be as vicious."

Stark snorted derisively. "What else was I supposed to do? Offer to polish his shoes?"

"We both could've been a little easier on his ego."

"Sure. Just like always. We go out to get shot at but the number one priority is protecting the damn General's ego. I never did figure out why something sitting back at headquarters needed more protection than my own butt did."

Vic laughed, drawing curious looks from the remaining occupants of the room, then smiled mockingly. "Lucky for us, we now serve a commander with no ego problems whatsoever."

"Very funny. You're a riot, Reynolds."

"You really think so?" she asked with feigned innocence.

"Funniest thing since nerve gas." Stark waved to his staff. "You guys can head home. Thanks for the backup. See you at headquarters. Chief Wiseman, keep those shuttles of yours at ready until those bozos who just left here are outside our orbital defenses."

"No problem. We love standing by." Wiseman saluted casually, then followed the soldiers as they left.

Campbell, looking like a man who'd just faced down death itself, came up to Stark and Reynolds. "I suppose that could have gone worse."

"Not a lot worse, but some," Stark agreed. "You did a good job of dealing with those jerks."

"I was scared stiff, Sergeant. I've never been a good poker player."

Vic appraised the civilian, her expression concerned. "You need a poker face when you're bluffing. Is that what's going on?"

"I'm afraid so." Campbell glanced over at his remaining advisors, talking animatedly to one another in one corner of the room, then back at the soldiers. "I don't have strong backing in the Colony. Truth be told, I certainly don't have majority backing for what I just said."

"How bad is it?" Stark demanded. "Just how strong is your support?"

"I've got roughly one-third of the Colony ready to back me in any action, up to and including a declaration of independence. But another third, either through loyalty or fear, wants nothing but reconciliation. The remaining third are fence-sitters, unsure and unwilling to commit either way."

"Great," Vic commented sourly. "What's it going to take to convince at least that middle third to swing our way?" Her gaze shifted to Stark. "Whatever way that turns out to be, that is."

Campbell shrugged, looking uncomfortable. "I'm not sure. This isn't exactly a routine political calculation, you know. We're dealing with very fundamental issues: a government's responsibilities to its people, a people's responsibilities to their government, family ties cutting across questions of loyalty and rebellion, and the simple economic fears driving everyone. Our jobs aren't stable, Sergeant. They never have been. A long time ago, civilians worked for the same employer for life, usually. Over time that changed into hire-on-demand and temporary employment agreements, and the resulting constant fear of losing a job or trying to find a better one has made many workers habitually cautious in any action that might impact on their work."

Stark nodded. "I remember my parents talking about that kind of thing. But there must be something that'd convince people it's time to take action."

"I'm sure there is, but I haven't been able to figure what that something is, Sergeant." Campbell looked intently at Stark. "Something must have motivated you to make your decision. What was it, exactly?"

Thousands of soldiers, marching steadily forward, dying in their tracks as futile assault followed futile assault. Faceless officers in the rear ordering more attacks, shredding the already decimated ranks of survivors as if by enough human sacrifice they could somehow alter reality to fit the fantasy worlds they'd concocted in the self-reverential cocoons of their plans and theories and simulations. Voices crying for help denied to them. Stark kept his face rigid with great effort, then spoke carefully, his voice almost toneless from his effort to control it. "I guess . . . what it came down to was . . . there was nothing I could do . . . except by doing something I wasn't ever supposed to do. I could've saved myself . . . but I had to save the others."

Vic grasped Stark's shoulder firmly, lending strength, but faced Campbell. "There's always been a contract," she explained. "An unwritten one. We'll die if we have to because that's part of the job, and we think the job matters. Our superiors broke that contract. It became obvious we were expected to die not to accomplish anything, but just because they said so."

Campbell eyed both soldiers as if he'd never seen them before. "I think I understand. We civilians all have contracts of one sort or another, but I think you're speaking of a contract in a greater sense. An understanding of why sacrifices are demanded and where rewards should lie. I need some way of convincing the majority of the Colony that our political leaders and corporate superiors have violated that sort of contract."

Vic nodded in agreement. "I hope you can manage that without watching a lot of them die," she noted quietly.

"I hope so, too. Sergeant Reynolds. I can't believe we're facing such threats over such issues. Do you think the people we just met with will have second thoughts and grant any of our demands?"

She smiled crookedly before replying. "Mr. Campbell, I think we're dealing with individuals who think they can make things happen because they want them to happen. Right and wrong has nothing to do with it. They're not going to calmly accept a requirement to do what we want."

"What do you think they'll do? Surely not an all-out attack."

"Your guess is as good as mine." Vic gestured to Stark. "Ethan, you know the civ side and the mil side. What's your assessment?"

"They'll try something." Stark stared around as if that "something" would be identified somewhere in the vainglorious art on the walls. "But they've gotta be worried. How much will all this cost them? Corporations only care about the bottom line, right? And the politicians must be wondering who's gonna get blamed for everything, especially if whatever they try fails. The mil? No, I mean the Pentagon. They're worried most of all. They've lost damn near two-thirds of their active duty strength, one-third when they tried to use Third Division as a battering ram and one-third when we told them to go to hell. They don't have the troops to do the things they've said they'll do, and all the public relations spin in the world can't get them out of that hole."

Campbell smiled with evident relief. "Then they're not likely to actually attack us? It's just a bluff?"

Both Stark and Reynolds shook their heads in negation. "You can't count on that," Vic advised. "They don't want to lose. They don't have enough soldiers and no likelihood of getting enough soldiers. But not attacking us guarantees losing, while if they actually try to hit us a miracle might happen."

"And," Stark added, "you can bet their senior intelligence types are churning out reports saying whatever the brass wants to hear the most, which is probably that we're likely to crumble when they push."

"But, that won't happen," Campbell objected anxiously. "Will it?"

"I'm gonna be perfectly honest with you, Mr. Campbell. I don't know what'll happen the first time my soldiers find themselves aiming at other American soldiers. I don't know what the other soldiers will do. I don't know what my soldiers will do. I hope to God I never find out because, whether they shoot or surrender, either way I'm gonna lose."

Campbell stared at the floor for a long moment, then looked up with a sardonic smile. "So it appears we're hoping for a miracle, too."

"Yeah. I guess so. Reckon we'll find out which side's in best with the Big Guy upstairs, won't we?"

"Mail call," Bev Manley announced, tossing a data coin onto Stark's desk.

"What?" Stark tapped the coin with one finger as if unsure of its existence. "We got mail?"

"Uh-huh. That official delegation brought it."

Stark frowned, rolling the coin back and forth. "That'd be our first real mail since Meecham's offensive, not counting the stuff that's been bootlegged up here. Why'd the authorities decide to be so nice to us?"

"Because they ain't being nice." Sergeant Manley pointed at the coin in Stark's hand. "Think about it. People we don't trust hand us letters allegedly from our friends and loved ones back home. Because they want to be nice all of a sudden? No way. It's because whatever messages are in that coin and every other one we got says whatever the authorities want them to say. I'd guess major league propaganda, heartfelt appeals to surrender, that sort of thing."

"Bev, my parents may not be the greatest human beings on Earth, though God knows I put 'em through enough to earn martyr status for both of 'em, but they wouldn't parrot some government line to me."

Manley shook her head, waving an objecting hand. "This has nothing to do with your parents' virtues. It has to do with the government's ability to coerce people into doing what they want."

"You saying they put a gun to my parents' heads or something?"

"I doubt it'd be that crude. More likely they told your parents 'read this script for us or we'll have to ask the Internal Revenue Service to audit your last twenty years of tax returns for any discrepancies.' You know, iron-hand-in-the-velvet-glove stuff. What are they gonna do? And if that coin's from a friend instead of your parents, the same thing applies. Listen, I'm gonna give you the same advice I'm giving every soldier who got mail: don't read it. If the government wants you to have it, you don't want to know what it says."

Stark sat silent for a moment, then nodded. "Can't argue with that."

"Want to give me the coin back?"

"No."

Manley smiled ruefully. "Didn't think so. Just be careful. Don't read it. If you do read it, don't believe it."

"Thanks, Bev. That's good advice. We get mail for a lot of guys?"

She shrugged. "Coupla hundred. Not much, not with thousands of soldiers up here, which is one more reason I'm sure the stuff is faked. If people were allowed to write whatever they wanted, we'd have thousands of letters. But it takes time and personnel to supervise scripted dialogues, doesn't it?"

"Should we be handing this stuff out then?"

"I wondered about that. But that'd mean keeping mail away from soldiers it's addressed to. If you want me to . . ."

"No. We don't hold mail." Stark glanced down at the coin again. "That'd be wrong. Like lying to them. I don't want to start down the road of thinking I can mess with these apes' personal lives just because I think it's for their own good. You do like you said, warn everybody that this stuff is likely poison, and tell them to talk to their superiors and friends and the chaplains if they need to after screening it. But we don't withhold mail."

"Thought you'd say that." Manley flipped a casual salute. "I'm off on my assigned mission, then. Commander Stark."

"Does that mean I got to order around an Administrative guy?

Maybe this job ain't so bad after all."

"Just don't let it go to your head." Manley smiled and left, leaving Stark alone with his mail.

Stark rolled the coin back and forth in his hand. *Yeah, it'd be real stupid to look at it. Just like Bev said. But I have to.* He leaned forward far enough to insert the coin in his palmtop, then watched the screen, trying to lock down his emotions as the still-familiar faces of his parents appeared. They were seated in what was surely the same apartment they'd lived in during Stark's youth, in a fairly anonymous suburb of the Seattle metroplex. Stark even recognized a few of the furnishings, though the couch on which his parents were seated looked new. His father looked like he had in the last coin Stark had received, older and thinner than the vision still stuck in his mind from his youth. His mother sat rigidly erect, surprisingly aged to Stark, who hadn't seen her image in over a decade, her face rigid with some unreadable emotion.

"Ethan Stark," his father began, the words falling heavily from his mouth, tinged with something like anger. "This is very unpleasant for us. We know what's happened up on the Moon. We know what you've done, and we are deeply, deeply ashamed." He paused, while Stark's mother remained uncharacteristically silent. "If you love us, if you care about us at all, if you have any decency, you'll surrender immediately to legal and lawful authorities. There's nothing else we can say. Please, do what's right." The screen blanked, leaving Stark to stare bleakly at white noise.

Is that really how they feel? Were they coerced into saying that? How can I know one way or another? He thought of his father, firmly admonishing him, so different from the halting pride expressed in his last letter.

Did you mean it then or do you mean it now? Or both? Couldn't you have given me some sign? Some indication if this is how you really felt? But his father had never been one for signs or subtlety. Like his universal gesture of contempt, the one Stark had seen a million times as a youth. His father would be watching the vid as some politician pontificated or some corporate ad rolled, and after a short time he'd throw down whatever he happened to be holding (or whatever was within reach) and declare "this is a bunch of crap." It had been one certain routine no matter the time of day or year. Political ad: "this is a bunch of crap" (wham). Smiling corporate speaker: "this is a bunch of crap" (wham). Earnest government representative: "this is a bunch of crap" (wham). Stark smiled involuntarily at the memory, then frowned thoughtfully.

Rewinding the coin, he watched carefully as his father spoke. "We know what you've done, and we are deeply, deeply ashamed." As the sentence ended, his father slapped down a bookpad on the table beside him. "If you love us, if you care about us at all, if you have any decency, you'll surrender immediately to legal and lawful authorities." The empty hand reached out as his father spoke, as if grabbing air, and making another throwing down gesture as if to emphasize the end of the sentence.

Stark rewound again. "Deeply, deeply ashamed." Wham. "Surrender immediately." Simulated wham. He watched the last two sentences carefully. "There's nothing else we can say." That could be read two ways, and Stark had a strong suspicion he now knew which one actually applied. "Please, do what's right." That, too. The government people who'd obviously supervised the making of this tape had no doubt believed that was pretty unambiguous, and it was, just not in the way they expected. Stark's father had all his life made it clear where he thought "right" lay, and that usually wasn't on the side of either big corporations seeking bigger profits or politicians in their pay.

He watched the tape one more time, focusing this time on his mother, sitting silently through his father's speech. That wasn't normal, either, not unless she'd changed a whole lot. *Mom always made it clear that even when she agreed with Dad, she wasn't going to let him do all the talking. So when she says nothing, that sends a message, too.*

Why you sneaky little devils. Never knew you could put one over on the government. The guys screening this coin probably thought Dad's throwing things emphasized his words real nice and figured Mom's silence was natural. Stark grinned, imagining the dialogue in his father's head as he'd spoken words he didn't believe: "this is a bunch of crap!" And his mother holding her tongue despite what must have been a powerful urge to say the same thing out loud. *How come we learn so much about our parents so late in life? Maybe we've got to get enough life under our own belts first to understand what we've always taken for granted. Do what's right. That's the bottom line. Okay. Got the message.*

"Ethan, time to meet with the officers."

Stark looked up from his work, blinking in confusion as his mind tried to surface through a haze of concentration and focus back into the real world. *Officers? Did the Company Commander call a meeting? No, wait. Wake up, Stark. They're gone. The delegation from the Pentagon? They left days ago.* "Officers? What officers?"

"Hellooooo, Ethan." Vic leaned down to peer into his eyes. "You are not getting enough sleep, soldier."

"Do tell. What officers?"

"The ones who volunteered to stay."

Oh, yeah. Those officers. "How many did we end up keeping?" That report had probably crossed his desk at some point, but Stark couldn't sort out that memory from a hundred others. *Too many damn reports. It's like the brass ordered reports on everything they could possibly order reports on. Gotta fix that.*

"Sixteen." Vic smiled encouragingly. "One of them is Conroy."

"Great." Stark stood, feeling muscles twinge as he stretched. "I gotta move more."

"You getting your resistance workouts in every day?"

"Mostly."

"Uh-huh. I'll see you this afternoon, and we'll work out together. Okay?"

"Thanks." Stark checked his scheduler, nodding approvingly. "That'll leave time for me to get prettied up for the dinner with my Squad."

"Don't get too pretty or your Squad won't recognize you."

"Har, har. When's the last time I told you how funny you were, Reynolds?"

"It's been a couple of days."

"Good. I'll make sure it's a couple more before I tell you again."

Vic smiled, then took another close look at Stark. "What's the matter? You look nervous. Don't worry, I'm sure that dinner'll happen on schedule this time, unless the Navy screws it up again."

"That's not what I'm nervous about. It's the officers who've joined us. Vic, I never faced a bunch of officers like this before. Giving 'em marching orders, instead of them ordering me around.

It's kinda . . . weird. You know?"

Instead of agreeing, she laughed. "Ethan, you've been telling officers what to do for as long as I've known you."

Her humor brought a self-mocking smile to Stark's face. "Well, yeah, but that was different. I was, whatayacallit, manipulating them to do the right thing. I wasn't coming right out and saying 'do this.' I couldn't."

Vic smiled reassuringly, reaching to pat his upper arm. "You've been doing fine giving orders. If these officers weren't ready to take them from you, they wouldn't be here."

"I guess that's right. Okay. Let's go."

The officers awaited Stark in a modestly sized room, one usually reserved for presentations or lectures to small units. Stark kept his eyes set straight ahead as he entered the room, then cursed mentally as Reynolds yelled "Attention!" behind him, bringing the officers to their feet. *She should've warned me she was gonna do that. But then if she had warned me, I'd have told her not to, so of course she didn't tell me.*

Reaching the front of the room, Stark turned, finally having to face the officers. Five Captains and eleven Lieutenants. Very few, counted against all the officers who had been assigned to Lunar Command, but a very large number compared to whatever amount of officers Stark would have guessed would volunteer to join a revolt against their fellows. He waited a moment longer, both Stark and the officers at attention, before realizing it was his responsibility to break the stalemate. "Uh, please, take your seats."

Captains and Lieutenants sat quickly, then stared back at him, faces carefully neutral. "I wanted to thank you all, personally, for offering to stay up here." His hesitation began to disappear as words started to flow. "I know what that kind of thing represents. I know you're taking a tremendous risk, and I know how tough it is to go against training and tradition, but I also think we all know there wasn't much choice any more. Whatever we make of this, and we want it to be something good, you officers have chosen to help us. We checked you all out, and every one of you were decent leaders and decent commanders when all the rules said you didn't have to be. In fact, you probably would've had more promotions if you had followed the rules. I thank you for that, too."

Stark paused, trying and failing to gauge the effects of his words on the officers before him. "You're all going to be paired with a Sergeant when you get to your new assignments. That's not because we don't trust you, it's because we want to make sure no enlisted tries to play games with you. Some of them have got in their heads that there'll never be officers giving them orders again. That idea's not going to last. We're training new officers, and we want you to show us the things you know, not the book learning stuff, but the things you get from experience on being officers. It's important. Being an officer's different. It's a different role, a different way of doing things. I know that. We all do, deep down. The Sergeants and other enlisted who are filling officer jobs will be looking to you for role models. Do your best."

Another pause, still unmarked by obvious reaction. "If any of you run into any problems, stuff like disrespect or mistreatment, I want to know about it. I'll also say something I'm sure you've already guessed, that I'll be getting reports on you, and if any of you try to play political games or abuse your troops, I'll find a new assignment for you where you can't do either." A series of small frowns appeared on the faces of the officers as they finally reacted, frowns whose meaning Stark could easily decipher. "That doesn't mean you can't enforce discipline. I said don't abuse your troops. There's a big difference between discipline and abuse, and if any of you don't know what it is, let me know right now." The frowns smoothed out, several heads nodding back at Stark in understanding or agreement.

"I don't expect this to go smooth," Stark finished. "Nothing else has. But I damn well intend to work through any problems. And I promise you I'll be fair. Any questions?" Memory suddenly superimposed visions of the same query, made by officers to enlisted at innumerable briefings. Now it was all mirror imaged, and Stark wondered if the officers would accept his inquiry as sincere or assume he'd adopted the senior officer stance to unwelcome questions. *Which is that any real question is unwelcome, of course. Hey, somebody's got a hand up.* "Yes, Captain?"

"What exactly are our marching orders if American forces fire on us?" the Captain demanded bluntly. "Do we treat it as if it were any other enemy assault?"

Stark looked over the officers' heads to where Vic stood by the door at parade rest, her own eyes fixed on him, then back at the Captain. "Exact marching orders haven't been promulgated. We hope to avoid any combat against American forces."

The Captain nodded slowly in response. "You realize that may be impossible."

"I know. Are you really asking me if I'm going to order you to fire on other Americans?"

"That's right. To be perfectly frank, I'm not sure I can do that."

"Me, neither," Stark agreed dryly. "My bet is the tougher we are, the harder we look to the authorities back home, the more likely they'll be to find a way to talk to us instead of fight us. Because if it does come to combat, nobody can take us unless we let them. We have to do our best to make sure the Pentagon knows that, too."

Another nod, quicker this time. "Thank you."

"Okay, then, that's all I've got. Good luck." He paused a moment, trying to think of how to send the officers on their way, then glared in exasperation as Vic Reynolds once again called out "Attention" and the officers sprang up from their chairs. "Uh, carry on."

"Hold on, Lieutenant Conroy," Stark called as the others exited. She came forward to stand stiffly at attention before him, a reversal of roles Stark found particularly disconcerting since he'd served directly under her. "Lieutenant, I never got to thank you for leading the platoon back to get me."

Conroy managed a half-smile. "We were all pretty busy. I never got a chance to thank you for saving my platoon. And me in the bargain."

"You got a lousy deal, Lieutenant, and now you're taking a real big chance on us. We'll treat you fair. I can't promise a helluva lot else, but I can promise we'll treat you fair."

"Thank you." Conroy smiled again. "We were all wondering, what is your proper title?"

"We're still working on that. Most people call me Commander. I'm damned if I want to be called General."

"Then I suppose I'll call you 'sir.' "

"Ah, jeez," Stark winced. "Don't call me 'sir.' I work for a living, Lieutenant."

This time she laughed. "It's your call."

"You know we're sending you back to Bravo Company, right? It's off the front line right now, just starting refresher training this week. Sergeant Sanchez is running the old platoon, and Sergeant Podesta is running the company. I think they'll be real happy to have you around to help show them the ropes."

Lieutenant Conroy nodded gratefully. "Thank you. It'll be much easier to adapt to this . . . situation in a unit I already know. But if I recall properly, I doubt Sergeant Sanchez will display much happiness."

"It's nothing personal, Lieutenant. Sanch don't display much to nobody. But he's a damn good leader. I'll see him tonight, so I'll let him know you remembered him."

"Thank you, Sergeant." Conroy colored slightly. "I'm sorry."

"Don't be. I like it when people call me that. And thank you again, Lieutenant. For coming back."

This time her smile reflected a mix of bitterness and sorrow. "After you led this takeover, a rather large number of my fellow officers clearly expressed to me their belief that I was at fault for not leaving you to die."

"Sorry, Lieutenant."

"That's all right. It made it easier to decide to stay."

"Commander?"

Stark halted his restless pacing, glancing around the dining room as he quickly palmed his comm unit. "Stark here."

"This is Sentry Post One, Commander. I've got a squad of soldiers who say they're here to meet you."

Stark relaxed, smiling. "That's right. You should have their names on your access list."

"Yes, sir, but they're carrying their weapons, and normally only personnel assigned to headquarters are authorized to have personal weapons with them inside the complex."

Stark frowned toward his comm unit. "Right. Put, um, Corporal Gomez on."

"Yes, sir."

"Sargento?" Corporal Gomez asked hesitantly.

"Yeah. What's with the weapons?"

"We were at the firing simulator this afternoon, and the thing broke, like it always does, so we had to wait until they fixed it 'cause we didn't want to lose our training slot, and that made us real late, so Sergeant Sanchez said we could just bring our weapons along tonight and get 'em back to the barracks afterwards. That okay, Sarge?"

If I can't trust these apes with weapons, who can I trust? "Sure, it's okay. Sentry, you copy that?"

"Roger, Commander. I'll pass them through."

"Thanks. And good job checking before you passed them." Stark looked over as the door opened and Vic Reynolds craned her neck inside. "My squad should be here in a few minutes. Anybody from my staff coming?"

"Manley begged off because her unit's having a get-together, too. Gordasa and Lamont are engaged in some sort of sim tournament. Tanaka's been running training drills all day, so I doubt she'll make it. I think Wiseman and Yurivan will be here."

"Great," Stark noted sarcastically. "My two favorites."

"And," Vic continued smoothly, "speaking of . . ." She moved inside, followed by Chief Wiseman and Sergeant Yurivan, then waved toward the bar. "Open bar, folks. Drink as much as you want, as long as it's not more than two beers."

Wiseman studied the bar carefully. "Do shots count?"

"Fraid so."

"Even small shots?"

"Them, too," Vic chuckled. "Don't worry, Chief, you can always tank up at one of Stacey's bootleg stills later on."

Yurivan managed to look offended. "I'm not operating any stills. Not at the moment, anyway. How come the limit?"

Vic waved toward Stark. "Our boss doesn't want to risk us all suffering from system degrades at the same time."

"Isn't he the same guy that told me 'no guts, no glory'?"

"That was different," Stark advised.

"And," Sergeant Yurivan continued, "the same guy who's always getting himself into hopeless situations that he survives by incredible luck? But he doesn't believe in taking risks? Hey, Chief Wiseman, what do you think?"

"I think," the Chief pronounced, "that it's a good thing he took a risk on us sailors when we came running here with warships on our tails. I know some of you mud-crawlers," she pivoted to point her beer at Vic, "didn't want him to, but I'm kind of glad he did."

"It wasn't anything personal," Vic stated in level tones. "You know that. It was simply a tremendous risk."

Stark nodded toward the Chief. "Yeah. And it was Vic's job to point that out to me, regardless of how she felt about it otherwise. But it worked out okay, and it gained us our own little Navy." *I don't need bad blood between those two. Wonder how Wiseman heard Vic had argued against letting her land? Some big-eared, loose-lipped watch-stander, I bet.* "There's just some risks you gotta take."

"I'm not denying that one worked out well. Chief Wiseman and her shuttles are a tremendous asset," Vic added diplomatically. "We just can't afford to take too many more risks like that."

"And I'm not arguing that, Vic. Keep reminding me of it. But I'm afraid sometimes we're gonna have to run some big risks."

Chief Wiseman cleared her throat. "Somebody who won't take risks can't win. That's a quote," she added with a grin.

"A quote," Vic repeated skeptically. "So who said it first?"

"John Paul Jones," Chief Wiseman declared, hoisting her beer. "That's the father of the United States Navy, in case you ground apes don't know."

"Hah!" Stark crowed, winking at Reynolds to show he was kidding. "See, Vic, I got the father of the U.S. Navy on my side!"

"Oooooh," Vic trilled with exaggerated awe. "I guess that settles that argument. Ethan Stark, you never took the Navy's side on any issue in your life."

"That's because the Navy was always wrong before. This time, they're right." Whatever rejoinder Vic might have manufactured was cut short by other arrivals. "Hey, Mendo, you got the rest of the Squad with you?"

"Yes, Commander Stark. All except Private Murphy, who is awaiting his own guest." Private Mendoza stepped aside as the other soldiers entered, most of them displaying their years of service experience by scanning the room, locking in on the bar, and immediately making a beeline toward it. "Sergeant Stark, this is my father, Lieutenant Mendoza," Mendo added with a gesture toward the man standing by his side, not trying to conceal his feelings as he smiled proudly.

"We've met a couple of times." Stark stepped forward with his hand extended. "Pleased to see you again, sir."

Lieutenant Mendoza shook the offered hand, nodding solemnly. "Thank you, Sergeant. Or should I call you Commander on this occasion?"

"Whatever you're comfortable with, Lieutenant. Hey, have you met Corporal Gomez? She's your son's acting squad leader."

The Lieutenant nodded again, this time to Anita Gomez as she came to stand with visible discomfort nearby. "I have not yet had that opportunity, but from all I have heard, Corporal Gomez appears to be highly effective in that role." Gomez's expression shifted marginally as she eyed Lieutenant Mendoza appraisingly. "My son advises me that the Corporal will accept nothing but the best performance from her Squad."

Everyone looked at Gomez. "That's what the *Sargento* expects, right?" she stated defiantly. "I'm not gonna let the squad go to hell just 'cause he's busy right now."

Sergeant Sanchez appeared, face calm and composed, waving a small greeting to Stark and Reynolds, as if he'd last seen them the day before. "Corporal Gomez's performance has been in the highest traditions of the service. I speak particularly of her defense of Mango Hill during an action prior to your arrival. She is indeed a good squad leader."

"Then my son is most fortunate. And you are a good platoon leader, I hear."

Sanchez shrugged, face and voice as noncommittal as ever. "I feel the responsibility to do my best in that position. However, I am merely an acting platoon commander, Lieutenant."

"That's true of everyone," Vic pointed out. "We're all just filling in at jobs we don't have the actual rank for."

"Sure," Stark agreed. "I'm the acting Commander, and we've got acting officers of every stripe. Some do real good, some don't. The best ones don't seem to need the acting rank to get the job done, so I'm not sure if acting ranks really amount to more than a hill of beans."

Lieutenant Mendoza smiled softly, the exact way Stark had seen Mendoza's son smile many times, but then, unlike his son, began speaking his inner thoughts unprompted. "There is a story from the American Civil War about that very issue. A battle had been fought over a long day, so the armies of the North and South were tired. Evening was coming on, and with the dimming light and the smoke from the gunpowder used in weapons at that time, the visibility had become very poor. At one critical spot on the Northern line, a train of mules was brought forward to resupply the Northern soldiers with ammunition. Just then, the Southern infantry launched a final attack against that very location. The Northern soldiers were weary. The attack might have succeeded and changed the course of the battle. But the firing of the Southern soldiers and the screaming of their battle cries panicked the mules, which stampeded directly toward the advancing Southerners. In the smoke-shrouded dimness, the attacking Southerners could see nothing, but could hear the thunder of hooves and the rattle of harness. They concluded they were being charged by an unseen force of Northern cavalry and retreated."

Stark laughed. "Stranger things have happened in battle. What's this got to do with acting rank?"

"After the battle," Lieutenant Mendoza explained, "the teamster in charge of the mules wrote the commanding officer of the Northern army. Noting that his mules had saved the battle for the North, the teamster asked that the mules' heroism be rewarded by promoting them to the acting rank of 'horse.' "

"Ha! Good story. That oughta keep us humble."

"Yeah, appropriate, too," Yurivan needled. "Even with acting rank, Stark here is still mule headed."

"Thanks, Stace. Not like you, huh? Tell you what, since you're doing half the job you should be, I'll let you be an acting horse, but only half a horse. You can guess which half."

Yurivan grinned, unabashed. "You keep sweet-talking me like that and Reynolds will get jealous."

Vic raised both eyebrows. "Jealous? I've been trying to get Ethan Stark interested in someone else for years so he'd stop following me around."

"Well, if you don't want him, I sure as hell don't."

Stark glanced sidelong at Lieutenant Mendoza. "You see what I have to put up with."

Lieutenant Mendoza smiled again. "You are fortunate that your staff has such high morale."

"Fortunate. I'll try to remember that." He looked around, then backed a step away. "I want a chance to talk to the rest of my Squad, you guys. Okay? I'll be back in a while." He turned, finding

Chen hovering near the bar with two soldiers Stark didn't know. "How's the hip?"

Chen grimaced, rubbing the spot. "Okay, I guess, Sarge. The docs claim if I get hit there again they'll just put a zipper in to make it easier to fix next time."

"I hope the last hip joint had a good warranty," Stark joked. "These friends of yours?"

"Sorta." Chen waved the other soldiers forward. "Replacements, Sarge. You know?"

Stark somehow kept his smile even though a cold ball formed somewhere in his gut. Replacements. He wouldn't see Hoxely here, or Kidd, or Maseru. He'd barely even had time to meet Maseru, a face fading too rapidly into oblivion. *It ain't right that a soldier dies, and you can't remember how they looked. It ain't right.* "Yeah," he finally agreed. "I know."

"This here's Private Josh Finley and Corporal Vince Caruso." The new soldiers nodded stiffly, visibly nervous. "They're originally from Third Division, Sarge."

"Third? You guys stayed, huh?" Stark reached to shake their hands, noticing how the simple gesture relaxed the two soldiers. "Thanks. I know it's hard leaving your old outfit."

Private Finley smiled, a brief twitch without humor. "There wasn't too much left of our old outfit to leave. Just three of us from our platoon still in one piece after Meecham's offensive. Gardiner didn't stay, but that was mostly because his girl is back home, and he couldn't handle maybe never seeing her again."

"I don't second guess anybody's decision on that," Stark noted. "My Squad treating you okay?"

"Sure, Sergeant. Uh, I mean, Commander."

"Sergeant's fine tonight. You apes relax and have a good time."

"Speaking of girls," Chen interjected with a grin, "looks like Private Murphy has arrived with his."

"Murph's got a girl? That's his guest?" Stark turned to see, remembering his conversation with the Private about dating civilian women. Murphy stood in the doorway, proud/nervous like a kid bringing his girl home to meet his dad, then stepped in. Stark stared briefly as he saw Murphy's date, then grinned hugely. "Robin Masood. Long time no see."

"Good evening, Sergeant Stark." Robin hugged Murphy's arm protectively, smiling up at him.

"This the civ who visited you while your arm was growing back, huh?" Stark asked Murphy, then turned to Robin. "I should've warned you that if you kept visiting soldiers in hospitals you'd pick up something."

"I'm glad you didn't."

"Murph treating you okay?" Stark demanded mock-seriously.

"He's a perfect gentleman!" Robin declared.

Corporal Gomez stepped close. "You made Murph a gentleman? Now you gone and ruined him, and I'm gonna have to turn him back into an ape."

Murphy beamed around at his audience. "I can still fight. Better than ever. I got somethin' special to fight for now."

Stark caught the flash of unease Murphy's proud words generated in Robin's eyes. "That's right. You got somethin' special to live for, too."

"Uh, sure, Sarge." Murphy turned away, momentarily distracted by his squad mates as they crowded around to tease and compliment him on his new relationship.

Taking advantage of the moment, Stark leaned in close to Robin, speaking quietly. "You sure you want to get into this? You ready for what comes with being in love with a guy in the mil?"

She flicked a quick look his way, then nodded. "Yes. I think so. Murphy is a wonderful guy, isn't he?"

"I never looked at him that way so I'd have to guess, but he's a good kid. That's not what I'm talking about. Being a full-time partner's hard enough without having to worry about your partner getting killed as part of his job. Can you handle that?"

She hesitated a moment. "I think I can."

Good. I can tell she thought about it before answering. "It's not easy. Believe me, all of us in here understand that. Don't be afraid to talk to someone if you get stressed out or just plain scared. Call me if you ever need to."

"Thank you, Sergeant Stark." She smiled suddenly. "I feel as if I'm talking to Murphy's father."

Stark smiled back. "Seems like that sometimes, I guess. Don't forget. Call me."

"I will."

Stark had agonized a bit over what food to offer his Squad, deciding eventually that a formal meal would just make them (and him) feel awkward. As a result, the trays a food service specialist wheeled in on a buffet cart carried the same sort of chow Stark normally ate.

Stacey Yurivan picked at her plate suspiciously. "This looks way too much like standard rations that've been prettied up a little," she complained. "Where's all that fancy food the senior officers used to eat?"

"You mean the steaks and lobster and junk?" Stark asked, hooking a thumb to point behind him. "In the same freeze lockers they were in when I got here. I'm not eating like a king while my people eat rations."

"You could feed your people steaks and eat rations yourself," Chief Wiseman suggested. "Then you'd really be virtuous. A true leader. Let's try it tonight."

"Sorry. I'm saving all the steaks in case we need to go on short rations. You can't stretch standard rations without making 'em inedible."

"That's 'cause they're already close to inedible," Private Billings agreed.

"Right. But good stuff can be stretched a lot."

Lieutenant Mendoza glanced around the table. "That is a lesson we learned all too well during Operation Eastern Steel. I thought everyone else present was too young to have participated in that campaign."

"We are," Stark concurred. "But we've all talked to veterans who were there. That's the sort of lesson that gets passed down. So, I'm saving the good stuff. Even the lumpia."

"Lumpia!" Yurivan howled. "Stark, you're a sadist."

Lieutenant Mendoza took a taste, chewing slowly. "Yet this food is better prepared than standard rations. Do you use the cooks and food service personnel who attended the senior officers?"

"A few," Stark admitted. "I mean, that's their jobs, and they're damn good at doing 'em. But I don't need all of those people. We don't have nearly as many soldiers in headquarters as they used to have officers, and I can carry my own plates and pour my own coffee. Most of the specialists are being rotated around to the other kitchens to teach the rest of the cooks how to make rations look and taste a little better. It's not much, but it's something."

Time sped by, Stark bouncing from joking with his Squad to serious talks with Lieutenant Mendoza. He felt nerves bundled into tight balls of tension slowly easing, the comradeship and support around him providing something more than simple conversation. It came as a surprise when Sergeant Sanchez walked up to stand half-apologetically before Stark. "I regret that I must pay my respects for this evening."

"So soon?" Stark glanced at the time. "I guess it's not 'soon' after all. Where'd the time go?"

"Maybe we shoulda had a timeline for this op entered in our Tacs," Billings joked.

"Yeah," Chen agreed, "along with orders on what to chew and when to chew each bite. You ever gonna cut orders to our Tacs like that, Sarge?"

"If I ever do, you apes come down here and beat me with your rifle butts until I regain my sanity." Stark smiled as everyone laughed, just as they would have at such a joke months before. "Okay, you guys, it's real late. Later than I meant to keep you. We've got plenty of spare rooms here in headquarters since we're managing to run things without all the officers they used to need, so if anybody wants to stay the night just pick a room to crash in. The empty ones don't have personal locks. You can get back to your barracks in the morning. That okay with you, Sanch?"

Sanchez inclined his head once in agreement. "I have no objection. Corporal Gomez, your squad members may feel free to remain this evening. For my part, I shall return to the barracks. I will be needed early in the morning at a training session."

"Understood. Thanks for coming, Sanch."

"*De nada.* In truth, I have missed the experience of watching Sergeant Ethan Stark conduct a private war against his superiors and enjoyed seeing how he has adapted to filling the role he once disdained." Sanchez kept his tone bland, only the barest twitch of a smile revealing his words as humor. "Until later."

Sanchez's departure triggered the others, as soldiers lined up to say good-nights and trooped out in small groups. Most, Stark suspected, would walk quickly from headquarters, detouring only long enough to stow their weapons at the barracks, and then head to the nearest bar in the Out-City portion of the Colony so they could extend their partying further into the night. *Well, let 'em. It's not like I wouldn't have enjoyed doing the same once upon a time.*

Murphy, smiling like he'd won the civ Set-for-Life Lottery, departed with Robin Masood still hanging on one arm. Lastly, Lieutenant Mendoza, his son, and Corporal Gomez came forward. The Lieutenant looked around the almost-vacant room, then back at Stark. "This was a good idea, I believe, Sergeant. Most commanders would benefit from real contact with their personnel, instead of staged events at which little actual interaction took place."

"That was part of the idea," Stark admitted. "But I also needed it, for personal reasons. These apes," he gestured to indicate Mendo and Gomez, "mean a lot to me. I'm still one of them."

"As you should be in many ways. I believe you already know those ways in which you can never be one of them again." Stark nodded. "Good night, Sergeant Stark." Lieutenant Mendoza turned slightly. "Sergeant Reynolds."

Vic smiled as if amused by the courtesy. "Where've you been all my career, sir? I could've used a Lieutenant like you."

"Perhaps that is why I was given an entire career of my own to enjoy that rank and not be promoted." The Lieutenant flashed a smile at the humor at his own expense.

"Could be," Stark agreed. "Lieutenant, give me a call later on. There's a lot of stuff I'd still like to talk over with you."

"In a few days, Sergeant?"

"Okay. Don't wait too long." Stark saluted precisely as Lieutenant Mendoza left, his son and Gomez following with nods to Stark, then he stood just outside the room watching his last guests depart.

Vic leaned against the wall nearby, arms crossed, watching Corporal Gomez walk away in conversation with Lieutenant Mendoza. "Now, that is a sight," she declared.

"What?" Stark asked, following her gaze. "What's the big deal?"

"Your Corporal seeking out the company of an officer? You don't think that's unusual?"

Stark laughed briefly. "When you put it that way, yeah. Wonder why she's doing that?"

"Oh, that I know. I saw her during this get-together. Your Corporal was watching you and your reactions to everyone. She saw you listening to Lieutenant Mendoza, treating him like someone you trusted, someone who knew stuff you didn't know, and she obviously took that assessment to heart."

"Huh." Stark watched the mismatched pair, along with Private Mendoza, walk around the corner and vanish from sight. "Gomez was watching me that close?" Vic nodded. "Well, smart soldiers learn from veterans, right? I just gotta tell her to be a little less trusting of me."

Vic's eyebrows rose. "Are you dangerous, Ethan?"

"To the wrong people, yeah, but that's not what I meant. I ain't perfect, Vic. Gomez shouldn't assume everything I do or say is right."

Stark's answer seemed to amuse Reynolds. "Hero-worship is a horrible burden, huh?"

"I am not a hero," Stark replied heavily, his words dropping out with flat emphasis.

"Maybe not, but you get the job done." She canted her head to indicate the hall. "Let me walk you home, soldier?"

"Sure." They headed for his quarters, moving together with the quiet acceptance of old comrades, until Stark broke the silence. "Hey, Vic, you think my old high school yearbook is still on-line?"

"Sure. Nothing ever comes off-line. It just sits there. Of course, we may not be able to access it from here right now. The authorities back home are restricting a lot of comms even though we're supposedly still talking. Why on Earth, or rather, why on the Moon, do you suddenly care about a high school yearbook?"

Stark shrugged. "I want to look up a teacher's name, see if I can find him some day and let him know he did make a difference, even if it did take a few decades for the lessons to work their way through a teenager's know-it-all skull."

Vic raised a questioning eyebrow. "What'd this teacher teach? How to revolt against authority?"

"Yeah. Sort of. He taught American history."

Vic paused, then laughed. "That is sort of the same thing, isn't it?" She paused at the door to Stark's room, gesturing him inside. "You calling it a day?"

Stark stood irresolute for a moment, then shook his head. "Nah. I guess I'll try to plow through some more of that paperwork."

Vic frowned in clear disapproval. "You need sleep, Ethan."

"I know, I know. I'm just sorta restless. I couldn't sleep right now if I tried."

"What's the matter? Are you worried about anything in particular?"

Stark thought, face disturbed, then waved one hand in negation. "No. Oh, I got plenty of worries, but nothing special that I can think of. Maybe I'm just keyed-up from seeing everybody tonight."

"Maybe. Promise me you'll try to sleep in a while?"

"Sure. It ain't like I don't want to get rest, you know." He smiled straight at her. "Thanks for setting up that get-together, Vic. It meant a lot."

"I live to serve, Commander Stark." Reynolds laughed at Stark's sour expression, waving in farewell as she turned away. "Sweet dreams, Ethan."

"Likewise." He settled at his desk, glowering down at the report displayed on his palmtop, then keyed the unit off. *I may be restless, but I'm not restless enough to work on this junk tonight.* Stark looked around the sparsely furnished room, eyes jumping rapidly from point to point, object to object, wondering again about the officers who had lived and worked here in the years since it had been hewn from lunar rock. *They're gonna come back. Try to take us down. I wish they'd try talking instead, but that'd mean admitting they'd screwed up enough to at least partially justify what I did. And the officers I'm used to never admit when they've screwed up.*

Stark slapped his palm unit irritably. "Security Central, this is Stark. How's everything look?"

"Really quiet, Commander. Nothing unusual. Oh, we did have some Private asking after you at one of the sentry posts an hour or so ago, but since it was so late we told him you'd hit the sack, and he should try contacting you tomorrow."

"He? You get his name?"

"Uh, something like Stone, I think."

"Stein?"

"Yeah. I mean, yes, sir. Should we call him?"

"No. You did right. I'll see what he wanted tomorrow. Keep an eye on things."

"Yes, sir."

That should make me feel a lot better. It doesn't. Stark studied his monitor carefully, using the command functions to pull up the security program, which granted access to vid from hallways and rooms throughout the headquarters complex. He sped through the images, outwardly identical rec rooms, halls, and working offices strobing past, almost all empty at this hour, until something caught his attention. Backing up, Stark peered at the vid of a rec room with three occupants. *What-daya know? Corporal Gomez, Lieutenant Mendoza, and Mendo. What're they looking at?* A 3-D projection hovered over one table, Mendo speaking as his hands traced movements along the projection, Gomez watching intently as he did so.

Where's the sound key? I gotta use security override for that, too, huh? I guess that's a smart restriction, but it doesn't look like they're talking about me so I don't figure there's any problem listening in for a minute. Still feels funny, though, like I'm some security officer looking for people making disloyal statements. But that's not what I'm doing. I just wanta know what's got Gomez so interested. Only half-convinced by his own arguments, Stark punched the override. Sound came, matching the vid.

Stark watched as Gomez drew a cup of coffee from the rec room dispenser, then glanced briefly across the corridor. "Hey, Mendo, don't let me forget I dumped my extra gear over there, okay?"

"It should be safe at headquarters, Corporal."

"There's a duffel bag with lots of ammo in there. That kinda thing ain't never safe unless you got a hand locked on it." Gomez sat down at the small table where Mendo waited. She raised one finger, moving it around the terrain map projected over the surface of the table. "I oughta be in bed," she complained, "instead of rehashing some battle a coupla hundred years old. What's this place again?"

"Gettysburg."

"Uh-huh. Same place where that big attack wasted a lot of infantry, right?"

"Yes, Corporal. Pickett's Charge. That happened on the third day of the battle."

"Yeah." Gomez glared at the map. "And they had to launch that big attack 'cause they let the other guys dig in on the good ground the first day. But I don't get it. Why'd they stop? Why didn't these, uh, Confeds take the high ground while they could?"

Mendo cleared his throat, glancing at his father for reassurance before speaking. "It may have been a failure of nerve or simple exhaustion after a long day of battle, but probably was due to overconfidence."

"Gettin' scared, that I understand. But overconfidence?"

"They had beaten the Union Army many times before and believed they had just done so again."

Lieutenant Mendoza nodded approvingly from his seat nearby. "Exactly. Winning too often can be dangerous. Lessons are learned from defeats."

"If you say so, but I still prefer winning." Gomez studied the map again. "So what'd this General, this Roberto Lee, what'd he do to the guys who stopped and let the Union soldiers dig in on the high ground?"

Mendo spread his hands. "Very little. Lee did not command by harsh measures. He was used to commanders who anticipated his wishes."

"Helluva thing to depend on. Sometimes you gotta kick butt to get things done."

Lieutenant Mendoza smiled. "Your Commander Stark, this is how he leads you?"

Stark frowned. He'd been absorbed in the conversation, but the question made him abruptly aware once more of his hidden observation of his friends. He reached to toggle off the audio, then hesitated in spite of his resolve as Gomez replied.

"The *Sargento!* Sometimes. Not always. We usually do things for him because we know he wants it, that's all. Not 'cause we're scared of him. But we also know what would happen if we let him down." She paused, thinking. "Only he wouldn't tell us we'd let him down, he'd say we'd let ourselves down. Nothing we can't do, that's what he tells us. Of course, he always mother-hens us anyways, tries to keep us out of trouble."

"That is the essence of good planning. Commanders must be bold in their concepts and actions, but also wise enough to take counsel of their fears." Stark's hand hovered over the audio cutoff as he concentrated on Lieutenant Mendoza's words.

Gomez frowned in obvious disagreement. "Sergeant Stark, afraid? He ain't afraid of nothing."

"On the contrary," Lieutenant Mendoza corrected softly, his words somehow carrying greater authority despite their gentle tone. "I have seen Commander Stark, and I believe he fears many things, yet he faces these fears and acts nonetheless in the manner he feels most correct."

"The *Sargento* is not a coward," Gomez stated firmly, each word heavily emphasized.

"Of course not. He is extremely brave, though I am certain he would deny that. No, his fears make him a better commander, perhaps a great one someday, for they make him question himself and his actions. This could easily paralyze a lesser soldier, as it has so many commanders in the past, did he not have the moral courage to act despite those fears."

"Well, maybe——" Gomez began.

Stark finally caught himself, appalled that he'd listened to so much, killing vid and audio together so his screen fuzzed into gray emptiness. *Why the hell did I do that? It was too easy. Just listen in like you're a fly on the wall. Find out what people think about you. Learn their little secrets. This is too damn . . . what's the word? Seductive. Yeah. Supposedly they put this vid and audio stuff in so they could run ops if headquarters ever got attacked, but I wonder. What boss wouldn't want to know how their people felt? What boss could resist checking every once in a while? I've got to get some kinda inhibit, put on this to keep me and anyone else who gains access honest. Or maybe just rip the whole damn thing out.*

Stark shut off his monitor completely, fighting down an unclean feeling from his covert spying on his friends. He fidgeted a moment longer, then jerked in guilty reaction as his comm unit buzzed. "Yeah."

"Commander? Security Central. We've got something pretty unusual to report."

"Unusual?" Stark felt the hairs on the back of his neck stiffen automatically.

"Yessir. We got a call from the civs at the spaceport, the ones who normally track the shuttles hauling stuff for the Colony. They wanted to tell us they'd seen some ghost images on one of their scans."

"Ghost images?"

"Something that looked like something might maybe be there, but then it wasn't. Our search gear at the spaceport gets that kind of stuff all the time because of all the electronic warfare going on nearby. You know, echoes of jamming and false signals from surface and orbital units."

"So why'd the civs tell us if that sort of junk shows up a lot?"

Security Central hesitated just enough for the pause to be obvious. "I dunno, Commander."

"The spaceport civs report a lot of this stuff to you?"

"No, sir. They never have before. Not anything. They don't talk to us unless they have to. You know civs."

Stark's eyes narrowed. "So why'd they talk to us this time? Did they say?"

"Uh, yessir. The civ I talked to said his bosses got word from the civs running the Colony to keep us informed of anything unusual they saw. New procedures, he said." Security Central paused again. "Commander, he also asked if there was anything else they could do for us."

"Sounds like that bothers you."

"Well, yeah, sir. It does. I mean, what kind of game are the civs trying to play?"

Stark smiled in self-derision. *Not too long ago I would've wondered the same thing. But I've been working with Campbell long enough to know these civs are mostly sincere even if they don't understand us too well.* "They're not playing any game. They want to help. I know that sounds pretty strange, but civs here are different than we got used to back on the World. I'd guess their boss, the Colony Manager, told them to work with you."

"Okay, Commander." Security Central's skepticism came clearly across the comm circuit. "But if they call us every time they see a scan ghost it won't help much."

"Understood. They don't know how we work, but it's nice they cared enough to call, right?"

"Yessir. You want us to do anything about the report, Commander?"

"I don't. . ." Stark paused, a memory nagging at his brain. *What was that? Some vid. Long time ago. Still a civ myself, I think. Someplace, a harbor or something, where the Navy got beat up bad because everybody saw all these warnings but everybody blew them off. But I can't jerk around my people every time the civs get nervous.*

"Commander?" Security Central prompted. "Like I said, we get this sort of thing all the time on our systems. It's no big deal."

The missing question finally popped into Stark's mind. "Did our mil scans see the ghost the civs warned you about?"

"Uh, I don't know, Commander. Probably not. The civs have different systems. You know, different pulse repetition rates, different frequency hopping algorithms—"

"Okay. Could the civs see something we didn't because something was hiding from the mil systems and reacting a little different to the civ systems?"

A longer hesitation this time. "Maybe. Sir."

Get my people spun up for nothing? Jump at electronic shadows? From civ warnings, yet? Everything Stark knew urged him to blow off the report. *And sometimes everything you know is more dangerous than what you don't know.* "Security, pass a warning to all posts. I want everyone extra alert. Somebody may be trying something."

"Yessir. If you say so."

"And make it a firm warning. None of that 'we're just telling you this 'cause we have to' stuff."

"Yes, Commander."

Stark slumped in his chair, annoyed with himself for overreacting to nervous civs. *They think they're helping when they're just getting in the way. But, hell, at least they're trying. Feels funny working with civs, though.* He sat straighter, then carefully retrieved his rifle from its rack and began painstakingly field stripping it. *Never know when I might need this thing again.* He worked carefully, focusing his mind on each step, forgetting moral ambiguities in his concentration on the task, relaxing slightly as the familiar process occupied his hands and his thoughts. Time passed, unmarked in the room buried beneath the lunar surface except for the soft, red glow of the digital clock counting down human minutes.

The blare of the Red Alert alarm seemed to jolt through Stark's entire body, reverberating from wall to wall before repeating its howl of warning. He slapped the last component of his rifle into place and was strapping on battle armor, moving by instinct, before the alarm had sounded the second time. By the third anxious bleat Stark had his rifle in one hand again while he toggled a comm circuit with another. "What's up?"

"Alert from Sentry Post Four," Security Central reported.

"Why? What happened?"

"We don't know. Could be the sentry triggered it by accident, but they're not answering—"

"Get a reaction force out here as fast as they can move!" Stark roared, heading for his doorway.

"Yes, sir. Sending orders. Wha—?" The sound of gunfire rang through the circuit. "Under attack. Repeat, we are und—"

Vic Reynolds stood outside her room, fully armored, weapon questing as if seeking targets of its own volition. "This a drill?" she demanded.

"No. We've lost at least one Sentry Post and probably Security Central." Stark stared through the blank fields on his Heads-Up Display, portraying nothing outside their own immediate surroundings. "I'm not getting any data relays."

Vic punched her comm unit. "Comms are being jammed now, too. Whoever they are, they took out all the relays already."

"Then I hope that order for a reaction force got out in time." Stark stood, indecisive, as several more staff members popped out of their rooms, only some armored but all carrying weapons. "Vic, what do you think they're after?"

"Whoever's attacking? They want to take down headquarters, and that means the Command Center. Unless it's an even more precise surgical strike, and they're after you personally."

"What if it's not? What if this is just part of an all-out assault?"

"Then we might have already lost, but I'd bet not. A large-scale attack would've generated some warning."

Warning. Stark stiffened. "You mean like scan ghosts?"

Vic shook her head. "More than that. You can hide a few shuttles from scan, but not a full-scale assault. Do you know something about scan ghosts tonight?"

"Yeah. The civs at the spaceport spotted some and warned us."

"You're kidding." Shots echoed down the halls, reverberating from an encounter an indeterminate distance away. "We've got to assume the exits are already blocked. We'll have to fight our way out."

"No." Stark pointed down the corridor. "The Command Center is that way and we haven't heard gunfire from that direction."

"Maybe they've already taken it," Vic argued.

"Then we take it back," Stark snapped. "My job is to command and I can't do that when my comms and information are limited to line of sight." He took off at a fast trot, gathering more headquarters personnel as he went, Vic following last with her weapon trained back the way they'd come.

Warning signals flickered on Stark's HUD even as Vic's weapon slammed several shots down the hallway. "We got company," she called. "Higgens. Fournier," she designated two Privates in battle armor. "Help me hold them."

Stark reached the Command Center, feverishly keying in his access code, then instinctively aiming his weapon straight at the door as it slid open. The armored figure standing on the other side of the door also had a weapon, bringing it up and around to center on Stark. He hesitated for only a microsecond, knowing IFF couldn't do a challenge-and-response in the time he had, then Stark fired, his bullets hurling the other soldier backward. Stark stepped forward, crouched low, aiming and firing in one motion at a second armored soldier guarding the other door, his HUD outlining the figure in bright detail, targeting sight centered on its abdomen. He held his breath, firing with vicious precision. Two bullets gouged holes in the doorframe near Stark, then his own rounds hit, sending Stark's target flailing back and to one side.

"H-how'd you know they were enemy?" someone stuttered. "That looks a lot like our armor."

Stark glanced over at Jill Tanaka, crowding close behind. "They were trying to kill me. That was all the ID I needed." He eased cautiously farther into the Command Center, rifle barrel questing for targets, then stood and waved the others forward. "Get in here. See if there's anybody we can help."

"What do you mean?" Tanaka dashed forward, then cursed as she caught sight of the night watch-standers slumped over their duty stations or huddled against the walls, bright pools of blood spreading around them. "Those bastards."

"They paid. Have somebody check for survivors. Get some sentries posted to guard that other entrance." He watched, eyes fierce, as Reynolds and her two Privates backed into the room, firing as they came. "Vic, you hold this door."

"Roger." Higgens jerked a couple of times, his body sliding back along the floor under the impacts. "Damn. Fournier, aim your shots and keep your head down!"

Stark pivoted, one finger singling out another soldier. "Corporal Abrakis, see if you can help Higgens." The finger shifted. "Sergeant Tanaka, get comms going in here."

"Roger," she acknowledged. "Sergeant Tran, get on it. We're being jammed, Commander—"

"I know. Get through it." The lights flickered, steadied, then died. Emergency lights came to life, glowing eerily. "How much of this stuff can run on backup power?"

"A few terminals," Sergeant Tran confirmed. "I will do my best, Commander."

Vic fired several more shots, each round aimed with cool deliberation, then halted. "I think that's the last of this bunch."

"How many were there?" Stark demanded.

"Four. That's how many we hit, anyway. Maybe five, if I nailed one in the corridor."

"That's all? We're dealing with professionals, Vic."

"No kidding. Hold here, stay alert," Reynolds barked at Fournier, then eased inside, slapping the control panel to keep the door from sealing behind her. "How many others are there? Where are they?"

Tanaka slammed her palm onto her console in frustration. "I don't know. Most of our sensors are inactive and internal comms are blocked, but we can't locate any physical damage. They must have inserted a worm into the system from one of the security stations."

"Then get the damn worm killed! We need to know what's going on out there!"

"I'm trying, dammit! Guerrero, try to build some workarounds while the watchdogs are hunting down that worm. Kloster, put together a manual picture from whatever you can pick up."

Stark glared, his frustration easy to see. "Vic, I'm supposed to be giving orders, and I can't."

"Then we'll have to do what we can." She raised her weapon. "At least we're good at it."

"Hey!" Sergeant Tran suddenly shouted, drawing nervous rifle barrels his way. "Don't shoot, dammit. Jill, these guys hitting us have got to be using their own systems for coordination."

"Yeah," Sergeant Tanaka agreed tartly. "So?"

"So we've got a couple of sets of their battle armor in here. Maybe we can use it to tap into their comms until we get our own working."

"Maybe we can. Good idea." Tanaka knelt next to one of the dead enemy soldiers, pulling off the helmet. Dark hair rasped against the Command Center floor as the head flopped back, eyes staring upward, still fixed on the target they'd seen when death came. "Commander?"

"What?"

"This *is* American battle armor."

"That's not our . . ." Stark's voice trailed off as he carefully looked at the equipment. "It is, isn't it? What is that, the new Mark V suits?"

"Looks like it. They didn't even send any Mark Vs up with Third Division because they supposedly weren't available."

Stark stared at the dark-haired soldier lying on the floor, the soldier who'd tried to kill him and died in the attempt. *Are we fighting*

Americans? He gazed around at the bodies of the watch-standers. *Did other Americans slaughter these soldiers?* "Vic."

She was already kneeling next to the body, studying it intently, then gestured at its shoulder. "Whoever they are, and wherever they got this armor, they're not American soldiers. The dogtag isn't where it should be."

Stark let out a breath he hadn't known he was holding. Every American soldier had what was still called a dogtag embedded near the left shoulder, carrying critical identity and medical information. "Thanks."

"I needed to know, too, Ethan."

Huddling with several other soldiers, Tanaka and Tran ran cables, scanned screens, and pulled other pieces of armor off the two bodies to plug them in as well in an effort to jury-rig a backdoor into the enemy comms. "Okay, Commander. We've got something. Apparently the worm the raiders inserted into our systems is not only blocking us, it's also hijacking our systems to relay the enemy comms. The worm's security subroutine is good, though. It keeps trying to kill our intrusions. We can get fragmentary vid, but only for one observer. I don't even know if it'll be real-time or Tactical records of recent activity, and it's going to keep shifting as the enemy worm figures out what we're doing and we have to tap into another data stream."

"Fine. How do I call it up?" Stark followed Tanaka's directions hastily, then triggered the vid feed.

Remote view, the vid from the spy tap grainy and dim. A big, elaborately furnished room. The Commanding General's suite. Vid shaking slightly as a weapon pumped rounds into the large bed, tearing smoking holes in the soft covers and revealing the absence of any occupant. Spinning now, moving rapidly, in the hall where the shocked face of one of the gardeners hung frozen for a bare moment before bullets hurled him back against the nearest wall. Disconnect. Gray static blurring in a chaotic mass, then the picture cleared on another enemy soldier's view.

A hall in the headquarters complex, the vid jerking in a manner that said the soldier was jogging rapidly. Unfamiliar symbology cluttered the HUD, then unmistakable threat warnings popped up. Stark watched, helpless, as a door slid open, the enemy soldier's weapon and combat system aiming at the gap. Brief glimpse of a woman staring wide-eyed, fancy civ hair marking her as alien to military headquarters, a vague figure barely visible over her shoulder bringing a weapon around, mouth wide open in a scream of warning. *Robin Masood? For the love of God, duck!* Vid broke into a million shards of static, then cleared into another view as Stark slammed a fist on his console in frustration.

"What happened?" Vic demanded.

"I don't know." The new view looked over the hunched shoulders of several other suits of battle armor. This raiding party seemed huddled behind a corner. Visible on the floor ahead were two bodies in the Mark V armor. Threat symbology snapped to life as several rounds tore small chunks of rock out of the corner, then the two nearest enemy soldiers leaned forward to fire, hurling bullets down the hallway around the corner. Vid bounced dizzingly as Stark's unwitting host jumped into motion, clearing the corner and charging down the hall, firing rapidly at a few figures just visible behind a doorway. *Is that Gomez? That might be the rec room she was in, so the other two would be the Mendozas.* The enemy HUD tracked the incoming fire, painting frantic warnings the soldier couldn't react to fast enough, then the view spun wildly up and down, back and forth, as bullets hit home. Vid shattered again, then went black. "Jill, I lost it."

"Sorry." She punched at her console frantically, then shook her head. 'The enemy worm ID'd the outfits we were using to gain access for our intrusion and froze them out."

"Damn."

"Ethan." Vic gestured angrily toward him. "What'd you see?"

"I tagged three groups of raiders, I think. One was chewing up the Commanding General's suite."

"There's nobody there."

"One of the gardeners was." Vic's eyes flared with fury at the obvious implication. "He didn't have a chance to fight, not that it would've made a difference, I guess. The second group was in some hallway. I'm pretty sure I saw Robin Masood and maybe Murphy. I dunno what happened to them." Stark had to pause a moment, getting his voice under control. "Then one more group, pinned down behind a corner. They were trying to get past some resistance. Gomez, I think, with the two Mendozas."

Vic thought for only a moment, then shook her head. "Gomez and the others can't have much ammo. Did Lieutenant Mendoza even have a weapon?"

"No, but he was shooting, if it was him. Probably Gomez's sidearm."

"Not enough weapons. Very little ammo. How long can they hold a hallway against a group of these guys?"

"I dunno." Memory of Stark's earlier eavesdropping came back. "She had extra ammo. But it's across the hall from them."

"How do you—?" Vic broke off as Stark's face closed down into stubborn refusal. "Never mind. Can they reach it?"

Stark remembered the enemy soldiers firing down the wide headquarters hallway, fast and accurate, toward the unarmored soldiers huddled behind the doorway. "Maybe. If somebody doesn't mind dying trying to get to it." He slammed one fist furiously into the other palm. "That vid didn't help. Just gave me enough information to scare the hell out of me."

"You couldn't have known that until you tried it," Vic reminded him. "At least we know parts of the attack are being held up."

"Yeah." *Held up by the lives of my friends. Don't think about Murphy and Robin. Whatever happened has happened, maybe even before I saw it. Nothing you can do right now. How long will Gomez and Mendo and his dad last? The raiders will push them hard. Holding them off will mean firing a lot. Pretty soon, no more ammo. Then they'll be toast. Be smart enough to run, Anita.* Even as Stark made that last, prayerful wish, he knew Corporal Gomez wouldn't run while she could still fight.

"I've got a sensor active," one of the watch-standers reported, face fixed with concentration as he scanned his data. "No. Dead again. It recorded firing in Corridor Six Delta before I lost it."

"Where in Six Delta?" Tanaka demanded. "Narrow it down."

"I can't, Sergeant! It was echoing. Without the main sensor grid I couldn't get a fix."

"Six Delta." Stark studied the map of the headquarters complex as Corporal Kloster manually placed a threat symbol in that corridor. "So maybe we have firing here, here, or here. Maybe.

What're they after, Vic? Just this place, or something else?"

She stared intently, then shook her head. "I can't tell. All the corridors intersect, and some of the enemy groups ran into our people before they reached where they were going. They already nailed Security Central and the Commanding General's suite. I'd guess this is the last one of their main objectives."

"Yeah. And anybody who hasn't run into our people oughta be here by now." He switched circuits, calling the sentry in the corridor outside. "Fournier, you see or hear anything?"

"No, sir. Real quiet, except for a lot of echoes. I don't—hey! Look out!"

The thunder of firing reached through the door as Stark called up vid from Fournier's battle armor, catching a brief glimpse of armored foes almost hidden by the threat symbology streaming from them toward the sentry. Then the vid died as Private Fournier did. "Everybody get down! "Vic, main door."

"Got it." She was already palming the door closed, shutting off a swarm of bullets that battered against the barrier like angry hornets, then yanked a grenade from her belt, crouching next to the doorway. Stark brought his weapon around smoothly, kneeling behind the nearest console to steady his aim on the entrance. Vic waited a moment, roughly gauging the timing, then activated her grenade, holding up first one, then two, then three fingers. On the third, Vic triggered the door open, then shut. As it bobbled open half a meter before halting to slam back, she tossed the grenade through the gap, then shoved herself away to escape the flurry of shots crashing through the temporary access.

By the time the rumble of the grenade's detonation died, Vic was back near Stark, also in firing position. A few moments later, the door shivered, light suddenly appearing on all four sides as an explosive strip tore it free, then fell inward with slow majesty under Luna's weak tug. Wood splinters from the ornate paneling on the outside of the door spun dreamily through the air, shaking as they flew from the shockwaves of bullets ripping past them into the Command Center.

Stark fired, almost continuous short bursts, vaguely aware of Vic doing the same. He caught momentary glimpses of targets being hit and falling back, his HUD painting a chaotic picture of fragmentary symbology as its picture shifted too rapidly to follow. *They're coming in through one door even though they know we've got it covered. Dumb move. Desperate move. They must be really pushing their timeline. How many of 'em this time? Fournier took out some. The grenade took out more. How many left?* The console next to Stark shrieked in complaint as answering fire slammed into it. The emergency lighting rippled again, then steadied.

An object flew into the room, arcing too high, a grenade thrown by someone not experienced enough in lunar gravity. The grenade bounced off the ceiling, angling down toward Vic, who released her trigger just long enough to swing her right arm up and around and slap the deadly sphere back toward the door. It detonated, spraying shrapnel both outside the room and in. Stark ducked beneath his console, feeling it shudder as metal impacted it, then surged up again to fire.

"Ethan. Hold it. Incoming fire's stopped." He paused, finger poised over his trigger, as Vic cautiously scuttled forward, coming to rest against the side wall near the gapping doorway, her rifle ready. "What do you think?"

"Maybe they're all down, but I could use some reassurance."

"Right." Vic dropped two grenades into her hand, hooking fingers from the other hand to activate both, then paused, counting. Her hand came forward, flicking to right and left in one smooth gesture before she yanked herself back away from the door. "Fire in the hole."

"Watch it," Stark added to the other personnel in the Command Center, ducking behind his console once again as the grenades detonated in a twin thunderclap in the hall. He waited, rifle lined up on the doorway, as Vic eased forward again, sticking one finger gingerly around the edge, the fiber-optic camera in the fingertip scanning for movement.

"All the ones I can see are dead," Vic reported.

"What about the ones you can't see?"

"I know. Look's like we took out this group, though."

"Anybody else coming?"

Her finger tip wriggled in search, then paused. "Nobody visible. Ethan, how are we going to secure this doorway now?"

"Hey, you guys," Stark gestured to the two nearest soldiers. "Pick up that door and prop it back in place. You got anything that'll hold it there?"

"We got duct tape," one offered.

"That's better than nothing. See how well you can fasten the thing to the walls again. Sergeant Tanaka, any progress on the sensors or comms?"

"No. The damn worm's got everything blocked." She frowned in thought. "Maybe the worm's blocking access just from our consoles, though. Maybe if we tapped into the remote feeds directly . . . Vreeland, you know exactly where the feeds are located?"

"Sure do," Corporal Vreeland declared, enthusiasm lighting his face. "The main bundle is right outside here, in the hall." He pointed out the secondary entrance, where two Privates stood nervous watch.

"Okay, Vreeland. Let's get them." Tanaka dashed forward, pulling the Corporal with her.

It took a moment for Stark to realize what Tanaka was doing, a moment to understand that for all her time on the Moon, she'd been serving in headquarters, not on the front lines where a moment of carelessness or a simple mistake could cost a life in the time it took enemy systems to register a target and fire. Vic, occupied guarding the other entrance, understood a bare instant after Stark did, turning to yell even as Stark shouted a warning. "Tanaka! Not out the door!"

Jill Tanaka spun at the warning, sudden knowledge of her error draining blood from her face, grabbing at Vreeland to yank them both back inside. The maneuver came too late, as the hall erupted with the crash of shots, bullets impacting all around the door area. Tanaka, halfway inside, went flying sideways as the enemy fire slammed into her, her hand still locked on Vreeland even as he jerked in time to hits on his body.

The Privates on guard fired frantically, one hosing down the hall on full automatic until Stark reached him and slapped his helmet. "Aim, damn it! How many are there?"

"I think there were just a couple," the other sentry reported, her voice shaking. "I'm pretty sure we got 'em both."

"Assume you didn't and assume there's more. We're in combat, people! Guard yourselves from the hallways!" Stark stared down where a couple of personnel were frantically trying to apply medical aid to Tanaka and Vreeland, made a motion to join them, then walked slowly back to his useless command console. *Do my job. Let them do theirs. I can't do anything more for the wounded than they can, except delay treatment if I insist on horning in.*

Vic's gaze met his, her eyes angry and frustrated. "Ethan, somebody's going to pay a big price for this," she vowed, her tone deceptively soft.

"Oh, yeah. One helluva big price. If we survive to make 'em pay." He looked from one entrance to another, face bleak. "They didn't expect to run into combat troops, Vic. They thought they'd be facing nothing but headquarters types without battle experience."

"You're probably right. Nice to know we surprised them, too."

Waiting had never been easy. Not when leading a squad. Not now with a lot more soldiers' fates riding on his decisions. Stark's hands moved restlessly, as if seeking some task, something he could do right now while others fought and died, then clenched in frustration. He glared at his blank, useless, command display. "I oughta be out there," he whispered. "Trying to relieve Gomez."

"You don't even know for sure where they are," Vic stated softly, drawing a surprised reaction from Stark. "Didn't know you transmitted that, huh? This is the hard part, Commander. Keeping yourself out of the action so you can command."

"It doesn't feel right."

"I know. I almost wish they'd hit the Command Center again so I'd feel useful."

"I'm not that desperate." Vic's words jabbed at his conscience, bringing up thoughts he'd tried to suppress. "How're the wounded?" Stark demanded of his makeshift medics.

"Tanaka's dead," Corporal Guerrero reported shakily. "We couldn't save her. I think Vreeland will make it."

"Damn." Stark brought a tightly clenched fist down on the panel before him.

"Commander?" Sergeant Tran gestured urgently. "The worm's been killed. We've got internal scan again."

"Thank God." *Why couldn't that have happened a couple of minutes ago, before Tanaka ran to her death? Why? Is anybody ever gonna figure out the answer to that kind of question?* Stark watched as the display flared to life, raising his hand to stab at the glowing symbology. "Vic, if I'm reading this right, if there's not another worm screwing up the picture, our own people are fighting their way in from the entrances."

"Yes. That's Taylor's company. They're rapid reaction for this area. Over here's . . . who the hell is that?"

"Scratch force," Stark decided. "Everybody who could get here fast." He clenched a fist in sudden elation. "Sanchez is in charge of 'em. He must have still been pretty close when the alarm sounded. Tran, we got internal comms yet? Yeah? Sanch, this is Stark."

"Roger." The response was weaker than it should be and riddled with static, but clear enough to be unmistakable. "Where are you?"

"The Command Center. We're holding it. We've got internal scan again. Can you tap in?"

"Wait. Ah. I have it. Shunting it down to my personnel. This will simplify our counterattack."

"Be careful, Sanchez," Reynolds cautioned. "These guys know

what they're doing. We've taken a lot of casualties."

"Understood. We won't take unnecessary chances."

"Is anything going down anywhere else, Sanch?" Stark demanded.

"Negative. The perimeter is quiet and all other military sectors are on full alert, but report no activity. The Colony leaders have offered any assistance we require."

Vic smiled sardonically. "Guess they've decided we're going to win."

Before Stark could reply, Sanchez did. "Sergeant Reynolds, the civilians made the offer as soon as they were aware of the attack."

Stark nodded to Vic, enjoying the brief look of surprise on her face. "Thanks, Sanch. Vic, bring Taylor up to date while I try to see what's going on."

As Reynolds quickly notified Taylor and her company of the internal scan, Stark fumbled with his display, cursing as he tried to pull up vid. "I think Gomez and the Mendozas were in this area, and we've got a gap in our scan there where somebody's still doing short-range jamming. Here. Look." The picture wavered, bands of random pixels running through it as the remaining enemy soldiers tried to jam signals in their area. It was the same hall Stark had observed before, but seen from the other end. More battle armored bodies than he remembered, all splayed short of the doorway where Gomez and the Mendozas had made their stand. "They're still there, Vic. They're still there."

Reynolds stared in disbelief. "Amazing. How'd their ammo last?"

"I dunno. It's gotta be almost gone. Where's Sanch?" Stark scanned the display, an empty space growing inside him. "It's gonna take him a while to get there. Isn't it?" *So close. So damn close.*

"Yeah," Vic agreed, frustration edging back into her voice. "Too long. The raiders have some guards at the other end of that hall they're in. Bet on it."

Bloody grass, waving before Stark's eyes in the red glow of the emergency lighting, intermingling with the multicolored patterns enemy jamming cast across the vid. Remembrance of help too far away and too late. Vid of the hallway trembled, steadied, then went back into its wavering dance. Stark eyed the figures in the doorway, then quickly tried to focus closer on them. "They're arguing. Why are they arguing?" Gomez had her hand up, pointing down and then across the hall, then back at herself. Lieutenant Mendoza shook his head, froze Gomez with a gesture, touched his son's shoulder. A moment later, the Lieutenant was gone. Stark watched, helpless, as Lieutenant Mendoza launched himself across the gaping hallway, body flat to minimize his exposure. Watched as the Lieutenant's body seemed to rock in midflight from impacts as the raiders poured fire down the hallway. "Ah, hell," he finally whispered, as momentum carried the Lieutenant on into the room his leap had aimed for.

Stark couldn't get audio from the rec room, but he could see Gomez firing and screaming in anger as she tried to cover the Lieutenant's movement. Then an object flew back across the hall, landing at her feet, and the Corporal dumped out ammunition clips, their shapes unmistakable even in the ragged vid, and began hastily reloading her weapon.

The raiders charged, figuring out moments too late why the Lieutenant had made his move. Gomez and Mendo cut the leading attackers down, a hail of bullets flaying chips from the rock walls, then vid blanked. "What the hell happened?" Stark shouted.

Vic punched her own panel repeatedly, shaking her head. "No response from the vid camera. It must have been hit by a stray round." She faced Stark squarely. "Don't worry. We saw what we needed to see. They'll make it."

Stark shook his head as if in denial of her words. "Two of them will. How bad did the Lieutenant get hit?"

"We won't know until Sanchez gets there. Lieutenant Mendoza did what he had to do, Ethan."

"I know that."

Vic nodded, clasped Stark's arm for a moment, then slumped back as if overcome with weariness. "Bad as it's been, I think we've won this one, Ethan. Any attacker still in headquarters is trapped, just like the ones Gomez has pinned down."

"Trapped animals can be real vicious, Vic. How can we be sure one last group won't try a real kamikaze on us here?"

"We can't. But maybe we can find out for sure who's still out there and where they were." Vic fumbled futilely at her console before turning to Tran. "Is there any system history for the last half-hour?"

"Uh, yeah. Fragmentary. The worm must have been shredding the system files when we axed it. Here it is."

"Look, Ethan." Now Vic's finger traced multiple paths. "They overran the sentry posts first."

"No warnings," Stark noted angrily, "except from Post Four."

"No. We'll have to find out why. Then some headed for the Command Center, some for Security Central, and some hit the Commanding General's suite."

Stark nodded grimly. "I saw part of that."

"Right." She indicated a motionless symbol. "Tran, can we get vid of this?"

"Yes. Got it."

The figure sitting against the wall seemed asleep, head hanging down on his chest, but the blood streaking his arms and chest told another story. "Damn," Stark breathed. "The gardener. I should have insisted on teaching those poor apes how to fight."

"It wouldn't have done that one much good if you did," Reynolds commented bitterly. "Okay, from there they headed toward . . . why that way?"

Stark indicated another section. "Rendezvous. They were gonna meet up with another group. These guys. But they stopped moving."

"Yeah. Let's find out why."

It took Stark a moment to grasp the picture even after it steadied. "Oh, God. That's Murphy. I did see him. He's down."

Vic nodded, adjusting the controls as quickly as her fingers could fly. "Scan says he's still alive. Barely. He's lying on something. No, someone. Protecting him?"

"Protecting her," Stark advised, his tone bleak. "That's his girl. See the hair?"

"Robin?" Vic glanced up, then down at the readouts again. "She's dead."

"You sure?"

"No question." Reynolds looked up, face drawn. "So are the attackers. Ethan, Murphy took out six of them."

"Yeah. He must have gone berserker when she got hit." Stark fought off a tight feeling in his chest that threatened to choke him.

"Why in God's name . . . get some medical help to him. Can we get a medic there?"

"I'll go myself, if I have to. Taylor? Your people are closest to this location. We've got a soldier down, badly wounded, scan shows no threat activity between you and him."

"Roger. I'll send a squad there on the double with our medic. Be advised we're still hearing firing off to our right."

"Your right?" Vic questioned, looking at the display. "No problem. Sergeant Sanchez is dealing with an enemy force in that area."

"He gonna push 'em into me?" Taylor demanded.

"Negative. The enemy is trapped between Sanchez and another friendly force. They won't be going anywhere."

"Okay. My medic's on the way. I'll keep a manual sweep going just in case anybody's hiding somehow."

"Good idea," Vic approved. "We still don't know how they got in here without being spotted."

Stark broke in, speaking with deliberate control. "Sanch, Corporal Gomez needs your help fast. They've taken casualties."

"Understood," Sanchez replied with apparent calm. "We are overrunning the rear guard for that location now. Corporal Gomez will be relieved momentarily."

"Thanks, Sanch. I owe you another." Stark let his hands fall limply, then looked over at Reynolds. "What else, Vic? What else should we be doin'? We're missing somethin'." *A ghost.* Stark stared upward, trying to divert his mind from recent tragedy, squinting as if he could see through the rock ceiling to space above. "There's gotta be a pickup out there, Vic. A shuttle hangin' around to drop in again and pull these guys out. Tanaka—" He bit off the name, glaring at nothing for a moment. "Tran. Call the orbital defenses. Tell them there's a shuttle out there we haven't detected. They've got to be spoofing our sensors, but the civs spotted it for a sec. Tell our people to do a manual scan and coordinate it with the civ scans. I want that shuttle."

"Yes, Commander."

"And tell Wiseman. One of our armed shuttles might be able to nail it."

"Ethan."

He stared at her, emotions running riot inside. "What?"

"We want prisoners." Stark looked away. "Ethan, we need prisoners. To interrogate. To find out exactly who launched this attack."

"Yeah. And get even with 'em. Everybody, listen up. I need some prisoners."

"These guys ain't surrendering, Stark!"

"I know. See what you can do." He glanced at Vic. "Happy?"

She shook her head. "I can't remember happy, Ethan. Not right now."

Stark hesitated another moment, then called up vid from Sanchez's armor. Smoothly gliding down a hall, a half-dozen armored figures just ahead, their backs overlain with comfortingly friendly symbology. Stopping. Kneeling, rifles aimed down the hall, where a cluster of enemy symbology displayed raiders firing around the next corner, still oblivious to the trap closing on them. Sanchez's vid shifted as he stood, then Stark heard him call out over his suit's external speaker. "Surrender immediately!" Then the vid dropped as Sanchez did, avoiding a wave of incoming bullets, the soldiers in front of him firing back, pausing as the enemy fire broke off, then leaping to their feet and charging forward. "They are trying to break out!" Sanchez commanded his troops. "Keep on them."

The end of the hall, a corner littered with expended ammunition clips and cluttered with bodies in Mark V armor, then around the corner, Stark fighting dizziness as he held on to Sanchez's vid picture. Over more bodies, a couple of them still dropping to the floor with nightmare slowness in the low gravity. Stopping, where one remaining figure stood, hands high, weaving slightly, bright red blood spreading slowly down its leg from a jagged tear in the armor near one hip. On the other side of the prisoner Corporal Gomez was visible, her weapon lined up, face rigid. Stark toggled a comm circuit as fast as he could, appropriating Sanchez's external speaker. "Corporal Gomez! Lower your weapon. Now."

She jerked in reaction, staring past the enemy soldier, then slowly brought the weapon barrel down.

"You believe she would have killed the prisoner?" Sanchez asked Stark.

"Sanch, I would've been real tempted in her place. Where's Private Mendoza?"

Sanchez repeated the question to Gomez, who pointed wordlessly to the room where Lieutenant Mendoza's leap had ended.

"Get a medic in there, Sanch," Stark urged.

"Of course." Sanchez raised one hand, a finger singling out another soldier and beckoning her forward. "In there, please. There are wounded. Commander Stark, we appear to have eliminated all resistance in this area of the headquarters complex."

"Roger. Taylor's company is running sweeps through the rest of headquarters, but it looks like we nailed all of 'em." Stark's voice sounded thin even to himself. "I'm coming down there. Just hold on a sec." Stark turned to Vic, fighting down another dark vision. "It's all over. I'm not needed here now." The words came out as a half-question, directed her way.

Reynolds nodded quickly. "Right. Go ahead, Ethan. I'll let you know if there's anything else."

Stark hesitated, one foot angling toward the door. "Murphy? They get to him in time?"

"They got to him. They don't know whether or not it'll be in time yet. The human body can only take so much punishment."

"I know." He ran, yanking aside the battered barrier, duct tape falling away in graceful, gentle twists and turns like some sort of clumsy confetti. The halls were oddly hushed now, without the din of battle echoing, and without the normal sounds of business being conducted by the men and women who lived and worked here. Stark reached the area where Sanchez waited, his helmet unsealed, his face emotionless. Gomez stood slumped, back against the wall, her rifle trailing barrel-down from one hand, her face bleak. "Anita. You okay?"

"*Sí, Sargento.*"

"Good Lord." Stark stared at the armored bodies lying about. In the rush of action, he hadn't bothered tallying symbology for dead enemies. Now he found himself shaking his head in wonder. "You did this?"

"Me an' Mendo, and his dad. The Lieutenant." Something about the way she said the last two words gave them a grim finality.

"The medic still in there? With Mendo and his dad?"

Gomez, her eyes hooded, jerked her head in negation. "No. Not anymore. The medic couldn't help. That Lieutenant, he saved us, *Sargento.*"

Stark stared wordlessly at the epitaph, then walked silently to gaze into the room where Mendo knelt next to his father, heedless of the pool of blood around him. Strange, yet oddly right, that tears fell so slowly on the Moon, as if only here could human grief slow time. Stark retreated silently until he stood beside Gomez and Sanchez once more. "Damn. Damn it all."

The words hung there a moment, then Sanchez began speaking quietly, the elegant phrases in strange contrast to his battle armor and ready weapon. "This evening there was no glory left, but the terror of the broken flesh, which had been our own men, carried past us to their homes.' "

Stark closed his own eyes briefly. "Sounds like you're quoting somebody, Sanch."

"Yes. An Englishman named Lawrence."

"A Brit, huh? Which war he fight in?"

"The First World War."

"I remember Mendo talkin' about that war." *Funny the things I don't know about Sanch even after fighting beside him for years. Funny how much we all keep inside.* "That war sounded even stupider than the wars we've fought." A moment more of brooding, then Stark turned to Corporal Gomez. "We'll make sure Mendo's got privacy, Anita. As much as he needs."

"*Sí.* That was one good officer, *Sargento.*"

"Yeah."

"Never thought I'd meet one like that. I never thought I'd care when one got nailed. I was gonna try to go. Me. Get the extra ammo we needed." The words spilled out rapidly, as if they had been held in by great effort. "The Lieutenant said no. He said a commander had to . . . had to choose the right person for a job. Said I was the best fighter, and Mendo was good, too. Then he said somethin' to Mendo, and he was gone. I couldn't stop him. Where are we gonna find another officer like that, *Sargento?*"

"Exactly like that? I dunno. But we're gonna need more officers like him, Anita. What about you?"

"Huh?" Gomez looked up in disbelief. "*Sargento*, I ain't good enough for that. I sure ain't as good as he was."

"You could be. At least you could try."

She glanced back to the room where Mendo grieved. "I guess, maybe."

"Think about it. How'd you realize these guys were enemy before they nailed you, anyway?"

"That's that Mark V armor, *Sargento*. I seen vid of it in a lecture, once. I knew we didn't have none."

"You saw it once." Stark exchanged a glance with Sanchez, who had been unable to prevent a brief but unmistakably impressed expression from flowing across his face, then focused on the dead enemy again, shaking his head. "Why'd they keep trying to come down here? Why not backtrack and take another route? It would have been easy to bypass this spot."

Sanchez followed Stark's gaze. "I can only guess, but I believe we will find their Tacticals mandated this approach, probably to ensure multiple attack routes were followed and any defenders such as your Corporal's group were tied down."

"That's right," Gomez agreed forcefully. "If they'd pulled back, we coulda just shifted to cover the next hallway. They couldn't move faster than us 'cause we had the, uh, interior lines of communication."

"Interior lines?" Stark stared at his Corporal again. "Where'd you learn that phrase, Anita? Another vid lecture?"

She took a deep breath, then smiled tightly. "No. From the Lieutenant. Like the North at Gettysburg, right?"

"I guess." Stark shook his head in disbelief, then slapped Gomez's upper arm. "You did great. You need time off now."

"No, *Sargento*. No. I don't need time to sit around thinking. I don't want to. Got a job to do."

"Yeah. Okay." He looked over at Sanchez meaningfully. "I'm sure you'll be kept busy. But don't forget the chaplains. And if you need some time to react, you let us know. *¿Comprendo?*"

"*Sí.*" She straightened, bringing her rifle up to port arms and facing the room where Lieutenant Mendoza lay. "Right now, I gotta do some sentry duty."

"One of Sanchez's people can handle that."

"No. My job. I owe it."

"Understood. Sanch, thanks for getting here."

Sergeant Sanchez shrugged noncommittally, even as the regular lighting came back to life, painfully bright after the diminished glow of the emergency lights. "I was not far away when the alarm sounded, and was able to borrow some armor."

"Lucky for us. Go ahead and hand this area over to Taylor's people and let your soldiers go. I've got some more stuff to do now, but I'll see you around."

"Certainly."

Sanchez began issuing orders to his soldiers as Stark strode away, trying to focus on the next task and not think of the friendly casualty count. "Vic. Anything happening?"

"Just running a final sweep for any lurkers. I've got Campbell standing by for you."

"Patch him in. Campbell?"

"Yes." The Colony Manager sounded a bit breathless, as if he had been the one recently engaged in combat. "Sergeant Reynolds told me everything is okay, now."

"That's right. Thanks for standing by us."

"Standing by you, and with you, is no longer an option, Sergeant Stark. We're in this together."

"Damn straight." Together. Mil and civs. *Maybe something good is gonna come from this whole mess.* "Gotta go. We're still picking up pieces, but everything's secure. I'll give you a full report later." Stark switched circuits again. "Vic? Anything else?"

"No, just—wait. Ah-hah. Wiseman found your shuttle."

Stark tensed. "Did she nail it?"

"Not yet. It's running like a bat out of hell. Never seen a shuttle with that kind of moves."

"Something special. Nice to know we rated the best, isn't it?"

"I could have done without that compliment," Vic stated bitterly. "I've got a prisoner count for you."

"How many?" Stark asked with forced mildness.

"Three. We count thirty-seven dead."

"So it was a platoon-strength raid." About the number of combat-loaded troops a single shuttle could carry. "Any wounded?"

"Those three *are* the wounded."

Only three, out of an attack force totaling forty. Not mercenaries, then, not that Stark had thought they were. Mercs didn't fight to the death, not when surrender was a realistic option. "Where are they?"

"Stacey Yurivan came in with Taylor's company. She's got the prisoners in this conference room." A symbol popped up on Stark's HUD, directing him to the location. "You sure you want to see them right now?"

"Yeah, I'm sure. I can handle it." Stark closed his thoughts down, blocking out emotion, focusing solely on procedure, then walked into the room.

Two fire teams from Taylor's company stood against the walls, weapons at ready, faces hard and angry. The prisoners, two men and one woman, stood rigidly erect despite their hands being bound behind them. Stripped of battle armor, their uniforms displayed no sign of rank or nationality. Stark eyed them coldly, not letting his fury show. "Who sent you?" Their eyes didn't even flicker in response to the question. "Where'd you get the latest American equipment?" Still no response. Stark singled out a tall, blond male with a huge bruise marring the left side of his face. "Where are you from?" Silence.

Whoever they are, they're pros, Stark thought bleakly. Professional soldiers, and very well-trained ones. *Not Americans, though.* Even without the evidence of the missing dogtags, they looked too much alike, carrying the similarity of nationalities that most countries still reflected. Only an American unit, drawn from generation upon generation of immigrants from everywhere on Earth, resembled all the peoples of the planet in its polyglot makeup. Some other country's military had provided these soldiers, hiring them out for the money it would bring and whatever American gratitude came with it.

"Okay. Have it your way." Stark turned to Stacey Yurivan, standing nearby with a wolf-snarl fixed on her face. She'd gotten to be pretty good friends with Jill Tanaka, he remembered. "Interrogate them."

Yurivan's snarl took on a hint of pleasure. "Will do."

Her words set off an alarm in Stark's mind. "Interrogate" could mean many things, many illegal and most of them painful. *So what? Make them hurt*, a voice in the back of his head pleaded. He fought it down with a savage shake of his head. "Keep it legal, Stacey. You're still an American soldier."

Her eyes flashed defiance. "These slime aren't."

He stepped close, matching her gaze. "They're soldiers. They did their job. These particular guys didn't commit any atrocities that I know of. Do you? Then treat them like we want our own people treated if they get captured in the future."

Stacey didn't flinch. "Nobody needs to know what happens to these."

"I'll know." Stark let the two words hang there between them, a challenge and a reminder, as Yurivan held her glare a few seconds longer.

"All right," she finally spat. "It'll be legal, but," she added with another glare full of promise at the prisoners, "just barely."

Stark stepped close enough to speak softly. "Scare them all you want, but remember, we want them to talk. If we get them to spill their guts we can do a lot of damage to whoever sent them here."

"Yeah." Her teeth showed in something that wasn't a smile. "Yes, sir," she added louder. "I'll do that."

Stark fought down a grim smile as her words brought a glimmer of anxiety to the otherwise stoic faces of the prisoners. *Let them guess what I whispered to her. A little fear of God and Stacey Yurivan might get some results.* "Let me know how it goes." The walls of the headquarters complex still felt alien as he walked back to the Command Center, passing small groups of soldiers with expressions of anger and shock on their faces. "Get to work, people," Stark commanded. "We need to clean this place up. Fix the damage. Get ready to get even." Heads nodded, hands saluted, and the world went on.

Vic awaited him in the Command Center, sitting in one corner, her face expressionless. "The shuttle got away. Wise-man couldn't catch it before it got far enough out to be covered by the big warships. She said she singed its tail-feathers, but that's all."

"That's okay. There's been enough killing today."

"Murphy'll probably live."

"Probably?" Stark felt his blood chill.

"He was shot up real bad. They've got him stabilized for now in medical, but his body took a helluva lot of damage. You know how it is. Technically, the docs should be able to patch someone up if there's anything at all left, but the body just gives out." She glanced directly at Stark, quirking a small smile. "The medic I talked to complained that they'd just fixed Murphy up and you were already sending him back."

"At least I know which medic it was. She should be able to save Murph if anyone can."

"Maybe. I think his heart took a bigger hit than his other organs."

Stark covered his face with both hands, blocking out the world. "No question," he finally agreed, slowly lowering his hands once again. "Robin was a good kid, Vic. Murphy's a good kid. They deserved a chance together."

"People don't always get what they deserve."

"I know. God, I know. Does Murphy know she's dead?"

"Dunno. He's not in any shape for talking, so it depends whether Murphy knew before he got shot up."

So maybe I gotta tell him. Sweet Jesus, why? "Civs aren't supposed to die," he finally whispered.

"No, they're not." Vic rose slowly, then came to stand beside him, hand on his shoulder. "It's part of our job description, and it still hurts like hell when we lose a friend. I guess when she decided to date a soldier she took on the negative side of things along with the positive."

"I warned her. But I thought it'd be about danger to Murphy. Not her." He glanced up speculatively. "It hurts you, too?"

"Of course it hurts me."

"But she was just a civ."

Vic glared down, eyes narrowing. "Okay. She was a civ. But she was our civ. She treated us decent, and she liked Murphy, and she died alongside us."

"That's right," Stark agreed, his tone unusually mild. "She died alongside us. Like an ally."

"Like an ally." Vic shook her head, then nodded wearily. "Yeah. A good ally. All right, Ethan. You were right all along. We and the civs up here are on the same side, and some of them are worth trusting. I guess their actions tonight proved it. Too bad Robin Masood had to die to make us see that."

"To make some of us see that, anyway," Stark noted, earning himself another glare. "At least she didn't die in vain, then. It meant something. It accomplished something."

"I'm sure that'll be a great comfort to Murphy."

Stark hung his head, feeling pain radiating from his entire body. "I gotta be there for him."

Vic's arm came around his head, cradling it for a moment. "Sorry. Sorry. Shouldn't have said that. Not your fault."

"Whose is it, then?"

"Whoever ordered this. Come on, soldier, let's get to work. There's a lot to do."

"Yeah." He followed her, walling off the pain behind a barrier of constant tasks large and small, knowing the barrier could only contain it and never make it go away.

Sometime later, as the artificial human day swung toward its close, Stark sat in his quarters, body worn out, brain still numb. "Commander?"

"Here." Security Central was mostly functional again. The attackers had been forced to leave most of its equipment intact so the worm would have time to work, and Stark's people had been able to deactivate the timed charges left behind before they could turn the whole place into wreckage.

"There's a visitor for you. A civilian."

"Who?"

"She says her name is Cheryl Sarafina."

Stark winced, then nodded silently to himself. "Let her in. Send her to my room." A short while later, Sarafina entered, ducking her head to avoid looking straight at Stark, before finally raising it so he could see her reddened eyes. "Pardon my interruption, Sergeant Stark."

"No problem. It's been a real bad day. Would you like to sit down? Can I get you anything?"

"No. No." Sarafina reached into her pocket, surfacing with a small object. "I was cataloging Robin Masood's possessions, and thought, perhaps, you might want to keep this." Her hand opened. A short, fat little figurine. Ridiculous smile, seemingly mocking, now. The paca Robin's mother had given her. A generation ago, the odd toys called pacas had been a fad. Stark's mother had owned one, too, like many other women.

He had last seen this paca when he visited Robin Masood's home and talked about the military with Sarafina and Masood. The paca had reminded him of his mother then, helping him to form an immediate if irrational bond with the civ women.

Stark shut his eyes for a moment, unable to bear the sight. "That was from her mother. It oughta go back to her."

"It seemed to mean something to you—"

"It does, but it ain't mine."

"I think she wanted you to have it. She mentioned a few times how you'd enjoyed seeing it."

He reached out slowly, touching the absurd little figurine. "Tell you what, I'll take it for now. But when Murphy gets better, I'll ask if he wants it. Okay?" *Murphy'll get better. Murphy'll survive. Just keep telling myself that.*

"Private Murphy? Of course. Ahhh, Sergeant." Sarafina blinked rapidly, wiping at the corners of her eyes with her fingers. "Why do such things happen to such people?"

"Because the Universe ain't fair, and even if it was, human beings would be in charge of this part of it, and they'd screw it up. I'm real sorry, Ma'am. If there's anything . . ." Stark's voice trailed off helplessly.

"Thank you, but you cannot bring the dead to life. Sergeant Stark, I must tell you, there has been much ambivalence in the Colony. Colony Manager Campbell told you of this. What should we do, how far should we press our cause, should we ally ourselves with the military you command." Sarafina's voice hardened. "That is gone. Robin was known by many, and well-liked. Her death has shocked everyone. The methods used by the authorities back home, hiring foreign military forces to attack us, to kill our own citizens!"

"They're kinda short of American ground troops right now."

"That is little excuse, and if Americans had been used it would have been even worse. No, Sergeant Stark, only a small minority of the Colony's inhabitants now still wants to place our trust in the authorities. Sentiment is hardening for a complete break."

"What does that mean?"

"A declaration of independence." Sarafina must have seen reflected on Stark's face the reaction her words generated inside him. "I know. It is such a major decision, to break ties with our country, even in the face of such provocations. Perhaps our leaders back on Earth will come to their senses even yet. Neither Mr. Campbell nor I are comfortable with such an extreme step at this time, but speaking for the citizens of the Colony I can now say we shall stand by you, together with you. For Robin's memory."

"Thanks." Stark turned the little paca in his hand, looking down at it with an exhausted sense of emptiness. "Funny how we'll do things for people after they're dead that we wouldn't do for them while they're still alive."

"The prisoners aren't talking," Vic informed him crisply, "and their battle armor systems all contained kamikaze watchdogs designed to wipe their programming. Stacey Yurivan's people have been able to recover enough fragments of the Tactical files to sketch a picture of their plan, though." She angled her display screen so Stark could view it. "Just like we saw on the sensor records, the primary objective was right there. The Commanding General's suite."

Stark frowned. "They expected to find me there, huh?"

"Right. You and me."

"What? It was the middle of the night. Why'd they think you'd be in there with me?"

Vic glared at him, plainly exasperated. "Ethan."

"Oh." For some reason, the innuendo amused him. "They know something about us I don't?"

"If they do, I don't know it either. Anyway, they apparently thought you lived there."

Stark made a face. "Too damn big and luxurious. You know that."

"You work in there sometimes," Vic pointed out.

"Pretty rarely, but it does have a nice desk and great comms." He thought about it, rubbing his chin, feeling stubble he hadn't remembered to shave off this day. "Did they guess I was using that place, or did someone see me working there and tell them that's where I lived?"

"Don't know. We'll have to find out, and if they were told, find out who that someone was."

Stark eyed the screen, his face grim. "So it was a decapitation raid. They wanted to take out our leadership. But decap raids are supposed to knock the enemy off-balance just before you hit them with an attack. Where's the follow-up?"

"I think this raid was always intended as a stand-alone." Reynolds sigh heavily, then glowered at Stark. "Ethan, if I've told you once I've told you a million times. You hold all this together. Nobody else is trusted enough among the ranks to function as commander. If they'd succeeded in blowing you away, they probably figured the rest of us would fall apart."

He thought about that, too. "I guess I'm pretty important."

"Duh! Hello, Ethan! Are the lights on in there yet?" Vic subsided, shaking her head. "So now you're going to be more careful? Finally?"

"No." Stark held up his hands to forestall another outburst. "Look, Vic, these apes trust me because they know I'll lead them. Okay, maybe that's not the only reason, but it's a big part. If I'm hiding down in a bunker, I'm not leading." He paused. "Besides, it's like leading my Squad, isn't it? You can't let the troops know you're scared, 'cause that'll scare them. I gotta be out in front."

Vic sat silent, her eyes closed for a long moment before they reopened and focused on him. "I can't argue with that, I guess. We have to keep you alive, but we also have to risk you. Why can't any of this be simple?"

"Because people are involved. So," Stark continued, "then those raiders hit the Command Center."

"Uh-huh. Apparently they were supposed to reinforce the two we found in there, trash the place, then bug out in the confusion. At least that's what they were told according to their Tacs. I don't see where they'd actually have had much chance to fight their way out."

"Nah. Not a big chance, but it might've worked," Stark conceded. "They were good, they had total surprise, they'd messed up our systems. We were lucky."

"Luck's a good word for it." Vic stabbed a finger at part of the display. "Though we have to thank the civs for the alarm that alerted us. The attackers had our internal codes so none of our sensors alerted us. But the sentry occupying Sentry Post Four got a warning off anyway." She glanced at Stark. "He was fairly new and apparently took the warning seriously when it was passed on earlier in the evening."

"Good thing I didn't blow it off."

"Yeah. And good thing the sentry was green enough not to blow off the warning you ordered passed." She paused. "I wouldn't have paid attention to it, Ethan. No veteran would've. I'd have just told the civs to leave us alone."

"I paid attention," Stark reminded her. "But you're right. My first instinct was to say 'yeah, sure, go away.' "

"Why didn't you?"

"Maybe because I've worked with the civs up here enough to know them personally. That makes a difference. Maybe because I grew up civ and know every civ is different, and most are decent human beings once they get to know us, too, and realize we're not players in some vid game." He remembered the old movie about the attack on the harbor. "Also maybe because I wasted part of my youth watching vids."

Her eyebrows rose skeptically. "Are you saying I should've watched more vids when I was growing up?"

"As long as they were the right ones. Anyway, these civs are on our team, Vic. They're learning to work with us. This victory, if you wanta call our surviving this attack a victory, is probably because the civs worked with us. We gotta learn to work with them."

Vic looked vaguely annoyed. "I know. Just one more anthill kicked over by Ethan Stark. I guess I can't get used to the idea of being in debt to the civs, though."

"Think of it as a payback for all they owe us." Stark thought a moment longer, focusing back on the details of the raid. "I guess the sentry at Post Four died anyway?"

"Oh, yeah," Vic nodded. "Never had a chance. But he did last long enough to sound the alert and delay the attack a few moments, which gave Security Central time to get a call out for reinforcements." She indicated another part of the headquarters schematic. "Even with that, we still needed a piece of luck named Corporal Gomez. Her and the Mendozas' resistance in this hall stopped a big part of the raider force from sweeping in to reinforce the groups that were hitting us."

"We barely held as it was."

"No argument here. And, of course, Murphy wiping out that one group single-handed didn't hurt. Between them, Gomez and Murphy took out or tied down half the attacking force. Good thing they happened to bring their weapons along that night. More luck." Vic managed a smile. "That old Squad of yours is hell-on-wheels, Ethan. What'd you feed them?"

"Common sense, training, and confidence." Stark shook his head, shuddering briefly. "Too close. Way too close. Those raiders should have taken us down, Vic."

"That's right." Reynolds nodded again, face hard. "Ethan, I don't like surviving just because we got lucky."

Stark stared at the display, his own expression reflecting growing anger. "So how'd *they* get so lucky? How'd those raiders get right on top of us without being detected earlier? How'd they land without being spotted by the orbital defenses and get inside the mil complex? How'd they pass through so many automated checkpoints where their IFF should have given them away? How was their shuttle able to spoof our sensors and remain undetected except for the ghost only the civ scan saw until we did a manual scan?"

She bit her lip. "I told you. They had our internal codes. That's the problem with automated systems, right? No common sense. They'd pass through the devil and all his demons if they flashed the right code response."

"Uh-huh. So they had our codes. And somebody most likely told the attackers I was living in the Commanding General's quarters. That can only mean one thing."

"Yes." Vic looked haggard now, as if worn out by the implications. "They had inside help, Ethan. Somebody compromised our own systems and fed the raiders information to plan their attack."

"Trasies?"

"He probably would've, but he never had access to mil systems. Believe me, that was checked out a long time ago. Besides, codes have changed repeatedly since we arrested Trasies. It had to be someone else. I've already told Stacey Yurivan to check it out."

"You sure we should use her for this? Stace is really mad about Tanaka buying it."

Vic shrugged. "That means she's motivated."

"I don't want a witch-hunt."

"Agreed. But Stacey won't settle for anybody but the guilty one. She wants revenge something fierce, and she wants the right somebody to be the one who gets nailed."

"Good, As soon as she gets an answer, I want to know."

The call came early the next morning, well before most humans were stirring. Stark dressed hurriedly, rushing to meet Sergeant Yurivan, Sergeant Reynolds joining him on the way.

Stacey Yurivan wore the look of weary triumph, which bespoke lack of sleep justified by results. "I've got your mole."

"Just one?" Vic questioned.

"I think so, yeah." Yurivan blinked several times, focusing through her fatigue. "Nothing's one hundred percent in this kind of thing, but since I had an idea what to look for I found some break-ins and traced them back. Once I cracked the protocol being used for the false accesses about a dozen fake identities spilled out. But they all led back to one real guy."

"A dozen?" Stark shook his head. "I thought our security was better than that. A dozen false ID's being used to penetrate—"

"Hold it, Stark," Yurivan snapped, then bit her lip. "Sorry . . . Commander. They didn't get through because our security was bad. No, they were real good. Nastiest stuff I've ever seen. I'll tell you all about a couple of the worms we found burrowed into the system when we have the time."

"Worms." Vic let the single word stand.

"Yeah. Real ugly ones." Yurivan grinned humorlessly. "I guess they were saving them for the main attack. Triggering them would have really caused us some trouble. They would've scrambled comm circuits, broadcast inhibits to all our weapons so they wouldn't shoot, screwed up our IFF so it mirror-imaged—"

"Mirror-imaged? What's that mean?"

"It means the IFF would have told us our friends were enemy targets and the enemy were our friends. Nice, huh?"

"Real nice."

"But they didn't use them during this raid, probably because they were saving them for the main attack, and now they're neutralized. You're welcome."

Stark managed a smile back. "Thanks, Stace."

"But these programs were very sophisticated?" Reynolds pressed.

"Best I've ever seen," Yurivan admitted. "No question this guy is an official agent. Only government code geeks could have generated that stuff. Now, you've got to tell me what to do. Do I leave the mole alone to see what else he tries and who he talks to, or pick him up before he does more damage?"

Stark pondered the question, frowning down at the table-top. "What do you think, Vic?"

"I think this mole has already done a lot of damage. I wouldn't want to risk more, tempting though it is to hope he exposes other spies."

"Yeah." Stark focused on Stacey Yurivan again. "Everything just points to one person? No indications of multiple agents?"

"No, which doesn't mean there aren't more than one. But it

looks like only one person was active."

"Are we sure this guy doesn't have access to weapons? Big stuff, I mean?"

She rubbed her chin. "Don't think so. I can't swear to it, though. Records on ordnance are never absolutely accurate, even for artillery shells. On top of that, a lot of stuff got used during General Meathead's offensive and when we shoved back that enemy attack soon afterward, and that ammo never got recorded right. Somebody could have carried off a small arsenal, and we wouldn't know for sure."

"Then take him down. Now. Do it clean and fast."

"Okay." Yurivan hesitated. "Something else I should tell you."

"What?"

"You ain't gonna like it."

Stark laughed, low and bitter. "I'm starting to get used to that kind of news. What is it?"

"This guy. The mole. You know him. His name is Grant Stein."

I can't feel anything. I can't feel anything. Kate, what the hell happened? "I want to see him. After you pick him up."

Yurivan stared suspiciously back. "Don't even think about going easy—".

"Shut up."

Vic took one look at Stark, then stood, gesturing to Yurivan, who nodded quickly and came with her. The door closed behind them, leaving the room silent.

It was much later when Grant Stein entered, wearing cuffs around both wrists, the chain connecting them looping down to fasten to another chain holding together shackles around his ankles. Even in low lunar gravity, no one could move quickly when chained in that fashion. Two MPs walked him in, one holding each shoulder, with two more standing a few steps behind, ready to assist if Stein attempted anything.

"Leave him," Stark ordered. "Wait outside." The MPs hesitated, eyeing one another uncertainly. "He's not going anywhere, and I can handle him if he tries something. Wait outside."

Four salutes, then the MPs marched out, and the door sealed. Stark stood, overtopping Stein, watching him for a long minute. "Why'd you do it?" he finally asked.

"I don't know what you mean."

"Drop the games. We got the evidence. We know you fed the raiders the stuff they needed to get through the sensor net. We know you planted worms in all our systems. Just tell me why."

Grant Stein stared back, his face slowly purpling with rage. "You left her to die when you could have saved her!"

Stark's own anger flared. "I did nothing of the kind, you stupid son of a bitch. She was already half-dead and wouldn't let me stay. I told you that!"

"Sure. Stark the hero, and any witnesses to what really happened dead on the battlefield."

"I never claimed to be a hero. I certainly wasn't on Patterson's Knoll."

The flat reply seemed to throw Grant Stein off balance. He glowered wordlessly for a moment, then shook his head vigorously. "You left her. I loved my sister, and you left her to die alone. You'll never know how that felt!"

Stark lowered his head for a long time, then raised it to look

Grant in the eyes once again. "Yes, I do. I loved her, too. Loved her enough to spend my life trying to make her death mean something. Kate never would have done what you did. No. Don't even try to interrupt me, or I'll beat you senseless. If Kate thought I'd betrayed her she'd have called me on it, face to face, not slunk around in the shadows looking for backs to plant knives in. How many deaths are you responsible for? People who in some cases couldn't even fight back. You proud of that? You think Kate would be proud of it?"

Grant Stein tried to stand straight despite the chains holding him in a slightly hunched position. "I'm her brother," he grated out.

"Yeah. Too damn bad." Stark hit the access pad, opening the door and summoning the MPs back into the room. "Get him out of here." He saw Vic hovering nearby, face emotionless. "Vic. I want a court-martial put together. We handle this legal."

She hesitated, then spoke cautiously. "Since the attackers killed a civilian we could hand him over to the civs for justice."

"No. He's ours. We handle it."

"You know what that'll mean." Vic didn't bother making the statement into a question.

"I know."

A military court-martial could be a complex thing or a simple thing, depending on the case, on the evidence, on the charges, and on the people running it. As acting commanding officer, Stark wouldn't be judge, jury, and executioner, but he did have the power to appoint the judge, select the jury, and approve or disapprove the sentence. As it was, he skipped the fact-gathering stage, ordering a direct move to formal General Court-Martial, letting Sergeant Bev Manley select the presiding officer and the other members of the court-martial to avoid any suspicion he might be trying to pack the court.

Then he waited.

Stark sat in the Command Center, momentarily alone while the watch-standers drilled in the alternate Command Center in another part of the headquarters complex. Every once in a while his eyes strayed as if of themselves to the spot where Sergeant Tanaka's body had once lain. It took him a moment to realize somebody was standing inside the dully shining metal door that now stood at the main entrance. "Vic?"

"Yeah." She came inside a few steps, standing with arms crossed. "What're you doing in here alone?"

"Trying to get some work done. You know. Going over these proposed improvements in security. We don't want a repeat of the surprise those raiders achieved."

"No." Reynolds came a little closer, but remained standing. "News of the raid has hit the press back home."

"How're they reacting?"

"Badly. What passes for political and military leadership these days is scrambling to disavow all knowledge of the failed raid. They're claiming it was some foreign power trying to take advantage of the confusion up here."

Stark snorted a short laugh. "A foreign power with our latest equipment and assistance from our government's agencies, huh? Anybody believe it?"

"Of course not. Civs back home are real unhappy one of their own got targeted. They're also unhappy the economy is sinking into a deep pit. Stock market took another big dive. Loss of confidence.

Apparently that matters to stock markets."

"I guess. Any word on military stuff?"

Vic shook her head. "No. But this raid telegraphed some of their intentions, don't you think? The Pentagon's hiring mercs to make up some for their own lack of personnel. And they're obviously planning to play rough. Assume we're going to face a major retaliatory attack, Ethan, as soon as they can put one together."

"I already had. I also assumed they'll have to cut more deals with foreign governments so they'll have a spot on the Moon to launch an attack on us from." Stark looked up at her, his eyes demanding. "None of those things is why you're here, are they?"

"No." Reynolds kept her voice level, her face unexpressive. "The General Court-Martial of Private Grant Stein has returned a verdict. Guilty of violations in time of war of Article 104, Aiding the Enemy, Article 106, Spying, and Article 106a, Espionage, of the Uniform Code of Military Justice. Recommended sentence is death by firing squad."

Stark couldn't breathe for a moment, then took a long, deep inhale, tasting the clean, sterile air. "That was pretty quick."

"The evidence was overwhelming. And he confessed. Simplifies things."

"I guess it does. Funny how we're trying to do this all legal, when we're in violation of, what, Article 99?"

"That's Misbehavior Before the Enemy, so I guess that applies, but they'd be more likely to lead with Article 94, Mutiny and Sedition."

"But I can't just let him walk," Stark stated slowly, as if to himself. "He caused a lot of deaths, among people who thought they were his fellow soldiers. I never did that."

"No, you didn't."

"Are we sure he acted alone? What about those other soldiers who came up with him?"

Vic shook her head, biting one lip. "We can't be sure he was the only one, but we've found nothing else. Our best guess is that the other soldiers were protective cover, allowed up here so Stein wouldn't stand out as a single exception."

Stark nodded, barely perceptible movements of his head up and down. "And we're doing this by the book, aren't we? Even if we do lack legal authority. We're trying to do it right. I suppose, though, legalwise the lawyers in the Pentagon could charge us with murder if I approve this sentence."

"I suppose. It's not like we're not already facing the maximum penalty because of the mutiny. What're they going to do, sentence us to death twice?"

"They would, just for the hell of it." Stark paused again, thinking. "Did he make any plea for mercy?" For some reason, he found it hard to say the name Grant Stein, but Vic had no trouble knowing who Stark meant.

"No. He knows it'd have to go to you, and he hates your guts."

"Yeah." Stark looked at his hands, lying slightly cupped in his lap as if bereft of the means to move. "All the things a guy does in life, good and bad, and I end up getting hated for something I didn't do."

"I can't make it fair, Ethan."

"I know that."

"I also can't make it go away." Stark sat silent, avoiding her gaze.

"You loved his sister, huh?"

"How'd you find out?"

"Stein kept flapping his lips after the MPs pulled him out of the room. He didn't believe you."

"No. He wouldn't. But I did love her. In a way. Never told her. Probably never would have."

Vic managed a sad smile. "She knew anyway."

"How the hell do you know?"

"Because I'm a woman, and men are never as good at hiding stuff as they think. So, Ethan, you've spent all the years since Patterson's Knoll proving you would have been good enough for her?"

"That's never what it was about," Stark objected. "Yeah, I've fought as hard as I can to make sure nobody else has to die like she did, but that's 'cause it was right. Nobody deserves to die like she and the other soldiers in my outfit did. Nobody. It's not about me."

"Then you done good, Ethan."

"And now all I have to do is condemn Kate's brother to death."

"Look, Ethan, what would you do if it was anyone else?"

"You mean like you? Or Gomez or Murphy?"

"You're avoiding the issue. They wouldn't betray you and everyone else." Stark sat silent. "Ethan, the only soldiers up here who didn't want Grant Stein sentenced to death by a court-martial were the ones who wanted him shot without bothering with a trial. He stuck a knife in the backs of his fellow soldiers. If I ever sunk low enough to do that, I'd want you to shoot me. Trust in each other is damn near all we've got, and it's been just about all we've had for a long time."

"Vic, are you trying to make me do this? Make me blame you for forcing my hand?"

"If I have to. I don't want it that way, but it's got to be done."

"You don't." Stark left the enigmatic reply hanging in the air for a moment, then leaned forward to key in his code at the command terminal, calling up the report from the General Court-Martial. Staring at the screen for a long moment, he finally punched the Send key so viciously the terminal shook as if in protest. *Forgive me, Kate.* "It's done. I confirmed the sentence."

"I'm sorry, Ethan. If there's anything—"

"There isn't."

"Want to go somewhere?"

"No. No. Not this time. Just leave me alone for a while, okay?"

"Okay." She left, the new door sliding silently shut in her wake, its clean metal standing out against the scarred wood on either side.

What have I done? What'd the soldier say in my dream? Where's our commander. Stuck on the Knoll, no way out, doomed. Is that what I've done to all the people who've trusted me? Hung 'em out to dry, stuck on a big rock with everyone targeting them? Even their former fellow soldiers? And now the civs up here are talking about declaring independence. That'd mean a long, full-scale war for sure. Just when we're starting to see some good things happen. Soldiers trusting their commanders. Civs and mil connecting like they're part of the same system. We could build something real good here. Show people back on the World how it should be. If we get a chance.

How are we—how am I—going to get us out of this? And how many people am I going to have to kill and watch die in the process?

Stark sat in the dimmed room, gazing emptily at the silent displays all around, displays that spoke of his power. Power of life and death. Somewhere outside, far from where the displays could monitor them, armies gathered. They would leave mankind's green home with its white clouds and blue water, and they would come to this place, this desolate Moon where black shadow met white light against dead gray rocks and dust, and they would die here.

Unless Sergeant Ethan Stark could think of something else.

The United States military forces on the moon have overthrown their high-ranking officers and placed Sergeant Ethan Stark in command. Instead of just issuing orders, Stark confides in his fellow sergeants in hopes of forging an army based on mutual respect. Now, in addition to fighting a merciless enemy on the moon's surface, Stark must contend with the U.S. government's reaction to his mutiny . . . .

The moon's American civilian colony has offered to assist the military with food and supplies on one condition: that Stark's troops back the colony's plea for independence. In order to survive, civilian and soldier must learn to trust each other as one man's cause becomes a crusade . . . .

STARK'S CRUSADE
JACK CAMPBELL (WRITING AS JOHN G. HEMRY)

THE THRILLING CONCLUSION TO
THE STARK'S WAR TRILOGY

He was sent into space to protect the US Lunar Colony. Instead, when faced with orders that would do nothing but get his soldiers killed, Sergeant Ethan Stark lead a rebellion. Now he and his soldiers must fend off deadly aggression from their own country without igniting a full-scale civil war.

"In a gripping space opera, Hemry delivers an intensely satisfying read. Strong characterization and well-executed action keep the pages turning." – RT Book Reviews

"Hemry has combined a keen sense of action with a fine look at the morality of following orders, and produced a groundbreaking story in the same vein as *The Forever War* or *Starship Troopers*."
– *Absolute Magnitude*

WWW.TITANBOOKS.COM

THE LOST FLEET SERIES

JACK CAMPBELL

DAUNTLESS

FEARLESS

COURAGEOUS

VALIANT

RELENTLESS

VICTORIOUS

After a hundred years of brutal war against the Syndics, the Alliance fleet is marooned deep in enemy territory, weakened and demoralised and desperate to make it home.

Their fate rests in the hands of Captain "Black Jack" Geary, a man who had been presumed dead but then emerged from a century of survival hibernation to find his name had become legend. Forced by a cruel twist of fate into taking command of the fleet, Geary must find a way to inspire the battle-hardened and exhausted men and women of the fleet or face certain annihilation by their enemies.

Brand-new editions of the bestselling novels containing unique bonus material from the author.

"Black Jack is an excellent character, and this series is the best military SF I've read in some time." – *Wired*

"Fascinating stuff… this is military SF where the military and SF parts are both done right." – *SFX Magazine*

"*The Lost Fleet* is some of the best military science fiction on the shelves today." – SF Site

WWW.TITANBOOKS.COM

THE LOST FLEET:
BEYOND THE FRONTIER: DREADNAUGHT
JACK CAMPBELL

THE FIRST VOLUME IN THE BRAND-NEW FOLLOW-ON SERIES

Captain John "Black Jack" Geary woke from a century of survival
hibernation to take command of the Alliance fleet in the final
throes of its long and bitter conflict against the Syndicate Worlds.
Now Fleet Admiral Geary's victory has earned him the adoration
of the people and enmity of politicians convinced that a living
hero can be a very dangerous thing.

Geary is charged with command of the newly christened First
Fleet. Its first mission: to probe deep into the territory of the
mysterious alien race. Geary knows that members of the military
high command and the government fear his staging a coup, so he
can't help but wonder if the fleet is being deliberately sent to the
far side of space on a suicide mission.

"Campbell combines the best parts of military SF and grand
space opera ... plenty of exciting discoveries and escapades."
– *Publishers Weekly*

"Another excellent addition to one of the best military science
fiction series on the market."
– Monsters & Critics

WWW.TITANBOOKS.COM

COMING SOON FROM TITAN BOOKS:

JAG IN SPACE
JACK CAMPBELL (WRITING AS JOHN G. HEMRY)

A JUST DETERMINATION
BURDEN OF PROOF
RULE OF EVIDENCE
AGAINST ALL ENEMIES

Equipped with the latest weaponry, and carrying more than two hundred sailors, the orbiting warship, USS *Michaelson*, is armored against the hazards of space and the threats posed in the vast nothing between planets. But who will protect her from the threats within?

He is Ensign Paul Sinclair, assigned to the USS *Michaelson* as the ship's lone legal officer—a designation that carries grave consequences as he soon learns that the struggle for justice among the stars is a never-ending fight…

"First-rate military SF… Hemry's series continues to offer outstanding suspense, realism and characterization." – *Booklist*

"Hemry's decision to wed courtroom drama to military SF has captured lightning in a bottle. He builds the story's suspense expertly." – SF Reviews